A KILLING IN THE MARKET

BY

JOHN BALL

EVERY INCH A LADY

BY

JOAN FLEMING

WITCHROCK

BY

BILL KNOX

Published for the
DETECTIVE BOOK CLUB ®
by Walter J. Black, Inc.
ROSLYN, NEW YORK

THE DETECTIVE BOOK CLUB®

Printed in the United States of America

A KILLING IN THE MARKET

BY

JOHN BALL

Though the action connected with the New York Stock Exchange is not usually the background for a mystery, it provides a novel and fascinating one when it is responsible for four murders and the near ruin of several other operators. John Ball, author of Police Chief, *likes to write about individuals who become unwitting victims of the workings of the powerful institutions of our time. His characters are affected for good or evil by the pressures of the Stock Exchange and he keeps the outcome a surprise . . . one the reader may or may not agree with.*

Doubleday and Company Edition **$6.95**

EVERY INCH A LADY

BY

JOAN FLEMING

Young, wealthy, handsome and six-months married, York Craig was found brutally murdered for no apparent reason. His wife was at the theatre with friends. Everyone, including her shipping magnate father-in-law, was sorry for the brave little widow, especially when it became known she had been cruelly deceived. But soon the widow takes matters into her small but unexpectedly determined hands with startling results.

G. P. Putnam's Sons Edition **$8.95**

WITCHROCK

BY

BILL KNOX

Webb Carrick, chief officer on the Marlin of Her Majesty's Fisheries Protection Service, gets involved with his dour skipper while on another official mission off the Scottish coast. They hear gossip about the so-called "Witch of the Isles." The talk circles around her influence on the death of a local law officer and other strange actions. Getting to the bottom of the rampant superstition and investigating what the locals may be doing because of their fear becomes a dangerous mission for Webb and the Marlin.

Doubleday and Company Edition **$6.95**

A KILLING IN THE MARKET

BY

JOHN BALL

Published by special arrangement with Doubleday & Co., Inc.

Chapter One

Two hundred feet after the lead car of the long commuter train had bitten into the half mile curve that ended at Boylesport station, the engineer began to feed compressed air through the triple valves precisely as he had done hundreds of times before. In response the steel brake shoes clamped against the spinning wheels and the screech of metal against metal shuddered through the air. The train had already dropped a good half of its original passenger load and the long coaches were no longer filled by the fetid air of New York City. Once again there was the illusion that Manhattan and all that it contained had been left forgetably far behind.

The station and its platform had been designed to perform a standard public function, therefore it was very like most of the other stations on the line with nothing about it to show that it had been selected to serve a privileged community. It ignored the fact that Boylesport had become synonymous with wealth; the real estate prices were astronomical, even for one of the most fashionable parts of the Long Island south shore. Boylesport was made up principally of estates, some paid for and some not, but all of them in varying degrees impressive.

The moment that the train braked to a stop, passengers began to dismount. A few were in a visible hurry, which was perhaps an index to their lives. Some were merely brisk. Most of the rest were carefully casual. Mr. Nathan Lockheim took his time so that he would not have to endure jostling or any other such indignities.

Along the station platform there was a long row of parked cars, waiting as they did each business day for their owners to return from the city and drive them home. As Mr. Lockheim walked with dignity past them, he noted as he did each time that the majority of them were compacts and small foreign cars. Some Volvos were in evidence, and an occasional Mercedes, but for the most part they were in the three to four thousand dollar bracket. The knowledge of this fact gave Mr. Lockheim a certain sense of inner warmth. They were something like troops with himself the reviewing general.

Mr. Lockheim's station car was a Cadillac El Dorado which gleamed with custom gold paint. He unlocked it with a sense of appropriate fitness; the ordinariness of the train he could not help, but now he was not about to be seen driving a Pinto.

Comfortably settled behind the wheel, he started the engine and listened to its contented purr. Satisfied, he adjusted the air conditioning and then turned on the stereo tape player. Immediately he was surrounded by soothing sounds of his own choosing as he pressed the automatic door lock that insured his privacy. When he was fully ready he backed out, cutting off a new Granada whose driver had to jump on the brake to avoid a collision, shifted the automatic transmission lever to *drive,* and rolled in comfort off the parking lot.

Mr. Lockheim was in a very good mood. His hard week's work had resulted in a handsome profit, one he had realized barely ten minutes before the market had closed. He had been ten thousand short on Sphinx Wire and Cable, a position it had taken him four days to acquire without tipping his hand. The stock had been up on the expectation of the passage of the Alaska Communications Complex bill, something that the military had been pushing for with all its muscle. When the bill had failed, due to some unexpected vote switches on the floor of the House, SXC had hit the skids for five and one eighth points. After he had covered his short positions, he had cleared an average profit of four and seven-eights per share. That was very close to fifty thousand dollars, and there were many many weeks during the year when he did not do as well as that.

He passed through the center of the small community at a dignified pace. He felt assured that the Boylesport Police would know better than to stop his car, but he drove carefully anyway since he was not a man compelled to hurry. His dignity was precious to him and he took pains to protect it. At the intersection where he always turned left he signaled and then made the corner just ahead of a housewife at the wheel of her Chevrolet station wagon, who had been coming the other way. When the Chevrolet swung in behind him, Mr. Lockheim pressed the accelerator and spurted away. The music kept him relaxed and contented.

Eight minutes later he slowed before the entrance drive to his own

splendid estate. It was a small ceremony to him, driving onto the
grounds that he owned and where things were maintained precisely
as he wished them to be. The moment that the public highway was
behind him, he would become, quite literally, master of all that he
surveyed. He had earned it, and it was his privilege to enjoy it. Since
two cars were coming toward him, he elected to use the turn signal. It
was proper, of course, and it also served to point out to those who
might be interested where it was that he lived. He raised his right
hand and flipped the lever down.

Instantly he was stunned by a sheet of flame that seemed to sur-
round him. A frightful shock of sound slammed against his eardrums
as the cushioned seat he was occupying erupted under him. He was
conscious that he was being thrown through the air as the impact of
unbearable pain smote him like a hammer. He landed hard with the
windsheld frame on top of him; searing heat tore at his legs.

He gasped for air and had to fight to get it into his lungs. A violent
sense of outrage filled him; his mind refused all other thoughts. As the
pain mounted he wanted desperately to fight back, but his body ignored his commands. Then someone had him by the shoulders and
was dragging him across the road, away from his flaming car. He
heard someone say, "It's all right; I called for help on my CB radio.
Just take it easy now."

He wanted to scream in protest, but the voice in his throat would
not come out. He began to see only a dim redness. He tried to raise
himself up to issue a command, but he failed in the attempt. The last
thing he heard was an approaching siren as he lay in his agony at the
edge of the public highway.

*   *   *

The first patrol car to respond was driven by Officer Frank Happs
who was 27 and who had been a sworn member of the force for a little
less than two years. Without getting out of his car he took a quick
look at what he had to handle and then radioed in for all of the back-
up that was available. The ambulance was already on the way; as he
pulled to one side he could see it coming down the road.

As soon as Happs' call came in Lieutenant John Harbizon knew
without being told that it was his baby. Not very much of a violent
nature occurred in the well-settled community, but when anything
did Harbizon was the acknowledged specialist to handle it. He had
been through the FBI school and he was the automatic delegate to

most of the law enforcement seminars to which the Boylesport Police was invited.

Harbizon responded in one of the three unmarked cars that the department had available. Because the community was limited in population they were useless for any sort of undercover work, but occasionally calls had to be made at some of the status conscious estates where a conspicuously marked police car might not be welcome. It took him a little more than five minutes to reach the scene; as he got out in front of the Lockheim estate he was very much aware that he was confronted with the first car bombing he had ever been called upon to handle.

Happs had his patrol unit properly positioned with the roof lights on, keeping traffic away from the grisly scene. A second unit, on the other side of the wreck, was doing the same thing. The ambulance men were standing by; they had covered the body with a blanket. At the gateway to the estate a little Latin-appearing maid was staring with huge, frightened eyes.

Harbizon lost no time whatever. He went first to the maid and spoke to her briefly, keeping his voice calm as he did so. "Please go back inside," he told her. "You can see that there's been an accident. We'll come in to see you shortly."

The little maid looked at him for a few stricken seconds, then she turned and almost fled back up the private driveway. Harbizon did not wait to watch her, as soon as he saw her start back he was intercepted by one of the ambulance men. "The victim is a Nathan Lockheim," he said. "He's dead, no doubt about it whatever. The man who pulled him away from his car is here if you want to talk to him."

"I do," Harbizon snapped. "And I need a doctor to pronounce the man dead."

"He's on his way."

"Good." He turned to Happs who was standing by. "Call in and ask to have a road block set up at each end of this stretch. Emergency vehicles and residents only to be allowed through."

"Got it," Happs said, and moved to obey.

The fire department had a single pumper on hand; the engineer in charge of it conferred next. "We foamed the fire and then left everything as it was," he advised. "We have a damn good arson man available if you want him."

"Ask him to come by all means," Harbizon answered. He knew

perfectly well that the arson man was good, but that was not the time to say so. "Stand by if you can; we'll want a washdown after the body has been removed."

The fire department engineer nodded and returned to his vehicle. As he did so, Harbizon walked rapidly to where the citizen who had pulled Lockheim away from his flaming car was patiently waiting, watching everything that was going on. "Tell me what happened," he invited.

The would-be rescuer was concise and accurate; he told how he had seen the big gold Cadillac slowing up, apparently to turn into the driveway. The turn signal had blinked once just as the car had exploded. The driver had not had his seat belt fastened, but it would have made little difference. He wasn't sure exactly how the dead man had come out of the car, but he had the impression that he had come through the windshield. He did remember that the windshield frame had been lying across the victim's body; he surmised that it had been a pop-out type that would let go in the event of enough force from the inside. He had seized the victim by the shoulders and had pulled him backwards, face up, to the side of the road. He had given a very quick call on his CB radio, but he wasn't sure that it had been effective. He had returned to his car and had put out a broadcast asking for police and emergency medical help.

Harbizon took his card and thanked him warmly for his timely and responsible action. Clearly the man was not afraid to get involved and in the greater New York area, that was a novelty. Undoubtedly he would turn out to be a member of some volunteer group such as the Civil Air Patrol; it would fit the pattern.

Harbizon went back to his car and took out some of the camera equipment it carried in the trunk. With a Rolleiflex he made a series of six shots of the car wreckage, planning them so that every angle was carefully covered. He had the cover removed from the body and took six more shots, following the same procedure. The exact position of the body would mean little, but he saw superficially that the way it lay fully backed up the story the rescuer had told him.

While he was working an intern arrived, bent briefly over the corpse, and then formally pronounced it dead. Harbizon nodded to the ambulance men that it could be taken away. The mess had to be cleaned up; the unsightliness had to be hidden, and the road reopened to normal traffic as soon as possible. At the fringes of the operation three wreckers were waiting, red lights blinking, each hoping for the bonanza of what would be an expensive job. One of the drivers even tried to begin operations before Harbizon abruptly waved him away. There was a police wrecker that was shared with two other nearby communities and the men riding it would know how to take care of evidence.

He wanted to explore the still warm wreck, but his judgment dictated that it would be best to let the fire department arson expert do that. Instead he bent over the body just before it was to be moved and extracted the wallet from the inner coat pocket. He flipped it open and examined some of the credit cards that it contained. He also checked the address. In Boylesport almost everyone was a person of some importance, and influence surrounded it like a corona. His thoroughness was his chief asset in addition to his professional training. In order to do his sworn duty in such an environment he had to be sure of every step that he took; he had learned that hard lesson many years ago.

By that time there were five officers on the scene, the road blocks were up, and things were working properly; the next job was to see the people in the house. Once more he turned to Happs whose ashen look had gradually disappeared. "I'm going inside," he said. "Care to come along?"

Happs had sense enough not to ask if it would be all right to leave his unit; the answer was obvious. Aware that the scene ahead of him might be a rough one, he fell in beside the lieutenant and walked up the driveway toward the house.

When they were still twenty feet short of the door it was opened by the same little maid; a butler stood waiting inside. A butler! Harbizon knew that there were a few in Boylesport and that most of them were there to support the never ending game of social upmanship that seemed to amuse the very rich, or those who just missed being in that category.

As the butler stepped forward, Harbizon held out his badge in its case. "I'm Lieutenant Harbizon," he said simply.

"My name is Harkness, lieutenant."

"Thank you. You're aware, of course, that there's been a terrible accident outside."

"Yes, sir, we know."

"I don't want to put this too abruptly," Harbizon said, "but are you also aware that there was a fatality."

"Yes, lieutenant, we understand that Mr. Lockheim was killed. Is that correct?"

"I'm afraid that it is."

For just a moment the butler hesitated, then he asked, "How was he struck down, sir?"

"It appears at present as though a bomb of some kind may have been attached to his car. You understand that that hasn't been established as yet."

"Yes, lieutenant, I understand perfectly. In what manner may I help you?"

Harbizon liked him, he couldn't help it. The man was obviously intelligent and he handled himself well. Of course there was no indication as yet as to how well he had gotten along with his employer. Presumably well enough, because Nathan Lockheim had been known as a man who liked to have things very much his own way. If the butler had not given complete satisfaction, no sentimental considerations would have interfered with his replacement.

"If I could speak with Mrs. Lockheim, it might be most helpful. I realize, of course, that she has sustained a very severe shock."

Harkness kept any expression off his face. "Madam is indeed terribly shocked, but fortunately she has . . ." The butler sought for words. ". . . great strength of character."

Harbizon caught the inference clearly and while Happs waited patiently in the background, he explored it. "Mr. Harkness, you understand that Mr. Lockheim's death is definitely a police matter."

"I am fully aware, sir that it was not an accident."

"Precisely. So before I speak with Mrs. Lockheim, if she can see me, I want to ask you a question or two in complete confidence." He turned toward his patrolman. "You understand that, Happs?"

"Yes, sir: not a word to anyone."

Harbizon chalked one up for his subordinate; that had been exactly the right answer.

"What do you wish to know, sir?" Harkness asked.

Harbizon checked that the maid was gone. "Has anyone, perhaps, been trying to win Mrs. Lockheim's affections?"

The Butler held his face immobile, but his voice was definite. "I very much doubt that, sir."

"Do you know of any possible interest Mr. Lockheim may have taken in, quite frankly, a married woman?"

There was a microscopic pause before that question was answered. "I know of no one offhand, lieutenant, who would fit that description. That is to say, a married woman in whom Mr. Lockheim was interested."

Those questions had been the warm up; Harbizon put the key one in the same tone of voice, almost as if it were an afterthought. "The relationship between Mr. and Mrs. Lockheim; I would appreciate your comment on that."

"Sir, you understand my position . . ."

"Absolutely, Mr. Harkness, and your confidence will not be violated. If I know now, I may be able to avoid more public exposure later on."

"In view of that statement, lieutenant, I might put it that Mr. and Mrs. Lockheim maintained diplomatic relations. I do not believe that they lavished a great deal of affection on each other."

"Thank you; will you see now if Mrs. Lockheim can see us." He almost said "receive," but caught himself in time.

At the moment the little maid appeared again, apparently to see if she were wanted. "Gretchen," the butler said to her, "Please inquire if madam can receive two gentlemen from the police."

As soon as the girl had gone, Harbizon put a one-word question. "Gretchen?"

"Her name, sir, is actually Maria, but madam desires her to answer to Gretchen, so she does so."

Harbizon did not comment on that as he followed the butler into a very large room that contained a huge grand piano, several oil paintings in massive gilt frames, and as weird a collection of furniture as he had ever seen. There were two or three antique Spanish pieces, a strikingly-styled Plexiglas table, three modern sofas that appeared to be custom-built, and a scattering of spindly French chairs. Harbizon concluded rapidly that the chairs were largely for show only; he could not imagine anyone wanting to sit on them. At Harkness' invitation he seated himself on one of the sofas and nodded to Happs to take the opposite end.

Approximately three minutes later he looked up to see a woman coming into the room. As he got to his feet he kept his features composed with an effort; she was the fattest human he had ever seen. She could not have been more than five-feet-five at the most, but she had to weigh more than three hundred pounds. Her head, thatched with carefully coiffured blond hair, was as flat and wide as a crabapple. Two features caught him, thick heavy lips that were painted a bright scarlet and a pair of small black eyes that radiated hardness and distrust.

Her massive figure was made up of piled mounds of flesh that were visibly compressed by what must have been steel-ribbed corsets. The dress she had on was made of an expensive flowered material, but the designer had given up on subtlety; he had tried only to avoid total disgrace. It was wrapped around her like a tent, reaching half way to her ankles, but even then it did not conceal the tree trunk legs that supported the whole gross body.

"Mrs. Lockheim?" Harbizon asked.

Without answering, the incredible woman eased herself down onto one end of a sofa that might have been specially built to hold her weight. Then her eyes glowed at him like live coals. "What do you want?" she asked in a voice that belonged in a fishmarket.

"I'm Lieutenant Harbizon, ma'm, from the police department. I would like to express our profound sympathy to you for what has just happened."

"Sympathy won't help a damn thing," she answered him. "My husband is dead, very suddenly, and everything is up in the air."

Harbizon detected no sorrow in her voice; she could have been speaking of the death of someone she had barely met and had not particularly liked. Perhaps, he thought, she was just case hardened and tough—the product of a hard childhood and possibly privation at one time or another. He wondered, because he could not help himself, if she had ever been normal-sized. Not slender, exactly, but able to pass muster as an attractive woman.

Still, with that face and those eyes, she must have been flint hard from the beginning. "Are you aware of the nature of the accident?" he asked, probing her for some sort of response.

He got more than he had hoped for; the woman leaned forward an inch or so, about as much as her body would allow, and her voice was suddenly armor plated. "Accident! Don't give me any of that crap. I was in my apartments upstairs and I saw out the window. It was an explosion and that, mister, was no accident!"

She lifted her left arm and looked at a wrist watch fastened by gold links around a wrestler's forearm. Harbizon saw it as she turned her arm; it had a square face that was completely surrounded by diamonds. On each side of the dial there were square projections like a pair of crude wings; their faces glittered with more diamonds set as close together as the maker had been able to manage. Harbizon thought that it was probably worth a mint and also that it was the most vulgar thing he had every seen. Her fingers were loaded with rings: there were still more diamonds, rubies, and two miniature carvings of Burmese jadeite. He had a sudden urge to find it all comical; with an effort he forced that thought out of his mind.

"Mrs. Lockheim," he tried again. "I don't want to distress you at such a time, but can you tell me if your husband had any known enemies?"

"Enemies? Everyone has enemies. Mr. Lockheim was very, very successful; to be that you gotta make enemies. Maybe hundreds, I don't know."

"Has anyone, to your knowledge, threatened your husband's life recently?"

She lifted her huge shoulders and let them fall. "Maybe. People got mad at him at times, but I don't concern myself with that. My husband could take care of himself."

Harbizon carefully refrained from pointing out the fallacy in that, instead he watched as the little maid appeared once more, this time carrying a dessert plate. On it was a large Napoleon; whipped cream had been added on top and what Harbizon took to be chocolate syrup. The immense woman took it without apology. "I have a stomach condition," she said. "Something like an ulcer. I have to keep food on my stomach or it becomes very painful."

She picked up a fork, skimmed off a large lump of whipped cream, and put it in her mouth.

Harbizon saw no reason to prolong the interview; he had too many other pressing things to do. As he stood up, Happs dutifully followed his example. "Thank you for seeing us at such a difficult time, Mrs. Lockheim," he said.

The woman looked up at him, her jaws working on a chunk of the pastry. "Call me Gilda," she answered.

When Harbizon got outside, the fire department arson specialist was waiting for him. The two men did not bother to shake hands; it was not a social occasion. "What have you got, George?" Harbizon asked.

"So far, it was a bomb, of course, and the man who made it knew his business. It was expertly installed under the driver's seat on the frame, and then hooked up to the right turn signal. That's a European trick, by the way, one of their special cuties. I did some thinking while you were inside. Lockheim drove home from the station and then went up right in front of his own place, fortunately where there was no one else to be hurt. I think that was intended. On the route from the station to here there are two left turns, but none to the right until he reached his own driveway. If it had been wired the other way, the bomb would have gone off right in the heart of town."

"Thank God for small favors. Any idea as to the type of bomb?"

"Not yet, because it could have been almost anything. The results are consistent with a neat plastic charge, but that's only a guess at the moment."

"So it comes down to one of two things: someone who didn't like Lockheim is an expert in the use of explosive devices, or else he knew how to get hold of a demolition man to do the job."

"That's how I see it too."

"And no chance of mistaken identity; that gold Caddie was one of the most conspicuous cars in the area. Parked at the station, it stood alone."

"John, that could be it right there. Somebody who saw that big flashy car at the station every day let it get on his nerves . . ."

Harbizon cut him off. "I can't buy that as a motive for murder. Not premeditated, as this one was. This wasn't a simple killing, just a butcher knife in the chest sort of thing. This one was planned, and very carefully executed."

The arson specialist accepted that. "I'll go over the wreckage and fill you in by noon tomorrow. Unless you need it sooner."

"That'll be fine," Harbizon answered. He checked the scene once more: the body had been removed and the burned-out car was about to be towed away. A fireman was standing by to wash down the roadway. He got back into his car, called off the road blocks by radio, and then drove back to the police station. As he walked inside he met the deputy chief who actually filled a captain's role in the department structure. At the chief's invitation he went into his office and supplied all the information he had. The chief listened intently, without comment.

"It's too late at night to do very much," Harbizon concluded, "but in the morning I'm going to start by checking for anyone who saw something being done to Lockheim's car. I don't have much hope; a lot of potential witnesses will deny seeing anything. And the man who planted that bomb was no fool."

"The FBI may be able to give us some help on known bombers."

"And after that, we can check on known enemies. His wife implied that he had some."

The deputy chief pushed back in his chair and pondered. "How much do you know about Lockheim?" he asked.

"Very little, as of now."

"Well, it depends, I guess, on how you view these things. He was a floor trader, a professional speculator on the stock exchange. So his career consisted in taking away other people's money, particularly the vulnerable small fly. Sometimes he lost, but largely he won. If you want to put it in harsh terms, he was a vulture."

"You could call that business acumen, couldn't you?" Harbizon asked.

"Yes, but you see so many of the so-called investors in the market don't want to gamble at all. A stockbroker somewhere recommends something and they buy it, hoping for a fair return and some eventual appreciation. But that can be like going for a beginner's swim in a pool of sharks. They don't know about the pros who are on the floor all the time for the sole purpose of skinning them. Lockheim undoubtedly broke a lot of people along the way; some of them were other pros who understood the risks they were taking, a lot of them weren't."

Harbizon had never heard his deputy chief talk that way and he searched in his mind for a possible reason. "How much did he take you for?" he asked.

The chief made his voice deliberately unemotional: "It was my fault, John, and there's no one else to blame. I thought at the time that I was making a conservative investment, but it didn't really matter, because Betty got a scholarship anyway. She's a bright girl, you know—a lot brighter than her dad most of the time. Thank God my stupidity didn't hold her back. From what I know now I take it that most of what I had went to add to Lockheim's profits. And I certainly wasn't the only one. So if you want to start tracking down his enemies, you may have quite a job ahead of you."

Chapter Two

In the stiffly cooled, softly lighted, carefully prepared atmosphere of the restaurant William San Marco felt himself very much at home. Because the location was well up into Westchester County, and on a carefully selected side road, it did not have quite the space problems it would have had to face on Manhattan Island. Consequently the tables were comfortably separated one from another and it was possible to talk without having total strangers on each side forced to listen to every word being said. He had careful plans laid for the young woman who was with him and to bring them about with his usual élan he had been more than glad to drive up from the city. He liked the country anyway, up to a point.

He had called and reserved a window table even though he had known that it would be close to dark before he would arrive. It gave a certain feeling of insulation from the outside because of the plate glass, and at the same time a lack of confinement that the center table could not avoid. The out of doors was there, behaving itself, but available if needed.

The drinks on the table were of the elaborate tropical variety that were called by exotic names and served in hollowed-out pineapples. They tasted of rum and fruit juices, but there were other ingredients that upped their potential considerably under the guise of mild flavor. San Marco knew that very well; so did the girl who sat across from him, even though she had never been to that particular restaurant. "Um, nice," she said in appreciation. She delivered the line well, making it sound unsophisticated and quite sincere.

"I thought you might like it," San Marco declared. "I believe in trying new things all the time. It makes life a helluva lot more interesting."

"Of course," she agreed as if the inner meaning of his remark had totally escaped her. "Anybody can do the same old things all of the time."

That answer pleased San Marco so much he decided at that moment to go whole hog on the dinner. If he spent four dollars on a drink he expected it to get him four dollars and fifty cents worth of results. That was the minimum. Some people he knew enjoyed spreading money around: it gratified their egos and those who accepted it responded with all of the necessary flattery. When he spent any of his own money, every dollar was calculated. It was an over-developed sense, perhaps, but it was his stock in trade and he made it work for him. The good things in life that he enjoyed all came from that semi-private instinct to protect himself at all times.

His decision made and firm, he leaned forward with a winning casualness. "How about chateaubriand for two," he suggested. "They do it exceptionally well here."

His companion smiled just as if she had taken a childish delight in his having proposed the most expensive item on the already costly menu. It had told her something she had wanted to know and the information warmed her on the inside as much as the unconventional drink had done. "I'd just love it," she answered.

San Marco summoned the waiter with a manner he had acquired only after careful practice in front of a mirror. He tried to make it combine equal parts of sophisticated youth, authority due to position, and the irresistible force of a well-stuffed wallet. He placed the order, specified Lyonnaise potatoes and fresh spinach on the side, and added rather loftily that they would have coffee later. He overdid it very slightly, but not enough, he was sure, to do anything but impress the female on the other side of the table.

She considered him a clown, but for the purpose she had in mind, she was willing to make allowances.

In point of fact San Marco was three weeks under fifty years of age. The anguish of his fiftieth birthday was something he had decided to circumvent by fixing in his mind that he was actually forty-seven and by never allowing himself to abandon that illusion for a moment. He did not like being forty-seven either, but he felt that he could defeat his numerical age by looking and acting as though he were still in his romantic thirties. He never visualized himself as anything other than romantic; he had chosen the name by which he was known with that in view. And he had certainly made out with the women. There his money had been of great help, but he had never paid for it, not directly. Women wanted him, women desired him, and that concept was almost more important than life itself.

Of course he had done his part. He had spent a fortune on clothes, cars, and on the cosmetic advantages that were available to a man. He paid a great deal to his hair stylist and to his barber who was positively brilliant with mud packs, facial massages, and similar refreshing treatments. In fact, for a man of forty-seven he was remarkably youthful looking and his hair transplant had been a considerable success.

As the dinner progressed he kept up the brilliant conversation that he knew would overwhelm the young woman he had chosen for his next conquest. She was something very special; if she proved to be as good as he dared to hope, he was prepared to take care of her for a while. He had a recently vacated apartment available and few additional arrangements would be needed. The apartment was well chosen and also well buried in his business expense records; he took a secret delight in the knowledge that he was also taking it off his income tax.

As soon as the dessert had been served, and everyone in the dining room knew that they were having cherries jubilee, he went into his well-rehearsed speech. "You know, Marcia, you can laugh at me if you like, but just having this dinner with you is a lot more than you might think. You're not an ordinary girl, you know."

He had never found a woman who wouldn't swallow that line.

She flashed him a smile with slightly pursed lips and bedroom eyes. "I think you're assuming too much," she told him. Inwardly she knew that it was true: she wasn't an ordinary girl as far as he was concerned. When he found that out, it might be the biggest shock he had ever known.

He picked up a spoon and began to toy with his cherries. "Look, Marcia, this is the first time that we've had dinner together, but I don't think it would be the last. I certainly hope not."

"Thank you," she responded.

"I'd like to get to know you a lot better, to see more of you." He pretended confusion as though the double meaning had been accidental. "Do you have any terribly serious commitment that would prevent it?" He knew, of course, that she didn't.

She pretended to think for a moment. "No, I don't think so. Not right at the moment. Of course . . ."

"We'll cross that bridge when we come to it. You told me that you write feature pieces to order, but that you don't have an assignment right now. Perhaps I can help; I know a lot of people."

"You must, I know, but I don't know how you've done it all. Bill, how old are you?"

He didn't think at all. "I'm older than I look, Marcia, I might as well admit that right away. I'm forty-five."

She looked at him as if she couldn't believe what she had heard. She had half thought of sending him a birthday card in three week's time, but thank the Lord she had avoided that blunder. "I'm amazed," she declared. "I though you were in your late thirties, possibly forty, but certainly no more than that."

He smiled what he considered his boyish best. "At least I'm not over the hill; not by a long ways yet."

"You'd never have to tell any woman that," she flattered.

It was going so splendidly he congratulated himself that he was combining both youth and experience in his best performance to date. Forty-five was older than he wanted to be, but it was true; he sometimes looked at himself a certain way in the mirror and he did look as though he were in his late thirties. A good James Bond age.

"I'm going to declare myself," he said, skipping by instinct much that he had so carefully prepared. "I am single again, at last, and I have the income to provide practically everything that anyone would want, but I'm not in the market for anybody. If you'll let me, I'd like to give you the time of your life for a while—until one of us says 'when.' And I can tell you right now, it won't be me." That certainly ought to be clear. Obviously, this was a girl who had been around enough to understand him and if she proved to be really good in the sack, then he might keep it up for a considerable while. She was an exciting wench.

"Let me think about it," she said.

For the sake of the impression it would make on her he left a very generous tip and was most gentlemanly as he made his way out. That was a part he had learned to perfection.

Outside the air was remarkably soft and warm. The very large parking lot held only a few vehicles; it was an off night. He handed a dollar to the parking attendant and said, "I'll pick it up myself."

He made a little ceremony of putting her into the huge black
Cadillac and then got in behind the wheel in the manner of a true
man of affairs. He turned the key and lowered the windows, letting
the inviting air inside. "Can we drive a little before we go back?" he
asked.

"Of course."

That was the key response—the implied consent. He had it made,
he knew it. Dizzy with delight at his own virtuosity, he slipped the
car into gear and turned up the road. He kept the speed moderate
so as not to upset her by blowing her hair too much; women were
funny that way. Within three or four minutes he had the road to
himself except for one other car well behind him that showed no
disposition to catch up and pass. If the other driver wanted to, he
would let him: he was in that warm a mood.

They reached the spot in twelve minutes time. He stopped at the
place he knew without the weakness of making an excuse and
turned to his companion. He rested his hand very gently on her
shoulder in the darkness and became as tender as he could simulate.
She came to him, not too eagerly, but in a way that showed she was
a real woman with all her internal fires banked, but burning. He
kissed her forehead and when she responded ever so little, he went
into his carefully developed routine.

The only awkward moment was getting her into the back seat,
but he managed it. When she came with him his last doubt was
erased and his loins were bursting with anticipation and eagerness.
Presently she was his in a way that was all that he could hope for in
the relatively confined space.

"Good evening."

The voice, almost in his ear, hit him like a thunderclap. For a
bare moment he was unable to move; he had never been so startled.

His mind was racing. A cop: it had to be a cop. Consenting
adults, that's what they were, and fornication wasn't an offense any
more. Embarrassing, hell for the girl, but she'd live through it. After
all, she'd been had a good many times before.

Then he felt a piece of cold metal press against his forehead and
terror flooded him until he couldn't even jibber.

"Don't move," the voice commanded. "Stay exactly the way that
you are."

He couldn't have moved for anything; it was all that he could do to keep breathing. Only his mind worked, and because he was used to tight corners he managed to speak. "My wallet's on the front seat. Help yourself; I'm insured." He started to rise.

"I said, don't move!"

He froze in compliance, despite the total awkwardness of his position.

The hard steel was still against his head. "Now, Mr. San Marco, you've come to the end of the road. You have just screwed somebody for the last time."

"No!!" he shrieked. The sound was still in his throat when the first silenced bullet hit him. He never felt the second.

The call that came in to the state police reported that there was an hysterical woman screaming in the middle of the roadway. The informant refused to give his ID, but he had taken the trouble to call the mobile operator from the phone in his car.

In response Trooper Stephen Petit was dispatched to the location. As soon as he was in the vicinity Petit began to cruise slowly, using his movable spotlight and with his roof lights on. A quarter of a mile further on he found her; sitting by the side of the road, sobbing, and obviously in some form of shock. He stopped his car beside her and went to her assistance in his most considerate manner. "Can I help you, miss?" he asked.

The girl replied by grabbing him savagely around the legs and hanging on with almost total desperation. Petit let her stay that way for a good thirty seconds before he did anything about it. Then he bent down and gently pried her arms free. "What happened?" he inquired, keeping his voice calm and soothing.

The young woman began to babble, but he could not understand what she was trying to say. He did grasp that she wanted him to go back in the direction from which he had come; she kept pointing that way. He eased her gently into the car, turned around, and began to drive very slowly toward the north. The girl was still inarticulate, but she continued to point ahead. As he drove, Peitit picked up his microphone and in careful language, because the girl could hear him, he reported the probable need for medical help.

He had just finished speaking when the young woman clutched his sleeve and pointed toward a turn-off on the left hand side. He took it at once without hesitation. He had turned his roof lights off, but he kept his movable spot on so that he could scan the area as he went.

Within a short two hundred feet he found the black sedan. After sweeping it with his spotlight he got out carefully, his weapon at the ready. He approached the semi-hidden car with full caution; when he was close enough he looked inside. As soon as he had done so, he hurried back to his own vehicle and reported what he had found.

The response took a little while because of the location, but in not much more than fifteen minutes four other vehicles had arrived, including an ambulance with an intern aboard. The young woman, who was still incoherent, was turned over to his care while the police personnel began a systematic investigative procedure. A trooper armed with a camera popped innummerable flash bulbs as he recorded the whole scene, both close-up and at a moderate distance, from every available angle. The doctor having quieted his patient examined what remained of William San Marco and pronounced him dead without hesitation. The victim was not a pretty slight, but policemen and medics in the greater New York area were all too familiar with violent death and to some extent they had gotten used to it.

The ID of the dead man was called in together with a request for the NYPD to supply as much information about him as its computers could print out from what was already stored in their memories. It was close to daybreak before everything that could be effectively done at the murder scene had been completed, the body had been removed, and the death car had been towed away to the police garage. Within a comparatively short time the road would once more be in normal use carrying its usual amount of traffic. Of the hundreds who would drive past during the morning to come, none would see any evidence that something out of the ordinary had taken place. And if they did happen to hear about the murder on one of the news broadcasts, they wouldn't greatly care.

After the shifts had changed, a considerable readout on San Marco came in from the New York Police Department. He had once been charged with rape, but the young woman involved had changed her story and withdrawn the complaint. He had had a considerable record of traffic offenses, but no warrants were outstanding. He had given his occupation as "financial specialist," a designation that covered a very wide area. He had also been twice divorced and had been named in another action.

Sergeant Charles Dietrich, the homicide investigator assigned to the case, probed deeper and came out almost at once with two interesting items. First, the victim had been employed as a "specialist" on the floor of the stock exchange; secondly, his true name was not William San Marco. He had been born just short of fifty years before, in the Bronx, as Moshe Feldman.

Sergeant Dietrich had never put any of his own money into the market and he was not sophisticated concerning the way that it operated. To find out precisely what the dead man had done he called on a stockbroker he knew would cooperate and asked for a full explanation with nothing omitted. He put it that way because he still did not have an inkling of a motive. He could think of several possibilities, but he had no evidence on hand to support any one of them.

"Since this is a police matter, I'll give it to you the way that it really is," the broker began. "The Stock Exchange puts out the idea that it is a trading facility, in fact if you go up on the balcony you can see an unbelievably juvenile display that shows how a farmer in the midwest, who has some stock he doesn't want, sells it, through the exchange of course, to a sweet old lady in New Hampshire who just happens to want precisely what he has and who finds the price to her liking. That's baloney. What really happens is this: each stock admitted for trading has what is called a specialist who handles all of the transactions concerning that particular company. A specialist may handle two or three stocks, but seldom more than that. So if you want to sell stock in the XYZ Company, you sell it to the specialist. If you want to buy some, you buy it from him. And he sets the price in both instances."

"In other words," the sergeant said, "he runs the only game in town."

"You've got it. When the market is going up, he may take his stock up with it, or he may keep the price down for a while. He has a lot of leeway. Without going into all the details about shorting, trading against the box, and other maneuvers, he usually manages to keep things in hand so that he comes out with a substantial profit. Sometimes he will get caught, but the specialists are sharp, they have to be, and you won't catch them in a corner very often."

"And it's the investors who pay him," the sergeant suggested.

"Correct. In many different ways. Just for example, John Doe buys a thousand shares of XYZ at thirty-five and then to insure himself against too severe a loss he puts in what is called a stop order, that is he authorizes his broker to sell the stock for him at a lower figure, but not too much lower. So John Doe puts in his stop order at thirty-one. If it reaches that figure he will be sold out at a loss of four thousand dollars, plus commissions, but that's all he can lose. Sounds great, doesn't it? But that stop order goes to the specialist who knows that he can buy a thousand shares of XYZ at thirty-one. So, if he wants to, he can usually manage to take the price down just to the sellout figure. The broker holding the stock follows orders and sells. The specialist picks it up and then lets the price rise again. Of course he can't bother to do that every time, but in the smaller stocks where there is not too much trading action, it can be a nice gimmick for him. The average, normal customers don't know this; to them the stop loss order looks like a very good idea, and under some circumstances it is."

"Just suppose that the stockholder simply decides mentally to sell if the stock reaches a certain figure and then keeps his eyes open?" Dietrich asked.

"That's doing it the smart way, of course, but few actually do go that route. The stock reaches the sell-out figure and they don't have the discipline to dump: they hang in there figuring that it will turn around soon and they won't have to swallow a bad loss. And down it may go until they become alarmed, at which point it's too late. Also, how many people have nothing to do but sit and watch the market all day? The professionals do, of course, that's one reason why they make out."

For another half hour the sergeant gathered information about the late victim's business activities, then he closed his notebook to leave. At the door he turned back and put one more question. "I forgot to ask," he said. "What was the stock that San Marco represented?"

The broker didn't know that offhand, but a single phone call produced the information. "Sphinx Wire and Cable," he reported.

Chapter Three

Lieutenant John Harbizon was practically prepared to sell his soul for one good cooperative witness. Everywhere he turned he ran into the New York syndrome that has as its basic creed *Don't Get Involved.*

No one at the railroad station was able to, or would, tell him a thing. Yes, it was recalled by one man that quite often car repair people came to the parking lot and worked on one of the cars there. It wasn't the railroad's business; the lot was provided as a convenience with no liability of any kind attached. Someone might have been on the lot, working on Lockheim's car, but he hadn't noticed. Furthermore, he couldn't recall any of the people who came to the lot at various times; he had other work to do.

Harbizon knew that it would be futile to check with the various available garages: the wiring job on Lockheim's car hadn't been done by any repairman who regularly provided service in Boylesport.

The report from the arson investigator gave him nothing new that he could use. The explosive charge had been put under the driver's seat, not in the gas tank as might have been expected. It had been a professional job all the way, with the added note, in case the lieutenant had forgotten, that the turn signal trick was a European invention.

Patiently, carefully, Harbizon built up his file. He was not a man easily discouraged. If it came simply, well and good; if it did not, he was prepared to do whatever was necessary the hard way.

When five days had elapsed, and the memorial services had been concluded, he braced himself for an ordeal and went once more to call on Mrs. Gilda Lockheim. As before, he was kept waiting until it suited her to present herself. When she at last waddled in, Harbizon rose to his feet like a humble petitioner. The sight of her in a pink pants suit was almost more than he could handle. He could not imagine what had persuaded her to wear a thing like that which, if anything, mercilessly emphasized her elephantine proportions. He guessed that she had issued a preemptory order concerning style and color and then had left the defenseless designer no choice but to commit artistic hara-kiri. She sank onto one end of the same sofa and fixed him with her hard, glinting eyes. "I don't know a damn thing more than I did last time," she greeted him. "What does your wife call you?"

He saw no need to tell her that like so many other policemen he was divorced. "John," he answered.

"All right, John, get on with it."

He began on a carefully calculated soft note. "I sincerely hope that Mr. Lockheim left you well-provided for."

She gulped the bait like a frog snaring one more fly. "You could say so. I inherit this place and about ten million after taxes, the way it looks now. With what I've already got, I should be comfortable."

"I sincerely hope so," he lied easily. Privately he thought it would be wonderful if she were compelled to go to work somewhere. She would make a good cashier, always providing that she could wedge herself into the appointed place. "Mrs. Lockheim—Gilda, I'm making a complete investigation of your husband's death. If I'm successful, I'll catch the man who was responsible. Or the woman. Right now I'm anxious to get every detail that I can."

"Somebody blew his ass off, that's all there is to it." Her voice held the emotion of a railroad spike, not a trace of sorrow showed. Apparently realizing that, she troubled to add something else. "He was a good provider."

"Obviously. Gilda, can you tell me how he got his start?"

His subject heaved herself into a fresh position. "Hell yes, I gave it to him. When we were married, it was my dough that set him up. He was young then, but smart and already he had some good connections. So I staked him enough to get on the exchange and have some capital to work with. It was a business deal, strictly, and we signed papers over it. He wanted it that way, he said for tax reasons. He made money almost right from the beginning."

"Gilda, did your husband ever do any other work?"

"Nat? No, he wasn't fitted for it. He was a speculator, but a damn good one. He used to tell me that he let others do the sweating, but when he was in school he was a theater usher once for about three weeks. Something about having to take a job for that long to get his degree."

"What was his degree in?"

"Investments and banking, I think; I'm not sure."

For a half hour longer Harbizon asked his questions and for the most part received candid answers. But with them came very little information that he could use. He asked the proper things, but most of the time his subject simply didn't know, or at least said so. He did confirm that the relationship between the dead man and his wife had been passive for some time, but since Gilda had held the purse strings to a considerable degree, a separation had never been mentioned. Harbizon thanked his hostess and left.

On the way back he laid out his next moves: first to get a list, if he could, of those persons who had lost substantially to Lockheim during the past six months—a year if the data could be located. Then he would check that list for any persons who had been in service and who had had demolition or other explosive experience.

Although it didn't help matters very much, it was evident to him that whoever the killer might be, he knew a lot about the stock market. The FBI had once examined two million pieces of handwriting looking for one suspect and had found him; compared to that his job should be relatively easy.

Also, the killer might be satisfied having taken his revenge on Lockheim, or he might not. He resolved to make a careful check of every reported homicide, or possibly related incident, that might involve a prominent stock market personality. Or a broker. That was a pretty good bet: a broker who had led a victim into Lockheim's fly trap might have good cause to be worried. There was a lot of work to be done.

When he reached his office, there was a note on his desk to call Sergeant Charles Dietrich of the state police. A direct Westchester County number was supplied.

When he had Dietrich on the line he identified himself and then waited.

Dietrich came right to the point. "I understand that you're handling the Lockheim killing in your jurisdiction."

"That's right. What can I do for you?"

"We've just had one up here that may be related. The m.o. is entirely different, the victim was shot at close range in his car—while he was humping a girl, as a matter of fact."

"What a way to die!"

"Right, and the girl blew her mind. The reason I called you: the deceased was involved in the stock market. He was a floor specialist if that means anything to you."

"Not at the moment, but go on. Who's the victim?"

"He was known as William San Marco; real name Moshe Feldman. Another one, I take it, who changed his name for business reasons."

Harbizon thought. "I think we ought to get together," he said. "I can think of two possibilities that might link these crimes together."

"So can I, and I don't like the second one one damn bit. I think the stock market angle is a good one, and that's what I'm following up at the moment. Incidentally, our killing was pretty tricky—not as simple as it sounds."

Harbizon reacted to that. "Fill me in," he requested.

"I said that our man was shot, and he was, but with an undersized bullet. You know the trick: you take, say, a thirty-eight cartridge and take out the bullet. In its place you put a smaller one, or possibly shave the original. It only works at short range, because it cuts way down on the accuracy, but it effectively prevents any kind of a ballistics test. As it is, I can't even say what calibre of gun was used."

"Was it dumdummed?"

"Good guess, it was. Whoever did the job isn't a casual killer. I'm running a check on all of the recent boy friends of the witness . . ."

"The girl who was getting laid," Harbizon interrupted.

"Yes. It's a pretty full list, but if one of those guys was pissed off, he'd get a gun, perhaps, and shoot San Marco. But he wouldn't go to the trouble of that trick shot. And he probably wouldn't know how."

"All right, Dietrich: here's something for you. The mechanic who did the job here was a pro and a cute one—probably European trained. Definitely not an amateur. Let's get together."

"I'll be with you in an hour," Dietrich said.

Harbizon welcomed his guest with a cup of bitter coffee that came out of a machine and spent five minutes in professional small talk. When that was over he knew the quality of the man who had come to see him and approved. Dietrich knew the homicide business: there was no doubt of that. After that he listened while the man from the state police laid out his case. He saw no point of real similarity: the stock market connection was the best bet, plus the remote possibility that he still held in the back of his mind. When Dietrich had finished, he gave him a briefing on his own case, including the details that had not been made public. The turn signal gimmick was one of them. The witness who had seen the explosion had not made that connection, or if he had, he had been careful not to mention it.

Dietrich listened with total attention. "Now we have two things," he said. "Both were stock market profiteers, parasites of a kind. A lot of people might have reason to hate them, but most of those who lost their money to them would never know their names. Or even that they existed. I had a broker brief me. Secondly, we have evidence that the killer in both cases was a genuine pro, someone who knows his business thoroughly."

"There's one other thought," Harbizon said.

"I know, lieutenant, and God forbid. Both victims were Jewish; it could just be . . ."

Harbizon kept his unbroken calm. "We've had the SLA, the Weathermen, and a number of other violent revolutionary groups. A Nazi kind of thing could be the answer. There are some organizations around."

"I know; we have files on them, of course, and the FBI has all kinds of information. I don't think that's it, because I presume that a good percentage of Wall Street operators are Jewish. And two out of two is a pretty small percentage."

Harbizon had an inspiration. "By any chance," he asked, "do you happen to know, yet, the name of any stocks that San Marco handled?"

"Yes, so far only one, but he specialized in it. Sphinx Wire and Cable."

"Eureka!" Harbizon snapped back. "That's the stock that Lockheim was involved in. I distinctly remember that name coming up."

Dietrich was elated and allowed it to show. "Out of eighteen hundred stocks they were both on that one. There's the connection: definitely. I won't buy a coincidence."

"Neither will I, what do you say that we hit the stock exchange together, in the morning?"

"You're on," Dietrich answered.

Three men were waiting for them when they arrived at the Stock Exchange. With careful formality everyone shook hands, then the small party settled into a conference room that had been designed for groups of from twelve to twenty. That made it possible for the five men present to gather at one end of the long central table with a suggestion of confidential rapport.

Harbizon opened his notebook and wrote at the top of a fresh page the names of the three men: Marcus, Fellini, and Stone. As he did so, his colleague from the state police opened the meeting.

"Gentlemen, Lieutenant Harbizon and I are heading up the investigations into the deaths of Mr. Nathan Lockheim and Mr. William San Marco, respectively. We know that both were active on the floor of the exchange and we feel that the killings may very well be related."

Marcus cut in quickly. "I understand what you are saying, sergeant, but simply because both men traded on the exchange floor it doesn't follow that their deaths are necessarily in any way connected."

Opposite the name "Marcus" Harbizon wrote *lawyer*. He looked up to see Dietrich looking at him, clearly putting a silent question.

He answered it affirmatively. "Gentlemen, you probably know this already, but both victims were associated in the trading of the stock of Sphinx Wire and Cable. That narrows the matter considerably."

The man called Fellini looked worried for a moment, then he spoke. "That certainly appears significant, gentlemen, and since this is a police investigation, I'll be completely candid with you on another point. I have informed myself in both of these killings insofar as the press reports permit. I know that Mr. San Marco was shot while . . . in the company of a young lady. Strictly not for publication, he had a reputation as a ladies' man. You understand what I'm driving at."

Opposite his name Harbizon wrote *PR*.

"We've already determined that, Mr. Fellini," Dietrich replied smoothly. "Two of our detectives are at work right now exploring that angle. Lieutenant Harbizon is also checking on the private life of Mr. Lockheim to see what may be significant there."

The one named Stone shifted slightly but did not speak. John Harbizon addressed him immediately. "In the confidence of this meeting," he said to the austere, white-haired man across from him, "if you can assist me there, I would appreciate it."

Stone took hardly a second before he replied, but it was enough for him. "I dislike very much discussing the private affairs of our members, but in view of the circumstances I will tell you, totally in confidence, that Lockheim was tied to his wife by legal commitments in addition to marriage. She is not an attractive woman, as you certainly already know. He did have a discreet lady companion whom he had maintained for some time. Apart from that, he was very circumspect in his personal affairs. I doubt if this has any bearing on your investigation; he provided very generously for his wife and the other lady involved, I happen to know, was most satisfied with the arrangement. I understand that she has no relatives."

Harbizon nodded his understanding and made a note. Opposite Stone's name he wrote *brass*.

Fellini cleared his throat. "Er, gentlemen, I do have something to tell you, but I'm somewhat hesitant. However . . ." He paused, pretended a moment's confusion. "You understand that the exchange is just that: we provide a trading facility and the necessary support functions, basically that's all. Many fortunes have been made here, and, unquestionably, some monies have been lost. But usually by investors who were not prudent in their selections or who, frankly, were speculating. Within the past ten days Mr. Lockheim received a letter, here at the exchange, from what appears to be a mentally deranged person. However, it does contain a death threat directed against him. Mr. Lockheim turned it in to us and our security people are investigating."

"Not the NYPD?" Dietrich asked.

Fellini spread his hands, dramatizing his Italian origins. "Gentlemen, if we turned over every crank letter we receive to the New York Police, they wouldn't have time for anything else."

"Of course," Marcus added, "if a letter were to come in, or any other kind of communication, that we had reason to believe was a genuine police matter, we would report it immediately."

"I understand," Harbizon said. "Incidently, gentlemen, Sergeant Dietrich and I have both been seconded to the NYPD for the purpose of this investigation. That's quite customary in cases of this kind. Now I would like to see the letter."

Fellini looked at Stone who nodded his head a half inch. The PR man opened a folder and passed the note across. Harbizon took it, checked the envelope, and then read the brief letter inside. When he had done so, he passed it to Dietrich and remained quiet while his colleague digested the piece of evidence. When he had finished Dietrich issued an order. "I'd like to have your security people fill us in on anything they have on this letter to date. Since it passed through the mail, it's federal. However, as I read it, it is more an expression of anger; the phrase 'it would be better if you were dead' isn't precisely a death threat."

"Quite possibly not," Stone said. "But we thought you ought to be told of it."

"Certainly," Harbizon responded. "Now a question at this point: how many letters like this come in here, on the average?"

Fellini looked once more at Stone who in turn was looking at Marcus. The lawyer answered. "Not very many, actually, because few members of the public have any idea who our floor traders are, or the names of the specialists who handle specific securities."

"But they can find out if they want to?"

Marcus hesitated. "Yes, I would say that they could, if they wanted to make the effort."

Dietrich had a question. "Since you are already investigating this letter from . . ." he checked the name once more . . . "Daniel Sisler, I presume you can tell the amount of his loss in the Sphinx Wire and Cable stock."

"Well, I'm not sure . . . . ."

"About eight thousand dollars," Stone cut in. "which, to a little man, could be quite a lot."

"I see. Mr. Stone, understanding that a double homicide is involved, and we have to consider the possibility of more if we don't stop this immediately, would you say that this particular stock had been manipulated?"

Stone did not blink an eye. "A pitcher manipulates a baseball when he throws it toward the plate, the term is very catholic. It is a matter of record that that particular security did have some rather dramatic fluctuations during the past several months. But there is no evidence whatever of any wrongdoing in that. When people buy, a stock goes up: when they sell, it goes down. Substantially it's as simple as that."

"Superficially," Harbizon responded, "that's true of course, but if there is a material change in interest rates, for instance, that can affect the market quite drastically, isn't that true?"

Stone did not move a muscle. "Perfectly true, Lieutenant, but I call your attention to the fact that the change in interest rates normally influences buying and selling and that, in turn, has an effect on prices."

In his notebook Harbizon underlined the name *Stone*. Then he stood up. "Thank you for your cooperation, gentlemen," he said. "I'm sure that we will be meeting again soon."

Outside the conference room there were two fairly young men waiting. As soon as Harbizon appeared they closed in on him. "Lieutenant Harbizon?" one of them asked. He could have been thirty-five; Harbizon's first impression of him was of slightly bug eyes and a complexion two shades lighter than it should have been. He wondered instantly if the man had been in prison.

"Yes," he answered. "What do you want?" The prison thought was still in his mind.

"My name is Bert Schneider, Amalgamated News. This is my partner, Gene Burroughs."

The light went on; Amalgamated News was new, aggressive, and making waves, even in New York."

"Burroughs and Schneider," Harbizon repeated. "I know the byline."

"Please, lieutenant, Schneider and Burroughs. Otherwise they abbreviate it BS. You see the point."

"I do. My colleague, Sergeant Dietrich, state police."

The two reporters shook hands. Burroughs, Harbizon noted, wore elevator shoes, but they were of a very expensive make. His suit was much better cut than was required for his job. A second look at Schneider confirmed that he was wearing what appeared to be a twenty-five or thirty dollar tie. He made an easy deduction that the well-known investigative reporters commanded pay checks commensurate with their considerable fame—or notoriety. "How did you ID me?" he asked.

Schneider answered him. "We learned you were on the case from the Boylesport Police. As soon as we had your name, we got a mug shot out of the morgue. We also read about the jewel heists that you cracked. Congratulations."

Burroughs took the conversational ball like a pivoting second baseman. "We're working on a new series about the stock market. It's been done before, of course, but during this last year there's been a major increase in stories of financial wrongdoing, a lot of them dealing with stock transactions."

Stone had disappeared, but Fellini was still present. He came forward with his hands half raised, palms toward the reporters. "Gentlemen, please. I told you only last week that we would cooperate fully with you, but harassing these officers at this time . . ."

The words were fine, but the way that they were spoken said something else entirely. Harbizon caught the difference clearly and it riled him. Also, the people of Boylesport, for the most part, were very conscious of press coverage—of the kind that they approved. "We've got another appointment," Dietrich said, then he caught Harbizon's reaction. "But we can spare you five minutes."

"That'll do it," Burroughs said, fresh crispness in his voice. "Let's go outside."

The brief interview was conducted in the police car that Dietrich had provided. Schneider opened a notebook, a gold Cross pen in his hand. "Look," he said, "to save time, we already know about the connection between the deaths of Lockheim and San Marco. That last is a phoney name, by the way."

"What connection?" Harbizon asked.

"How did you find out?" Dietrich added. The two speeches almost overlapped.

"They both dealt in Sphinx Wire and Cable. Lockheim was the trader, San Marco the specialist. They worked hand in glove, a couple of savvy parasites." Schneider seemed to savor the words.

"Aren't you being a little hard on them?" Dietrich asked.

Burroughs was ready with an answer. "San Marco was a cocksman: he only beat a rape charge by buying the girl off, and that isn't all that he had to pay. When he was seventeen he was up for manslaughter—traffic accident—but he beat it and managed to get the record sealed. Juvenile. Legally yes, but his little girl friend was pregnant at the time."

That was one Harbizon had missed, but he gave no indication. "What do you want from us?" he asked.

"First, any suspects?"

"None in custody at this time."

"How about the girl Marco was having when he got it?"

"Our next step; we haven't talked to her yet."

Schneider took over. It was an effective technique: one man questioned while the other formulated his questions to follow. "Are both of you going to stay on the case?"

Dietrich answered. "Until we're told to stop."

"And what might cause that?"

"The right suspect in custody, with all necessary evidence to prove his guilt."

"Aren't you the Sergeant Dietrich who solved the Fleisch killing about three years ago?"

"I was on the team. It was a combined effort."

"As I recall the suspect confessed."

"Not in words, but he shot himself just before we got to him."

Burroughs was warmed up and ready. "Do you believe that the fact that both of the murdered men were in the stock market, professionally, is a significant factor in the two cases?"

"That's a possibility, certainly," Harbizon answered. "We intend to check out all of the leads we can uncover."

"One more. In general terms, are you aware of the number of major stories in the Wall Street Journal dealing with stock market frauds and manipulations that have appeared recently?"

Harbizon had a dead safe answer for that. "I don't read the Wall Street Journal. Gentlemen, that's all."

The reporters got out of the car and took the trouble to express their thanks as they left. When they were out of range Dietrich commented. "They're sharp."

"Yes, I agree. But we didn't give them very much."

Dietrich pressed his lips together in grim irony. "Just how much did we have to give them?" he asked. "Let's go and see the girl."

The building on the west side was in the sixties not too far from upper Broadway. It had once had a moderate dignity, but that had been stolen by spray cans of black paint that had defaced it with words and symbols against which it had no defense. The few steps up to the door might have been scrubbed during some long gone decade, but now they were hopelessly overlaid with dirt that seemed to have penetrated deep into the stone, vivid stains like spilled cofff-fee, and some that were eloquent of passing animals. It was four stories tall and neither man had to be told that there was no elevator.

The lobby, such as it was, had a broken tile floor and a worn out door that still hung on its hinges and made a pretext of protecting the interior. A small row of mail slots was on the right hand side; a few had cut off cards stuck in their name slots, all of them were decorated with more rust than paint. There was an odor of stale to-bacco smoke and a suggestion of urine. Dietrich checked his notebook and then pushed one of the buttons that had no name card to identify it. After some delay the remote latch of the inner door buzzed.

The girl who called herself Marcia Churchill lived on the third floor. The steps up were steep and hard; there were fittings still in place that had once held carpeting, but they had been unemployed for a long procession of dreary years. The neighbourhood had gone down, Harbizon concluded, to the point where the landlord refused to spend anything that wasn't essential on his building. He would still have tenants.

Although it was approaching noon, Marcia was wrapped in a thin pink robe that was faded from many washings. She had combed her hair and had used some cosmetics, but even in the less than adequate light of her doorway the signs of accelerating age and hard urban liv-ing marked her like acne. As soon as Dietrich had introduced himself and Harbizon, she admitted them listlessly and planted herself in a worn chair for the inevitable recounting of her story. The front room was small and looked out over the street: it was a toss-up whether it was worth looking through the window or not. There was a fake fire-place that had once been a half attempt at elegance, now it admitted itself to be a fraud and earned its Lebenstraum by displaying a small assortment of pictures and a carnival stuffed animal that had a thin veneer of plushness.

"I've been waiting for you," she said, "I knew you'd come, sooner or later. I can't tell you a lot."

There was an undertone Harbizon caught, a fighting against nonentity, a desire not to be just another police interviewee. It didn't take him a second to shape his response to it. "Miss Churchill," he said. "We both realize that you've been through a frightful experience; we appreciate your receiving us here in your home."

It was her home, to a point, as long as she paid the rent promptly and accepted the inevitable increases that were periodically imposed. But it was drained dry of pride: it was a small area in which to live from day to day, from week to week, until something broke, one way or the other.

Dietrich followed him perfectly, he said nothing but he radiated sympathy and understanding. And, as Harbizon had hoped, the girl fell for it. "It's nice to be treated like a lady," she responded. "I know what you're after; do you think that if I give you all that I can you could go easy on me? The wrong publicity could kill me right now."

"Answer two questions first," Harbizon countered. "First, do you know who killed Mr. San Marco?"

"No."

"As far as you know, did you have anything whatever to do with his death?"

"No."

John Harbizon sat back and visibly relaxed his manner. "In that case, I think we can leave it that two gentlemen know how to treat a lady."

She drank up the implied flattery like a starving kitten with a saucer of milk. "You're all right," she said. "Are you sure you're cops?"

Without comment both men displayed credentials. She shook her head. "The smart thing is never to talk to cops, but I want out. I want to get free of this thing as fast as I can."

"Perhaps," Dietrich suggested, "if you do give us all that you can this time, it may not be necessary for us, or anyone else, to come back." Harbizon gave his temporary partner a strong vote of confidence; the state police sergeant knew his business. And, essentially, he had spoken the truth.

The girl tilted her head back and stretched her arms out along the back of her chair. When she spoke, she could have been addressing the ceiling. "You can look me up, I know it, so I'll save you the trouble. My real name isn't Marcia Churchill, I'm east European and I come from Pittsburgh. My parents were immigrants. I'm thirty four and trying my damndest to pass for twenty-six or seven. Once I had ideas about a career, but that's all blown now; all I'm after is a man to take care of me and get me out of this." Her gesture included the room and, by implication everything about the apartment, the building, and the street outside. "For a while I was a damn good looking doll, but I blew it and married the man of my dreams. There are different kinds of dreams."

"Such as nightmares," Harbizon suggested.

"Right on, brother! Let's skip the details. I'm not a call girl, I've never been. Nobody has ever bought a piece of my ass for cash like that. You know I was getting laid when San Marco, if you want to call him that, was shot. So there's no point in being coy about it. If a man can do something for me, then he gets something in return, I don't think that's too bad."

"How long had you known Mr. San Marco?" Dietrich asked. His voice was gentle, as though he was primarily interested in her.

"Not too long. But long enough to have looked him up." She shifted her position and looked at Dietrich directly. "Let's lay it on the line: I told you that I was looking for a man who could take care of me. I can pass as good looking, and young, for maybe another year or two; after that, who knows. I found out that he has a plush apartment over on the east side where he puts up his mistresses. None of them last too long, but in the beginning, when he's trying to score all the points he can, he likes to play the bigshot and be generous. I know the girl he had a year ago. She told me that I might be able to make a play for him and get him to keep me. The ride might be good for six months if I really worked at it. Meanwhile, I could build up a nest egg. There's only one cushion that will soften the bumps in life and it's cash. Green beautiful money. I need some, badly. He was a fifty-year-old egotistic freak, but he had the money. He was determined to spend some of it on a girl who would tell him that she couldn't believe that he was forty-five and pretend that no other man in the world could screw her so magnificently. That's why I let him have me that night—so that I could look him in the face and tell him that it was the greatest sex I had ever known, that I hadn't imagined that it could be like that. If he bought it, and I was pretty sure that he would, then I had my six months of comfort and whatever I could gather on the side,—legally of course."

Harbizon nodded. "I don't blame you a damn bit for trying," he said, and half meant it. The apartment he was in would have driven him out of his mind in a week's time. "Miss Churchill, how did you meet Mr. San Marco?"

"The girl I told you about set it up. She made it look accidental."

"She wasn't jealous?"

She shook her head vigorously. "No way: she had had her ride, or just the opposite, and there was nothing more there for her. You see, this man was an egomaniac, he had to have new girls all the time to convince himself that he was young and dashing, and irresistible to women. He'd had his face lifted and a hair transplant; my girl friend told me all about it."

"However, he was apparently a good stock trader."

She waved a hand in the air, letting it move however it wanted. "I don't know anything about that, except that he did have a lot of money. And he told me that he was making it hand over fist, but a lot of guys give you that line. Helen, that's my girl friend, told me something else: he liked to appear to be splurging, but he never spent a dime unless he thought he was getting something for it worth at least fifteen cents—or more."

"Marcia, just for the record, I'd like your girl friend's name." Harbizon had been holding that question, waiting until the moment was right.

"I didn't want to tell you that."

"Probably we won't need to talk to her at all," Harbizon said, trying to sound as though he meant it—and succeeding. "It's mainly so we won't have to come back and bother you again."

"Helen Chow: she's Chinese. Her father runs a provision company on Mott Street, or somewhere in Chinatown."

He nodded as though he were completely satisfied. Then, casually he asked for and got her number.

He looked at his subject and for a moment smiled at her, as though he knew that he was a policeman on duty, but if he had not been, he would have liked to have asked her out. He radiated understanding and masculine approval of a desirable female. "You told me," he said, "that you didn't know who killed your escort on that . . . night. I accept that. I wonder, however, if you have any ideas or thoughts of your own. You're a very intelligent young lady, and I want to hear anything you have to say."

It worked. Marcia Churchill sat silently for several seconds, then she spoke very cautiously. "I'm not sure, you understand, and when it happened I was, well, upset isn't the word."

Both policemen remained graveyard still, so as not to break the spell.

"You see, Helen had this boy friend who was pretty stuck on her. But he couldn't take care of her, not the way that she deserves. Of course a lot of men like her, she's exotic and very, *very* pretty. I only saw the gunman in the dark and I only heard him speak a few words, but when he said, 'That's the last time that you'll screw anybody,' I thought for an instant, just thought, that it might be him. His name's Harold Horowitz and he works in Wall Street."

Chapter Four

When Harbizon got up in the morning it was pouring rain. The steady downpour came out of a low lead sky that sucked the energy out of his body and gave him the feeling that whatever he attempted to do that day was foredoomed to defeat. And whenever the rains came traffic incidents increased dramatically as though the Boylesport drivers had never learned to cope with wet streets, as indeed they hadn't. For the most part they were people who were not used to inconvenience and who could not understand when it was thrust upon them.

The trains would run late because it would take the passengers so much longer to get on and off at each station. In New York itself cabs would be impossible, the subways would have the musty odor that wet weather always brought out, and the supposedly greatest city in the nation would virtually slow to a crawl. Decisions that were made were much more likely to be negative and no one would say that it was good for the crops.

As he shaved, Harbizon listened to the news There was little reported that he did not already know. The market was reported down almost four points on the Dow; profit-taking was given as the reason.

As he drank his morning instant coffee and ate toast he reviewed his plans for the day. Charlie Dietrich had agreed to run down the threatening letter addressed to Lockheim because the writer lived up his way; there was no question of Dietrich's ability and if there was anything to find, he would get it. Meanwhile Harbizon had accepted the tedious task of trying to ferret out those persons who had lost heavily during the past several months because of Lockheim. At the same time he planned to try and find out just how ethical the speculator had been in his business dealings. The fact that he had been a professional gambler on the exchange, and that was the word for it, didn't necessarily make him a scoundrel as well.

From his office he made a call in to the NYPD and talked to a Lieutenant there who was working bunko and who was a specialist in stock market operations. The city man was already informed about Lockheim's death and the fact that Harbizon was working on it; he maintained good files. He suggested that they get together; Harbizon answered by promising to catch the next train.

The miserable weather continued all of the way into the city and showed no signs of a letup for the next several hours. Harbizon accepted it as part of a policeman's lot and made his way to the office of his colleague hoping that there might be a cup of hot coffee waiting when he got there. It would be bad coffee, that was automatic, but it would be warm and stimulating.

The man he met was big, very wide in the shoulders, sandy-haired, and surprisingly young. Or at least he looked it. He had a reddish complexion, more than a hint of freckles, and the build of a professional wrestler. He extended a quick, cordial welcome and led the way into his small office without a shred of formality. "It's John, isn't it?" he asked.

"Right." Harbizon passed over his card.

"Ted. Nobody can pronounce Walchewski anyway. So you got yourself into a can of worms."

"It looks that way. You know the problems with a bomb case: you can't set the time that the charge was planted, the man who did it can be miles away when it goes off, and if the job is successful, there's nothing much left to work with; the evidence destroys itself."

"It was a pro job?"

"Definitely."

"Then our MO files may help out. In the meantime, you want to know about Lockheim."

Harbizon settled down and took out a fresh notebook. It was a larger one than he usually carried and he was all set to begin on page one.

"Some coffee, John? It's not so hot, but what the hell."

Knowing the way that things were, Harbizon dug into his pocket for change. His host shook his head and left the office. While he was gone Harbizon studied the large bulletin board that all but covered one wall. At the top of semi-permanent sign read. *No Polish Jokes.* That was the only evidence of levity; thum-tacked below there were fifteen or twenty news stories clipped from various media. All of them reported admitted frauds, actions taken against member firms of the New York Stock Exchange, censures by the Securities and Exchange Commission, and investigations of white collar crime. The name *Equity Funding* was prominent in some yellowing columns.

Walchewski came back with two paper cups of coffee. He planted himself behind his small desk, tossed two packets of sugar where Harbizon could reach them easily, and relaxed. "So Nat Lockheim is no more," he said almost cheerfully. "I'm sorry, of course, that his passing has given you a nasty job."

"Were you building a file on him?" Harbizon asked quickly.

"Not on Lockheim himself as much as on the whole Sphinx Wire and Cable mess. A lot of people were badly caught on that one. Some of them asked for it, but most of them were innocent investors."

"Fill me in."

Walchewski put his massive forearms on the desk. "The company itself is a sound honest outfit that turns out good products for the military. They're a prime source. About six months ago Sphinx came out with an annual report that was a sensational job; the agency that produced it made the company sound like an ideal holding."

"Exaggerated half truths, that sort of thing?"

"No, not really: all of the facts were valid as far as I know, but the tone, the bubbling optimism, was overdone in view of the general climate defense suppliers have to face right now. But to get back to the subject: with a company like Sphinx a rumor of congressional action, or a veto, can make its stock act like a Mexican jumping bean. And the traders who are just a jump ahead of these rumors, or who feed them, have practically sure bets."

"What I'm after," Harbizon declared, "is some first class suspects. Some who lost heavily to Lockheim not too long ago. I just might find one who had learned demolition in Nam."

"Well, John, you've got yourself a job, because stock market customers come from all over the country, and other parts of the world. And think about the brokers too: if they recommend something to their clients and then the roof falls in, where are they?"

"I thought they had big research departments to back them up."

"To some degree, but look here: a brokerage firm gets a big position in a stock that it wants to unload. So it puts the word out to its salesmen to push it. The salesmen, or brokers, follow orders unless they want to lose their outside telephone lines. They shove the cats and dogs onto their customers like a waitress promoting last week's roasts as barbecued beef bones. They have stock in trade like everyone else, only most people don't know that."

"Was Lockheim a distinctive individual, or are there others like him?"

"Plenty, unfortunately. There are lots of traders who use their wits and who have the privilege of buying and selling without having to pay commissions. If a stock goes up or down even a half a point they can make money, and they frequently do. If you or I go for the same stock, it will have to move a point or more before we can break even with our commissions. So the traders have a big edge."

"Getting down to specifics," Harbizon said, "I'd like to get a list, if it's at all possible, of people whom Lockheim took to the cleaners. Or Lockheim and San Marco as a team. Not the small fry in Burning Stump, Oklahoma, but here in New York and the surrounding areas."

"I'll try," Walchewski promised. "I'll see what I can find out."

That was what Harbizon wanted to hear. He said the remaining necessary things and then excused himself. He was anxious to talk to the bomb specialists and to consult their Mo files.

Mr. Simon R. Korngold was in a particularly vile mood. He was not a man of even temperment and he suffered from a permanently inflated ego, so when things turned against him, as they did at times, he became unbearable—often even to himself. For almost a month he had carefully been building a heavy short position in one single stock where he knew that the earnings reports were going to be a serious disappointment. He had paid for that information and then had built up his account on the short side, some of it visibly, much of it through straw men and stock held in street name. He had what he knew to be a sure thing.

He had overlooked the fact that the president of the company had spent the four years of his college career living in the same fraternity house with a significant government official. If he had checked the sports records, he would have learned that the government man, as quarterback, had passed to the company president, as tight end, for the winning touchdown during the last eighty seconds of play in a memorable homecoming game. Mr. Korngold didn't give a damn about sports and that, in part, was his undoing.

He had never imagined that the smaller, definitely dark horse candidate for a major contract would be able to get the ear of the powerful man who would make the final decision. Once more the quarterback put up the ball, once more the tight end was there, this time with a sound proposition and the low bid. At a news conference the company executive released the important news. Almost immediately it hit the broad tape and when it did, the company's stock that had been depressed for months, crashed through its resistance level and soared. Korngold had been badly caught and had had to cover with heavy amounts of cash. His month's careful maneuvering had been wiped out and he had had to swallow the biggest loss of his career as a professional trader.

He did not wait for the market to close; he could not stand it to be on the floor for another minute where other traders could look at him and know that he had at last guessed totally wrong. He got out of the sight of those who could ridicule him and headed outside, the whole middle of his body feeling as though hot lava were running through his intestines. When he was at last in the open air he ignored the fact that it was still pouring rain. He almost tripped as he reached the sidewalk and recovered himself awkwardly. That tiny incident inflamed him even more: it had made him look ridiculous for two or three seconds in the eyes of a few others who didn't know him and who cared even less.

It became a burning necessity to him to exert his authority; to issue commands that would be instantly obeyed because of his position—and his money. There was a lot less of it now, but he blocked that intolerable fact out of his mind. His head down against the pelting of the rain, he saw a cab coming with its top light on.

Out of the corner of his eye he saw that he had a competitor for the cab; the driver was already pulling over in response to his signal. Korngold knew well that the first passenger to hit the rear seat would win the cab and the right to use it; with total determination he leaped forward to grab the door handle and jump inside before the other man awoke to what was happening.

An odd thing happened. Another cab, that had been apparently parked momentarily, suddenly accelerated as fast as the wet pavement would allow. It struck Korngold with its right front fender hard enough to throw him off his feet and a short distance through the air before he hit the pavement. For a second or so the cab swerved as the driver fought to regain control, then it spurted forward still faster until it reached the corner. It turned against the light and disappeared into the stream of traffic that was moving northbound. Simon Korngold lay still and bleeding on the side of the street.

Because everything that happens in New York is seen by someone, and because Wall Street is a jugular of telephone lines, someone called the police. A car responded shortly and an ambulance was summoned. Simon Korngold, still living but in very critical condition, was lifted off the pavement and taken to the nearest available receiving hospital. There he was undressed and cared for while his wallet was searched for evidence of medical insurance that would pay the charges. When nothing was found, the business office became very upset, but it was too late to stop treatment.

Dr. Robert McKinley did his best: there was no time to assemble a team of specialists and young Dr. McKinley therefore had to cope alone. For a resident with limited experience in the emergency ward he did phenomenally well; the case-hardened nurse who assisted him was markedly impressed. When after three quarters of an hour of intense work on his behalf Simon Korngold breathed his last, Dr. McKinley rested his chocolate-colored hands on the body of the man he had fought so hard to save and despite his years of training very nearly wept.

John Harbizon was patiently going through the long involved MO lists when a young officer tapped him on the shoulder. "A call for you," he said.

Dietrich, who was on the line, was brisk. "I have the dope on Daniel Sisler, the man who wrote the letter to Lockheim."

"Any good?"

"Could be, he had demolition training in the military and he has no immediate alibi, but there's something else. About two hours ago a man was knocked down by a a hit and run cab in front of the Stock Exchange. NYPD has a good and apparently very reliable witness. There are some suspicious circumstances; the car that made the hit could have been lying in wait for him."

"Does the victim fit the pattern?" Harbizon asked. He knew he would be understood.

"Yes, very closely, based on first reports. I'm going down there now; do you want to sit in?"

"I'm on my way," Harbizon said. "When and where?"

They met in an office that was temporarily vacant: in addition to Dietrich there were two homicide men from the NYPD and the witness. The strong atmosphere of the police station did not upset the man in the least; within seconds of meeting him Harbizon knew that he was a gem. He obviously had his head on straight, he was articulate, and he had no fear whatsoever of becoming involved. He was Mr. Ideal Citizen; his name was Henessey.

When the introductions had been made and the door had been closed, one of the New York men took over. He was small and slender with a thin head of hair that refused to stay on top of his head. He wore it slightly long to cover his baldness with the result that it kept constantly falling over his forehead. He looked like an unemployed typesetter which was strictly protective coloration; he was thoroughly experienced and competent. His partner, a younger man, was obviously new in detectives and smart enough to keep still and listen. Harbizon picked him as a comer.

"Mr. Henessey," the older man said, pushing his hair back with his right palm. "You've been very good to wait here until these gentlemen arrived. Now, if it isn't too much trouble, will you please repeat what you told us for their benefit?"

"Certainly," the witness answered. "My name is Chester Henessey and I'm a printing salesman. I spend a good deal of time in the street, Wall Street that is, and in the surrounding financial area. We supply letterheads, vouchers, receipt books, and a wide line of specialized forms for the use of financial institutions." He passed across two of his business cards.

"This afternoon, at approximately two-ten, I came out of a building below the Stock Exchange and on the other side of the street. I had a midtown appointment at two forty-five; I had just started to walk toward the subway when I saw a cab coming with its light on. That was a break I hadn't expected, particularly on a rainy day. I signaled the driver and he began to slow up and pull toward the curb where I was."

"Was anyone else trying to get the cab at that time?" Dietrich asked.

"No, not as far as I could see. Apparently I had been lucky. Just then I saw a man across the street slip and for a moment I thought he was going to fall. Then, with his head down, he dashed into the street toward the cab I had just hailed."

"In other words, he was trying to beat you to it," Harbizon commented.

"Yes, I believe that's correct. It's grossly discourteous, but you know this city. I should say that I had noticed another cab pulled against the curb a little farther down the street, apparently waiting for someone. I didn't actually see that cab start up, but I caught its motion out of the side of my eye as it came up the street, accelerating rapidly despite the wet pavement. Then, without slowing at all it hit the man in the street with its right front fender. I distinctly saw him thrown through the air for a distance of about six feet."

"Can you describe that cab?" Dietrich asked.

"I'm sorry, sergeant, outside of saying that it was yellow, I can't. I was frankly shocked and by the time I had recovered my wits, the cab had sped down the street and was much too far away for me to get the license number. I saw it go through the red light and turn into the uptown traffic stream. As far as I could tell it was a standard-sized cab and not too new, but that's all. Of course any pursuit on foot would have been futile."

The senior New York detective nodded his agreement. "We certainly agree with that, Mr. Henessey. Tell these gentlemen the rest."

"There's very little more, actually. Someone phoned the police, obviously, since they came very fast. I went to the help of the man in the street, but I'm not medically trained and there's very little I could do."

"But you did stay until the officers came."

"Yes, of course. The ambulance came very quickly also, I was still talking with one of the officers when the man was taken away."

"What happened to your cab in the meantime?" Harbizon asked.

Henessey looked at him. "I don't know lieutenant, I didn't think about it until this moment."

"One last question, Mr. Henessey." The homicide specialist pushed his hair back off his forehead once more. "You've given us a very lucid account of what occurred. Now, in your opinion, was it an accident, or is it possible that the victim was deliberately hit?"

Henessey considered that for a few seconds before he replied. "I would have to say that the way the cab started up, so rapidly, and on wet pavement, certainly wasn't normal. It could have been an accident, but there is no way that the driver couldn't have known that he had hit someone, I remember now that his cab definitely swerved after the impact."

"That's important."

"Thank you, sir. In answer to your question, it was either a hit and run, or something that had been planned. But, in the latter case, considering the way that the man ran into the street, headlong and without looking, even if it was deliberate and you were able to catch the driver responsible . . ." He stopped realizing that he was getting tangled in his sentence. "What I mean is, I'm not a lawyer, but with the given circumstances, I don't see how you could ever get a conviction."

The deli-restaurant wasn't crowded; its worn booths had held countless forgotten customers since they had first been installed, but two of them were empty when Harbizon sat down with Dietrich to compare notes. They ordered and then relaxed. Harbizon traced a finger across the scarred Formica and banished from his mind, as best he could, the fact that his wife had left him two years before on the same date.

He was not a handsome man, he had no illusions about that. He tried to make up for it in the way he dressed and the manner in which he conducted himself. He was not yet forty, but there were lines in his face that had been etched there permanently. They were not signs of dissipation, or even of long late hours on the job, they came more from hard work and dedication. Someone had once told him that he looked like a mountaineer. When he contemplated the massive pile of work that his profession entailed, he sometimes felt like one. He was surprised that women frequently found him attractive, and told him so.

Dietrich opened his notebook. "I've had a talk with Sisler. He readily admits having written the letter to Lockheim, but he insists that it wasn't threatening per se. Frankly, I have to agree with that. Also he signed it with his right name and gave his return address and I can't believe he would have done that if he had contemplated any violence against him. However, it is a fact, and Sisler admits it, that he served in Nam and he has had training in demolition. He has no satisfactory alibi to cover the whole time period during which the bomb could have been planted."

"Are you satisfied that he's out of it?" Harbizon asked.

"Pretty much so. He was very straightforward; he admits that he was enraged when he lost his money through Lockheim's manipulations and he sounded off. He had a right to; it's still a free country, thank God."

"How did Sisler get onto Lockheim in the first place?"

"I've been waiting for you to ask that. He saw a column head with the name Sphinx Wire and Cable in it, so naturally he read it. The column had a lot to say about Lockheim and his heavy profits when the stock plunged. In language that stopped just short of libel it said that he had had advance knowledge and therefore manipulated the stock to his own considerable advantage."

"Was San Marco mentioned in the article?"

"Yes, but not as prominently."

Harbizon bit into his pastrami sandwich. He chewed until he could talk easily once more, then he asked the other question that Dietrich was expecting. "Who wrote the column, Schneider and Burroughs?"

"That's right," Dietrich said.

The city of Boylesport is limited in size and in population, but it is disproportionately important as a center of both wealth and influence. It has a tax base which makes possible a level of municipal services considerably above average, the police department among them. When the Lockheim killing became a major *cause célèbre* in that carefully controlled community, the word was put out quietly, but with authority, that no expense was to be spared to bring about its resolution. The city manager had had several calls promising him all the backing he might need, but pressing for action.

The city manager called the police chief who had been expecting to hear from him on an hourly basis for the past three days. Without any external indications of applying pressure, the city manager made his point clear and then asked some questions, all in a very restrained manner. "Who have you got on the case right now?" he asked.

"John Harbizon," the chief answered promptly. "He's very well qualified, as you know. And he's been relieved of everything else until the Lockheim killing is solved."

"Would you like some extra help?" the manager asked. "I can request assistance from the state police and call in some private specialists in consultation."

"I certainly appreciate your support," the chief responded, "but for the moment I'm going with Harbizon. He's already working with the state police on the case, by the way. You know the salary we had to offer to get him and he's more than proven that he's worth it. If he asks for any more back-up, I'll see that he gets it. Right now our budget is in good shape."

"Then lets leave it this way: as long as the Lockheim murder remains unsolved, I'd like to suggest that you keep Harbizon on it full time and with all of the expense account he may need. I want him to follow it all of the way through. That can be done, I believe."

"Yes, it can be done, even if he might have to go into some other jurisdiction. I'll keep him on it unless it reaches the point where there is nowhere else to go. If that happen's I'll let you know."

"Fine. In the meanwhile, the city's official position is that we have put our top detective on it and that there isn't a better man anywhere. If you have to, you can leak the fact that we hired him at a premium salary to be sure we would have a man of his stature available if we ever needed him."

"Perfectly understood," the chief said. "One suggestion: I think the city should post a reward. It will look good, and it might be helpful."

"Damn good idea," the manager responded. "About ten thousand?"

"Right on, I'd say."

"I'll make some calls," the manager promised, and hung up.

By morning John Harbizon knew that he had carried his investigations in Boylesport per se as far as they would go. He had searched for additional witnesses and had all but exhausted the ones he did have. Someone had remembered seeing Lockheim's conspicuous car passing through town on its way toward its owner's estate, but that was of no practical help. An exhaustive examination of the burned out wreck that that car had become yielded nothing new. The most tenacious questioning of every possible known person who had been on or near the railroad parking area on the fatal day got nowhere. A stakeout that had been set up just in case the bomber might decide to try again had been futile as far as the murder was concerned. A thief who was stealing electronics under the guise of a repairman was nabbed, thereby clearing up an annoying problem for several other communities up and down the railroad line.

The chief sent for Harbizon and was diplomatic. He knew that his best man could probably get a job with more prestige, and possibly more pay, almost anywhere he chose. "John," he said, "I've had a talk with the city manager and some members of the council. The upshot is that to a man they have every confidence in you and they're going to continue to have it. They understand, in short, what you're up against."

"But."

The chief shook his head. "No 'buts,' John, just the opposite. I've been instructed to give you full back-up in any form that you need it; I'm to call in any help that you want. Furthermore, the city is putting up a ten thousand dollar reward for information leading to the arrest and conviction of the bomber. Also, until further notice you have total mobility with all necessary expenses. They want the Lockheim killer."

Harbizon uttered a very soft, drawn out whistle. "Evidently they don't know who might be next."

"That's part of it, certainly. Lockheim was popular to a degree, but I suspect that it was his money that was the attraction."

"Did you know him?"

"Slightly. Within this office, I didn't care for him, and he indirectly cost one member of this department a lot of money he couldn't afford to lose. And his wife is an obscenity. She got abusive with a delivery boy about six months ago and had to pay him off to avoid a lawsuit. The kid told me that he had never heard language like that in his life, and he wasn't tenderly reared. But Lockheim was totaled out in our fair city and his killer must therefore be brought to justice."

"I'll do my best," Harbizon promised.

As soon as he could get away, he took the train into the city. As he rode he thought, and cemented in his mind the idea that the killing of William San Marco, or Moshe Feldman, was closely related and offered a more fertile field of investigation. Also there was his Chinese ex-mistress to be followed up, and her boy friend. He was relieved to know that he had been given an almost totally free rein; it could easily have gone the other way if the community had insisted on a sacrifice.

When he got off the train, he was slightly astonished to be met by Sergeant Charles Dietrich. "Let me guess," he said, "you called me at my office and they told you I was on my way into the city, probably on this train."

"This is the second one I've met," Dietrich admitted. "We have a break; believe it or not, the NYPD has made the cab that hit and killed Korngold. It may be related: he was a floor trader and speculator, noted for his temper and his ruthlessness."

As they walked together toward the street Harbizon asked the question he wished he could ignore, and to which he already knew the answer. "Was he Jewish?" he asked?

"Yes, definitely. I checked to make sure. The first readout is that he was a very hard case who would rather bite your head off than talk to you. A minor record when he was younger, principally an assault charge. He couldn't buy out of it, the victim was a police officer."

"New York born?"

"No—Europe, Russian extraction. He was apparently born somewhere in Eastern Europe. Came here with his family when he was fifteen. He was seventeen when he tackled the cop."

Dietrich stopped for a moment and took a newspaper from under his arm. "Read," he said, and pointed to a good-sized display ad:

REWARD
$5,000.00
Will be paid for information leading to the arrest and conviction of the person or persons responsible for the violent deaths of our valued and esteemed members:

Nathan Lockheim
William San Marco
Simon R. Korngold

(In the case of Mr. Korngold, the above reward will be paid as specified if it is established that his death was deliberately caused. If the proper authorities determine that his death was accidental, $500.00 will be paid for information leading to the arrest and conviction of the driver of the cab responsible for his fatal injuries.)

"That's interesting," Harbizon said when he had read the announcement. "But even in an ad they had to slip in the small print."

"What the big print giveth the small print taketh away," Dietrich said. "But it's immaterial because the police have the driver already, I think unaided. Now, maybe we'll get somewhere in this damn case!"

Chapter Five

Miss Helen Chow was not at all what Harbizon had expected her to be. He had somehow visualized a tiny, slim girl with wide almond eyes who would look all innocence and who underneath would be a hard, calculating little bitch. Instead he found himself confronted by a young woman who wore her black hair in a soft swirl around her face which was open, friendly, and altogether lovely. She was of medium height and her figure was at once intensely feminine. The dress she wore was informal, but a model of good taste. Her Chinese descent was evident in her features, but it was secondary. There wasn't the slightest hint of the Orient in the way that she held the door open or the manner in which she made him welcome. Within seconds Harbizon knew that she was highly intelligent and that if he didn't watch himself she would have him captivated.

Her voice was like water running under snow. "Lieutenant Harbizon? Please come in. I'm Helen Chow."

He walked into the room following his hostess. She gestured toward a settee and when he had sat down she placed herself more or less beside him. He could detect her perfume then and the man inside the policeman hammered to be let out.

"What may I offer you?" she asked. "Hard, soft, hot or cold?"

"Soft and cold." There was no drinking while on duty in Boylesport and he automatically refused to take advantage of his position. He was alone for a minute or two, then Helen came back with two tall glasses filled with ice and some red-colored liquid. "This is a special fruit punch we have," she said. "See if you like it."

Harbizon obeyed, took a careful swallow and his taste buds reeled with delight. "It's marvelous," he declared.

He received a smile in return that would have made the Trojan horse stand up and rear. He found it a strain to believe that this appealing girl had been William San Marco's mistress. But the fact was definite, according to the information he had received. For one bitter moment he wished that policemen were compensated in the same manner as Wall Street speculators.

Helen folded one leg under her body as she turned sideways to face. "I assume you want to talk about Bill San Marco."

"Yes, if you don't mind."

"I'd rather not, obviously, but I realize that a murder investigation takes precedence over my personal feelings. So go ahead, Lieutenant, and I'll be as helpful as I can."

Harbizon began to recover his form. "That's very kind of you, Miss Chow, and in return let me assure you that I will protect your privacy as much as I'm able. I'm not here to collect gossip."

"My name is Helen, Lieutenant, and I think you must be a very fine policeman."

"Why?"

"Because you're obviously a gentleman, you're conscientious, and the way you put that indicates to me that you're probably an excellent psychologist."

"Are you a psychologist, Helen?"

"No, I'm a fashion designer—in furniture and decorative fabrics."

"I suspect that pays quite well."

"It does, inspector, up to a point. But I'm not implying by that that I've found it necessary to augment my income in other ways. Much older ways."

Harbizon saw the trap and sidestepped neatly. "Tell me about Mr. San Marco," he invited. "Whatever you'd care to say."

She drank some of her punch and set the glass down with precise care. Harbizon noticed it and deducted something of her mental processes from that simple clue. "Bill San Marco was a leech," she began. "Not only in his business dealings, but in the way he managed his life. He had a gigantic ego and the principal reason why he went after money was as a means to gratify it. He was a notorious woman chaser, less for biological than statistic reasons. He saw himself as a perpetually young, dashing, romantic lover that no female could resist. Actually he never fitted that description, I'm sure, at any time in his life."

"Was he a religious man?"

"I doubt if he ever went near a temple, at least for the last thirty years. I know for a fact that he didn't observe the high holy days, because the point arose during the time that I was living with him."

That was a deliberate lead-in that she had given him and Harbizon knew it instantly. "Since you know the first question I'm going to ask, suppose you answer it," he invited.

Helen lit a cigarette and let the smoke drift silently upward. When she put it between her lips her mouth curved into a shape that was for a bare moment totally tantalizing. Then she blew the smoke out as if to say that what was visible was unobtainable. "I met San Marco at a party where, as usual, he was trying to cut a swath wider than anyone else. His trick was to play up to me, to show how he could captivate the exotic flower who was present in a black dress. What he did not know, and never learned, was that I had gone there specifically to meet him."

She paused, but Harbizon was far too experienced to interrupt her with a comment.

"You see," she continued, without any visible emotion, "He had once badly cheated someone in our community. You may have heard that we tend to have very strong family ties."

"I know it for a fact," Harbizon said.

"Quite simply, I decided to deal with the matter. Roger Han, a stockbroker friend of mine, made the necessary arrangements. He knew about San Marco and had met him once or twice. At that time I was twenty-nine years old, still unmarried because I still hadn't found the man that I wanted, and being normal in all respects that I know of, I was not a virgin. Does that statement disturb you?"

"Not at all; I find it comforting."

She looked at him. "Why?"

"Because of what I know about San Marco. I would not like to think that he received an honor he didn't deserve."

"The man who received the honor, as you put it, took it without consulting me. I was sixteen. Subsequently, of course, I occasionally made my own choices, not always successfully I might add."

Harbizon opened his mouth to say, "Try me," but he caught it in time.

Helen took a final puff from her cigarette and then neatly put it out. Harbizon was glad, because it had spoiled the aura of her perfume.

"I let San Marco, which was a self-chosen name as I presume you already know, make the necessary advances. I dined with him twice before he asked me to occupy the apartment he maintained for his kept women. His ego demanded that I accept. I made it clear to him that I had never accepted such a proposition, which was true, and that it would take a great deal to make me look with favor on his. He told me that I was priceless and that he could afford it, a rather visible contradiction in terms. During the time that I was supported by him I allowed him limited sexual contact, and no more, until I had recovered the entire sum that he owed, with appropriate interest. And some additional for my inconvenience. Then I contrived to have him get rid of me, otherwise he might have become difficult, or even annoying."

"And that was the end of it."

"Almost. A member of my family sent him a receipt for the money he had unintentionally repaid. We desired that he should know."

"Was Mr. Horowitz aware of these—arrangements?"

"Marcia probably told you that Harold is my boy friend. We are good friends, but it doesn't go beyond that."

"Still, I'd like to talk to him."

"By all means, if you would like. For your information, Harold's family is strictly orthodox, which is to say that they will never approve of any girl who is not of similar religious background. I don't qualify and Harold will never go against their wishes. Therefore we keep things within bounds. We both like medieval music, so we go to The Cloisters together and some other places. However, I can tell you right now that on the evening when San Marco was shot, Harold and I were together until quite late—very late, in fact. And if you need them, I think that I can produce witnesses."

Driver Abraham Schwartz sat in the hard chair that had been provided for him, twisted his greasy cap in his hard, muscular hands and wished to hell that the detective talking to him would stop pushing his hair back on top of his head all of the time. Every time he tried to think the damn cop would start fussing with his hair some more and make him forget what he intended to say.

He was in a damn tough spot and he knew it. He was fifty-four years old, he had had no other occupation but driving a cab for the past twenty years, and the man before him could take away his "face:" the license that permitted him to drive a hack in the city of

New York. Hacking made some money, of course, but Abe Schwartz had a number of sidelines closely connected with his work that were much more profitable. Dropping tourists at certain bars, keeping special trips off his route sheet; there were all kinds of angles. But he had to keep his face to stay in business and if he lost it he didn't know what the hell he could do. He wasn't fitted for anything else. Outside of New York he would have perished like a water-starved canteloupe.

The detective took a comb out of his pocket and arranged his hair formally; as he was putting the tool back in its place, part of his thin crop of hair fell over his forehead once more. It nearly drove Schwartz crazy.

"Now let's go over it again," the detective said. "Do you deny that you dropped a fare in Wall Street shortly before two yesterday afternoon?"

Schwartz felt that his only defense was to clam up, so he did.

"I don't remember, look at my route sheet."

There was a tap on the door that in itself told the detective a great deal. He got up without hurrying and looked outside. A voice that was out of sight of the cab driver told him, "The witness is here, and ready to make the identification."

That didn't scare Schwartz; he knew too well that fares never noticed a hackie's face or remembered his number. They usually didn't give a damn.

The witness who came in was a man, dressed in a business suit, with eyes behind steel rimmed glasses that were hostile and cold. The witness surveyed Schwartz as though he were a fish on display in the aquarium and spoke in a flint-hard voice. "You've got the right man. I'm positive. I'll testify to it."

"How are you able to recognize him?"

"I saw his cab come around the corner against the red light. It forced its way into traffic and forced my car almost into a collision situation. The man had his window open despite the rain. He leaned out and made an obscene gesture to me, then he cut in front of me ruthlessly. I memorized his face and then took his license number. I followed him for two blocks while I made sure of it."

"Did you write it down?"

"I did. I have it here, the same piece of paper. I wrote it on the edge of the *Times* that I had on the seat beside me."

That was bad. Two or three times before a witness like that had caused Schwartz serious trouble. He was had and he knew it. The only way out now was to cop-out for as little as possible. If he persisted in evading questions and remaining silent, they'd have his face for sure.

The detective sat down calmly, brushed his hair back on top of his head, finger-combing it as he did so. Schwartz could have climbed up the wall. "Now you can tell me about it," the detective said, "or we can go the whole route. You know what that means." He touched a folder. "Your record is bad already; you should have been off the street before now."

Schwartz began to sweat. By nature he was extremely stubborn, he hated cops automatically, and his usual rule of life was never to give an inch. But the detective across the table from him had him by the balls and the harder he squeezed, the worse it was going to hurt. A sharp bite of acid hit his stomach and he tried once more to find a way out without giving anything.

"Another witness is coming in," the detective said, almost as though no one else was in the room. "The last fare you had, the one you dropped in the street. He had an appointment and he noted the exact time."

That did it. Schwartz felt the agony in his stomach grow. His rock hard stubbornness urged him to hang on no matter what, but he knew that would lead to worse disaster. His hatred for cops, as a fragment of the whole human race, flamed within him, but he had never been able to get completely away from people because driving them around was his business. And suckering them for extra bucks whenever he could. He disliked everyone and trusted no one, he had grown up that way, but no matter how he felt, he had to do what was best for himself. Like a prowling big cat, that was the only thought that predominated in his mind.

"All right," he said. "But if I help you out, I gotta walk out of here and nothing more in there." He pointed a stubby, dirt grimed finger demandingly toward the folder.

The detective was suddenly as hard-minded as he was himself. "You get no deal of any kind. You're caught dead to rights and if, just if, you don't spill wide open and all the way, we'll look into you a little more. You'd be surprised what we can dig up when we put our minds to it. I've got enough right now to pull your license permanently." His voice abruptly was like glacial ice. "You've got fifteen seconds before I throw you in the can."

The stubbornness inside of Abe Schwartz cracked and yielded. The world was against him, as he had always been against it, and the bile in his stomach was boiling.

"I picked up this fare," he said, "near Lincoln Center. He wanted to go to Wall Street. It was bad because it was raining and when it's raining, I can make twice as much, on short hauls. But this turkey sticks me with a long one. Still I had to take him. So I did. By the time we got there, with the rain and all, I had about six and a half on the clock. When I pulled up, he handed me a five and told me to wait.

"I couldn't do nothing about it, so I sat and waited. If I went off, I'd lose a buck and a half on the clock and the tip to boot. So I sat there for ten, maybe fifteen minutes. I had read the guy as good for it, but there was no way I could find him in that building and I couldn't leave my cab. And I was losing too damn much money sitting there."

"But your meter was running."

"Of course, damnit, but that does me no good if this turkey blows! By the time I had waited twelve or fifteen minutes I knew I'd been had; I was a damn fool to wait for him at all. I was burning mad and you'da been too."

If he expected sympathy or understanding, he got none whatever. "So I said to hell with it and hauled ass away from that curb. I could get another fare in thirty seconds, but it was dead where I sat. I was mad, I admit it, I had a right to be. Then this brainless idiot jumps out into the middle of the street right in front of me. God couldn't have stopped in time. I knew I brushed him, but what the hell, it was his damn fault; no way was it mine. So I got the hell out of there. I took more than a four-buck loss on the meter and in that time I could have made five with a tip. It wasn't any of my business because it wasn't my fault."

He tried to look as if he believed it, and failed.

The detective got up and opened the door part way. "Take him away," he ordered.

Abe Schwartz got to his feet and cursed the world that had hated him from the day of his birth. He only endured it because there was no other place to go, at least not anywhere he could make a buck. He felt sharper pains still in his stomach as he was led away.

John Harbizon fed a quarter into the slot of the vending machine and pulled the appropriate plunger. In response a small package dropped into the tray in the bottom; he picked it up without much hope. The so-called sweet roll on display looked as though it had been defeated before it had ever been started as dough. Across the top it had a thin brushing of what passed for glaze. Harbizon had bought it anyway out of a certain sense of desperation. He had not had any breakfast and he wanted something that was presumably edible to go with the cup of bad coffee the next machine would provide.

While he waited for Dietrich to arrive he peeled the wrapping off the roll and took an experimental bite. He had expected very little, but the roll was worse than he had imagined. He looked at it for a moment, wondering how with all of the skills of modern science a product could be turned out that was so utterly tasteless. He would have thrown it away, but the only other available selection was a packet of four tiny cracker sandwiches with a minute amount of peanut butter for filling. He had tried it once and found it ghastly. As he made the best of the inevitable situation he wondered why something better could not be provided for the men and women whose job it was to see that the city did not cannibalize itself with crime. Take away the NYPD and in a month there wouldn't be anything left of the supposedly greatest city on earth.

Harbizon ate the miserable sweet roll and drank his acid coffee until Dietrich came in. Neither of them properly belonged in a Manhattan police station, but they were officers of the law and as such were welcomed. They might even write a letter to somebody about the food.

Dietrich was ready with a report. "I talked with Harold Horowitz, the Chinese doll's boy friend. In essence he confirmed everything that she told you: the nature of their relationship, the religious barrier to it developing any further, and the statement that they were together on the night that San Marco was shot. He said that they could produce witnesses, but when I asked for some, he couldn't come up with anything definite; he said that he would try."

"Which could mean that he wants to look for someone to lie for him."

"Exactly. At this point he's probably out of it, but I would like to see that alibi cemented down. He admitted knowing Marcia Churchill and said that he had talked to her several times, so the idea of her recognizing his voice is still a possibility. And there's motive: he's a very intense person and no matter how he may have accepted it on the surface, he hardly liked the idea that San Marco had been laying his girl friend. And you remember what Davenport said that the gunman told San Marco, 'That's the last time you'll screw anyone.' "

Harbizon had his own notebook out. "That remark could be taken two ways, of course, as you realize. Literally, or figuratively."

"Or both, John. Literally in the sense that he had just had a girl, figuratively in the sense that he had made his living for some time in some possibly questionable activities, in cahoots with Lockheim."

"If Horowitz can come up with a valid proof of his alibi, what's our next step?"

"I say we hit the stock exchange again and find out all we can about the victims' associates and particularly trading opponents. I presume they had some."

"Lockheim, probably, but I'm not so sure about San Marco: he was a specialist, remember."

"I have that clearly in mind and we can expect to encounter the grand cover up if anything at all was out of line. What are your ideas?"

"We could do that together, but if you want to ferret alone, I'll see what I can get out of those columnists we met. It's their job to dig up the dirt about the market, so they have to know a lot about what's going on."

Dietrich snapped his notebook shut. "Done. I'll go down and sweat that PR man, Fellini. If he doesn't come through, I'll threaten to go upstairs to Stone who I'm sure is his boss. Stone knows that we have a double homicide that's definite plus the Korngold thing, so he isn't going to try to be cute."

A New York detective came into the coffee room, a coin in his left hand. With his right he brushed his hair back from off his forehead. "Speaking of Korngold . . . ," Harbizon said. When the New York man had his ration, Dietrich signaled to him and he joined them.

"I'm sorry," Dietrich said, "I didn't get your name last time."

"Elliott."

"What's the latest on the Korngold matter?"

"I was about to call you on that," Elliott answered. "We had a witness, another one, who came forward and ID'ed the cab that made the hit. We brought the driver in and I just finished questioning him a few minutes ago."

Harbizon and Dietrich were both listening intently.

"The driver is a hard case, known to us. His name is Abe Schwartz and he's on file for suspected minor racketeering, running errands for the mob now and then, and clipping tourists when he isn't otherwise occupied. He feeds john's into the come-on bars and is a short change artist. He has one MO: grab the buck."

"What's his story?" Dietrich asked.

Elliott summarized the interview, carefully including every pertinent point. It took him less than a minute.

Harbizon worked the muscles of his jaw while he thought. "What you're telling us," he said, "is that if the driver's story stands up, the killing was an accident."

"You've got it," Elliott told him. "We have him, of course, for felony hit and run, so he'll be off the street for good. But as of now I can't see murder and what's more, it was at least partly Korngold's fault."

Harbizon remained silent, still thinking. "Let me tell you what's been bothering me," he said at last. "I'm sure that Charlie has had the same thought, although we haven't discussed it. There are a lot of far-out organizations around; you remember the SLA, then there's the American Nazi Party, and a lot more. All three of the victims were Jewish. I've been hoping to God that it was a coincidence, because if it wasn't, we might be up against the worst thing we've ever faced."

"Exactly," Dietrich agreed.

"The apparent fact that the Korngold killing was accidental takes off some of the curse: it shortens the odds a great deal. And a man named Abe Schwartz is more likely to be Jewish than gentile."

"I thought of that, of course," Elliott said. "Terrorism is something that we have to watch out for on a continuously alert basis. I'm inclined to agree that we're dealing with a not too strong coincidence, because admittedly there is a high percentage of Jews in

Wall Street. But when it looked as though there might be three in a row: well, I didn't get much sleep last night."

"Welcome to the club," Harbizon said.

From that point everything appeared to go downhill. Fellini at the Stock Exchange, went through all of the motions of being helpful, but when Dietrich left him, he went out by the same door that he came in.

When Harbizon tried to make an appointment to see Schneider and Burroughs, he learned that Bert Schneider was out of town and that his partner was up to his eyeballs in work. Burroughs offered to cooperate fully and then asked that the conversation be restricted to five minutes. He wasn't putting on an act, he had a deadline to meet.

The upshot of that conference was that there was so much hanky panky going on in the market that the case of Sphinx Wire and Cable was more representative than unique. "Read the files of the *Wall Street Journal* and see for yourself," the columnist advised. "We have scrapbooks full of clippings of financial wrongdoing, and there's no end in sight."

"When you have a few more minutes, could we talk about it then?" Harbizon asked, his voice mild.

Gene Burroughs relented. "O.K., I guess I've been letting things get to me a little too much lately. Look at the picture this way: you save up some money or come into an inheritance and what do you do? You can put it in the bank or the savings and loan and get some interest. The big plus is that your funds are safe and you can count on some return. The bad part is that the rates of inflation we've had to live with for the past several years have so reduced the buying power of the dollar, savings deposits have often shrunk in value despite the interest they earned.

"What the market professes to offer is a hedge against inflation, plus a return. The theory is simple: a hundred shares of stock in a sound company are worth so much buying power, therefore if the value of the dollar goes down the price will go up. If it worked that way it would be great, but the market is fuelled by literally billions of dollars. That much cash in turn attracts every kind of vulture and parasite who thinks that he can get a chunk of it, usually by taking it away from someone else. So the price of a stock doesn't rest simply on the value of the company it represents or even its earnings; furthermore speculation is encouraged by all kinds of tricks and devices: option sales, trading against the box, and you name it. The pros set it up and they usually have a continuing field day, especially if they don't have to pay commissions."

"You know my present assignment," Harbizon said. "I need some help. I'm not an expert in the stock market; you are. Narrowing it down to Sphinx Wire and Cable, who else was involved? Did Lockheim have a trading rival, somebody he beat out? Were any of the Sphinx executives themselves hit hard? I know that company officers often have sizable stock holdings in their own firms. Is there anyone else at all in the picture whom you might know about?"

Burroughs thought hard. Harbizon knew that he didn't want to answer that question, not when it contained within it the built-in suspicion of murder. Finally, when the answer came, it was with considerable reservation. "I want to do all that I can for you, but I don't want to be sued. So please, treat this as confidential. What I mean is, don't give me, or Bert and me, as the source."

"Depend on it," Harbizon said.

"All right. There's a man named Cecil Forrester. He's a respected stockbroker who for years handled some very large accounts. His track record was one of the best. Then somehow he was cornered by this Sphinx Wire and Cable thing. You see, it's basically a very good company, soundly financed, and with an excellent product line. The kind of thing you or I might buy for ourselves. I can't give you the details offhand, but Forrester was very badly hurt; his clients suffered and naturally they blamed him. He made a considerable stink and seriously talked about filing a complaint with the SEC. He's just heavy enough that he might make it stick and put some very important people squarely on the spot. There was even talk that he might force a congressional investigation of the whole securities business. If that were to happen right now, the pavement would be littered by window jumpers who wouldn't be able to escape the heat."

"This must be common knowledge, then," Harbizon noted.

"It is, everyone in the street knows it. But they don't know Forrester. He has an interesting background: before he took up his present occupation he was, according to a limited rumor, a James Bond type. At least I'm pretty sure that he worked for some years for British intelligence."

Chapter Six

During the three months that he had been head of the Beverly Hills office of *Williams, Sloan, Furman, & Brown* Ben Sorenson had already cut a wide swath. As soon as he had been promoted to his new job he had been made a vice president, a title that was highly impressive lettered on the glass paneling that enclosed his comfortable office. The customers who read it were not always aware that the big Stock Exchange member firm had a multiplicity of vice presidents and that the title as it stood had largely come to mean head salesman.

Ben sat with a full view of the many cubicles in which his sales staff was housed, like so many bees in a hive. On the far wall a long, narrow electronic board kept up a continuously traveling display of quotations that reflected the activity on the trading floor of the New York Stock Exchange. Underneath it a somewhat smaller panel reported the transactions on the American Stock Exchange. Lastly, a projection device supplied a readout of the broad tape: the more or less continuous news wire that supplied business news likely to affect stock prices.

To one side a number of chairs had been placed to accommodate the tape watchers, some of whom sat there by the hour trading what was left of their eyesight for the continuous stream of financial information. Sometimes, when he was sure he was speaking to someone who would sympathize with his viewpoint, Ben liked to refer to that section of the office as the Home for Elderly Hebrews.

At thirty-four Ben was already successful and in his own opinion he deserved every bit of it. He was indisputably handsome, an asset that had been of incalculable value in forming new romantic attachments. He stood an even six feet, wore expensive clothes that displayed his youthful figure, and had cultivated the habit of speaking in a way that won the confidence of men and the admiration of women. He felt that he could hardly ask for more than that. He had a very good income from his own commissions, his override bonuses when they came, and those transactions he made on his own account when he was equipped with some special information. Nature and circumstances had both been very good to Ben Sorenson; and he had neglected no opportunity to translate his existing assets into hard cash or other things that he wanted. To have done less would have been to ignore the endowments he had been given.

Jack Rampole, an unspectacular but steady salesman, paused at the doorway and when he received a nod came in. "We've got another idiot letter, this time from Mrs. Betty Williamson. Remember her?"

"Vaguely."

"She came in off the street ten or eleven months ago—before you joined us. She had some securities left to her by a brother; she wanted us to handle the account."

"I remember now," Ben said. "She gave us full discretionary powers, didn't she?"

"In writing. Of course she said all of the usual things: she wanted dividends, stocks that would be sure to hold their value with a chance for growth, and personal attention to her account. For her first trades I put her into a hundred of Bethelem and another hundred of Kodak. When she was happy with that I gave her a thousand of Pacific Oil Exploration. You know we were to unload that."

"A thousand was a little much, five hundred would have been better. Did you call her first?"

"Yes, she told me whatever I thought was right for her she would approve. So I made it a point to put her into an electronics outfit where she gained three points; that made her very happy. But now she's written threatening to write to the president of the company about the Pacific Oil."

"What did she buy it at?"

"Nineteen and five-eighths."

Sorenson punched a machine on his desk. "It's back up to four and three-eighths," he said. "Call her and tell her to hang in there—that we expect the stock to recover any day."

"I've already done that."

Ben leaned forward. "All right, give me her number. I'll call her myself and tell her that I'm taking over her account personally, that ought to shut her up for a while. And do me a favor: call Marisconi's and have them reserve a table for me at one-fifteen. Today is Thursday and that's the abalone special."

"Right away," Rampole responded. For a moment he wondered if he were going to be issued an invitation, then he knew better. It would be that girl from the university, of course.

At three o'clock Ben made a show of returning to his office. He made the stroking call to the Williamson woman and confidently assured her that he would give her account his complete personal attention. He listened with amusement, carefully kept inside, as she again recited her complaint and then warmly thanked him for his personal interest. "I do so need help," she said. "You see, soon my investments are going to have to be what I will be living on."

He made a note on his pad to put her into something where she would make two or three hundred dollars. He could usually find a way to do it, and it would shut her up for a long while. After that she'd have to take her chances like everyone else. The name of the game was commissions and that was his catechism.

Most of the office being empty, he called Wanderlust Inc. and spoke directly with the president of the small house trailer manufacturer. Although they had never met, the executive was quite open and honest with him. "Yes," he said. "Our backlog is up a little and now that the fuel shortage fears are over, at least for the time being, it's getting easier to sell our products. We do make very good units and our prices are competitive."

"I assumed that, sir." Ben was all polished smoothness on the line. "And I know your stock is available over the counter . . ."

"Yes, but in very limited supply. This is largely a family held business, although we did officially go public three years ago. Three or four transactions could affect the price noticeably, so please bear that in mind."

"I certainly will," Sorenson declared, truthfully. "I want to come down and see your plant one of these days."

"Do that, sir, we're not too far. And if you see one of our models that you like, perhaps we may be able to do something for you."

"That's most enticing. Thank you very much."

As soon as he had hung up he called his contact at the Pacific Stock Exchange and directed him to buy three thousand Wanderlust, Inc. for his own account, on margin.

That was enough work for the afternoon. In the morning he

would call about fifteen people whom he knew would buy anything that he recommended and tell them that Wanderlust was going to report new high earnings and that he had advance information of the date. If that resulted in ten or eleven buys of Wanderlust, and that was practically a certainty, it should push the price up two and a half to three points—perhaps even more. The rise, in turn would trigger more orders which he would fill from his own holding; if he played it right he should be able to clear several thousand on the deal. And the stock might stay up there a while which would give some of his pigeons a chance to make a buck also, that is if they had the sense to sell. If they didn't then they would ride it right down again, but they would have no squawk coming because he had told them that it was going to go up and it had. Of course not all of them could get out, because the sell orders would drive the price down once more.

He got into his Porsche and drove to the house in the canyon. Dorothy wouldn't be there for some time, but it didn't matter. It was a common enough name, but it was attached to an uncommon girl. She had money in her own right and the small canyon house that featured a spectacular view. She was a spectacular view herself when she walked around casually naked in the living room, as she often did for his entertainment. Despite the fact that he had been living with her for almost a year, he had not yet tired of the sight of her body. Perhaps because she was also the most sensational lay that he had ever taken to bed. Whenever she gave him her all, he was left as wrung out as a spawned salmon.

As he let himself into the house, the damned dog that she insisted on keeping came running up to offer him wet and unwanted affection. The beast was all over him, thinking he was his master and therefore a close relative of God. Sorenson hated the animal; it had once jumped onto the bed just at the moment when he was reaching one of the greatest climaxes of his life, and had licked one of his bare buttocks. From that moment forward the dog had to go. But Ben knew that Dorothy was aware of his dislike for her pet and he did not dare to kill it until the time would be right. Then he would pitch its body over into the bottom of the canyon where it would lie undisturbed for weeks, even months. No one ever went down there; it was too overgrown and thorny to encourage exploration.

He made himself a drink and sat down with a sense of easy freedom. He liked the house very much and it afforded exactly the kind of privacy that he valued so much. None of his clients would ever be able to find him where he was and his office had strict instructions to call him only in the event of a real emergency.

As if to match his thoughts, the phone rang. Since the number was in the most restricted category, he answered, with a plain "Hello."

Dorothy's voice came over the wire. "Lover, I'm roped into the damn thing in San Diego. I've got to leave in a few minutes and I won't be back until tomorrow afternoon. Can you make out O.K.?"

Damn right he could make out, but he had to check something first. "How about clothes and things?" he asked. "You'll be coming for those, won't you?"

"No, I packed a bag and brought it with me this morning—just in case. I'm sorry."

Ben Sorenson left her with the feeling that life would end for him until she returned, then he hung up. When the dog came and put his forepaws in his lap, trying again for a return of affection, the wild idea hit him that right then would be a good time to strangle the damn mutt, but then his salesman's sense told him that it would be wrong. The way to do it would be to leave his office sometime during the hours when he would usually be there and get rid of the pesky creature. Then he would arrange to be delayed until after Dorothy had come home. She would be all upset because the dog would be missing and he would help her search. It was ideal, because he had to leave before six every morning in order to be in his office at seven when the market opened in New York.

He shut the dog in a back room where it could stay and die for all he cared and then he picked up the phone once more. When the answer came he said, "Marion?"

"Yes?"

"Ben. You remember the little business matter I've been trying to arrange?"

"Yes."

"The contract has just been signed. I'll see the other party again late tomorrow."

"I see. Perhaps we should celebrate."

"I'm all for it. Can your husband join us?"

"No, I'm sorry, Phil is out of town again—somewhere in the mid west. I don't expect him back until Sunday night."

It was perfect; she was willing, her husband was out of the way, Dorothy was gone, and there was nothing whatever to interfere. "Come anytime," he said. "We have lots to talk about."

Marion breathed something over the line that he ignored; when a fish was hooked it was hooked and that was all that mattered.

When she arrived he showed her in with proper formality just in case anyone was looking. That was all but impossible since the canyon house was quite isolated, but he never took any unnecessary chances. Once the door had been closed he went into his "I couldn't wait another moment" routine which, this time, was close to the truth. He had dreamed of having her ever since he had met her and Phil at a party somewhere in Malibu. Every time that he had watched her walking across the floor he had had an insatiable desire to have her despite her six foot three, two hundred and twenty pound husband who had once played professionally as middle line backer.

She would be number one hundred and he could not think of anyone he wanted more to be the hundredth woman he had screwed. Even the fading Hollywood actress he had had three weeks before for all her fame wasn't quite up to it. Marion was.

He made some immediate drinks and then spent the next fifteen minutes showing her how totally considerate and charming he could be. He turned on his most winning smile, the same one that had sold ten thousand shares of Pacific Exploration to a normally sharp-witted attorney, and ignored the whinings of the dog that was pleading to be let out.

Then Marion looked at him with a face that he hadn't been able to erase from his mind. "I want to tell you something," she said. "This is the first time; I've never cheated on my husband before."

He knew better than to say anything in response to that; instead he sat down very close to her and sent out vibrations to tell her that this hallowed moment meant at least as much, if not more, to him. He put his arm around her and kept the thought in his mind that they were true mates; if she had anything in her at all she would read it out and respond. And after he went through his standard program she did.

He wanted her to stay the night, but she was too afraid that her neighbour would notice that she had not come home. If that happened, the neighbour would be certain to mention it to Phil sometime when he was out in the yard, just to see if she could create something exciting. It was too much risk. They had two more drinks, and because he had decided that return engagements would be well worth the arranging, he took her to dinner at a restaurant noted for its privacy and intimate atmosphere. She saw no one whom she knew, but just in case, they agreed that he had been advising her on some possible stock investments.

He went back to the house in the canyon enormously well satisfied with himself. He knew for a certainty that Wanderlust, Inc. would have to go up during the next two days and he already knew how he was going to hide his profit from the Internal Revenue Service.

He was deeply asleep when an inconspicuous car parked a quarter of a mile away down the canyon road. People often did that sort of thing at odd hours and most of the canyon residents paid little attention. The man who got out had a bag with him, but at that hour everyone who might have noticed was sound asleep. Even if a police patrol had come past there was nothing to attract attention. It hardly mattered because the man with the bag disappeared over the rim of the road and was out of sight, somewhere in the tall growth of the canyon, within seconds.

With the assurance of someone who knows precisely what he is doing he made his invisible way through the scattered brush until he was just below the house where Ben Sorenson lay asleep, wild and undisciplined erotic dreams running through his head. He was alone with a girl called Evelyn, and his adventures with her were so exciting he was actually contemplating marriage. She wanted her sex life and he wanted his, but together they could reach Himalayan summits. A wide smile curved his lips as he turned over and took a fresh position between the satin sheets.

The man with the bag surveyed the ground and then set about his work with neat, careful precision. When he was sure that everything was under proper control, he climbed up thirty more steps until he was under the house itself. That was easy, because it was semi-cantilevered over the canyon rim. The ground was totally dry and his deliberately wrong-sized shoes left the faintest of impressions on its parched surface.

From the bag that he carried he took out a small arsenal of electrician's tools and two short lengths of substantial insulated wire which were equipped with alligator clips at both ends. It did not take him long to tap a section of flexible conduit; with pliers he peeled away a small part of the spiral casing and after separating the wires it contained, he fixed one of the biting clamps onto each one. Since the two short lengths of wire he had brought were then energized, he kept them well apart. He was twenty minutes early, but he was completely out of sight and the chances of anyone taking an interest in the car he had parked were almost nil. If a police unit were to run the number, the readback would report that it was rented and that everything was in order.

Because the flooring above him was not insulated, he clearly heard the alarm clock ring in the master bedroom even though it was well to his right. After a half minute he heard the sound of footsteps across the floor. Mr. Benjamin Sorenson, who would sell anything to anyone for a commission, had wakened for the day.

Sorenson went into the bathroom which, not by accident, was directly above the place where the man underneath had done his work. With controlled patience the unseen man waited until he heard the toilet flush, then the intermittent running water as Sorenson shaved. He checked his watch and discovered that the time was within four minutes of what he had anticipated. His man still had to brush his teeth which would take a minute and a half. When that time was up, Sorenson entered the shower. Within a few seconds there was a rush of water and the drain pipe under the house began to give off sounds.

With neat care the man attached one of the alligator clamps to a drain lug, securing a good ground. Then he put on an insulating glove, took a careful grip on the other lead, and listened for a few seconds more. The sounds that came to him were partially distorted by the steady flow of water, but apparently the man in the shower was singing. It would have been appropriate if it had been a penitential hymn, but the man underneath the house very much doubted that it was. Then he opened the other clip and let it close over the hot water pipe.

The singing was instantly interrupted by a sudden mounting

shriek, but it was cut off in mid flight. Three seconds later there was a muffled thud against the flooring above.

The man under the house let the current flow for a few more seconds, then he disconnected his kit. With the pliers he carefully rewrapped the spiral covering of the flexible conduit; when he had finished the repair was so neat it was all but invisible. He put all of his tools back into the bag together with the wire leads and the insulated glove. Then, his work done, he went back down the pathway he had chosen, brushing away his tracks behind him. Hardly ten minutes later he drove quietly away in his rented car. It was just six and in that moneyed area there was not another soul awake to take note of his presence.

The body was not discovered until that evening. The first indication was a series of female screams loud enough to be heard elsewhere in the canyon. That upset someone enough to call the cops; a LAPD black and white cruiser responded with officers Jerry Abarian and Frank Toth aboard. After ringing the bell several times they were admitted by a young woman who was holding a tall, half-filled glass in her shaking left hand. "I just came home and found him there," she burst out without preliminary. "I didn't touch anything—I couldn't."

Officer Abarian went in the direction she was pointing. He was the senior man and much more experienced in the sight of sudden death than was his younger partner. He found the body quickly; the water was still running and there was a considerable amount on the floor. He noted that when the nude man in the shower stall had collapsed he had done so in a way that had not forced the door open; consequently the water had gone steadily down the drain which, also by chance, had been left clear.

A first quick examination of the circumstances indicated that it had been an accidental death, but Abarian noted that the deceased was a quite young man, well muscled, and not a very likely heart attack victim. Since the now cold water had been running on the body for an unknown period of time, the usual tests for body heat would be out the window. He phoned in and reported the circumstances.

Homicide investigators Marlow and Hatch were part of the second response. While Officer Abarian sat in a chair carefully printing his report in block letters, Marlow talked in a soothing manner with the young woman who had discovered the body and calmed her down as much as he could. He was a known expert at that sort of thing and presently she was anxious to supply him with all of the details she knew.

"His name is Ben Sorenson," she began. "We've been living together here for about ten months. He is—was—a stockbroker, a vice president and head of the Beverly Hills office of his firm."

"A stockbroker, you say?"

"Yes. He must have been a very good one because he made scads of money. He was very, very smart and he was always talking about some deal that he was putting over. Don't ask me about them; I only pretended to listen when he described them, but they were always complicated. I was away yesterday, in San Diego, and I only got back a little while ago."

"Just when was that, Miss Abrams?"

"Within the hour; my God, I wasn't watching the time! I'd better take Valium." She got to her feet, took three steps, and then stopped. "They're in the bathroom," she said.

Marlow went and got the small bottle for her. She gulped two of the tiny pills and then washed them down with her highball. Marlow wondered about the overdose, but it was actually none of his business.

"When did Mr. Sorenson usually get up in the morning?" He asked.

"Before six: you see, he had to be in his office by seven, because that's when the market opens in New York. When people call him at the opening, they expect him to be there."

"The last time you saw him, was he in good health?"

"Oh yes, he's the healthiest man I know."

"Did he ever complain to you about dizziness or pains in the chest?"

"No, never."

"Do you know the name of his doctor?"

"We never discussed that."

"What about his next of kin; was he married?"

"He was, but he isn't now. He has some family back in Minnesota, but I don't know anything about them."

"Did he get his personal mail here or at the office?"

"Everything went to the office; no mail for him came here at all."

Hatch came back into the room. He nodded to his partner and then spoke in a matter of fact voice that was easy on the nerves. "The medical examiner will be here shortly. He won't be long and then the body can be removed." He looked at the young woman who was again resorting to her drink. "Excuse me," he asked, "but have you had any girl friends staying with you here recently?"

Dorothy gave him a quick, penetrating look charged with suspicion. "What did you find?" she asked.

Hatch moved a hand in a casual horizontal gesture. "Nothing, really. I was just wondering."

"You found something, I know it. This is my house; I own it, and I'm entitled to know."

Marlow knew that her continuing cooperation was essential and that there was no way that anything could alienate her from her boy friend any more. "Tell her," he advised. He had a pretty good idea what the evidence might be.

"Just some long blond hairs in the drain," Hatch said. "They're new."

Dorothy swallowed hard and, despite herself, she raised her hand to touch her own naturally chestnut-colored hair.

Chapter Seven

John Harbizon sat quietly in the outer office under the eye of a secretary-receptionist who had obviously been chosen, at least in part, for eye appeal. By her accent she was British and the way she quietly sat at her desk suggested that she was experienced in her job.

The room itself was wood paneled, probably with synthetically-coated plywood, and decorated with a dignified reserve. There were no plastic plants gathering dust in corners where no living thing of its supposed kind could possibly grow and no forced effort to carry out a "theme." The chair in which Harbizon was sitting was comfortable; it had been designed by someone who was more interested in its function than in a wish to produce a striking appearance. Harbizon chalked the whole room up as a point in favor of the man he was waiting to meet. The more ostentatious types usually had decor smeared on by a heavy hand with nothing else allowed to intrude.

A light glowed on the telephone and the receptionist rose. "Mr. Forrester is free now," she said. "I'm very sorry you were kept waiting."

"That's quite all right," Harbizon responded, then he walked toward the door that she was courteously holding open for him.

Cecil Forrester rose from behind his desk to greet his guest. He was quietly and neatly dressed; as he stood up Harbizon decided that he was carrying perhaps ten pounds more than he should, but it was well distributed. He might have been fifty, and when he shook hands Harbizon had a definite feeling that he was exceptionally fit for his age. The secretary closed the door and they were alone.

Harbizon passed over his card. Forrester took it and then asked if he might see some credentials. As Harbizon produced his laminated card he decided that the man before him might very well have been with British intelligence; most people would have accepted his card as proof of identity which, of course, it was not.

Forrester indicated a chair. "Sit down, lieutenant," he said, "and tell me what I can do for you."

"I understand, Mr. Forrester, that you are a stock broker."

"Financial advisor, lieutenant, which is quite a different thing. I do make transactions on behalf of my clients, but I go through a member firm of the New York Stock Exchange when I do." His accent was definite and presumably British, but to Harbizon's untutored ear it could also have been either Australian or South African. He had been fooled on that point before.

"But you are fully familiar with the securities market," Harbizon suggested.

"Yes, that's true, but I am naturally stronger in some areas. What do you have in mind?"

"Mr. Forrester, I am investigating the recent death of Nathan Lockheim. By any chance, did you know him?"

"No, I did not." The answer was prompt, but carefully given.

"Are you aware how he died?"

"According to the news reports, he was blown up in his car."

"That's correct. Not long afterwards another man, William San Marco, also died violently under unusual circumstances."

"If you are implying a question, I didn't know him either."

"Did you know of either of these men?"

Forrester nodded, his composure unruffled. "Yes, I knew of them."

At that point Harbizon deliberately shifted his tack. "Mr. Forrester, I know very little about the stock market, but I do know that both of those men were involved with the same stock."

It was clearly a baited question, but Forrester answered it anyway. "You mean Sphinx Wire and Cable. San Marco was the floor specialist; Lockheim was a heavy trader in the stock."

"A speculator, in other words."

"Yes."

"Now . . ." Harbizon leaned forward just a little. "I'm conducting a murder investigation, so some of the niceties have to go by the board. Not for quotation, what was Lockheim's reputation?"

"About the same as a cobra at a Sunday school picnic," Forrester answered without turning a hair.

"Did he manipulate the stock?"

"Yes, of course he did. Technically everyone manipulates whenever they buy or sell any security, but that's beside the point."

"How did he manage it?"

"By means of capital." Forrester broke his formal tone for a moment. "I take it that you want a candid answer that I won't be liable for later."

"Yes, both ways."

"Very well. Nate Lockheim had some money of his own, but not enough for large scale speculating until he married a woman who had all the money he could possibly need. After that, he became an almost sure winner."

"Why?" Harbizon asked.

Forrester turned in his chair a little, preparing himself to answer that. "I ran into a man once on a train who offered to match pennies with anyone interested. You know how that works: you stack up whatever pennies you have, he does the same, then you compare piles. If the two top pennies match, you take then; if they don't, he does. And so on down through the pile. Before long he had won all of the pennies of everyone who had played with him."

Harbizon thought. "But if the game was honest, the odds were exactly even."

"That's right, lieutenant, but it's also very deceptive, because the man who started the game couldn't lose except by a miracle. Look at it this way: you are going to fight an enemy who has one hundred soldiers, all equally grave and skillful. You have an army of only ten men."

"But that isn't the same thing."

"Oh, yes it is. Your ten men engage ten of the enemy; the other ninety enemy troops are held in reserve. According to the law of averages, if they fight until every man is wounded or captured, what will the outcome be?"

"I will lose five men, and the enemy will lose five."

"Exactly, but you have now lost fifty percent of your total resources, your enemy has lost only five percent. Even if your army wins six to four, or even seven to three, you still lose because the enemy only takes a seven percent loss while you sustain thirty percent. The man on the train won constantly because he had two or three hundred pennies. No one else had anything like that number."

Harbizon digested that, and saw the logic behind it. "What you are saying is, a man with ten thousand dollars can't defeat a man with a hundred thousand."

"That's it—barring a miracle."

Harbizon shot a quick question. "Was Lockheim in cahoots with San Marco?"

Forrester laughed, and gained a little time. "An unusual word, lieutenant, but I know what it means. I would say that it was likely. Off the record, of course. I won't so state in court."

Harbizon declined to discuss that. "Can you see revenge as a motive for the killing of those two men?"

"That's in your field of specialty, Lieutenant, not mine. But clearly, it's a possibility. You can also take it a step further and consider whether or not someone might have wanted simply to clean up the scene—keep the weasels out of the chicken coop."

Harbizon had thought of that, and often. He tried another shot. "I heard, strictly unofficially, that you were once in a field close to law enforcement."

Forrester appeared to ignore that. "I presume that you've heard about the incident in California last night."

"What incident?"

"It's probably totally unrelated, but a stock broker with not too good a reputation died very suddenly under suspicious circumstances."

"Where in California?"

"Los Angeles. Of course, that's a long way away."

"It takes less than six hours to fly to Los Angeles," Harbizon snapped. "And there are a number of planes every day."

That new information so absorbed his attention, he was left unaware that his carefully timed key question had been left unanswered.

When he called his office, there was a message to phone Sergeant Dietrich. He presumed that it would be about the California thing and was a little embarrassed that he hadn't heard of it sooner. He got Dietrich on the line and waited.

"John," the state trooper began, "I've been at work checking out some of the people we've encountered in this case. Right now, about the only one who couldn't have shot San Marco is Marcia Churchill who was otherwise engaged at the time."

"It's still a possibility," Harbizon warned.

"I realize that, and she did have the opportunity to get rid of the gun. She told a story very embarrassing to herself, but it could have been a pretty cute piece of misdirection."

Harbizon immediately felt better. "I believe that part of it, because the medical examiner confirmed that the deceased had had very recent sexual intercourse."

"Granted, but suppose she let him lay her and then while he was getting his breath back, she shot him. She got out of the back seat first and *pow*. It all fits."

The trouble was, it did.

"What do you know about this California thing?"

"Not much. I've talked with LAPD and they don't have very much so far. The victim, if he was one, was in his early thirties, in apparently excellent physical condition. He dropped dead in the shower and was found there."

"After exercise? Tennis, something like that?"

"Apparently he was taking his morning shower when he keeled over."

"Same type of guy?"

"Same type of guy, a wheeler and dealer in the market. But there's one big difference."

"Yes?"

"His name was Sorenson. That checked out as his real name, so thank the Lord, he probably wasn't Jewish."

Harbizon hesitated before he went on. "What else have you got?"

"Daniel Sisler, the letter writer who told Lockheim he would be better off dead, has been moonlighting a little. Using his skills as an explosives expert. He has had access to some quite interesting material."

"Alibi?"

"Nothing checkable. He states where he was, but it can't be proven. Do you remember Harold Horowitz?"

"Yes."

"Then you remember that he and his Chinese girl friend alibied each other. I believe they said that they could produce witnesses. I invited him to do that, just to keep things tidy."

"And he couldn't."

"That's right—he couldn't. And the more I talked with him, the more uncomfortable he became."

"A tag might be a good idea."

"He's got one on him now. At the moment, I'm very interested in that young man. And in his lady friend, I gather she has plenty of nerve."

Harbizon could have said something about that, but he didn't.

Detective Marlow, who was assigned to homicide investigation by the LAPD, was named Emil. That was the way that he was listed in the official records of the department, but none of his associates could recall any time when that name had been used. From the day that he had signed on and had been sent to the academy he had been tagged with the name Philip. He rather liked it and during his twelve years as a policeman there had been three of four instances of his being taken for the fictional character, despite the fact that Chandler's creation was a private eye.

With his partner Hatch he went to work on the Sorenson case with a thoroughness that was well known both to his superiors and within the grim walls of San Quentin. Unless the coroner advised that the cause of death was a natural one, he considered that the circumstances warranted the closest attention. He examined the premises where the victim had met his end and determined a number of things to his satisfaction. One of them was the interesting fact that Sorenson had apparently entertained at least four different women at the house where he lived with Miss Dorothy Abrams. The other women of whom he found evidence could have been the overnight guests of the owner, but he very much doubted it.

On the second full day of his investigation he visited the office where Sorenson had worked and was slightly surprised to find that his successor had already been installed. A few minutes conversation with that gentleman convinced him that some footprints were being neatly covered up; he countered by inviting the young woman who had been Sorenson's secretary to lunch. She accepted gladly and at once, before her new boss could flash her a signal to the contrary. By the time that the coffee expresso had been served, Marlow had found his guest to be a fountain of information, much of it definitely usable.

"I want you to understand," she said, "that I don't discuss my boss's business outside the office. That's an absolute taboo at our company. However, Mr: Sorenson is dead now and you are a police officer checking on the circumstances. That makes it a different ball game. Ask me what you need to know and if I can answer you, I will."

"Fair enough," Marlow conceded. "Anything you tell me will re main confidential if there's any way to keep it that way. What I mean is, I won't repeat anything unless I have to."

"I understand."

"How did Mr. Sorenson treat you?"

"Well enough. He tried awfully hard to make me, and he promised me some pretty nice things if I would go to bed with him, but I don't believe in mixing pleasure with business. And to be honest, I didn't like him that much. He was too much of a professional smoothy."

"Do you think that he always tried to handle his clients' accounts in their best interests?"

She almost laughed at him. "Of course he didn't. Every now and then he had some stock to unload and then he would get on the telephone and sell it all to people who believed in him."

"Did many of them lose money?"

"Oh, a lot did, some of them large amounts. I know of one client who came in with a hundred and twenty thousand dollars he wanted to invest, not speculate. Three years later, his account was down to less than thirty thousand."

"That's a pretty heavy loss," Marlow said.

"I know it, and he wasn't the only one. But of course Mr. Sorenson made a great deal in commissions. The oftener he could persuade a client to trade, the more he made. And he was very persuasive."

"But you continued to work for him."

"Yes, because the pay is very good and of course I'm not involved with the market trading in any way."

"Do you have any brokers in your shop whom you consider really honest and capable? Any who you would let handle your own money?"

"Yes, Mr. Jarvis is very honest. One time Mr. Sorenson wanted him to push some Pacific Oil Exploration and he refused. He said that it was a lousy investment and he wouldn't do it."

"How are Mr. Jarvis's sales compared to the other brokers?"

"Very good, he's second in the office in volume. But he has more clients than most of the men."

By the time that he dropped the young woman back at her office, Marlow had an increasingly clear picture of the man whose death he was investigating. He also understood why a number of people might have wished to have seen him out of the way. That thought was largely subjective until he returned to his office and put in a call to the county coroner. He had learned from experience that he could attach a high degree of credibility to anything he got from that source.

The conversation he held was not a long one, but it was definite. He was told that the cause of death had been electrocution. Otherwise, the deceased had been in excellent physical condition with no significant pathology. One more detail was added: he had recently had sexual intercourse, probably more than once, but that was in no way a contributory cause of death—unless an irate husband had happened on the scene.

A whole attic full of difficulties blew away as soon as he had that information. He simply had not been able to accept the idea that a physically sound man in his early thirties had dropped dead in the shower, particularly when he had just risen from his bed. He called Hatch, who was buried in a mountain of paper work, and with him went out to the canyon house to which he now had a key. On the way there he did some thinking, with the result that the first thing he did was to check all of the electric clocks to see whether or not their telltales had turned from white to red. He found five clocks that all told the same story. He picked up the phone and dialed the number for the correct time. His watch was almost exactly one minute slow. Allowing for that he checked the clocks once more. Taking an average reading, he satisfied himself that the current had been interrupted for only a very brief time. But a few seconds would have been enough.

It took him more than forty minutes to find the place where the flexible cable had been tapped. He missed it the first time, but when he rechecked his work in that highly unlikely location, he found it. As soon as he had done so, he went into the house and phoned for lab help and a police electrician.

The wiring expert confirmed his findings. "This is absolutely a new one on me," he admitted, "and pretty close to foolproof. You know the familiar hazard of having a radio, or something like that, fall into bathwater. Normally water pipes are good grounds, but whoever energized the hot water side got results without ever entering the house and probably without even being seen. It was damn tricky, because there is probably some way that the water heater itself prevented a direct ground. In any event, it obviously worked. Someone knows some very special dirty tricks."

"Where would he learn them?"

"Possibly in the CIA, but I would think the KGB much more likely. The red Chinese could have dreamed it up. The British are also very good at such technical matters." The police expert shook his head to emphasize his point. "Your man is handy with tools; the rewrapping of the flexible conduit was beautifully done. A month from now, with ordinary corrosion and dirt, it would have been almost literally invisible."

Marlow made a careful entry in his notebook. "What you are saying is, we are dealing with a professional."

"Hell, yes," the electrician agreed, "and one who has had some very sophisticated training. An experienced intelligent agent, or something very close to that."

John Harbizon went back to his office to check his mail and messages, if any. He had spread quite a wide net through various law enforcement channels, knowing that to go much further he would need some outside help. In addition, the reward posted by the City of Boylesport might produce some usable result, though he tended to doubt it. At the best, it might serve to loosen the tongues of otherwise reluctant witnesses. There were a lot of people who were willing to get involved for ten thousand dollars.

He parked his car in the available slot that by unstated precedent was his and went inside. His mind was full of the California thing: he knew very little about it and he wanted to get all that he could despite the distance.

There was a message to call Lieutenant Walchewski at the NYPD.

A Mr. Henry O'Connor wanted him to call. He didn't know the name.

Investigator Elliott, also of the NYPD, wanted to talk with him.

And Investigator Phil Marlow, LAPD, wanted him to call as soon as convenient.

The desk man who handed him his messages had one more item. "There's a young woman here to see you. I put her in the reception area. She seemed quite upset. I told her that I didn't know when you would be in, but she decided to wait for you anyway." He checked a slip of paper. "She's a Miss Helen Chow."

Harbizon managed to keep any unusual expression off his face, which was a minor achievement. He took his messages and then went to the washroom for a few moments before he did anything else. He was vain enough to comb his hair and brush his sleeves with the palms of his hands before he left the room. Having done the best that he could for himself on short notice, he went to the small reception area and found Helen Chow. He had anticipated that she would be upset, the circumstances of her visit indicated that, and very obviously she was. But that did not rob her of her dignity and when she rose to speak to him, he reacted in her favor because he couldn't help himself.

"Lieutenant, I want to see you very much if I may," she said.

Damn right she could see him, but he was careful not to let that show. Instead he welcomed her formally and led the way to his office. There he provided a hard chair, the best one available, and asked if he could get her anything. Most of the stuff in the few machines was terrible, but there were canned soft drinks and coffee of a sort. "No, thank you," she responded, "I just need to talk with you."

As she sat down, Harbizon closed the door. He prepared himself for anything from an appeal to leave her alone to a full confession. He only knew that she would not have come all of the way to Boylesport without an appointment for something trivial. He sat down behind his desk and put on his most sympathetic manner. "What can I do for you?" he asked.

She folded her hands in her lap and looked at him steadily. "I'm about to destroy completely any respect that you may have for me," she said quite candidly. "You can't think very much of me in the first place, since I admit to having been William San Marco's mistress."

"You had a reason," Harbizon heard himself saying. "Throughout history a good many other young women have done the same thing. For king and country—and all that."

Helen Chow eyes him from under lowered lashes; he could not read her expression. "You're being overly generous. I've also had sex at times simply because I wanted to. I am not a babe in arms, Lieutenant."

"You didn't come here to tell me that."

"No, I didn't." She composed herself and smoothed her skirt over her crossed knees. Someone had once remarked to Harbizon that oriental girls had crooked legs; it had been a slander.

"Lieutenant, on the night that San Marco was killed, I was with Harold—Harold Horowitz. We had dinner together."

"You mentioned that last time."

"I know that I did. I also told you that we were together most of the night—and that we could produce witnesses."

Harbizon was well ahead of her then. Dietrich had already told him that Horowitz's alibi hadn't held up; the promised witnesses had not appeared. So now the girl had come, sensing that he was interested in her enough to take more than casual notice, hoping to make a confession and thereby enlist his sympathy. But he kept his face under control and appeared to be all considerate attention.

"I can tell you where we ate, and the staff will remember me."

"Perhaps it would be a good idea to do that."

She reacted to the hardening of his attitude as though she had been expecting it. But she did not allow it to show in her voice. "Harold is Jewish and I am Chinese. We share a common heritage in one thing: a close attention to matters concerning money. While we ate, Harold had an interesting idea to suggest to me. First, he was considering dropping his orthodox faith in order to marry me. He put that in the form of an announcement."

Harbizon took a moment or two. "As I remember it," he said, "you were quite anxious to marry him and only the religious problem was keeping you apart."

Helen lit a cigarette with careful ease. Harbizon did not smoke, so he had no light to offer her. As she blew the first lungful out of her mouth in a thin stream, he wished that she would stop the habit. It disturbed him.

"At one time that might have been true, but Harold has been a great deal more self-centered lately. To the point of forgetting to ask whether or not I wanted him to make such a sacrifice."

"I see."

"Anyhow, he had a suggestion. He reminded me that I had allowed an unspeakable person to take me to bed with him. After that he made his proposal: that I accept a very limited number of lovers, each at a very high fee, and that we then invest my earnings together. Harold works in Wall Street—I told you that. He had an uncle who was a financial wizard; according to Harold this man would take my earnings, if you chose to call them that, and build us a considerable sum on which to get married. He was certain that my exotic appeal would command a premium price."

"Had he ever talked to you like this before?"

"No, never. You should have known the answer to that, Lieutenant, you are a detective."

"Meaning that if he had, you would not have gone to dinner with him on that night."

She answered by taking another puff from her cigarette, then she carefully put it out. "I'm sorry," she said. "I see that my smoking bothers you."

"Now you are the detective."

"I would like to think that it was concern for me, rather than the irritation of the smoke itself."

"That's quite true—and I'm not being gallant."

"If you were not a policeman, and I your suspect, it could be quite interesting."

He did not fall for that. "I am a policeman, Helen, and I intend to stay one, despite the very considerable enticement. Now you are going to tell me that you walked out of the restaurant and therefore can't account for any of Mr. Horowitz's actions for the rest of the night."

She nodded, with a certain respectful deference that was as hard to ignore as a salaam. He was a romantic at heart and the girl before him reminded him of some of the lurid literature he had read as a boy, and had found captivating. He turned that off forcefully and came back to reality. "Where were you after dinner?" he asked.

"I was home—alone. That is the truth, but I can't prove it."

"Did Harold subsequently tell you where he had gone, or what he had done, after he left you?"

"After *I* left *him*, Lieutenant. Permanently."

"Did he tell you who his uncle was: the man who was to enrich you both?"

"Yes: his name was Simon Korngold. He was killed recently, in a traffic accident."

Harbizon did not allow his face to betray a thing. "Two questions, Helen. Am I right in assuming that you didn't dispose of your former patron, to use the polite term?"

"You put that very graciously, thank you. I didn't kill Bill San Marco."

"Or anyone else?"

"Or anyone else."

"Do you know who did?"

"I have no idea."

Harbizon waited for a moment, not wanting to dismiss her. But he had to. "Thank you for coming to see me," he said.

Helen rose, quietly and gracefully. "Do you believe me?" she asked.

"At the moment I'm inclined to, but that's as far as I can go."

"It's quite enough, Lieutenant. I've noticed the way that you have been looking at me, and your careful restraint. Are you married?"

"I was."

"Is there a particular girl at the moment?"

"Why?"

"Just asking."

"No, not at the moment." He should not have told her that; it came out before he thought.

"When this is all over, and I am no longer your suspect, perhaps you will let me cook dinner for you, at my apartment. Just dinner, but it might be pleasant."

"I'm sure it would be," he answered her, and then showed her out before he committed himself to anything more. After she had gone, it took him a good ten minutes to get himself fully under control once more.

Chapter Eight

Lieutenant Ted Walchewski was much less composed than he had been the first time that Harbizon had been in his office. At that time he had appeared to be in the position of a man fighting the good fight for the sake of a lost cause. Now what he had lost in composure he had gained in confidence. He had a tight, tense enthusiasm that refused to be held under too much restraint.

"Have you got a good line yet on who killed your stock speculator?" he asked as soon as Harbizon had settled down into a hard chair.

"No," Harbizon answered, "not yet." His tone implied that that was an interim answer, one that would definitely be revised later.

"I'm wishing you all of the luck in the world," Walchewski came back. "Meanwhile, a helluva lot is suddenly going on. You see, there have been four deaths, all by violence, of stock market figures who were big on rimming the public. One might have passed relatively unnoticed, but the sum total of four has put a damn bright spotlight on the whole thing. Schneider and Burroughs, in that column of theirs, have been running a full background on each one and the composite picture is a real fireworks display."

"I know," Harbizon said. "Since the Lockheim killing, and meeting them, I've been following them daily. Apparently the Korngold death, the traffic victim, took the lid off the worst mess of all."

Walchewski nodded energetically. "It sure as hell did. I know that all the evidence points to accidental death, but it fits too well into the pattern. Now this thing in California—how much do you know about it?"

"I've talked to the man whose handling it out there, an investigator named Marlow. We've compared notes."

"First name Philip?"

"Yes, I think so."

"Does he spell Marlow with an 'e'?"

"I don't know, but he's a cop, not a private eye. To be serious for a moment, he feels that the killing out there was triggered by what has been happening here, but he doesn't think that the same man is responsible."

"Do you agree with that?"

"No, for two reasons. First, the killing was expertly done by an unusual method—one that requires sophisticated training. Secondly, I discount the physical distance; it's a matter of a few hours to go to California and you can buy a ticket under any name you like."

"But the M.O. wasn't the same."

"No, it wasn't, but the technique was. It's like a good pianist: if he can play Chopin, he can probably also play Liszt."

Walchewski considered that. "A nice point. And there is another thing: the stock market hotshot. I presume you noticed that of the murder victims—the known murder victims—one was a speculator, one a specialist, and one a broker. And each was as parasitic as they come. This guy in Los Angeles: Marlow found out that he had just put in a big buy order on a sleepy little stock called Wanderlust, Inc. He checked that one out thoroughly: the company is small, decent, and turns out a good product. Sales have been up encouragingly, but not anything to arouse excitement. Shortly before he died, Sorenson, that's the victim, phoned Wanderlust and talked to the president. He was told then that even a few transactions in the stock would have an effect on the price."

Harbizon was ahead of him. "So he intended to tout the stock, thereby shoving it up, and then unload his own holdings before anyone learned what he was doing."

"Exactly—perfectly legal, probably, but it was a clear case of manipulation. Marlow said that he could have cleared ten grand easily if the deal had gone through."

Harbizon leaned forward. "Ted, don't quote me on this, but there is one aspect of the California thing that I like very much."

"Sorenson wasn't Jewish."

Harbizon moved Walchewski up another notch in his esteem. "Exactly. I've been spending some time with the FBI looking at the anti-Semitic lunacy fringe. Now, if the California thing can be tied in, that lead goes up the flue, thank God."

Walchewski let a few seconds pass, then he changed the subject. "I've got some developments you may not know about. Indirect, but interesting. One: there is a sharpie who has been making his living for some time devising tax dodges and shelters for the very rich. He is Jewish, incidently, and the interesting thing is, he has applied for police protection."

"Are you going to give it to him?"

"Are you nuts? He worked a lot with Lockheim, now he is genuinely scared. He thinks it is a red group of anti-Semites that is doing all this. Against the capitalistic system and down on his people. He has asked the FBI, his legislative representative, and the SEC to investigate."

"What happens if they investigate him?"

"I'd like to be around to see that. There's more. The SEC has put out a release about stricter controls to be imposed on stock transactions in the near future; the brokerage houses are in agony. The new commodity regulating commission is flexing its muscles, and it should—that business is gambling pure and simple no matter how much they call it speculation. Personally I think they should slam the door on the whole thing. And some very interesting reform bills are being rushed onto the floor of Congress."

"They did not die in vain, then."

"No, apparently they didn't, though I won't say that publically. But I will say this to you:—if there is one more killing, and it's another rip off artist, then everything will hit the fan for sure."

"Do you think that's a possibility?" Harbizon asked.

"What's your guess?"

"I'm expecting it at any time," he admitted.

In California Phil Marlow was talking with Mrs. Betty Williamson, whose stock account had diminished drastically while it was in the hands of Williams, Sloan, Furman & Brown. She was an intelligent woman who knew how to express herself clearly when she was giving an official statement.

"For a while," she said, "I wasn't unduly alarmed, largely because Mr. Rampole called me very frequently and reassured me that I did not need to worry. I should explain, Sergeant, that at that time I regarded my stockbroker in the same light as I regard my attorney or for that matter anyone else whom I turn to for advice and counsel. For example, Mr. Sorelli at the bank."

"Did Mr. Sorelli ever advise you concerning your stock holdings?"

"Only indirectly. I told him, not too long ago, where I had my account and asked his opinion. He told me, rather cautiously now that I recall our conversation, that I was with a reputable brokerage firm, but he strongly advised that I stay in blue chips. Therefore when Mr. Rampole called me about Pacific Oil Exporation I asked him if it was a blue chip and he told me that it was even better. He talked about the continuing energy crisis and said that he felt that company would be one of the saviors of our economy. So I invested as he advised."

"And lost your shirt," Marlow said, without thinking.

Mrs. Williamson did not let it throw her. "Yes, I lost quite heavily, and you understand, Sergeant, I didn't want to speculate—I wanted to *invest*. In sound, secure stocks."

"You made that clear to the broker?"

"By letter, at the time that I opened my account. And I have a carbon."

"Excellent! After you became disenchanted with Mr. Rampole, then Mr. Sorenson took over your account, is that right?"

"Yes, he told me he would handle it personally and he implied strongly that he would recover what I had lost very quickly. I did gain almost two hundred dollars that month, but of course that isn't very much in light of what I have lost."

"Do you still own your Pacific Oil Exploration stock?"

"Yes, I do."

Mrs. Williamson was the seventh Ben Sorenson client Marlow had interviewed and the picture that each had painted was the same. Every one of them had been ruthlessly exploited. When he thanked Mrs. Williamson and went outside, he wondered if he really wanted to catch the man who had so neatly eliminated Ben Sorenson and had removed him from his place of public trust and confidence. But murder was murder, and he knew that he would go on with his investigation until he hit pay dirt, unless he were pulled off the case for some as yet unforeseeable reason.

John Harbizon was grateful for the fact that his abilities were respected and he was kept free of pressure from above. Consequently, when the chief asked him to come in, he knew he had no cause for concern.

In that he was right. The chief made that clear immediately and put him at his ease. "Have you got anything definite yet?" he asked, simply as a conversational gambit.

Harbizon shook his head. "I'm at that stage when I'm doing all the plodding work and praying for a break. I'm getting some help in running down known car bombers who might be involved. Running ex-intelligence agents is a much harder job, but I do have one man in my sights. He was in intelligence work and he's a stockbroker."

"Any other connection?"

"Yes, he got badly burned by Lockheim and his manipulations, but against that is the fact that he is a very solid citizen, he checks out all the way, and dozens of people will vouch for him."

"Alibi?"

"Nothing that can be solidly checked. Incidently, he offered to take a polygraph test if I wanted him to. He understands the situation and he is fully aware that he has both technique, presumably, and motive."

"Usually the innocent invite polygraph tests," the chief said, stating what they both knew, "the guilty refuse them."

"I considered that."

"Anyone else?"

"Yes, I'm very interested in an aggressive young man named Harold Horowitz. He works in Wall Street and has a Chinese girl friend who at one time was the mistress of that man who was killed up in Westchester County."

"Is she the one who came to see you here?"

"Yes. She isn't common, quite a principled young lady as a matter of fact."

The chief eyed him. "You seem a little defensive on that point."

Harbizon had no choice but to admit it. "I am," he conceded. "And I might as well add that she has given me a wide opening for social contact—after this is all over."

"That's quite interesting, John. Are you going to follow through?"

"I haven't made up my mind as to that."

"I didn't see her," the chief said, "but those who did were impressed."

Harbizon handled that easily. "You would have been too. She's quite something, and at the risk of being caught out again, she isn't promiscuous—I've had a check run. She's offered me dinner at her apartment—dinner only."

"Is she an active suspect?"

"I don't think so. It doesn't add up and if the California thing is related, she was here at the time. The account she gave me of her relationship with William San Marco, the murder victim in Westchester, is accurate. I've interviewed several of his friends and he complained to them that his very expensive mistress wasn't putting out."

The chief thought for a moment. "I think you should cultivate her," he said.

Harbizon was cautious. "Just on general principles?" he asked.

"No, for practical reasons. If you've been fortunate enough to catch the young lady's eye, then she might prove to be a valuable witness. In my experience ladies who have changed their affections frequently become quite talkative. I've been reading your reports and I know about her boy friend who tried to make her a call girl. Incidentally, how about his connection with the traffic victim, I believe his name was Korngold?"

"Coincidence, as I see it. I've been in close touch with Elliott of the NYPD and he is convinced that it was a felony hit and run and nothing more. There was no way that the man who killed Korngold could have known that he would leave the trading floor before the end of the session. And there's no connection at all between the driver and Korngold."

"The driver could have been hired, but I agree that it looks very much like a coincidence that Korngold was killed. He was a viper, I understand."

Harbizon nodded. "Like the Mikado, none of the victims will be missed."

"A point," the chief said, then he broke off the conversation.

Robert Jarvis was willing to talk. He arrived promptly at the place Marlow had suggested, a bar in the valley well away from the offices of Williams, Sloan, Furnam & Brown in Beverly Hills. He shook hands and then sat down in a quiet booth to face the inquisition that he knew was coming.

Marlow led up to it carefully. "Mr. Jarvis, your name was given to me as a strictly honest stockbroker in what was Ben Sorenson's office. Is it true that you refused to push Pacific Oil Exploration onto your clients when you were asked to do so?"

Jarvis was uncomfortable with the question and took some seconds before he answered it. "Yes, that's true, because I knew that it was a potential bad loser. And that's how it turned out."

"Your company had a position in the stock and wanted to unload, is that right?"

"Yes."

"Does this sort of thing happen often?"

"Every day."

Marlow asked a number of additional questions and warmed his man up for what was to come. He was satisfied that Jarvis was an unusually honest person, honest enough that he obviously did not want to embarrass his employer any more than was necessary. When the time was right, Marlow dug in.

"Mr. Jarvis, since you've been in this business for a long time, how do you rate your late boss? How did he compare with other men in similar positions?"

Jarvis considered that carefully. "He was a very good salesman," he began, "and he certainly appealed to the women. Many of his clients were female. You already know that he was very fond of the ladies in bed and he had a great many affairs."

"Were any of his clients also his mistresses?"

"I don't think so: most of his female clients were well past the point of being attractive as bed partners. Ben was very discreet, he had to be."

"Would you describe him as a good financial advisor?"

That brought a dead stop and Marlow wondered if he had gone too fast too soon. Then Jarvis answered him. "Ben and I often disagreed on the value of certain securities. Of course that is to be expected. I will say, though, that I was right a little more often than he was. In particular there was one stock he was pushing while I was almost certain that it was being manipulated and therefore dangerous. Some of his clients lost very badly, although Sphinx Wire and Cable is, basically, a good company. But that often means very little when the speculators step in."

Because he was a complete professional at his job, John Harbizon did not shrink from the meticulously detailed investigation work that any difficult major case entailed. He also knew that good hard thinking was a large part of any successful operation of that type and he was not the kind of man to substitute impulsive judgments for careful analysis. For that reason he sat alone in his house at nine o'clock in the evening refusing the enticements of the TV. He was fed up anyway with being sung to by car salesmen. Finally, when he was reasonably sure of his ground, he picked up the phone and dialed the chief's private number. After brief preliminaries he said, "I think I would like to go to Los Angeles and confer with this man Marlow of the LAPD. I've been giving the matter some thought and I think I see a connection."

"If it will help, by all means go," the chief told him immediately. "Strictly off the record, I'm glad you made that decision. The council will be pleased to see the evidence of extended action. So will the mayor. A lot of the citizens keep calling in to ask what is being done."

"I understand," Harbizon told him. "But this is strictly business; I'm not packing any sun tan lotion."

"Do whatever is necessary," the chief concluded. "Just keep me in the picture if you learn anything."

"Depend on that," Harbizon concluded, and hung up. He called TWA and made a reservation for Los Angeles at four the following afternoon. He still had one important thing to do before he left and he wanted to allow as much time as he might need.

Bert Schneider was in and waiting when he got there the following morning. The reporter offered coffee which was several grades superior to the product available to New York's finest and made small talk until his partner arrived. Burroughs came in within the next five minutes and the meeting was able to get down to business.

"I saw your column on the front page this morning," Harbizon began. "I read it coming in on the train. This whole business must have been an indirect boost for you."

"It has been indeed," Borroughs agreed. "We had been interested in the stock market for some time as a fertile field for some investigative reporting when Lockheim was blown up. We already knew about him, and about San Marco. So when San Marco got his, our readership jumped way up in the continuing surveys. It's still climbing."

"Did you get any reaction from the Korngold thing?" Harbizon asked.

"Yes," Schneider responded, "very much so. It damn near made us as big as Woodward and Bernstein in Washington. We had been gathering material on the Sphinx Wire and Cable fraud—and that's the word for it—when we ran across Korngold and the kind of thing he was pulling. We latched onto him and we had a thick folder full of good stuff when he bought the farm. So all we had to do was to put it into the typewriter."

"How many more are there like him?" Harbizon asked.

Burroughs shook his head. "Here in New York a whole nest full. Around the country a few more, but the majority of the worst manipulators operate off the floor of the Exchange. In that way they don't have to pay commissions."

"Now I've got a big question," Harbizon prefaced. "Think before you answer it. A stockbroker was erased in Los Angeles, you know all about that . . ."

"Yes, we do," Schneider cut in, a little too quickly. His partner picked up the ball. "Off the record," he said, "we're on that right now. We think there may be a connection and to be honest about it, we're hoping to break the story."

"And you see me as a possible hazard to that," Harbizon supplied.

"Yes, in a way. You see, we're both investigating the same thing. Only we don't have police powers."

"And I don't have the power of the press," Harbizon added. "I'll make you a deal: why don't we try to help each other. You are good at digging up things and I understand your desire to break any important news in your column. Insofar as I can, ethically, I'll return the favor. I can't be more specific than that, and you know why."

"It's a deal," Schneider said immediately. "And if you like, we'll make our first contribution right now."

Harbizon looked at Gene Burroughs who nodded his agreement. "What have you got?" he asked.

Schneider answered. "First, the killing on the Coast was a very cute job, using a little-known technique. It wasn't an ordinary homicide."

"I know that," Harbizon said, "but how did you find it out?"

"Probably the same way that you did," Burroughs answered, "By having friends in the business. We make a lot of long distance calls."

Schneider went on. "For a while we were hot on the Jewish angle; I'm Jewish and naturally we were both very concerned."

"So was I," Harbizon admitted. "Dietrich and I have been checking out all of the crackpot organizations, and individuals, who might be trying to start World War III. So far we haven't turned up any positive leads. Now the Sorenson death, if I can establish that it's related, shoots that angle down, thank God. Sorenson was his real name and he wasn't Jewish."

The two columnists looked at each other, then Schneider spoke for them both. "Two things that might help you. First of all, there is a heavyweight financial advisor who knows a lot of important people in Washington. For some time he has been conducting a quiet campaign to have the rules of the New York Stock Exchange, and the work of the SEC, overhauled and made a lot less favorable to speculators. If they want to gamble, let 'em go to the horse races, that was his attitude. We discovered that he is an old friend of the president of Sphinx Wire and Cable."

"I missed that," Harbizon admitted.

"You met him, then?" Burroughs asked.

"Yes, Cecil Forrester. I interviewed him. I also know that he put some of his clients in that stock and they lost a bundle."

"Do you know why?" Schneider asked.

"You tell me."

"Sphinx is a good sound outfit; we've been out there and talked with the top people. They're on the rails and they know what they're doing. Their financial position is very sound and the order backlog is substantial. The products check out as superior. So all the way it should be a good investment, if you go by the fundamentals. But Lockheim and San Marco got together and between them they screwed everybody. The stock went down the tube for no valid reason and a lot of good people got hurt. Lockheim made a mint, and undoubtedly San Marco did too. Forrester and his clients took it on the chin."

Harbizon came to the point. "Are you suggesting that Forrester was responsible for correcting this situation—either personally or indirectly?"

"That would be accusing a man of murder," Burroughs answered immediately, "and we're not about to do that. Another thing: he's been working through legal channels and he has a lot of clout, and so do his clients. He handles some very big portfolios and the people who own them often make substantial campaign contributions. What we are saying is that he is prominent in the scenario. He may be keeping a few things to himself."

"Not guilty knowledge," Schneider added, "but information, you might say."

Harbizon made a note. "If I find out anything interesting on the Coast and I can, I'll let you in on it," he promised, thereby easing his conscience. He had offered a deal and he would have to hold up his end.

"When are you going out there?" Schneider asked.

"Later this afternoon. I want to see if I can establish a firmer connection than I have now. By the way: can you offhand think of any person or persons who might be likely victims in the future if this thing continues? Any conspicuous candidates for elimination in the class of San Marco or Lockheim?"

Burroughs shook his head. "Lots of candidates, too many, but not anyone conspicuous."

"Would you say that Lockheim and San Marco were conspicuous?"

"Within the financial community, yes, a lot of people knew about them." Burroughs looked at his partner who turned his head sideways a bare fraction of an inch. Harbizon was not looking at him, but he still caught the movement.

"Of course San Marco could have been eliminated by the husband or boy friend of one of his conquests," John said easily. "He was a hell of a womanizer."

"And how," Burroughs agreed. "He was a rapist too, but he beat the rap. The funny thing is, he was never attractive to women. He got it when he bought it, and no other way. He spend a fortune on his women. We know about one mistress of his who took him to the cleaners for a very round sum and gave him almost nothing back. He had it coming, he had damn near ruined someone in her family."

Harbizon keep his face very still and for a moment watched his breathing. "Then we have to consider that his involvement in Sphinx Wire and Cable may have been a coincidence."

The columnists exchanged open glances and then Schneider spoke for the team. "That's possible, yes, but the odds are way against it. We do have something that you may not know, and as we see it it's damn important."

Harbizon was fully attentive. "What is it?" he asked.

"The man who was killed in Los Angeles, Sorenson was his name, was into Sphinx Wire and Cable up to his neck."

Chapter Nine

The West Valley Police Station in Los Angeles had a considerable spread of green grass in front and a large parking lot in the rear with plenty of room for the attached personnel to leave their private cars. When he saw it Harbizon was slightly envious, but not on his own behalf. His own office in Boylesport was not too bad, but the facilities provided in New York, where he had recently spent so much of his time, were not worthy of the men and women who were asked to work in them. He went inside, showed his credentials at the desk, and asked to see Phil Marlow.

Marlow and Hatch both came out to meet him. As they went down the corridor together to the coffee room, Harbizon sized up his opposite number. Marlow was of average size, with thinning sandy hair and a slightly round face that could be either cherubic or stone hard as the circumstances might require. He wore a brown suit that might have stood a pressing, but it was of high quality and had come from the hands of a good tailor or else a first class men's shop.

Hatch was taller by two or three inches, dark-haired, and well muscled. He was clearly a physical type, but that aspect was subdued by a patina of obvious education and training in his profession. Harbizon felt better almost at once. He had been fortunate in Dietrich and now it was clear that the West Coast situation was in good hands.

As soon as they were seated together, and Hatch had produced three cups of coffee from a convenient machine, Harbizon opened up. "I came out here to see you because I think the Sorenson killing is tied in with two homicides I'm investigating back home."

Marlow responded to that as though they had known each other for some time. He spoke deliberately, because that was his style. "We've been operating up to now on the theory that your homicides may have triggered the one we have. You know how that works. Also, the m.o.'s are entirely different and Sorenson doesn't fit the pattern of your two victims."

Harbizon used the device of beginning with agreement. "I had the same idea, until I got something else just before I left. Sorenson was heavily into a stock that was closely tied to my two victims. I realize that we have three different m.o.'s, but they're alike in that they are all tricky and show an expert's hand. Look at it the other way: so many homicides are routine affairs—family quarrels, shootings, and you name it,—but how often do we get one that is in the assassination category? Not very often. Now we have three of them and all three victims were stock market operators heavily involved in the same security."

"Looking at it that way," Hatch said, "I can see why you came out here. Suppose you fill us in on your end of this thing."

In careful, well-organized detail Harbizon described the killings of Nathan Lockheim and William San Marco and his subsequent investigation. He told them about Dietrich's work and about the apparently accidental death of Simon Korngold, the one that had done the most to trigger a massive reaction against many of the existing stock market practices. He filled in the several items of information that had not been made public. When he had finished he had told it all, including what he knew of Harold Horowitz and the pertinent details concerning Helen Chow. He didn't tell of her call on him at his office.

"All right," Marlow said, "here's what we've got at this end." He told his own story with equal care and thoroughness, laying out the principal points of investigative interest and soft pedaling those which were of background value only. Before he finished Harbizon had confirmed his earlier judgment that Marlow was a top man. Hatch had remained silent most of the time, which was probably good judgment on his part.

When the recital was over, Hatch got the full file on the Sorenson investigation and gave it to Harbizon to read. That task took the rest of the morning; he was still hard at it when Hatch came in to ask him if he would like some lunch.

When he returned to the police station, there was a message for him. Sergeant Dietrich of the New York State Police wanted him to call. Harbizon got on the line, gave his credit card number, and was talking to Dietrich almost at once. "What have you got?" he asked.

"You asked to check on Cecil Forrester, your financial advisor friend. On the day that Lockheim was blown up there is no way to prove conclusively where he was. Reportedly he was in his office, but his secretary was out sick that day and it seems he had no visitors. Don't say anything, I know what you're thinking. But he's definitely out of the San Marco thing: on the night that the victim had his last piece of ass, Forrester was delivering an address to a women's club in Jamaica. So forget it. I know that it was a long shot, John, but he did have motive and presumably the techniques."

"He could have hired someone," Harbizon suggested.

"I doubt it; in the first place he would have had to hire someone to commit murder and it isn't that easy. He would lay himself open to blackmail for the rest of his life if the killer got away. If he didn't, he would have to stand trial for murder himself. No way."

"I was thinking of one of his intelligence pals. Someone who, perhaps, owed him a favor."

"Possibly, but you'd have a helluva time proving it."

Harbizon thanked him and hung up. He had not placed much faith in the idea of Forrester in the first place, but it was, or had been, a visible lead and he didn't intend to overlook anything.

He spent two hours of the afternoon with Marlow and Hatch discussing the whole matter with very little productive result, other than the fact that they understood each other thoroughly and agreed to coordinate efforts as long as the cases remained open and active.

Marlow summed up how things stood on the West Coast in very simple, clear English. "First, we don't know who totaled out Sorenson. Secondly, even if we did we'd have one helluva time proving it. As of right now we have no witnesses. We don't have a single lead to go on. We know that the man was handy with tools which cuts the suspects down to about twenty million or so. There are a lot of good mechanics around. We learned that Sorenson had had some married women at that isolated canyon house, but no enraged husbands are in the picture. He had a woman there the night before he was killed, but we haven't any idea of her identity and she isn't likely to come forward."

"Informants?" Harbizon asked.

"Nothing: zero. This wasn't the kind of thing that gets out on the street. We've talked to every canyon resident for more than a mile in both directions. Blank; nobody saw anything and in this instance I believe them. So where do we go from here?"

"I have one suggestion," Harbizon said. "If we are right in assuming that the three killings are related, then the motive lies in Sorenson's stock market activities, not in his womanizing, granted that one of our victims was heavy on the sex side also."

"That's logical," Hatch conceded.

"Then there are the people who lost money through him, but narrowed down, perhaps, to those who lost on Sphinx Wire and Cable. There can't be too many of those, not with a single broker."

"We're hitting that right now," Marlow said. "I grant that we haven't been concentrating on Sphinx, because we still entertain the idea that the Sorenson killing may have been triggered by your New York jobs. But we will look at the Sphinx investors very closely and we'll keep you posted."

The ended it for the day. Harbizon went back to his motel and was on the point of checking out and heading toward the airport when the idea hit him. He didn't know where it came from, only that it was suddenly there, like Minerva, full grown and ready for battle. He sat down and forced himself to think, to make sure that he was not about to run off half cocked. When he had satisfied himself that he knew what he was doing, and that took very little persuading, he took out his notebook, checked a number, and called Forrester's office in New York.

Because of the time difference the office was closed, but an answering service came on the line—possibly in answer to Harbizon's prayer. He identified himself and asked to be patched through to Mr. Forrester at home, stating that it was urgent. The authority of his position got him through and within a minute he had the financial advisor on the line.

He identified himself and stated that he was speaking from Los Angeles. "I have just had a brainstorm, Mr. Forrester," he said, "and I want to ask your immediate cooperation."

"Anything I can do," Forrester responded.

"All right, sir: you know the financial community and certainly you are familiar with the Sphinx Wire and Cable stock and how it has been manipulated."

"To my sorrow."

"This is in very strict confidence, but so far the police investigation hasn't turned up very much that will help us to end this thing. I'm now convinced that we have three killings, all related to that particular stock, and all three victims used it to their profit. So my question is: who is left that might be the *next* victim? Are there any more people who have been conspicuous in manipulating the Sphinx Wire and Cable stock? Anywhere in the country?"

Forrester saw it immediately. "I understand. I can't give you a list offhand, but I could call you back in an hour if that will be all right."

Harbizon gave the number of the motel, and his room, while a sense of impending excitement grew within him. Forrester could well be the best man in the country to forecast who might be the next on someone's list, and now that he was out of it himself, he could be safely consulted.

Forty-two minutes later the phone rang in Harbizon's room. He picked up the instrument with his notebook open and his pen in hand.

"I've thought carefully," Forrester told him, "and I made one or two calls to people whom I completely trust without telling them a thing. I have a total of eleven names to give to you. In one case, all three of us nominated one individual. All the others got one vote each."

"Give me the runners-up first," Harbizon asked. He listened and wrote the names down, with addresses for each one. When he had done that, he asked for the name that had gotten all three votes.

"He's a man in Chicago," Forrester said. "He publishes one of the many tip sheets that are put out, usually for about two hundred dollars a year. He's in the self-fulfilling prophesy business: when he touts something it often goes up or down as a result, whichever way he predicts. He makes his real money by riding his own forecasts. Enough people follow him to cause a predictable fluctuation. Of course he only does this with smaller firms, he never plays with anything like General Motors or DuPont."

"Was he in the Sphinx thing?"

"He certainly was, and possibly still is. As I hear it, he boosted it to the skies, helped to get it run up, and then sold short. When it came down many of his clients lost heavily; he made a pile."

12   Harbizon was a calm man, but his pen almost shook as he held it over the paper. "What's his name?" he asked.

"Irving W. Brown. As I said, he's in Chicago, but I only have a Post Office box address."

Chicago was soaked in rain; it came down out of a lead gray sky that shrouded the city at low altitude from horizon to horizon and kept up an unrelenting downpour. Air traffic was severely restricted and during most of the day the airports were closed. When Harbizon's flight finally managed to get in it was early evening and the rain had not relented; the few available cabs were themselves water-soaked and the street traffic was constantly tied up by accidents.

It had been Harbizon's intention to go first to the police facility nearest to the Post Office where Brown had his box, but the almost impossible driving conditions caused him to change his mind. He resorted to the telephone and made a number of calls. There was no Irving W. Brown listed in the directory, but he had expected that. By the time that he had finished, he had formally notified the Chicago Police Department that he was in its jurisdiction and he had ferreted out his subject's telephone number. He called it and waited while the phone rang for some time. Finally he was rewarded by an abrupt, "Yes?"

"Mr. Brown?"

"What is it?"

"This is Lieutenant Harbizon of the Boylesport, New York Police Department."

"Who gave you my number!"

Harbizon bore down a little harder. "Mr. Brown, I've come to Chicago expressly to see you. It's very important that I do so as soon as possible."

"I don't see anybody, I'm too busy. Sorry." He hung up.

Harbizon called him back and waited patiently for almost twenty rings until Brown at last came back on the line. At that point he wasted no more time. *"Mr. Brown, you'd better see me immediately if you want to keep on living."* His voice carried full, urgent authority.

"Are you threatening me?"

"No, sir, I'm trying to warn you. You may be in very acute danger, as of this minute."

Brown softened very slightly. "Tell me about it."

"Not over the phone, but I will come and see you. Give me your address."

"You haven't proven to me who you are."

"I'll show you my full credentials when I get there. Is there a doorman at your building?"

"Yes."

"I'll show them to him."

There was a pause. "All right, I'll see you sometime after nine-thirty—not before. I have to go out first."

"Nine-thirty," Harbizon repeated. "I'll be there. What's your address?"

Brown supplied it and specified the twenty-third floor. That automatically told Harbizon that it would be an exclusive and expensive apartment, in all probability somewhere near the lake shore. Residential buildings of that size were usually located in choice areas.

When he had finished phoning he went to the airport police facility where he was able to consult a map of the city. As soon as he located his destination he saw that his deduction had been correct: it was south of the loop area and less than a quarter mile from the lake. Presumably Brown had a nice view of the water on clear days.

Because of the weather conditions, the airport police advised him to go into town via the limo service and then catch a cab, if he could, downtown. That made sense and Harbizon rode in a seat by himself, with much almost continuous splashing and occasional skidding, into the central part of the city. When he got there he discovered that he was hungry; he checked his watch and then chose a quick service restaurant where he ate a not very satisfactory dinner. Unfortunately he was used to that and insofar as food went, Chicago was little different from other major cities.

When he had finished he checked the time once more, considered the still drenching rain, and decided not to wait any longer. He could not predict how long it might take him to reach the address, and getting a cab was probably going to be a problem.

It proved to be a worse one than he had anticipated. He tried from under a canopy for a while with no luck at all; one or two cabs did come by, but they were grabbed by others who had been out waiting in the street despite the continuing downpour. Resigning himself to what he had to do he stood out in the street himself, with no protection from the rain whatever, and tried to keep his patience. He was there nearly twenty minutes until two cabs appeared almost together. Someone else rushed out and flagged the first; he got the second.

As he sat miserably in the back, Harbizon was still grateful that he was out of the weather for a little time at least. He would have a short dash into the building which wouldn't matter and presumably the doorman would be able to get him a cab when it came time to leave. The worst, at least was behind him. As he felt the wet on every part of his skin, he planned what he was going to say to Brown.

He was not watching outside—he had seen enough of that for one night, when he felt the cab coming to a stop. He leaned forward and saw the tall building that was undoubtedly his destination a good block ahead. "Something wrong?" he asked.

Before the driver could answer a uniformed policeman bulking large in his rain gear loomed beside the car. "You'll have to stop here," he said.

Harbizon rolled the window down so that he could speak. "What's the problem?" he asked.

"Police road block," the man outside answered, and turned away.

"Wait!" Harbizon called. When the patrolman turned back, he held up his badge. "Does this help?" he asked. "I've already reported in."

The officer outside took it for a moment and then handed it back. "All right," he said. "Go ahead."

The driver fed gas, the cab moved, and for a few more precious seconds of relative dryness Harbizon was inside. There was a canopy over the entranceway that provided some shelter; the driver pulled under it, moving around at least two police cars that were flashing rotating blue lights into the soaked, unimpressed night. Harbizon handed the driver a five and saw him pick up another passenger almost immediately.

A plainclothes policeman in a plastic raincoat confronted Harbizon. "How did you get through?" he asked. Once more Harbizon produced his badge and saw it examined. The plainclothesman handed it back as though it had been something of a toy. "Now that you're here, what do you want?" he asked.

"First, suppose you tell me what the flap is. And what's your rank?"

"Sergeant. A suicide. From the looks of the body he jumped from a great height—near to the top. It happened about ten minutes ago."

Harbizon was fully alert and was aware that his heartbeat had picked up. "Who's the victim?" he asked sharply.

"We don't know yet, there's no I.D. on the body."

"Need any help?"

"No." With that the plainclothesman turned away.

Harbizon was about to go inside when he saw a bit of action that interested him: another man, obviously a policeman, was escorting a reluctant lobby attendant out of doors. The man had no rain protection, but that did not appear to matter. As Harbizon stood carefully still and watched, the attendant was taken over to where a form lay covered with a blanket on the sidewalk. He was made to bend down while a corner of the blanket was lifted.

Despite the darkness, and the rain, Harbizon saw the man react, jerking himself back as though from something unclean. He was quite elderly and his thin body offered little in the way of physical stamina to support him. He covered his face with his hands as if to blot out the gruesome sight he had just seen and then, with great reluctance he spoke. "I think so," he stammered. "I can't be sure, the way he looks now, but yes, I think I know him."

At that moment with the sure instinct that had guided him so many times Harbizon's last doubt was removed. The odds against it being the man he had come to see were probably at least two hundred to one, considering the size of the building, but his subject was about to be warned of a possible attempt on his life. And suicide was often the first guess in many homicides. Without ceremony he walked three brisk steps to where the attendant was standing and asked. "Is it Mr. Brown?"

The attendant looked up, grateful that he did not have to pronounce the name himself. "Yes," he said. "It's him."

Almost at once Harbizon was tapped on the shoulder. He turned to find a man he had not seen before, a large and impressive man who was in no mood to play games. "Come in here," he said with sharp authority and led the way into the lobby. As soon as they were both out of the rain he turned and confronted Harbizon.

"How long have you known that man," he asked, his voice quick and abrupt.

"I never met him. I talked to him on the phone about four hours ago."

"Who are you and what do you want?"

Once more Harbizon produced his credentials. "I've already advised your headquarters that I'm in your jurisdiction. I came here to see Brown, the man who jumped—if he did."

His interrogator picked that up immediately. "Do you doubt it's suicide?"

"At the moment, yes. I'd like to check one or two things about the body, if I may."

"All right, come outside." The speaker did not bother to introduce himself, but Harbizon overlooked it. It was a vile night for man or beast and few people could remain courteous under such circumstances.

With a wave of his hand the big man cleared Harbizon to look at the corpse. Harbizon folded the blanket back and surveyed the body for a few seconds, noting that the deceased man had been a sizable man himself. Since the body had struck face down, there was almost nothing left of the features. The hair at the crown of the head showed male baldness enough to indicate an age of perhaps fifty. When he had noted all that, Harbizon bent down and carefully examined the dead man's shoes. He looked especially at the soles. The shoes were quite new and obviously expensive: they could even have been custom made.

"If you want to examine the shoe, take it off."

Harbizon accepted the invitation without looking up. He slipped the shoe off and then got to his feet. "I don't want to butt in here," he said, "but if I may, I'd like to see the place he came from."

Despite the continuing soaking rain, the man who had been talking to him softened his attitude. "I don't see any harm in you're giving us a hand if you'd like," he said. "Come on along."

Thoroughly wet to the point where his clothes clung to his skin, Harbizon went back into the lobby where his guide punched an elevator button. The doorman stood back, wanting to say something, but knowing that he had better not. It was his job to see that *no one* was admitted into the building until a tenant had requested it, but the police were another matter. He only hoped that they would finish quickly and then go away before too many people saw them. He also hoped fervently that the body outside had been removed, or would be within the next two or three minutes.

Harbizon pushed the button for the twenty-third floor which got an immediate reaction from the Chicago detective. "How did you know?" he asked.

"Brown told me; I made an appointment with him by telephone."

"For what time?"

"Nine-thirty this evening. I got here at nine-fourteen."

"You're pretty precise."

"My job."

"What's your field?"

"Major felonies. We have a small department. Before I signed on, I did homicide for eight years."

"No wonder."

When the elevator door opened the Chicago man led the way down the hall to the proper door. He knocked sharply and waited briefly for an answer. When none came, he fitted the key that the desk had given him into the lock and opened the door.

The apartment was a definition of luxury. Despite the streaming rain, Harbizon could see that in better weather it would command a spectacular view of both the lake and the loop area; he estimated the rent at two thousand dollars a month unless it was one of those deals where you own your apartment outright. The carpeting was thick to the point of being sybaritic and the furniture was of top custom quality. Obviously the late Mr. Brown had lived very well indeed.

There was a cunningly lighted bar at one end of the long living room; Harbizon went there immediately and looked carefully at the bare top. "Have one if you want to," his companions said. "He won't miss it."

Harbizon turned. "Suppose you had a bar stocked like that and you were about to jump over the railing and end your own life. What would you do?"

"I'd have a good stiff belt or two to brace myself. But he could have carried the glass somewhere else, even outside onto the balcony."

"Would he carefully put the liquor bottle back in place first?"

The Chicago detective stood stock still for a moment or two, then he nodded agreement. "You know your business," he conceded. "I'm glad you're here. I'm Lieutenant Hanratty, watch commander."

Harbizon offered a quick handshake and then deliberately fell behind as his companion walked toward the door that opened onto the terrace. There was a small throw rug dropped in front of it as though it were used by the fastidious owner to wipe his feet before venturing back onto his thirty-dollar a square yard carpeting.

Hanratty opened the door and let the outside wind come in. It blew quite strongly, but carried little water; the overhang of the terrace above offered some protection from the constant rain. On the terrace itself, which cantilevered out from the building like all the others, there were two or three pieces of aluminum patio furniture minus their covers. Surrounding them was the railing which was about four feet high.

Harbizon took in the scene, then without asking permission he got down on his knees and gave minute attention to the place where it was most likely that Brown had stood before taking his fatal plunge. He chose the spot directly in front of the doorway: a man about to kill himself would come out and go over, not walk around in the rain first. He had loved luxury—that was all too apparent—and even in his last moments he would not have subjected himself to the wretched weather.

After three or four minutes of the most careful examination he reached his conclusion. During the time that he had been occupied he had entirely ignored the rain, the wind that came with it, and the terrifying drop directly in front of his face. When he got to his feet, he stepped inside where Hanratty was patiently waiting for him to finish. "Well?" the watch commander asked.

"Call out your homicide boys," Harbizon answered. "I'm almost certain that it's murder."

Chapter Ten

For a few seconds Hanratty did nothing except stand still and look at his colleague—evaluating him. Then he spoke. "Give me a for instance."

Harbizon was ready for that. "Three things, to start with. The shoe. The absence of any scratches on the deck outside where he went over. And the misplaced throw rug."

Hanratty picked up the shoe, turned it over, and studied the sole. When he had done that he went to the telephone and called the homicide people. "I know that it's a foul night," he said, "but it looks like a killing. The victim was a big shot."

He hung up the instrument and turned to Harbizon. "Now what?" he asked.

"I'd like to talk to the doorman; can you get him up here?"

A call on the house phone took care of that. Three minutes later the bedraggled doorman, his wet uniform hanging like a sack, came to the door. It was wide open and the owner of the apartment was dead, but he still knocked. Harbizon gestured him to come in without suggesting that an ordeal was to follow. In response the doorman entered, cautiously, and waited to see what was wanted of him.

"Did Mr. Brown normally receive many visitors?" Harbizon asked.

"Some, sir. Not a great many."

"Of those appointments, from your observation would you say that they were mostly of a business kind?"

"I would think not, sir."

"I take it that Mr. Brown was not married."

"That's right, sir; he was divorced three times."

"Did he tell you that?"

"No, sir, but it was common knowledge in the building. It has been in the papers."

"I see. Now, the man is dead and nothing you might say can hurt him. Remembering that, was he in the habit of entertaining young women from time to time?"

The doorman hesitated a half second before he nodded. "We're not supposed to discuss the residents," he said, "but that's true."

"Any one young lady in particular?"

"I don't think so."

"All right, now pay very close attention to this. I called Mr. Brown earlier this evening and made an appointment to see him at nine-thirty."

"I know, sir, because Mr. Brown went out earlier and left word for you. He said that if you arrived before he got back, you were to wait in the lobby."

"Did he give you my name?"

"No, he just said that a gentleman would be calling. I assume he meant you, sir, because I saw you arrive by cab shortly after . . ."

"I understand." Harbizon turned to his Chicago colleague. "You see the point, of course. Brown definitely intended to see me. He gave me an appointment. If he had wanted to duck me, he wouldn't have left word for me to wait; he would have said that he wouldn't be back tonight at all."

He turned again to the doorman. "If a tenant doesn't want to see somebody, is it usual for you to say that he's out?"

The doorman bobbed his head. "We do it all the time. It's orders."

Hanratty picked it up. "I get it: if he was expecting you and wanted the meeting, he wouldn't pick that time to jump. But there's a hole in it: suppose he learned something while he was out that made him decide to kill himself immediately. In that case he could have hurried back here, braced himself with a couple of good strong belts, and gone over the railing."

"That sounds logical," Harbizon agreed, "but Brown agreed to see me only after I told him that his life might be in danger. That shook him. As of three hours ago, he very much wanted to live: enough to let me come and drip all over his expensive white carpeting."

Hanratty looked at the doorman. "This isn't the time to hold anything back," he said. "Do you know where Brown went tonight?"

The doorman didn't want to talk for the sake of his job, but he knew he had no choice. "I put him in a cab, and I heard him give the address."

"Did you recognize it?"

"I'd heard it before."

"Give it to me."

Once more the doorman let his misery show, then he supplied the information. Harbizon went to the telephone, picked up an index that was beside it, and began to check the pages. Within a minute he found the entry he wanted. While Hanratty released the doorman and got rid of him, he dialed and waited three rings until a feminine voice answered.

"This is Lieutenant Harbizon of the police department," he said with calm smoothness. "This is just a routine check, are you Helen Heinemann?"

"Yes. What's happened?"

"We're simply verifying the movements of Mr. Irving Brown earlier this evening. Can you confirm that he paid you a visit?"

"Look, I don't want to get involved in anything!"

"You have nothing to worry about, all we want to affirm is that you saw Mr. Brown this evening."

"All right, he was here. But you can't prove we did anything we shouldn't."

"Miss Heinemann, I don't give a damn what you did, just answer one question: did anything happen while Mr. Brown was with you to upset him? Did he receive any phone calls?"

"He didn't get any calls and there was nothing wrong with him. He left here happy; he always does. Ask him."

"Thank you, Miss Heinemann, you've been very helpful." He hung up. "Nothing shook up Brown while he was with the girl," he reported. "She let me get off the line without flooding me with questions. If she had been lying, she would have been a lot more curious."

Hanratty went to the bar. "What'll you have?" he asked.

Harbizon was still wet and chilled from his inspection on the balcony. "Scotch and soda," he answered.

Hanratty was surveying the bottles. "You should see the stuff; nothing but the best." He reached for a bottle. "You're getting twelve year old, will that do?" The Chicago detective filled two glasses with whiskey, ice, and soda, then passed one of them to Harbizon. "It's a helluva night," he commented.

As they clinked glasses sounds in the corridor announced the arrival of the homicide team. The four additional men who came into the room didn't crowd it in the least. While his colleague began to set up more drinks on the bar, Harbizon briefed the investigators despite the fact that he was not in his own jurisdiction. "About the shoe," he concluded. "A check of the sole by eyesight alone showed some tiny particles pressed into the leather. It was wet, of course, and that may have softened the leather a little. If Brown had deliberately jumped to his death, he would either have had to climb over the railing or else take a kind of running leap. In either case there would be some traces on the concrete deck; it's freshly painted. There's nothing there; I checked it carefully.

"Something else," he continued. "There's a small throw rug by the door to the terrace. The rug belongs in the bedroom; I can show you the spot."

He was interrupted by a question. "You mean, someone put the rug out there, got him to stand on it, and then yanked it away?"

"Something like that. Obviously, I don't know how it was done—not yet. But if you check, you'll see that the rug is wet."

"But that doesn't make sense! If Brown was supposed to have jumped by himself, why try to prevent any scratches on the terrace?"

"I didn't say that the idea was to conceal any marks, only that the absence of marks indicated that a rug was used. Brown certainly didn't do it himself."

Another of the homicide men spoke up. "Don't you agree that, on principle, he'd be very conscious of that relative low railing and the wet deck on a night like tonight?"

"Yes, but remember that he lived here and presumably was out on that terrace a good bit of the time. He was familiar with it and the vertigo would have worn off."

Hanratty stated the obvious. "We'll have to check the whole building for guests and any tenants who might have had it in for Brown. And there must be two hundred apartments."

As Harbizon was allowing himself to be grateful that that wouldn't be his job, Hanratty touched him on the shoulder. "I'll fix you another drink," he offered, "then I want to talk to you."

They went into the huge bedroom, taking their glasses with them, and sat down on luxurious wool chairs so soft that they seemed to have no frames. "There's a few things you haven't told me yet," the Chicago detective began. "First, what's your connection with Brown? Why did you tell him his life was in danger? And why are you so far away from your own jurisdiction?" His tone was casual, but that didn't dilute the firmness of his questions. Obviously he wanted answers.

Harbizon tasted his drink without a pang of conscience and then took it from the top. He described the first homicide that had brought him into the case and added as much information as was necessary to bring Hanratty fully up to date on the stock market killings. "Since I didn't have any leads to work on, I checked to see who might be next on the list," he concluded. "Three different people suggested Brown as a likely candidate. I was going to warn him, then ask if we could get together to have him covered; the time seemed about right. He died a few minutes before I got here."

"Do you think that it all ties in?"

"I'd like to look through his papers if I may. The second bedroom is fitted out as a study and there's a big desk in there."

"Go ahead. Officially, you're cooperating with us."

"No other way," Harbizon agreed.

The blustering rain had quieted to a slow drizzle and a lead gray dawn was struggling to take over when he finished. During the long night Harbizon's eyes had grown heavy and then had smarted painfully, but he had kept on with his work. He found a private account book of records that was kept in a very simple code; in a matter of minutes he worked that out and the figures were revealed before him. And he read and studied them, he had to fight with himself to keep from becoming emotionally involved. The chicanery was blatant as the week to week records revealed. The market letter that Brown had published had been a cunning device to support his own ends to a degree Harbizon could hardly believe. And running through for the past four months there had been a steady thread that dealt with Sphinx Wire and Cable. Then, at a little after six, he found the letter, marked TOTALLY CONFIDENTIAL and in a double envelope, that had come to Brown from Nathan Lockheim. It was absolute proof that any jury would have accepted at full value, but it was worthless except for possible civil actions since both men were dead.

When he went back into the huge living room, the homicide crew had left: Hanratty was asleep in one of the massive chairs. He had his head thrown back, his mouth open, and he was softly snoring. As Harbizon looked at him he knew that it was part of the life of a cop: a constant, endless process of slogging work without regard to normal hours, murderous overtime, and precious little thanks of any kind. He wondered for a moment why he had chosen this life for himself, then he wiped that thought away, as he had so often before, with the statement to himself that it was his chosen profession. Without the police department, any major city in the nation could be reduced to an area of total disaster in thirty days. He wondered what kind of a family Hanratty had and whether they had any home life at all.

He shook his colleague awake and said, "Let's get out of here."

Outside the morning air held no encouragement,—there was less rain, but that was all. Harbizon carried a large manila envelope with certain of Brown's documents in them. Hanratty woke up his rain-soaked car, coaxed it into unwilling life, and drove to an all night restaurant that was a standard code seven stop. Eggs, sausage, toast, and hot coffee helped to make the day seem a little brighter; because he had a liberal expense account, Harbizon insisted on picking up the check. Both men were unshaven and utterly weary, but Harbizon turned down the idea of a hotel; instead he asked to be dropped off where he could catch the airport bus. Hanratty offered to take him all the way north to the terminal, but Harbizon refused. Somehow he rode back to the field, checked in with the airline that had the next flight to New York without caring which one it was, and went through the boarding gate into the waiting 727. He slept fitfully all of the way to Kennedy Airport and thereby got a little uncertain rest.

Forgetting the expense for once, he took a cab to Boylesport and his own waiting bed. As he rode, despite his acute fatigue, something was nagging in his brain. He tried to bring it forward into his consciousness, but he couldn't do so. Tantalizingly it told him that there was something he had missed back in that high rise, luxury apartment in Chicago. Something he should have seen and grasped when it had been right in front of him.

He tried to think about it, but his overladen mind refused to oblige. It reminded him again, sharply, of the utter desirability of his own bed, of cool, clean sheets, and of undisturbed rest.

When he got home he did not even take time to read the accumulated mail. He got out of his clothes, washed, and then climbed into bed at close to noon, utterly exhausted. His last waking thought, which barely had time to catch him still conscious, was that there was *something,* plain and apparent, that he had missed.

He awoke somewhere in the middle of the night, his body aching and with the beginning of a cold. He got into a bathrobe and made himself something to eat. As soon as he had the food inside his stomach he drew a hot bath and soaked in the tub until all of the stiffness had gone and he felt fully relaxed. He toweled down carefully, went back into the bedroom, and climbed back between the sheets, planning just to lie there and think. The bed was too warm and too soft for that; he went to sleep once more and didn't wake again until the very early dawn.

There was nothing important in his mail, but he was sure that there would be messages at his office. After he had shaved and dressed he went in, arriving while the thin graveyard shift was still on duty. As he had expected, there were a number of messages, some of them casual and others of prime interest. It was too early to place any calls, but he was rested now and ready to charge in against whatever obstacles he might find in his path. Part of his energy came from the fact that he had found a possible new angle to the case.

When at last it was eight-thirty he put in a call to Charles Dietrich who had phoned twice while he had been out of town. "I'm back," he reported simply. "What have you got?"

Dietrich was all business. "First, I had a nice long talk with Harold Horowitz, the boy friend of the Chinese doll. He's a slippery guy, totally self-centered, and very much money oriented. He admitted that he tried to package his girl friend as a super call girl and still can't understand why she refused all that loot. Anyhow, he finally gave me an account of his movements on the night that San Marco was done in. He had had a tiff with the Chow girl, so he had gone off tomcatting to see what else he could find. He ran a girl down in a bar and she provided his entertainment for the evening."

"Have you been able to locate her?"

"No problem; she's a professional working girl known to the precinct vice boys where she operates. She passes on some very useful information from time to time, so they leave her relatively alone. She fully confirmed her evening with Horowitz."

"There could have been another occasion."

"I did think of that, John, I wasn't born yesterday. The bartender who made the arrangements was cooperative and confirmed the fact that Horowitz was in the bar for some time. So I don't think Horowitz is guilty and even if he is, there's no hope of a conviction."

"How about the Chinese girl herself?" Harbizon asked. "Have you talked to her."

"Yes, I have. I discovered that there are inner depths to you, my friend, she spoke of you in quite complimentary terms. Something about being a gentleman, I didn't get quite all of it, because I had other matters on my mind. If the Churchill girl is to be believed, it was a man who shot San Marco, so the field is narrowed down a little."

"Go on," Harbizon invited.

"I went to see Elliott of the NYPD. The Korngold case has been closed. They're satisfied that it was a bona fide traffic accident despite the fact that the Korngold killing touched off a major reaction against stock market manipulators and the like. The driver involved, a guy named Abe Schwartz, was nailed for felony hit and run. He's off the street and has a trial coming up. He was unlucky; he was picked up in his own car for a minor traffic violation. He made such a case of it, the officers involved considered it probable cause and shook down his car. He was running a small load of heroin, about sixty balloons packed for street sale."

"I take it he's inside."

"Warm and dry. He hasn't a prayer of beating the rap since the probable cause is O.K. The charge is possession for sale and since he was on bail at the time, he's looking at about three years."

"Anything new on Forrester?"

"Yes, but not to be discussed over the phone. It seems he has some friends."

"Mutual friends?"

"You could put it that way."

"We'd better talk about that."

"I want to. Which reminds me: Ted Walchewski of the NYPD wants to see us both ASAP; can you come in?"

Harbizon made an appointment for just after lunch and then turned his attention to the accumulated paper work that was on his desk. He cleared it away and then headed for the city; he had a new angle and he wanted to explore it without any more delay.

He went first to the newspaper office where he hoped to find either Gene Burroughs or Bert Schneider in. He could have made an appointment, but he had his reasons for not doing that. Luck was with him, both of the columnists were in and what was more, they seemed glad to see him. "Have you got anything for us?" Schneider asked.

Harbizon looked around for a moment. The two reporters had taken him to a vacant corner office that was stark, cluttered, and partitioned by clear glass that didn't reach all the way up to the ceiling. It was a private sanctuary only by courtesy; it was more like a half-filled goldfish bowl. "Maybe I do," he answered. "I've been on the Coast and in Chicago."

"We know about Chicago," Schneider told him. "We get the first info off the AP wire. How did you happen to be there at exactly that time?"

"I've been asking myself the same question," Harbizon answered. "One possibility is that the man went over the railing rather than see me, but that's hard to accept."

"Wipe it off," Burroughs advised. "No way. If he didn't want to see you, badge or not he could have kept you out. Unless you went and got a warrant. The tenants of those expensive high rises pay for protection, and they get it."

"How much of the story have you got?" Harbizon asked.

"A lot," Burroughs answered. "Irving Brown jumped from the terrace of his apartment shortly after nine at night. It was raining heavily, but despite that it's hard to believe that he slipped."

"For one thing," Schneider added, "people don't go out on open terraces in that kind of weather. Anyhow, he jumped. But, get this, sometime later the homicide people were called in, on a suicide. You're a cop, what do you make of that?"

"Suspicious circumstances," Harbizon answered promptly. "A suicide is always subject to suspicion unless there are several things that point to it. Known difficulties, a note, two or three other things. In this case Brown wasn't known to have any reason to kill himself and, off the record, no note was left."

"And that was enough to trigger a homicide investigation."

"There were some other things, but I didn't come here to talk about the Brown death in Chicago. I've got a new angle. Can I discuss it strictly off the record?"

"Off the record," Schneider answered promptly. "You ought to know, we've never broken that commitment."

"Then here it is: of the four known victims, not counting the traffic casualty, three have turned out to be heavy womanizers. San Marco kept an apartment just for his mistresses. The guy in Los Angeles was living with one woman and screwing several others on the side. Brown, in Chicago, regularly entertained young women in his apartment at night."

"How about Lockheim?" Burroughs asked.

"That's why I'm here," Harbizon replied. "I know that he did have a regular girl friend and having met his wife, I sympathize with that completely. But was that all? I'd like to know if Nathan Lockheim had sexual activity other than his regular mistress and to what extent."

"You see an irate husband or lover?" Schneider asked.

"I didn't say that, but it could be that someone objects to the victims' stock market activity *and* moral character. There are a lot of crackpots, and some not so cracked who have strong views. Or, sometimes there is someone who has been sexually deprived and who 'get's even' by taking out those who have more than their share."

Schneider was thinking. "Look," he said. "That might just hold water. The last thing San Marco heard, just before he was shot, was his assassin saying something like, 'that's the last time you'll screw anybody.' That could be taken literally."

"We know about it," Burroughs explained, "because we read the police report. You know the policy on that."

Harbizon nodded. "We let the press read our reports, too, if there isn't anything in them that's confidential. Now, if you guys want to help me, see what you can dig up on Nathan Lockheim's sex life. If you hit anything juicy, let me know. Thousands got badly stung on

Sphinx Wire and Cable, but if we're looking for a prude or a fanatic as well, it might help a lot."

"Count on us," Burroughs said. "If there's anything to be found out, we'll get it. If we do and it jells, then we get the story,—agreed?"

"Agreed," Harbizon said.

Lieutenant Walchewski looked like a quarterback who had just completed a forty-four yard touchdown pass to take the lead in the scoring. He had seen action and he was thirsting for more. Dietrich was already in his office when Harbizon arrived; Walchewski picked up his phone and passed the word to Sergeant Elliott the meeting was about to begin. Two minutes later Elliott came in, brushing his hair back although for once it did not need it.

Because it was his office, and because he was charged up for the conference, Walchewski took the floor. "As of this moment we have five men dead who've been up to their necks in white collar crime. Some of it may have been technically within the law, but it was crime just the same. Don't quote me, for God's sake, but these deaths have triggered a reform movement that's the best thing that has happened for years. Whoever has been knocking these guys over has done a major service for his country. That doesn't mean that I condone it, but the facts are there. Are you all up on what's been happening?"

Harbizon shook his head, so did Dietrich. "All right," Walchewski continued, "Let me give you a fast once over. You know about the commodity trading markets. As far as I'm concerned they're pure gambling: people buying and selling things they have no use for and never expect to take delivery on. They bet against each other, which is their funeral except for the fact that it raises hob with food prices, farm income, and a lot of other damn important things. Well, the Commodity Trading Commission has suddenly gotten tough. The old argument that all the speculating created a stable market place has gone down the tube. There's a bill being prepared in Washington that will outlaw all speculative trading in commodity futures. If it passes, the only people who will be allowed to buy and sell are those who have a legitimate interest in the commodities they are dealing in. From now on, the speculators can bet on the horse races instead."

Harbizon drew a deep breath and let it out, but he did not comment.

"Up until now," Walchewski went on, "most of the major brokerage firms have been openly advertising tax shelters, which is a helluva note if you ask me. Schemes and devices to get around paying the taxes that the rest of us all face. Anyhow, there are about six bills pending in the congressional hopper to wipe out these shelters and to make it illegal to advertise ways and means of beating the Internal Revenue Service. The upper income brackets are screaming, but the public is getting more aroused every day, and that's a force no special privilege group can stop. Nixon found that out."

Walchewski picked up an out of town paper off his desk; it had been folded open at the editorial page. "Listen to this," he said. "The editorial is called *justifiable homicide?*. It starts out by saying that there is such a thing in law: circumstances that excuse homicide. Then it goes on to say that while these Wall Street killings can't be condoned per se, they have brought about a long overdo reform movement that has great momentum, coast to coast. And that out of these illegal acts, it can't be denied that a great deal of good has come."

"I've got one for you," Dietrich cut in. "I haven't even told John about this yet, I haven't had a chance. Lockheim's widow has been hit with a massive class action lawsuit. I don't know how valid it is but Sphinx Wire and Cable is a party to it. And, since they're a government supplier, the Justice Department just might get involved. It all has some fascinating possibilities."

"Some lawyers are going to make out; that's for sure," Elliott said. "I'm only sitting in because our finding that the Korngold death was accidental is being challenged. They don't have a prayer, but apparently he was some kind of an operator."

"His estate's been attached," Walchewski said. "The government is interested, because it seems that he was using a tax shelter that isn't valid. At least Internal Revenue is going after it full bore.

"How about the San Marco estate?" Harbizon asked.

"So far there's no action there, but the clean-up wave is gaining by the hour and a lot of floor traders are suddenly getting religion."

"It's a field day for Burroughs and Schneider," Dietrich said.

Walchewski made his chair creak under him. "Hell yes, they've got enough stuff right now to keep their column going for months ahead. They were sniping at the market and getting nowhere when this all started. Believe me, the New York Stock Exchange and the other market places have their defenses. But when Korngold, in particular, died, what was uncovered then was enough to turn the whole thing around. Now the NYSE is changing its rules, making them a lot tougher. They may even ban margin trading and option sales. It will bust the brokerage houses, but the public could be millions ahead."

"The brokerage houses have a legitimate function," Harbizon said. "At least it seems so to me at the moment. But there is obviously a lot that needs fixing."

"There's one key bill," Walchewski said. "If it passes, the brokerage houses will have to follow the clients' instructions as to the type of stocks they recommend and offer. An investment client, for example, that's registered that way, can't be sold a speculative or volatile stock unless he first signs a waiver stating that he knows that the stock in question isn't investment quality. Then the monkey is on his back. You guys aren't involved with the market, so the technical details won't mean a lot, but it boils down to the fact that the stock and commodity markets are through as national gambling halls, the way things are going now. The widows and orphans are going to be protected for a change, as well as some of the rest of us who try to put something by whenever we can."

"But no matter how beneficial the result, you can't go out and knock off people because they are sharpies and manipulators," Harbizon said.

"Of course not," Walchewski agreed. "I said that it can't be condoned, but how would you feel if someone had succeeded in shooting Hitler early in the game. It would have been murder, but I'd like to sit on the jury that tried the man who did it."

"What we're talking about is the judicial process," Harbizon said. "Thank God we're not part of that game. I once spent seven months, off and on, and finally nailed a child molester that was an animal. I went to court with an air tight case and a confession. He got off because he claimed that he hadn't understood his rights because they weren't read to him in Spanish."

Dietrich calmed him down. "We've all had cases like that," he said, "You don't have to tell us about it. But the killings have got to stop. Either that or admit that we no longer live in a civilized society."

"We'll stop them," Harbizon promised. "At the moment I don't know how, but I promise you it will be done. Wait and see."

Chapter Eleven

As he waited a moment before he pushed the bell, John Harbizon asked himself, almost savagely, if he was behaving like a damn fool. By her own admission Helen Chow had been the bought and paid for mistress of William San Marco, and her touching story about having done it in order to get back money that was owed to her family was just a little hard to believe. She had the looks, the youth, the polish, and the other ingredients necessary to be a first class, high priced call girl. Ruthlessly he told himself that he was a middle-aged policeman with nothing whatever that would attract such a girl to him, professional or not. Therefore it had to be something else: something that she wanted.

He rang the bell and waited, steeling himself to ignore the physical appearance he knew she possessed. She had invited him, she wanted something, and if he handled things the right way, he might end up with some vital information concerning his case. Miss Helen Chow knew more than she had told.

When she opened the door and he saw her, his hard resolution fled. She had on a simple black cocktail dress with a white scarf around her throat that set off her black hair. Her skirt flared just a little in a way that emphasized her femininity. A silver and turquoise Navajo ornament was pinned below her left shoulder. "Good evening," she said. "I'm glad you could come."

The first hard thought that hit Harbizon was that he could not have any part of the very high quality merchandise that was on display. Women like that were reserved for the very handsome and gifted, for the very wealthy, and in most cases for a combination of the two. For reason of her own she was allowing him a little of her company; the reason for it would emerge later. The fact that she was Chinese in origin had nothing to do with it at all; the quality was there and that was all that mattered.

Harbizon came in, aware that he was trespassing. "Thank you for asking me," was the best he could manage.

"Please sit down, Lieutenant, and let me fix you a drink."

"Since this is a purely social occasion," he said, "I suggest we drop the title. My name is Harbizon, or John if you would like."

"What would you like, John? I have scotch, bourbon, vodka, gin, and white wine."

"A scotch and seven."

"Coming up."

She disappeared for a few moments; when she came back she had two glasses in her hands. When she gave Harbizon his, he touched her slender, tapered fingers and felt an immediate reaction to that limited physical contact. He sat down on the sofa with her, but at the opposite end so that there was a space of several feet between them. He tasted his drink and found it, as he had expected, excellent.

For a few seconds he felt awkward: he was no good at small talk and he was embarrassingly aware of it. His hostess seemed to understand that and spoke in such a quiet way that answering her was no strain at all. Within a few minutes his hesitation had been broken down and he was much more comfortable. He had resolved before he came that he would not discuss police business in any way unless she brought it up or else gave him an opening he could not pass by. To his amazement, before he had found the bottom of his first glass he was telling her the bare bones of his marriage and why it had broken up so disasterously.

"It wasn't Gwen's fault," he explained. "It was mine—and the kind of work that I do. I was a sergeant then in a big city department, which meant that the pressures were constant. Sometimes I was gone from the house for two or three days and she had no idea where I was or what I was doing. She had every right to be worried, and upset. Gradually it just got worse until we both knew that it was no go any longer."

"Where is she now?"

"Living in St. Louis, I think; I'm not sure."

Helen Chow refilled his glass, then she went out into the kitchen of her apartment. She had already set a small table for two in her living room a little way back from the windows; it gleamed with white linen and shining silverware; he could not remember when anyone had set a table like that for him. As if to underline his thought, Helen came back in with a bottle of wine in her hands. She poured out two glasses and then put the bottle in a holder that was waiting to receive it. "Do you have any eating taboos?" she asked.

Harbizon shook his head. "None at all. I'll like whatever you have."

She smiled her appreciation of that, left, and came back with a tureen she put on the table. "To start," she said, "I have birds' nest soup. It really is made from birds' nests, but it's thoroughly purified in the cooking and we consider it a delicacy. I hope you will like it."

He sat down after putting her into her chair, laid his napkin on his lap, and then tried the soup. He put completely out of his mind what it was and thought of it only as the start of his dinner. The first taste told him that it was delicious. He was much closer to Helen Chow now and her proximity, touching distance away, had a decided effect on him. But he could not dismiss the idea that she was treating him this well because she wanted something from him—something important to her.

Then she began talking with him again and once more he found that he could respond easily. She mentioned literature and music, sounding him out as to his own interests. He had the feeling that this disturbing young woman could see directly through him and knew without asking which subjects he liked and how much he knew about them.

The main course she offered him was duck stuffed with some kind of tantalizing filling. He had no idea what the dish was, he had never had it before, but it was clearly something special.

"Did you make this yourself?" he asked.

"Yes, I did," she answered. "I like to cook, I enjoy good food, and I hope you're impressed."

"I am—very much."

"I believe that it's very important a man think of a girl as a good cook. It could carry a lot of weight." Her mouth quirked a little as she said that and he knew that she was playing with him—she knew her own beauty and her appeal and she knew too that he was a plain-faced man with no special virtues and certainly no brilliant future. He would never be able to provide mounds of money, social glamor, and the kind of jet-set living that her superior assets could capture for her. She wouldn't always be this beautiful, but oriental women, he knew, hung onto it longer than anyone else. She would be a knockout when she was fifty,—and beyond.

"You are a fine cook," he said. "And a brilliant conversationalist. I'm enjoying my evening very much."

"I'm so glad." She said it as if she meant it. Later they moved back to the davenport where she provided tiny thin glasses of an after dinner liqueur. Harbizon sat as he had before, half facing her and at one end of the sofa. The rich, powerful liquid he tasted sent warmth through his body and he wished, for a moment or two, that he might have been born into a situation where he could live like this every day. It wasn't his lot, but he allowed himself a very brief dream.

"What else do you do besides cook, design, and all of the other things we talked about?" he asked.

"I'll tell you later," she promised. "Right now, there are all sorts of interesting things I want to ask you. Have you ever been to the Far East?"

Harbizon lost track of the time. All that he knew was that he was having an evening completely apart from his work; an evening free of abrupt telephone calls, sudden disasters, and the other hazards of his profession. He was out of his class, far out, insofar as women were concerned, but he had this utterly desirable young woman for his companion pro tem and he was making the most of it. He allowed himself to imagine that he was entitled to the kind of life she typified and talked of things that he would never dare to mention to his colleagues on the police force. He had read quite a good bit and it seemed that every worthwhile thing he had picked up somehow came into the conversation.

He had another liqueur or two—he didn't bother to keep count— and he knew that his inhibitions were considerably softened, but still he managed to satisfy himself just by conversation and enjoying the immaculate, gently perfumed, and fully compelling beauty of his hostess. He had ceased to wonder why she had invited him, he concentrated instead on being the best possible guest. For a little while he allowed himself to think that this kind of woman was his just due: that he was equal to any man who might compete for her attention. Subconsciously he knew that it wasn't true, but he played the game and found that it came more easily than he could have hoped.

When he knew that it was close to the time when he would have to get up and break the spell by leaving, he returned without knowing why to the question he had asked her almost two hours before. "What else do you do?" he repeated. "I really want to know."

She looked down at her lap and ran an ivory white hand across her skirt before she looked up. "Sometimes, John, I read minds."

"In what way?"

She looked at him face to face, their eyes meeting as she spoke. "Shall I tell you what you have been thinking these last few minutes?"

"Yes, please."

As he spoke, he hoped to heaven that she couldn't do it. His private thoughts were his own and he didn't want her to know them.

"Very well. I caught something in your manner: you looked at me for a moment and then there was pain on your face. Not a lot, but a little. You clasped your hands together and forced them down between your knees, as though you were trying to push a thought away. You were thinking, I believe, that I had once granted some privileges to William San Marco and wondering why that man, with all of his flaws of character, achieved something that you can't have. Am I right?"

He drew a tight breath and held it for a second or so: she had come so close to the mark he did not dare to deny it. Since it was true, he gave the simplest answer he could. "Yes," he admitted.

"John, I want to tell you something. All men—all normal men—look at girls and think about them as sexual partners. It's the most natural thing in the world. Some men achieve a good many of their ambitions in that direction. A lot of them are crude, overbearing, and demanding. They think it's being forceful. You, John, are a fine and decent man, a gentleman. Consequently you don't attack girls by trying to seduce them regardless of anything else. It's always been that way: the decent honorable types behave themselves and they don't make the grade. They won't push and fight or hand out a line of pure bull in order to get what they're after. Men like you look for sex only from their wives; if they don't have a wife, they go without."

"Just suppose," Harbizon said, "that I had laid a strong campaign for you after dinner. Suppose I had forced myself on you, and played the part of the mean, hard man who wouldn't be denied.

The kind they are using to illustrate the cigarette ads at the moment. Would I have gotten you into the bedroom?"

She looked at him. "Possibly—if I wanted it that way; not otherwise. But the question is academic, because if you were that way, I wouldn't have invited you here. I never cooked a dinner for San Marco; I made him take me out. He asked me to prepare a meal for him once; I gave him hot dogs and canned beans."

The thought of that took a little of the bitterness away. It was all so near, but actually so far because she was right: he would never force anything, it wasn't the way he wanted to live his life.

He stood up and faced her. "I have a long way to go," he said. "I've had a wonderful evening."

Helen Chow stood up and came toward him. Without ceremony she put an arm across his shoulders and lifted her face toward him.

He knew that he was expected to kiss her, but he knew also that she would turn her head quickly and present him with her cheek; so many women did that. As he drew her to him, actually touching her for the first time, a kind of fire seemed to run through his fingers. It was far from the first time that he had held a woman other than his wife, but none of his previous experiences approached this time; it was utterly different.

And she did not turn her head away from him, she tilted it just a little and pressed her lips on his. Her body was beside his and his whole being responded. He was careful not to kiss her too hard, but he was not gentle. He broke the contact for a moment, looked at her, and then came back for more. At that moment he didn't give a damn for the case, what she might know, or anything else. He had not had a woman that close to him in too long a time, and never one so utterly appealing.

He did not know how long it lasted, he was on some plain suspended at an unknown point in space where ordinary considerations did not apply. It could have been a minute, two minutes, or as much as five. The thing that encompassed him was the fact that she was not simply giving him a goodnight kiss; she seemed to welcome the contact between them. At last he recovered himself and stood, still very close to her, but with his arms at his sides.

She looked at him evenly and openly, an intelligent young woman talking to a mature and capable man. "You're welcome to stay if you'd like," she said.

Her bed was very soft; it fitted itself perfectly to his body and gave him the feeling he had never known such luxury before. As soon as she had left him and had gone into the little dressing room that was one of the features of her apartment, he had washed and stolen a little of the mouthwash that he found in the bathroom. After that he had gotten out of his clothes quickly and had climbed into her bed with a strong sense of unreality. He had seen her carefully lock and bolt the only door, but he could not dismiss concern from his mind. It could be some kind of a trap. Then he came to his senses: he was about to go to bed with a damn goodlooking woman, and that wasn't even a misdemeanor any more.

She had set the light in the bedroom very low, but it was enough. When she came out of her dressing room she was a milk and ivory goddess. He watched her as she came toward him, bent down, and folded her side of the covers back. Then she was in bed beside him. He took her into his arms and from that moment every second of delay was a precious agony.

Never had he resorted to a professional, but he knew at once that while she was experienced, she would never be in that category. Her teeth stung his earlobe slightly and her fingernails found his back. He buried his face in her neck, his lips against her warm flesh.

When he awoke he was lying on his back. His left arm was at his side; his right arm was outstretched and pillowing the head of Helen Chow. He became aware of daylight in the room, otherwise the hour was meaningless. He turned his head then and saw her face looking into his own. He was more conscious of her eyes—large, very dark, and limpid. Her lips formed a very slight quirk, more a silent communication than a smile.

John Harbizon was aware of several things at once: his hair was unruly, his face had to be covered with stubble, and his breath, in all probability, was not at its best. He looked at her again and the same eyes were looking back at him: silently, apparently approvingly, and intimately. It was then that he became fully aware that her body was still close to his and with a warmth for which there is no substitute.

"Good morning," she said.

He turned his body a little. "Have you been awake long?"

"No; I awoke just now. How do you feel?"

"I can't tell you," he answered, "because I never felt like this before."

"Even when you were married?"

He didn't want to say an unkind thing about the girl who had shared a few years of his life, but he couldn't think of any evasion that would work. "No," he said, "not even then."

"I'll be back in a minute," she told him and then the warm bed was suddenly terribly empty. When she returned he got to his feet and went into the bathroom, still not knowing what time it was—or caring. He used the mouthwash again and hoped that it would be effective. He was conscious of looking his worst and would have given a great deal for a shower. Then he remembered what awaited him and the same feeling of disbelief came surging up once more.

But she was there, the upper sheet covering only part of her bare shoulders. "I used your mouthwash," he confessed.

"In the cabinet there's an electric razor," Helen said. "Before you jump to conclusions, it's brand new."

"Then how do you happen to have it?"

"I bought it for you."

That was the answer he had dared to hope for. He got back into bed, gathered her once more in his arms, but was content for the moment just to hold her that way. He kissed her quietly and gently, just to be sure that he could, and liked it so much that he did it twice more, asserting himself. Then he ran his fingers through her hair, admiring the texture of it and its shining blackness. "I want to know something," he said. "It's very important. I think you could have any man you ever wanted, discounting those in holy orders, so why did you ever allow—chose me? I don't possibly deserve it."

She kissed him effortlessly, making it a simple caress, more to please herself than him. "But you do," she answered. "And I'll tell you why."

She snuggled her head against his shoulder, making herself intimately comfortable, taking possession of him even if for only a short while. "I told you about Harold's plan: how I was to become a very costly and exotic call girl. And how he and his uncle were going to invest my earnings for us to get married on. I came home that evening alone, and sat here thinking. One of the questions I asked myself was this: of all of the men I have ever met, which one would be the least likely to offer me that kind of proposition. Several different people I knew ran through my mind, and then I came to you. There wasn't any doubt; you were the one: the exact opposite of the man who wanted to package me and sell me like merchandise. So I thought about you."

She stopped and looked at him again; even in the early morning light, unwashed and without make-up, she had not lost an iota of her beauty.

"So you invited me to dinner," Harbizon said, speaking quietly toward the ceiling, "prepared a fabulous meal, and laid in a brand new electric razor."

"That was a gamble," she answered. "Not a very big one. I didn't know whether I would invite you to stay or not; I wanted to know you a lot better first. I'm not a call girl, you know. I think you may have had the idea that I was—because of the way we met. I'm not, and I never will be."

She paused, but Harbizon was very careful to say nothing; she read him too well.

"I'm a designer—remember?" she went on. "I make a good salary, much better than you might think. And I pay my own rent. To an uncle of mine: he owns this building."

The kiss he gave her then lasted longer. In his heart he had the feeling that this would never happen to him again, therefore he was making the most of it during the one chance that he had.

"I believe in sex," she said. "I think it's one of the great blessings we have. Adults, like ourselves, should be free to enjoy it together, properly, without any censure from anybody."

"That's quite a declaration," Harbizon said.

She traced a finger across his chest. "I didn't want to sound formal; what I meant was, no obligations—either way. Some girls can only see sex as part of love and marriage; I see it as part of living."

"How about in the morning?" he asked her.

"Good!" she breathed. "Before I cook your breakfast."

On the way back to Boylesport Harbizon tried to reassess himself and the fixed boundaries of his life. He had no intention whatever of changing his profession, but he allowed himself to relive in his mind the past fifteen hours and lock them permanently in his memory. Even their light-hearted conversation at breakfast, while he had eaten the bacon and eggs that she had so skilfully prepared.

"I supposed you've heard that ugly rumor about Chinese women," she had chided him.

"With utmost disbelief."

"Well, now you know it isn't so, don't you."

"Yes I do, but I'd like to be reassured from time to time."

She had smiled at that, but she had said nothing in reply.

He was glad that he had stopped at a florist shop and had ordered something sent to her.

As the train took him closer and closer to his base of operation, the case that had been engaging his full attention forced itself back into his mind.

The scenery outside the window was so totally familiar he did not see it at all. Instead he was standing, mentally, in the middle of a huge, luxurious living room on a pouring night in Chicago, seeing something that he could not recall—something that danced maddeningly at the very edge of his memory. To capture it he went back to the first moment when his cab had pulled up before the high rise building, after he had cleared the police line that had been hastily thrown up in the foul weather.

Patiently he retraced every minute: everything that he had seen or done, every word that had been spoken, every tiny thing he had noted. He missed it the first time through and he knew, somewhere he had inadvertently skipped something. Once more he brought back the rain, the wet, jouncing cab, the policeman who had stopped him and had let him through only after he had identified himself.

The entrance to the building, the still drenching rain, the plain-clothes man in the plastic raincoat who had challenged him, the reluctant doorman who had been taken out to see the body. The squashed thing that had been a man, the shoe he had taken off . . . .

The body.

Something about the body.

He knew now where the thing was hiding, but he still didn't have it in his conscious mind.

Then it came. The body: the remains of a big burly man crushed horribly from a fall that had been something like two hundred and fifty feet through the sopping wet night, through the blackness, without a scream that had been heard, a plunge of several seconds that had ended with the instant transformation of a healthy, muscular man into a squashed corpse that had been dreadful to look at. It had not been easy to take off that shoe, even though he had kept his eyes away from the main part of the body while he was untying it.

He returned to his office with a whole new channel of investigation opened to him. He had a great many things to do and he would have to be extremely careful not to let his own foot slip. One mistake now and the whole thing would be forever out of his reach.

Chapter Twelve

After he had cleared the top of his desk and had picked up his routine for the day, Harbizon went to see the chief. There was little protocol in the Boylesport Police Department; he picked a free moment to walk in and sit down knowing that he would be welcome. He exchanged a few of the usual agreeable remarks and then came to the point. "I'm not making any promises whatever," he said, "but I may have found the end of the tunnel in the Lockheim killing. I believe that I know who did it—and why."

The chief did not let it show too much, but he was close to elated. "John, that's wonderful! I don't know how in the world you did it, but accept my congratulations. You are certainly a major asset to this department."

"Thank you, but I haven't earned all that yet."

"I'm sure you will. What are the chances for arrest and conviction?"

Harbizon shook his head. "It may not be possible. If everything works out, we'll be able to report in due time that the case has been solved, but owing to circumstances we can't reveal, the guilty party may not be brought to trial."

"Do you think the citizenry will buy that?"

"If we put it the right way, yes. We might leak it out that a suicide was involved; that almost always closes a matter."

The chief thought for a few moments while his lips unconsciously reflected his thoughts. "Nat Lockheim was not a popular man. He belonged to the yacht club and all that, but few people actually cared for him. I'm inclined to think that the suicide idea will satisfy almost everyone. Discretion is very much appreciated in this community."

Harbizon was grateful for that. The attitude of the chief, and that of the whole department, was one of the reasons why he was contented to remain with a very small organization where the major crimes were not often encountered. It was a police force that knew how to do its job, but kept its cuffs clean in the process. There was a lot to recommend that approach whenever the community being served made it possible. On Manhattan island it would have been out of the question.

"Tell me," the chief continued. "That man who jumped to his death in Chicago: had he anything to do with the case?"

"I think so—yes. I have a letter that he received from Lockheim, written just before Lockheim died."

"I'd like to see it."

"You will. Let me put the whole package together first; it will make more sense then."

"You handle it your way, John."

Harbizon got up, spoke his thanks, and left before he had to say any more.

Because he hadn't given the matter any advance thought, Harbizon had expected Harold Horowitz to be some kind of a kid. Possibly the fact that Helen Chow had referred to him as her boy friend had influenced him, but he should have known that any young woman of her sophistication wouldn't have been tied up with a juvenile. As it was, Horowitz was close to forty and had the philosophy of a pile driver.

"I don't know why in hell you've come to see me," he said. "I don't know a damn thing about the death of San Marco. I told your partner, Dietrich, that when he came down here and took up more than an hour of my time."

His office was a small one, uncarpeted, and with no particular amenities. It didn't suggest that Harold Horowitz' time was as valuable as he himself seemed to think. He was officially a statistician, but that didn't appear to limit the scope of his activity.

"I'm sure you were willing to give an hour to help clear up a murder." Harbizon's tone was deceptively mild.

"Damn it, I'm getting sick of this! Just because I used to go with San Marco's mistress, now I'm being hounded by you city employees. You're exceeding your authority, mister, I don't like you, and I don't give a damn what you're trying to do. Is that clear enough?"

"It's clear to me that you're a complete horse's ass," Harbizon snapped back. "Any time reasonable questions are put to you by duly constituted authorities, you'd damn better answer them. If you get handed a subpoena, you're required to answer it. It's part of the price you pay for the privilege of living in this country. And that's one of the most valuable things you'll ever have."

Horowitz sneered at him, and made sure that Harbizon saw the curl of his lips. "The only thing I gave a damn about is money. Money means power, and that's the name of the game."

Harbizon had a reason for appearing to remain patient. "There are some things money won't buy."

"Nuts. Fifty grand will get you a degree from any college in the country; an ambassadorship costs twice that." He waved a rejecting hand in front of Harbizon's face. "You haven't any, because you're only a cop; already you're done for. Now how about getting out of my hair; the market's open and I'm not making a dime sitting here talking to you."

Harbizon timed it as he got up; he started to turn and then suddenly faced Horowitz again. "One question: isn't it true that you had demolition training in the Army?"

"So what of it," Horowitz snapped. "Can I help it if I was drafted?"

Cecil Forrester received Harbizon with the same dignified and courteous manner that he had used at their first meeting. He showed his guest into his private office, picked up the phone, and instructed his secretary to hold all of his calls. That done he settled back in his chair and offered his full attention. "How are you coming with your investigation?" he asked.

Harbizon maintained a completely relaxed attitude. "Quite well, all things considered. I came by to get the answers to a very few questions, if you don't mind. I've been spending most of the past three days gathering further background material on some of the people who figure in the case."

"Am I included?"

"Yes, Mr. Forrester, you are."

That caused the financial advisor to lean back in his chair and reflect for several seconds. When he finally spoke, he chose his words most carefully. "It was my belief that I was assisting you, in a small way, with some professional information about the stock market. I was not aware that I was a suspect."

Harbizon answered with equal care. "I didn't use that word, Mr.

Forrester, nor do I intend to. But I would appreciate some answers, as I said."

"All right; go ahead."

"At my request, you made some inquiries concerning a possible next victim in this series of stock market murders. You mentioned that you were very discreet."

"I was."

"You did consult two other people."

"That's correct, but I put it on the basis that I wanted some information for purely personal reasons. You see, I too had a connection with Sphinx Wire and Cable, but in my case it was a disaster. I covered myself by asking if I might be a likely candidate to be eliminated."

That was an angle Harbizon had not considered. "You covered yourself very well indeed, I have to agree. In your opinion, Mr. Forrester, could either of the people you consulted unintentionally have mentioned your inquiry?"

"Absolutely not. One of them is the president of Sphinx, a man I have known intimately for many years and trust completely. The other is a financial adviser like myself whom I have also known for some time—well before I got into this business, as a matter of fact."

Harbizon appeared to be thinking carefully. Actually he was, planning just how he was going to put the next key question. "This is absolutely off the record, sir. It is my understanding that you were once in intelligence work. Could this other gentleman possibly have a similar background?"

Forrester became extremely cautious. He waited some time and then spoke totally without visible emotion. "We were once associated for some time under conditions of great mutual trust. That's as far as I'm prepared to go. He did not, and will not talk, I'll guarantee it. You have my unreserved word that I did not. Even my secretary, who is totally trustworthy, doesn't know about those calls."

"Thank you very much."

"You're welcome, Lieutenant. I'm sorry that everything I had to tell you was negative. I fear that I wasn't much help."

Harbizon stood up, calmly and easily. "On the contrary, sir, you've brought me quite a bit closer to my objective."

He fully expected after that to have Forrester ask him if he knew who had done the killings. When that obvious question didn't come, his opinion of the investment specialist rose proportionately. He left the office after making the usual polite statement, got back into his car, and headed up to see Dietrich.

In Los Angeles Hatch and Marlow wrote up an interim final report on the murder of Ben Sorenson. It contained a good deal of data, particularly bearing on the private life of the dead broker, and included all of the definite evidence that the capable team had been able to gather. Every canyon resident had been seen and questioned, most of the people in Sorenson's office had been searchingly investigated and all of them had been interviewed in depth. Several lady friends of the deceased, married and otherwise, were compelled to unburden themselves concerning their relations with the dead man. When it had all been summed up it gave a very clear picture of Ben Sorenson, the considerable swinger, the girl with whom he had been living at the time of his death, and the exact way in which the killing had been done.

But it did not contain the name of the man who had been under the house. It did contain the statement that until some new evidence or fresh data came to light, the investigation was suspended. A murder case is never closed until it is solved, but every available avenue had been exhausted and is wasn't only a case of insufficient evidence—it was a case of no clues whatsoever as to the identity of the killer. As luck would have it, every one of the eleven clients of Ben Sorenson who had lost heavily on Sphinx Wire and Cable had been able to prove a clear and solid alibi for the time of the murder. Without exception they had been asleep in their homes and had other family members to back them up.

Marlow send a copy of the report to Harbizon together with a covering letter. He asked to be posted immediately on any new developments.

In Chicago Hanratty had also come to a dead end. The tenants of the high rise apartment dwelling where Irving Brown had lived were notably uncooperative. They were paying premium rates for privacy and they had no interest whatsoever in the dead man who had embarrassed them by splattering himself on the sidewalk in front of their exclusive building. The Brown apartment was sold within a week to a new tenant, or rather two: a pair of young men who were the owners of a highly successful small chain of beauty parlors. They charged astronomical prices and paid a good share of their earnings to a most efficient publicity agent. None of the other tenants took the least notice of them when they moved in.

Medical examination of the dead man had yielded very little. He had been drinking, but only moderately. Definitely he had not given himself one or two strong jolts before going over the railing. The amount of alcohol in his blood stream had been consistent with what he had drunk at his friend's apartment, according to her account. Brown's own apartment had yielded no clues other than the misplaced throw rug and the unmarred surface of the new paint on the terrace.

No one had been seen going either in or out of the rear service entrance, but it had been a foul night and understandably no one had been looking. Delivery vans were always coming at all hours; in particular liquor store deliveries were often made well after midnight. Not a single witness could be found who would admit to having seen a stranger in the corridors, or anything unusual at all. Hanratty knew well that if any of the tenants *had* seen anything, they would never admit it to the police and thereby get involved. They all knew that it was a murder case and they wanted no part of it.

Hanratty put it on the back burner; there were too many other things that cried for his attention.

Then the grinding work began. Harbizon patiently put in day after day, often until late at night, searching for fragments of evidence that might help him to make a case. Time after time he ran into a dead end, but when that happened he made a note or two and then started off on a new track.

He made a trip to the Sphinx Wire and Cable Company and talked to several of the company officers, notably the comptroller. He was taken on an extensive tour of the plant facilities and formed his own estimate of the efficiency of the firm in producing its military hardware. He went to Washington and talked with some procurement specialists. From them he obtained records and a large amount of other data.

A broker in Boylesport supplied him with a price chart of the stock of Sphinx Wire and Cable. He spent more than a day correlating the purchase orders, the delivery dates, and the payment schedules with the fluctuations of the market price of the stock. He got a complete set of the publicity releases that the company had put out for the past year and studied those in reference to the stock price chart.

Lieutenant Walchewski of the NYPD helped him to obtain records on the transactions of Nathan Lockheim, Simon Korngold, and Ben Sorenson. It was less easy to trace the transactions of William San Marco because he had been the stock specialist and therefore every transaction, legitimate or otherwise, had passed through his hands. As he worked, he made it a business to read the *Wall Street Journal* every day; he was rewarded by a barrage of news concerning new regulatory bills in Congress, SEC actions, new trading restriction proposals, and other reforms that appeared to be coming from all directions.

From the New York Public Library he obtained a list of all the available works dealing with explosive demolition and tried to track down who had drawn out those particular books during the past several months. That proved to be too mammoth a task and he was forced to abandon it. Trying from the other direction, he found that the library was unable to tell him all of the books that a certain card holder had taken out. It was explained to him a number of times that the city was in acute financial straits and many normal services had been suspended.

It was slow, it was energy-sapping, but all of it had to be done. He did glean a few fragments here and there, all of the circumstantial nature. He felt consciously that he probably could have built some sort of a case against every person connected with the whole matter, but the real conclusive data, information that would tell him that he was at last on the right track, could not be found.

When he had done all that he could, and had put together as much as he had been able to glean from every source, he decided that it was time for him to fulfil an obligation. He had given his promise and he was the kind of a man who considered that an unpaid obligation. He put in a call to the office of Burroughs and Schneider and asked when they could get together.

"Have you got something for us?" Schneider asked, quick interest in his voice.

"Possibly yes, but we will have to meet somewhere that's out of sight and where we won't be interrupted."

"Just tell me one thing," the columnist asked. "We're busy as hell right now: will it be worth taking the time? No offense, but it's never been like this before."

"If I were you, I'd come," Harbizon said. "I have something to give you, and I warn you that I'm going to ask for something in return."

"Fair enough. Hang on."

The line was quiet for almost a half minute, then Schneider was back. "Is it hot?" he asked.

"It's hot."

"Then we can make it this afternoon, after three. Where?"

"On the parking lot of Pallisades Park. Don't look for a police car."

"Hey, man, that's in Jersey."

"I know, but your faces are too well known everywhere in New York. Even though it's just across the river, Jersey is a different matter. Have you got wheels?"

"Oh sure, no sweat about that. O.K.. on the lot at four o'clock; how's that?"

"Fine. One thing: don't tell *anyone,* except your partner, that we're meeting."

"Depend on it. And you know that we'll protect a source if we have to go to jail for it."

"I appreciate that," Harbizon told him, "because some of this is police sensitive."

"Say no more. See you at four."

The line went dead.

Harbizon took his lunch in a bar that specialized in much better than average food at a price that had prevailed five years before. He had hoped to eat quietly and in peace, but a television set that was on kept intruding itself into his consciousness. He had seldom seen television during the daytime and the barrage of commercials that bombarded his composure and peace of mind made him gratefully aware of what he had been missing. He tried to give his full attention to his food and to the important matters that he wanted to review in his mind, but the ubiquitous TV continued to hammer at him like a mechanical being that would go on and on witlessly until someone either threw a switch or pulled out the plug.

With a burst of electronic siren sounds the set launched into the second half of a many times rerun police drama. Actors in uniform, doing their best to look like policemen, carried on their procedures as the screen writer had imagined them to be. In the position of a captive audience Harbizon watched and generously decided that the several absurdities were not the actors' fault; they were only doing as they were directed.

When the suspects appeared on screen, they were prototypes for Professor Lombroso's concept of criminal man. They snarled with well-schooled technique, jumped into a car, and took off in a burst of burning rubber.

Harbizon made a determined effort to ignore the tube and return to his lunch. He would have walked out, but the food was good and he was still hungry. He ate and drank to wash it down, forcing the voice of the TV out of his mind. He did it so successfully he managed to ignore the next two commercials completely. Then the volume level dropped and the police drama was resumed.

The car chase was on. It was good visual stuff with the stunt drivers coaxing the maximum performance they could out of their specially equipped cars. At last the chief suspect was trapped on a bridge. He whipped out a gun and fired several shots at the police who were closing in on him. He hit no one, despite the fact that the usual precautions essential in such cases were not followed. Then the hero cop of the series raised his hand gun and fired.

It was obvious that the suspect had been fatally hit. He tetered for a few seconds at the railing, then the camera shifted angle as the stunt man did a carefully managed fall into the river. The police turned away; no one seemed interested in recovering the body and the available witnesses were ignored. The tube cut to a model who danced in a thin gown in the sunlight to show how beautifully her hair had responded to the sponsor's shampoo.

Harbizon finished his meal, paid, and left.

As he drove in toward the city he reflected on the police drama that he had just seen: so similar to hundreds of others conjured up to formula to entertain an audience popularly supposed to be at a mental age of ten years. There had been exceptions: brilliant exceptions, but they were too few and much to far between, as far as he was concerned.

The ending of his own case, when it eventually came, would not be a spectacular chase ending in bursts of gunfire: the great arrests of history had often been made quietly. Some of the most desperate criminals taken into custody had been asleep or had yielded without a struggle. But that sort of thing did not make the overt TV fare that the sponsors presumably wanted, or the networks, or the producers of the often all but machine-made shows . . .

That kind of thinking was getting him nowhere; he had a job to do and what was more, it would have to be very carefully done. He was about to skate on some very thin ice indeed and he would need to have all of his wits about him to pull off the deal for which he hoped.

He drove across New York with the feeling that he knew the city intimately, but that the city would never know him. He remembered the once world famous film star that he had encountered in a Times Square hot dog stand. The place had been crowded with people, but no one else appeared to have noticed what had been a major entertainment celebrity. New York as a city, he decided, had one policy: it didn't give a damn.

The George Washington bridge took him across the Hudson and into New Jersey, the state that had not asked to adjoin New York but did. Harbizon could not help feeling for the tens of thousands who lived in the shabby houses that hugged their tiny bits of costly real estate under the pretext of being homesteads. It was a way of existing week to week, fighting the bills, the unrelieved parade of rate increases, and the near hostility of computers built to order lives by electronic means.

But nobody had built one yet that could get a willing girl pregnant, and maybe that was the salvation of mankind.

Also, computers didn't murder people. They came pretty close at times, but they were dispassionate mechanical beings who did as they were programmed, perhaps the first manifestations of the Orwellian world to come.

As he drove nearer to the place where he hoped to make a deal, he looked again at the parade of totally uninspired houses crowded together to provide for as many people as possible within a minimum of space and wondered if the people who lived in them were sentimental about their homes—if to them one of the identical structures seemed any different than the others.

"And this is the room where our Alice was born . . ."

"I spent the better part of five months fixing up these cabinets, but now it's like a new kitchen . . ."

"Dad—mother—this is Cecile, the girl I've been telling you about . . ."

". . . just two days after our fourtieth anniversary. He felt just fine when he went to bed. He drank his coffee just like always, then about two in the morning . . ."

He jerked his mind away from that channel and thought once again about the beautifully produced Annual Report put out by Sphinx Wire and Cable. The agency had done a fine job of that; the messages to the stockholders over the signatures of the principal officers of the company told in just the right confident tones of the increased profits for the past year, of the satisfactory disposal of a small division that had not been returning a profit, and of the very substantial backlog of confirmed government orders that would keep the plant at close to capacity for the next three and a half years.

He wondered, savagely, if many of the people who lived in these uninspired, depressing homes had read that glowing report, had put their faith in it, and had invested their money in the company that had to do well because of the government orders. The United States Government would not go out of business; it was the world's best and most reliable customer. And, according to the report, the quality of Sphinx products had never been higher and the new line of shielded cables was a major advance produced by the research division.

He could well have put his money into Sphinx itself. And at the end of the report there had been the auditor's statement that the whole thing had been examined by them and, in their opinion, it was a true and accurate statement of the company's condition as of the close of business on . . .

It *was* a good company and he knew from his visit to the Pentagon that its products were first rate. The stock should have held its value, it should have advanced, and the stockholders should have been rewarded for their confidence and trust. But then Nathan Lockheim had begun his manipulations and suddenly SXE had begun a series of gyrations, aided and abetted by William San

Marco, the man who found his own name inadequate for his daily use.

Lockheim had made money, great amounts of money to keep that obscene wife of his in French pastries and whipped cream. He had made the money, but by no standard that Harbizon knew had he *earned* it; he had taken it away from people who had never wanted to play his game in the first place—people whom the stock market called "investors."

Probably almost all of them had bought what they had thought of as "securities" and then had watched the papers, hoping for some gradual appreciation. They had ended up losing millions and then Nathan Lockheim, in the words of his wife, had had his ass blown off. As far as Harbizon was concerned, he would be briefly mourned and little missed. His sole contribution to society had been to take other people's money away, and that was not much of an obituary.

It was ten minutes to four when Harbizon reached the amusement park, giving him a little time to put his mind in order and to make sure that he knew what he was going to do. Five minutes later another car arrived, circled and then came up to where he was waiting. He saw at a glance that both Bert Schneider and Gene Burroughs had come, so they had taken him at his word when he had told them that he had something hot to give them.

Harbizon got out of his car and walked the short distance over to where the other vehicle had stopped. He bent over and spoke to Burroughs who was driving. "Have you got your car equipped with a tape recorder or anything like that?" he asked.

"Absolutely not," Burroughs said. "You have our word on it."

"Good. But somebody might still be interested in what we're doing here, and I don't want to have to identify myself. There's a coffee shop a short distance from here that has a large back room with private booths. At this hour it should be close to empty."

"You lead the way, we'll follow."

Harbizon got back into his car and drove to the coffee shop. His surmise had been accurate: the rear section was empty and closed. A word to the manager took care of that and when he sat down with the columnists they were entirely by themselves.

A waitress came and took their order for coffee and some Danish rolls; that was enough to guarantee their being left alone for a few minutes. When the food had been served, and the waitress had left, the two columnists looked at Harbizon, waiting for him to speak.

"In the first place," he began, "in the state of New Jersey I am relieved of certain restraints. I'm a peace officer in the state of New York, but my authority doesn't extend across the Hudson."

"Understood," Schneider said.

"Now, this whole business of stock market killings has been quite a bit different from the usual murder investigation. There is no legal excuse for taking human life promiscuously, and it can't be condoned no matter how much some particular individual offends society or outrages the people around him. If he commits a capital offense and is convicted of it, then society will dispose of him. If he is in a position where the law doesn't reach him, then the proper remedy is to change the law."

He stopped, but neither of his listeners interrupted the silence. He had put himself on record and they understood that.

"Now we come to some specifics," Harbizon went on. "I'm going to keep my promise to you and give you certain facts. Under no circumstances are you to refer to me as the source."

Both of the columnists spoke at once, but it was Schneider who came out on top. "No court in the land can make us talk," he said. "And that issue is pretty well settled by now. If we ever did start talking, that would be the day we would be out of business."

"Then we understand each other. Now here are the facts that I promised to you. You can publish them if you want to, and I don't have to caution you to watch the laws of libel. You may be walking pretty close to the edge."

Harbizon broke off a piece of roll and took his time eating it. He was in no hurry and he wanted to keep the pace of the conversation as he had planned it. He drank a little coffee and then began once more. "There was a man in Chicago named Irving W. Brown. He ran a market tip sheet and did a good deal of business on the side as a trader himself. He was splitting commissions with a brokerage house in Chicago, but that's incidental. He was heavily involved in Sphinx Wire and Cable. He knew Nathan Lockheim and I have a letter that Lockheim wrote to him shortly before Lockheim died. That last is off the record, you know nothing of any such letter."

"Agreed," Schneider said.

"Now, the evidence of the letter, plus a very careful check of what happened to the Sphinx stock shortly thereafter, indicates that Lockheim had promised some sort of deal to Brown. At least Brown's tip sheet played right into Lockheim's hands."

"I don't see why Brown would do that," Burroughs interrupted. "If he deliberately printed the wrong information in his tip sheet, then he would lose subscribers and his reputation would be damaged."

"Exactly the way I see it," Harbizon agreed. "I think, therefore, that Lockheim crossed him up. Brown was smart enough to catch it in time and save his own bacon, but the letter was out and he couldn't recall it."

Schneider whistled softly. "You've been doing your homework," he said. "And it is one hell of a story."

"I think there's more," Burroughs said. "Please go on, lieutenant."

"Some more facts, and I emphasize that they are facts not necessarily related. It is next to impossible to establish the time when a bomb is rigged or planted, because if it is successful all of the pertinent evidence is destroyed. In the case of Lockheim's car, I do know that the bomb was wired to it sometime after he parked it at the station, but I haven't been able to narrow it from there. No one saw anything, and I can't come up with any evidence to the contrary."

"Leaving an open period of eight hours or more," Burroughs declared.

"True. Now, gentlemen, I have been able to establish one thing. Brown lived alone and didn't report his movements to anyone. But according to his mistress, on the day that Lockheim went up in front of his estate, Brown was out of town. She thinks that he was in New York. What's more, he had said something to her about seeing a man who had badly crossed him up."

"Eureka!" Schneider said, keeping his voice down.

"How about the time when dear Mr. San Marco got his?" Burroughs asked.

"Brown was still out of town," Harbizon said, "but he was often out of town, gathering information for his tip sheet—or so he said. In the absence of his own testimony, and that isn't available, Brown has no alibi for the time of either of the murders. He was in Chicago when Simon Korngold was run down, but that has been put down as an accident and therefore the timing isn't important."

"There was another killing in California," Burroughs said. He ventured that cautiously, leaving it to Harbizon whether he wanted to talk about it or not.

"As far as I can trace, Brown was in Chicago when that happened. However, the man who was killed, Ben Sorenson, was laying every female he could find to go to bed with him, married or otherwise. He also was a market operator and cost a lot of people some huge sums, enough to make him some very strong enemies."

"You're suggesting, then, that his death was not directly related to the Lockheim and San Marco killings?"

"I could make a good case for that theory."

Schneider was thinking intently. "If what you say is true, and the Sorenson death was a separate thing, then that could revive the Jewish angle. I hope to God that I'm wrong, but it could be a combination—a campaign against men who were stock market manipulators *and* Jewish . . ."

"You can drop it," Harbizon said. "I don't believe that there is a Jewish angle, and I'm as grateful as you are. Brown, incidentally, was also Jewish, so I checked exhaustively on all known bigoted organizations and violent individuals. I'll stake my reputation that religion had nothing to do with these murders."

"We'll buy that," Burroughs said. "Please go on."

Harbizon did. "Now let me give you a possible reconstruction. Irving Brown got a letter from Lockheim laying out a plan. Brown went along and published in his tip sheet exactly what Lockheim had asked for. Brown took a position himself in the Sphinx Wire and Cable stock and all looked well. Then, according to the phone company, Lockheim called Brown in Chicago."

"When?" Burroughs asked quickly.

"Two days before he died. Thereupon Brown left town, presumably for New York."

"Is there any evidence that Brown knew anything about explosives?" Schneider asked.

"He was never in any branch of the service, he managed to duck it, and I didn't find any other lead in that direction."

"But he could have been briefed, or he could have hired someone."

"The briefing is possible, but I can't see him finding a man to do that job for him. Too risky. Now here's some more: I dug up Brown's name, never mind how, and went to see him. I called him from the airport and asked for an immediate appointment. He refused until I told him that I was a police officer and that his life might be in danger. At that time I specifically told him that I was from the Boylesport Police. He didn't ask me why anyone from that jurisdiction wanted to see him, he didn't even ask where Boylesport was."

"He would have known that Lockheim lived there," Schneider interjected.

"That's true, of course. Now Brown told me that he would be out earlier in the evening, but to come to his apartment house and to wait in the lobby. When I got there, a little early, Brown was dead, lying on the pavement where he could well have hit had he jumped from his own terrace. Those are the facts that I promised to give to you."

The waitress came and warmed their coffee cups. Harbizon smiled his thanks and then let the reporters consider the information he had just given them.

"It all makes very good sense," Burroughs said at last. "Brown was double-crossed by Lockheim and his whole position was undermined. He went to New York. Lockheim thereupon died and so did San Marco, who we know was involved with him in the stock manipulation. Brown returned to Chicago. After a while a lieutenant of the Boylesport Police is suddenly in town and wants to see him that same night. Personally I would have run for it, but Brown went the other route."

"And you can't arrest a dead man," Schneider said.

"No, I can't."

"Now, can we print the facts that you just gave us, except the part about the letter?"

"Yes."

"I take it that we have this exclusively," Burroughs said.

"That's right—you do."

"Lieutenant, I don't know how we can thank you enough."

"Never mind that. Do you agree that I've lived up to my part of our bargain?"

Both columnists spoke at the same time, then Schneider stopped and let Burroughs go ahead. "Absolutely. But before we print, we've got to get some more background on Brown. We don't know what kind of a man he was."

"Not a lot different from Lockheim and San Marco," Harbizon supplied. "I ran quite a careful check on him. He was a heavy trader and used his own tip sheet to increase the odds in his favor. He had a reputation for ruthlessness."

"Did he play around with a lot of women?"

"No, not according to the picture that I got. He had a steady lay and that seemed to satisfy him."

"Then why didn't he marry her?"

"He couldn't."

"Oh!"

"Her husband's in service overseas. Sit on that."

There was another silence. When it had run its course, Harbizon broke it with a question. "Would you care for a little more?"

"Hell, yes," Burroughs answered.

"Then I'd better begin by telling you something further about police work. A crime is committed and we are called in. From that moment on we have, substantially, two jobs: we have to find out who is responsible for the crime and determine the motive. Then, after that, we have to get enough hard evidence, by strictly legal means, to establish proof in court of his guilt. We have to give the District Attorney a case solid enough that he knows he has a good chance of securing a conviction despite anything that the defense may try, and you can take it from me that they will try anything."

"I think we both understand that," Burroughs said.

"I hadn't quite made my point," Harbizon came back. "Because of certain legal rules, and some court decisions that have been handed down in the past, we often find ourselves in the position of knowing who committed a certain crime, but for one reason or another we can't make a case strong enough for the DA to take into court."

Schneider wasn't paying full attention. "There's something I can't figure out," he said. "How did Brown ever manage to put that bomb on Lockheim's car without somebody seeing him?"

"I think I can answer that," Harbizon replied. "It goes back to Mr. Chesterton and his invisible man. What is the most common thing you could see anyone doing to a car, by way of repair that is?"

"Changing a tire," Burroughs responded.

"Exactly. No one would notice or pay any attention to someone changing a tire. This is pure speculation, but I can see a service truck or van, or even a private car, pulling onto the lot and then going about changing a tire on Lockheim's car. The risk factor would be relatively small, because no one would notice Lockheim's tires unless one happened to be conspicuously flat. The repair truck drives on the lot: out comes the jack and the wheel is lifted off the ground. From that point on it looks perfectly all right, because a flat tire, once it is jacked up, almost always resumes its normal shape."

"He would need a key," Schneider said.

"Yes, or a small tool that would pop open the trunk for him. Remember, he knew that the car was going to be wrecked, so a few extra scratches wouldn't cause him any great concern."

"And under the guise of changing a tire, he could attach the bomb."

"Something like that. Any ordinary tire change wouldn't even be noticed, or if it happened to be seen, it would be forgotten almost at once. We don't remember things unless we take some note of them first."

"And if the car was parked some distance down the line on the lot, no one would be able to recognize Brown later anyway." Burroughs contributed.

"Quite right, any more than he would be able to recognize you. Now let me back up for a moment. I thought at first that these killings were someone's revenge for having lost heavily on Sphinx Wire and Cable; later I discarded that theory and I saw that particular company more as a thread that leads all through the case. It is a definite connecting link, but the death of the broker, Ben Sorenson, on the Coast should have narrowed the possible suspects down to his own clients."

"I thought you said that the incident in California wasn't part of the picture," Schneider cut in.

"No, I didn't say that. I said that I could make a good case for that theory, but I didn't say that I bought it. As a matter of fact, I believe that it was very much a part of the whole picture."

Both columnists remained silent, even though Harbizon gave them plenty of time to comment if they wanted to.

"Now there are certain pieces of information that I collected which fit together in quite another way," Harbizon continued. "First of all, it was clear from the first that whoever was behind these deaths had a much better than average knowledge of the stock market. The point was made to me that a person could find out who a floor specialist in a certain stock was, but that it was almost literally never done. A cheated or disappointed investor would blame his stockbroker first of all, then perhaps his brokerage company, and possible a publicized speculator. You remember the Insull case and more recently Cornfeld. These men were well covered by the press and their manipulations were exposed over a wide area. But Lockheim had never had any such publicity and San Marco was virtually unknown except on the trading floor of the exchange. So it is an obvious conclusion that it was not merely a furious investor who had lost because of these men's activities. It had to be someone who had a much greater knowledge of the whole stock market set-up."

He stopped and drank a little coffee, waiting for any questions. Both reporters were listening to him intently now, which was the way he wanted it.

"Now the Lockheim killing was very neatly done by someone who knew his business, but it is surprising how much information you can get on almost any subject if you take the trouble to really look it up. You know that, of course, being reporters. The San Marco killing had something about it that disturbed me, and that was the manner in which he was shot. The man who killed him carefully used an under-sized bullet trick that is very cute indeed, but there was no need for it. Ever since Saturday night specials became a drug on the market, almost anyone can obtain one, use it once, and then throw it away. So I asked myself; why would anyone go to the trouble of working that particular trick unnecessarily. The only reason would be to prevent the identification of a known gun, or one that the police could obtain if necessary. But no such gun has appeared anywhere along the line. For example, neither of you has a licensed firearm, I looked it up."

"What's your conclusion, then?" Burroughs asked.

"I think it was done to confuse the issue, or else to display virtuosity for its own sake. You see, it's an interesting aspect of these killings that the m.o.'s differed so radically. One man was blown up, a second was shot, a third was electrocuted, and a fourth was pushed over a railing. In all four cases some refined technique was used, possibly to suggest that some undercover agents, friendly or otherwise, were at work. Or else someone who had had that kind of training."

"Most interesting," Schneider said.

"Now I also noticed another fact," Harbizon went on, "At one stage of the game I wanted to contact someone for some detailed information about the stock market and I consulted you. You will remember that, I'm sure. You were kind enough to give me the name of Cecil Forrester and then, in the next breath, you supplied the rather unusual information that he had an intelligence background—that he had been, in your words, 'a James Bond type'."

"For men trained to keep your mouths shut about confidential information, that was an astounding thing for you to tell me. Later, when I saw Mr. Forrester, I brought the subject of his intelligence activity up twice and both times he very carefully avoided making any statement, even though I had assured him that our conversation was totally confidential. You can see the obvious conclusion that I drew; I didn't think that you were trying to implicate him, because he's a man who keeps a careful schedule and he was able to prove an alibi when I asked him for one. But there was a certain odor about it, one that is commonly known as red herring.

"Now, gentlemen, a most interesting little point. I've already established the fact that Sphinx Wire and Cable stock was a thread, carefully maintained, that runs through this whole case. With that in mind you will remember that I asked you if there were any more like Lockheim, San Marco, and Korngold, you gave me a generalized answer that there were probably some on the floor of the exchange and possibly a few more scattered around the country. I noted at the time that although the Korngold killing was accidental, you had built up a thick file on him, you told me so in so many words. In view of later events, I wonder how you ever overlooked telling me about Brown in Chicago. Especially since he published a nationally distributed tip sheet that you couldn't possibly have missed. And, as I just told you, it ran recent material on Sphinx Wire and Cable to please Nathan Lockheim. You do know that tip sheet, don't you?"

"Yes," Burroughs answered.

"I might add, if you're still interested, that I managed to obtain three other opinions on who might possibly be the next victim. All three of my consultants came up with several names, but Brown was the only one who was mentioned by all three; *they* certainly knew of him. And he was a prize bet because no other name was duplicated even once. Subsequent events would seem to prove that my information was correct: Brown was indeed the most likely next victim."

"I thought he was a suicide," Schneider said.

"Come now," Harbizon answered, "I just told you a few minutes ago that he was pushed; if you wanted to question the point, that would have been the time. No, gentlemen, he was pushed, and something about his body lying on the sidewalk gave me a very important lead. I already knew that he wasn't a suicide; I had seen evidence of that in his apartment."

"Naturally we're most interested in what you're saying," Burroughs declared.

"I thought you might be. When I was in Chicago I had the feeling that I was missing something, but I couldn't bring it into focus. Later it came to me. As I saw Brown's body, even though it was badly squashed, I noticed that he had been a big burly man. He had been in the prime of life and he maintained a steady mistress, so he was a definitely physical individual obviously of much more than average strength and vigor. He definitely didn't want to die, I checked that out thoroughly.

"He died when he was somehow compelled to stand on a small rug on the terrace of his apartment and then he was levered over. I was supposed to know that, because the rug had not been replaced where it belonged and that would only have taken a few seconds. So I began to reconstruct. Certainly he didn't go out on the terrace willingly, it was a wretched wet night. I worked out several possible ways that it might have been done, but the interesting feature was that in every case two people were required. Would you like to hear the theory I like best?"

"Please," Schneider said.

"Very well. I see two men coming into the apartment house through the rear entrance. Presumably they were making a delivery, but I've already established that although the front door is constantly watched to keep out unwanted visitors, the service entrance is often left uncovered at night—a bad breach of security. Nobody saw them, which was their good fortune, but few people were going in or out that night. They got into Brown's apartment, and I admit I don't know if they picked the lock or had gotten hold of a key. Then they checked through the apartment, found the throw rug, and made very good use of it. From that apartment they could see people arriving or leaving the building, you remember that Brown's body was just a few feet from the front entrance. When they saw Brown arrive, or someone who might be Brown, they went into their act.

"When Brown came in, he found what he believed to be burglars ransacking his apartment. One of them put a gun on him, took his wallet, and ordered him to go onto the terrace. As a wild guess, I would cover a small bet that it was the same gun that sent San Marco to join his ancestors. Anyhow, with a gun held on him, Brown was forced to obey. When he had been seen coming, the rug had been put on the terrace. Then the other supposed burglar came, said something like, 'let's get out of here,' and then yanked the rug when Brown wasn't expecting it. I don't say that it happened that way—that's only one possibility—but I am confident that no one person could have overpowered Brown or forced him to jump from his own balcony. He would have to be tricked since it is obvious that he wouldn't willingly kill himself against the threat of a gun. A man of his build would have rushed the gunman and taken his chances of only being wounded. Also, his temperment was not meek and submissive; a single attacker would have had his hands very full with Mr. Irving Brown.

"So that is what put me on the track of a possible collaboration. The only other alternative was a gang type of thing and that didn't fit the evidence at all. Now you can begin to see the picture emerge: a job that obviously required two people, persons well acquainted with the stock market and its many aspects, and what's more, persons with a very close mutual understanding. It did come to me that whenever we've talked together, neither one of you has ever said 'I'—on every occasion, including today, it has always been 'we'."

"In all candor, wouldn't you agree that what you're suggesting is a bit far fetched?" Schneider asked.

"I don't know," Harbizon answered, "you see there's one other thing that was quite significant. The death of Brown was mentioned in the papers, particularly in the *Wall Street Journal.* No weather report was attached to the story. But when I talked to you gentlemen about it, you brought up the point that it had been a particularly foul and rainy night in Chicago, a rather clear indication to me that you had been there. Weather is never mentioned in a newspaper account of that kind unless it was a contributing factor, such as reporting that a plane crash took place during heavy rain and dense fog."

Harbizon drank the last of his coffee in an almost casual manner. "By the way, two other small points," he added. "You made the mistake of giving me a description of the building in which Brown lived; you wouldn't have known that unless you had called on him at some time and if you had, you would have mentioned it before now. We must have missed each other by a fairly small margin. And perhaps you remember that once when I came to see you both, Bert was reported as being "out of town" and I talked to you, Gene, instead. That was the time that you gave me Forrester's name. And, interestingly enough, while Bert was gone, Ben Soreson died in Los Angeles. That was a one-man job and I must say, it was very expertly done."

Speaking very carefully, Gene Burroughs took up the conversation. "While we've been here," he said, "you made out quite a good case against Brown as the man behind these untimely deaths. Then you turned around and theorized about us. As a starter, you can't possible have it both ways."

"Of course not," Harbizon agreed. "I gave you some information about Brown and I'm afraid that I did present it in a way that could be construed as implicating him. The man is dead, he left no family, and there is no one to suffer in the possible event that he is eventually thought to be the stock market killer. You see: as I told you no case can be advanced against a suspect unless there is enough hard evidence, or some reliable witnesses, or both, to support a prosecution."

Schneider cut in. "There's a point you mentioned before, when you were telling us about police work. You said specifically that your first job in any investigation was to find out who had done a certain thing, and establish the reason—determine the motive in other words. What motive would you ascribe to us, for instance?"

Harbizon retained his very casual manner. "As to that, I do have in mind a conversation we had together when you told me that the stock market killings had done wonders for your circulation and readership. As I recall, you said that these developments had made you almost as well known as Woodward and Bernstein in Washington. Some people could call that an extremely strong motive: being right on top of a continuing major story, like the Watergate scandal that brought down the Nixon administration, could make a lifelong major reputation.

"Then there is another angle, one to which I have given a lot of thought. I told you that murder cannot be condoned, no matter who the victim is, and that is the law's position—and mine. In the case of the stock market killings, the victims were all exploiters of the public, human sharks who took advantage of our financial system to commit something close to legal robbery. Their elimination was a selective process, it is obvious, a kind of vigilantism that might have a small measure of justification in some people's eyes. You remember the old 'unwritten law' that we still hear about from time to time; these killings had even less justification, but the victims themselves are not too likely to be missed—I noted that. Only Lockheim was married and that, I was told, was strictly a business arrangement. I interviewed Mrs. Lockheim twice, once right after her husband had been killed, and she showed no signs of grief at all."

"So what happens now?" Schneider asked.

Harbizon became a bit more brisk. "Oh that is all laid out. As I told you before, when we don't have enough evidence to make an arrest of a known guilty party, we lie in wait more or less for him to make his next move. Almost invariably we get him then. We're forewarned, we know who we're after, and under those circumstances we can gather damning evidence without any waste of time. In my previous job, before I came to Boylesport, we had a known hit man who had committed three brutal murders. When we had him pinpointed we kept a careful watch. On his fourth try we nailed him and incidently saved the victim. And we had more than enough evidence for a conviction."

"Did you get it?" Burroughs asked.

"He copped out; there was no trial."

Bert Schneider looked at his partner and then went through the motions of stretching his legs under the table. "I don't know," he said, "it's just a feeling I have, but with all of the reform action that's going on now, the major clean-up that's been fifty years overdue, the new regulatory bills in Congress, and the sudden show of guts on the part of some governmental agencies, I don't believe that there are going to be any more violent deaths. What do you think, Gene?"

"I'm inclined to agree," Burroughs answered. "If, for instance, the major reform now going on had been the real objective, certainly it's already been achieved. From now on the public is going to be protected and the Locheims won't be able to exist any more."

"There's a basic lesson behind all this," Harbizon declared. "Someday when you have a good opportunity, you might put this in your column. Every now and then some citizens become upset, angry, and even violent, but there is a remedy available to them. If certain judges consistently let off obviously guilty defendants on one pretext or another, they can be voted out of office. The same goes for politicians who put through legislation drastically reducing penalties for major crimes. You have the power of the press behind you; use it to expose the people in office who deserve to be defeated or recalled. You can do that for the rest of your lives and stay completely within the law. They give Pulitzer Prizes for things like that."

"It's a good thought," Schneider agreed.

"You mentioned Woodward and Bernstein: you know what they did and everything after that went strictly according to the Constitutional process. Ford became President, a new vice-president was named, and there was no violence whatever. As I see it, that's the way to do things. The means are there and with your column, you can, as they say, move mountains. I hope that you will."

Burroughs signaled to the waitress. "This little refreshment is on us," he announced. "I hope we'll meet again soon."

"I hope so too," Harbizon answered. "Unofficially."

He left them and went outside by himself. Without looking back he got into his car and headed toward the George Washington Bridge. When he was once more on Manhattan Island, he pulled up at a convenient corner and made use of a phone booth.

Helen Chow answered on the third ring. When he heard her voice on the line it gave him a little stab of satisfaction. "This is John Harbizon," he said.

"Hello, John."

"I've been working on the Lockheim case and now, I believe, I've got it wrapped up. That goes for the death of your late friend, San Marco, also."

"I'm so glad to hear that!" There was real warmth in her voice.

"We had talked once about getting together after the case was over. I wondered if by any chance . . ."

"As it happens I am, free that is. Where are you?"

"Upper Manhattan."

"Then why don't you come down and we'll have a drink together."

"And then I'd like to take you out to dinner."

"All right."

After she had hung up Harbizon pressed his lips together with satisfaction. She had had the very good sense not to ask him any questions over the telephone. If his luck held out, she might be intelligent enough not to ask him anything at all, knowing that if he wanted to tell her he would.

As he started up his car once more, a major weight that he had been living with for some time had been lifted away.

Also he had a most pleasant evening in prospect: dinner with a charming companion and then whatever might come after that. He would never have met her if it had not been for the series of events that had begun in Boylesport.

He realized then that whatever Helen Chow had done in the past didn't mean a damn to him. She was more woman than he had ever known before, and he was more than willing to settle for that.

At that moment he knew that a policeman's lot could also be a happy one.

The End

EVERY INCH A LADY

BY

JOAN FLEMING

Published by special arrangement with G. P. Putnam's Sons.

The First Part

CHAPTER I

"What a life!" Police Constable Bacon blew thoughtfully upon his tea and sighed heavily. He had already told his wife a trifle sharply to turn off the television; she gave him a keen look.

"Life's no joke!" he said heavily a few minutes later.

The arrival of a plate of fried fish and chips in front of him interrupted his philosophizing; he gave it a sickened look, pushed it aside and asked for more tea.

"It's not like me to be put off me oats," he observed, "but it's been a nasty day. Very nasty. I reckon I never ought to of been a policeman," he mused.

"What's got into you, Sam Bacon?"

"I'm getting a sissy in me old age." Bacon smiled at the absurdity of his suggestion. "I've seen some sights in my time, but honest, I've never seen nothing what got me like today's job."

He took a long draught of tea. "It's all over the evening papers. And it'll be tomorrow's murder, so I'm not giving nothing away when I tell you there's been a slap-up, full-dress murder, with all the knobs on, in one of those posh new houses on the edge of the heath. Putney's never known anything like it, not in my time it hasn't. What a job!"

Mrs. Bacon disapproved of shoptalk; she took a pride in the sanctity of her home and liked to feel that when Sam came home he left his work behind him. She now felt, however, that this was the moment for a wife's sympathy and understanding. She popped the plate of fish and chips back into the oven, turned the gas to its lowest, and sat down at the table with an expression of receptive interest.

"Life's a terrible thing," he told her. "Why should such things

happen to them more than to you and me? Oh, I know they're rich
and all that, but all the time I was standing there, on duty, I was
thinking: 'Here's a couple just like Doris and me!' They've not been
married so long; the wife's only a kid and a nice one at that. It went to
my heart to see her, straight it did. In the midst of life we are in death,
amen."

During the pause Mrs. Bacon made another, this time successful,
essay with the fish and chips. But when the meal was over her husband's mood was still heavily lugubrious.

"He was savaged," he said at last, "stabbed all over the back like he
was a pin-cushion, and the stuffing coming out," he added, looking
awed by his own description.

"Sam Bacon!" his wife cried. "I don't want no talk of that sort in
this house, I don't!"

"You're a funny girl," Sam said good-naturedly; "spend hours
reading them shocking murder stories and then, when you get a bit of
real life, you come all over nice. Upon my word, standing there looking at the horrible scene I thought: this is like one of Doris's bits of
literature, *Death of a Fat Man* we'll call this one."

"But those stories I read are all a bit of fun. Things like that don't
happen."

"Oh, don't they!" Sam stirred his large frame uneasily. "Don't
they! Except that there's one happened last night not a couple of
miles from here!"

Interest having worked its way through her prejudices, his wife
asked: "Robbery with violence? Armed robbery, or what?"

"No robbery. all violence. At least no robbery as we could see. No
forced entry as we could see. Nothing taken as far as the wife was able
to say. It was like this. They've been married six months, this young
couple; husband around thirty-two; wife, say, twenty-four. They
asked another couple in for cocktails, seeing it was the six months'
anniversary of their wedding, and the chap they asked having been
their best man, like. The idea was that after they'd finished having
their cocktails they'd drive up West for a meal, see? The four of them.
Then the husband backed out, said he was too tired, maybe drunk too
much, said he didn't feel like it, so off he goes, presumably, to bed,
and the other three say ta ta, and off they goes up West, has dinner,
goes to a show. The friends bring the wife home in their car, say good
night to her on the doorstep; she says come in and have a drink, they

say no thanks, it's late. Wife goes upstairs—they've no servants, by the way—looks into her husband's room . . ."

"Husband's room! Don't they sleep together?"

"Posh folk don't; not all night they don't. The husband has what they call a dressing room, with a bed in it, in which, I presume," Bacon said primly, "he sleeps. Don't laugh, Doris, this is no laughing matter. Wife listens outside husband's door, all silent, she opens it a crack, light out, silence, everything okey dokey, she goes off to bed keeping as quiet as she can so's not to disturb her husband. See? Wife sleeps late. The husband usually wakes her with a cuppa tea, but today no one wakes her so she sleeps on. Arrival at nine ack emma of Mrs. Whozit, the lady help, who lets herself in with her own key. No breakfast remains, nothing to wash up. Mrs. Whozit guesses they've overslept, goes upstairs, wakens wife, pulls back curtains, excetra. Goes into husband's room and what does she find? Darkness, curtains drawn close. She draws back curtains and very near faints. In fact, when we got there she was in hysterics."

"Dead?" Mrs. Bacon whispered.

"Dead! But not only dead . . . he was lying with his head inside the open wardrobe, which is one of those big built-in things they have in these modern houses; he'd fallen down half inside the wardrobe as though he'd been attacked from behind just as he was stooping down to get something out. There was some travel kit underneath him when we moved him at last, and it looks like he'd been getting it out. But his back, Doris! There was stab wounds all over it, through the stuff of his suit; it was like someone had stabbed him over and over again like Grandma used to prod the top of her cottage loaves before she put them to rise. He's a great hefty chap, fifteen stone or more; it took four of us to lift him when they'd finished taking photographs. And then we found the canvas grip and the case underneath him, soaked in blood. It wasn't that that upset me, oh, no," Bacon explained. "I'm used to the sight of blood, I got over that long ago. It was the young wife and the way I kept thinking it was like you and me, and how you'd carry on if it was me'd been found murdered. She's just a slip of a little thing, Doris, no more than a kid. She was that brave, I'd have been proud of her if she'd been mine. Which she ain't," he added hurriedly.

"You could see her heart was well nigh broke but she kept a marvellous hold of herself: 'Yes, Officer, no, Officer.' She was white like a sheet of paper; it would of killed you to see her and how she was trying to keep up. And then the father-in-law turned up, in a bloomin' great old-fashioned Rolls-Royce. I've never seen a man take on like it. They had to go to one of those blocks of 'ar-la' flats behind the Ritz in Piccadilly to find him, and he insisted on coming right away. He's a shipping magnate, so they tell me, and this here chap was his only son. He acted like a madman. Pandemonium! Sir Jason bloomin' Cragg, they call him, and he's not that old to be the father of a son of thirty-odd. Good-lookin' chap too, when he's normal."

"Who do they reckon done it?"

"No idea at all. Between you and me, Doris, I could see my old man was flummoxed, though he looked as though he'd got a lot of private information up his sleeve. They went around looking busy, taking fingerprints on doorknobs, on handrail of the stairs, excetra. But I'd have laughed if I hadn't been upset. They'll get nothing. Whoever did it entered that house with a view to doing it. There was no row nor nothing, no fight. This chap went in with a pair of kid gloves and a sharp knife, did his job and got out, quick as quick."

"But you said there was no sign of entry."

"I said, nothing we could find. To me, in confidence, it looks like it was a chap he knew called after the others had gone off to the West End. Maybe he was waiting outside the house in the dark, watching until he knew the Cragg chap was alone, then ringing the bell and being let in normal, like. Maybe the Cragg chap was expecting him. That's my view, anyway, and for why? Because Doris, my love, he was fully dressed. Said he'd stay at home to go to bed, but did he? Just up your street, eh, ain't it?"

"Do they reckon they know how long he'd been dead?"

"Only rough, very rough. The central heating was on, they've got one of them expensive oil-heating outfits, and the place is like a bloomin' oven. Makes it difficult to estimate exactly how long a body's been a corpse, if you get me."

"Well, dear me," Mrs. Bacon murmured thoughtfully.

"There's a group of those new houses, all alike but very exclusive, built in what used to be the grounds of that big mansion called Silverdale they pulled down a year or so back, remember? They're called Silverdale, One, Two, Three and Four. And there's a block of service flats, Nero Court, very modern, what actually overlooks the back of the Craggs' house. Today they've been to the other houses, asking questions, and tomorrow, I believe, we're going right through that block of flats with a fine-tooth comb, asking if anyone knew the couple, heard any unusual noise, saw anything funny. There'll be the usual busybodies say they've seen this, heard that, we'll spend hours interviewing thousands, and it'll all add up to nothing, you'll see. A dark night, everyone indoors watching the TV. Anything could happen. Not long ago there was a so-called furniture van went to one of those grand houses, on the other side of the heath it was, some time after business hours; the chaps broke in, all dressed in their white coats like real removal men, and they took every rag and stick out of that house, and there wasn't a soul noticed them, or if they did, thought there was anything up. So what hope have you of finding the murderer? None whatever, though it wouldn't do for anyone to hear me say so. Progress, that's what we're supposed to have, with police cars fitted up with radio so's they can be on the spot before you can count sixty. But the job's done by that time. There's nothing to touch the old bobby on the beat, believe me. He sees a chap lurking round aimless, takes a sharp look at him, passes again to see if he's still there, and if he is, he wonders, and if he's not—then he still wonders. And when a member of the police force starts wondering, well, that's something, anyway. He'll remember that face; maybe he'll never have to, but one in twenty times, maybe, he'll be shown the photographs at the Yard: 'Is it any of these?' 'Yes,' he'll say, 'it's that one.' And it's in the bag! Progress . . ."

Police Constable Bacon had talked himself into a state of comfort. Mrs. Bacon went to wash up and left him musing upon the horrors of progress.

CHAPTER II

She lay face-downwards on the bed, listening to the sound of policemen tramping up and down the polished stairs, of motor cars stopping and starting, the sound of lowered voices, the policeman at the door talking to the visiting reporters. The policewoman was kind, frequently bringing her cups of tea and having little friendly chats about nothing. "Now you must try not to think about it, dear. Your husband is out of pain. You must be brave. Try to bear up for his sake."

The short winter day drew to its close about five o'clock and the darkness put an end to police activity out of doors; the police cars drove away leaving two police constables on duty in the stricken house.

Sir Jason, heavily under the influence of the tranquillizing tablets he had been taking at frequent intervals, tapped on the door.

"May I come in, Easter?"

She raised her head and turned over, her face blotched with red from pressure against her arms.

"My poor dear girl," he said gently, "get some night things into a bag and let's go."

"Go?"

"Yes, you're to come back to Arlington Street with me; I've made arrangements."

Easter shook her head. "No, thanks."

"No nonsense, child. Of course you're coming."

"No, I'm not, really. Thank you, but . . . this is my home; in spite of everything, I still regard it as my home. I don't want to leave here, Jason, truly."

"You can't possibly stay here after what's happened," he told her sharply.

"They're leaving a policeman to guard the house, aren't they?"

He nodded, on the verge of argument.

"Well, then," Easter said reasonably, "I shall be quite all right; don't worry about me."

"Look here, it's impossible to leave you here alone . . . "

"Oh, don't *fuss*," she said irritably.

He looked searchingly at the ravaged young face. "Very well, if that's the way you feel about it . . . I shall find a pair of York's pyjamas and sleep in the guest room, not that I shall sleep!"

"There's no need for it," Easter protested.

He sat down on the edge of the bed and took her limp hand. "Look, you and I have only got each other now; you've no other relative in the world, have you?"

She did not answer but looked away.

"Have you?" he urged, shaking her hand. "And I've only my club friends, business friends and acquaintances; it is blood relations that matter at a time like this, and you're the nearest thing I have to that. Besides, I feel . . . there's nothing left of my poor boy but you. We must stick together, Easter, it is the only comfort we shall have; that and . . . bringing whoever did it to justice. Up to now I've been a firm abolitionist but, my God, it makes you wonder. It's easy to talk about abolishing hanging so long as your only son hasn't been murdered. But when he has—" he coughed—"when he has . . . hanging seems a lot too good for the bloke that did this. Practical experience makes all the difference," he added wryly.

He went across to the window and drew aside the heavy lined curtain, looked out into the darkness for a minute. Sir Jason Cragg was of the same build as his son, York, had been; not tall, he was powerfully built and well covered so that it would not take much in the way of excess to make him a fat man. That he was well tailored and well groomed afforded him protection from that description as a rule, but upon this particular evening there was no doubt that he looked a distracted fat man. He peered this way and that into the darkness.

"Who knows? He may be watching the house, like the proverbial dog returning to its vomit. He may be out there now, crouching in the bushes, watching and waiting, or he may have been disturbed at his task when you came back, Easter. Or perhaps he lay hidden in the darkness somewhere in the house, waiting for an opportunity to look round. Or, when he saw that it was hopeless without waking you with sound and lights, he may have let himself out by the front door, planning to come back some other time, when the house was deserted."

"Oh, do stop it!" she cried. "Are you trying to frighten me, or what?"

"But if he comes back," Sir Jason went on discursively, "I shall kill *him;* it will be my turn."

He let the curtain drop back into place and picked up the photograph of his son from the dressing-table. He stared at it for a long time. Then he went slowly from the room without another word.

CHAPTER III

John Ramsgate had been at Cambridge with York Cragg and was now a member of Lloyd's. Both he and his wife Jill were able to give a full and frank description of the evening they had spent. The Ramsgates had two young children, one of whom had whooping cough; on the evening of the murder, this child had had some bad paroxysms of

coughing and the nannie had stayed up in order to talk to the father
and mother on their return about the desirability of asking the doctor
to come at that late hour to give the child something to calm him and
so enable everyone in the house to get some sleep. There was, therefore, no question as to what hour the young couple had returned
home; the doctor was telephoned for within a few minutes of their return, he came at once, and the child was attended to in the presence
of his father and mother.

Since the movements of everyone connected in any way with the
crime had to be checked, the Ramsgates were able to produce a couple of acquaintances who corroborated the fact that they had met the
Ramsgates and Easter Cragg as they came out of the Windmill Theatre together not long after eleven.

At about seven-fifteen, York Cragg had telephoned to his father, it
being a few minutes after his wife and the Ramsgates had left the
house. He had arranged with his father to go to Southampton the following morning to meet the *Queen Elizabeth* which was arriving from
New York with an important client of the Golden Fleece Shipping
Company on board. His father was, within a minute or two, in no
doubt as to the time his son had telephoned; he had been expecting a
friend to dine with him in Arlington Street at seven-fifteen, and was
keeping an eye on the clock as he spoke to his son on the telephone.

The staff of a Hungarian restaurant in the West End had no difficulty at all in remembering the couple who, in the company of a second young woman, dined there before going on to the theatre.

York Cragg, therefore, had been alive at seven-fifteen, some fifteen
minutes after his wife and friends had left the house; some time between then and nine o'clock the following morning, he had been
murdered. The police discounted the possibility of his having been
killed within at least four hours of his body having been found.

As Mrs. Cragg had been at home from midnight onwards and
would have heard any unusual noise, it was fairly safe to assume that
Cragg was killed some time between the time of the telephone call,
seven-fifteen, and the return of his wife, midnight.

Starting with these premises, the following morning then, the police began their more intimate questioning: "I do want you to understand, Mrs. Cragg, that we are, if anything, more anxious than you to
bring this criminal to justice and that everything you can possibly tell
us about your husband's private life may be of value. Sir Jason will,

we assume, be able to give us any information there may be with regard to his business life, but I must rely on you for the rest."

"I'm afraid there is very little I can tell you, Officer. I do assure
you—" she smiled a little wanly—"that my husband did not lead a
double life. I think I can safely say I knew everything about him.'

"Ah, yes." The inspector loooked thoughtful as his assistant scribbled busily in his notebook.

"We went racing from time to time, but don't get the idea that he
was heavily involved; it was only for pleasure. You will see from his
bank statements that everything was above board. My father-in-law,
Sir Jason, paid a generous salary to my husband for his services to the
Golden Fleece."

"Shipping company, that is."

"What? Er . . . yes . . . of course. The Golden Fleece Shipping
Company."

"What about friends?"

"John Ramsgate was his best friend. As for the others
. . . well . . . we had the usual group of friends, mostly young
people. If you like I can look out the list of people we asked to
our Christmas Eve party; about thirty of them. But I don't think
you'll find any of them are possible murderers, Inspector."

"Anyone, my dear young lady, is a possible murderer; and someone," he said cryptically, "is a positive one. You see, your husband *has*
been murdered; therefore, someone murdered him. It's as easy as
that."

"Easy!" she repeated thoughtfully. "I think you will find, Inspector, that this will turn out to be a crime without a motive. My husband wasn't blackmailing anyone, he wasn't the possessor of valuable
jewels or documents, he wasn't an heir to a fortune, he wasn't the father of an illegitimate unborn baby, he wasn't a homosexual, he
wasn't even—" she said with the ghost of a smile, "—an identical twin.
And motiveless crimes are so much less easy to solve, aren't they?"

The inspector remained impassive. "There's something you've left
out," he reminded her gently, "the 'friend' sent to gaol for a crime
which he did not commit who, when he is released, hurries to take the
vengeance he has vowed during the years of imprisonment towards
the really guilty man."

"You won't find that, either," she returned equally gently; "he was
incorruptible, incorrupted."

"Yes, Mrs. Cragg. But you don't really expect me to take your word for it, do you? I shall investigate all the possibilities you have suggested because, you see, as I have just reminded you, he *was* murdered, so there *must* have been a motive."

She simply shrugged and waited patiently for more questions.

Later the inspector said: "She's a very remarkable young woman, that Mrs. Cragg. They tell me she was an air hostess; if I was falling through the sky in a burning plane and I had her hand to hold, it would help, believe me, it would!"

CHAPTER IV

"My son and his wife adored each other," Sir Jason told the police. "From the moment they met, ski-ing in Austria, they were just like that." He clasped his hands together to show how close the couple were. "I knew York would never marry until he felt he had found the girl he really wanted. He was run after quite considerably by pretty girls and their fond mamas. Once or twice, it looked as though he were falling, but it never came to anything. I was anxious for him to marry, naturally, I want . . . wanted a grandson. I asked York more than once when he was going to marry and he always answered: 'When I meet the right girl, Dad!' Finally he met my daughter-in-law last spring at St. Anton, floundering about, so I am told, in the snow. She was never any good at ski-ing; my son was first class in spite of his build. Well, there it was. They knew each other out there for, let me see, about a fortnight. York brought her to see me as soon as they got home; it was hardly to ask my permission to get married, but it was a gesture which I appreciated. I took to her at once, who wouldn't? She's a great gal; she's got everything, looks, character, ability. She'd no money, of course, but, fortunately, it didn't matter about that. One thing—I'm perfectly certain she didn't marry York for his money; she's not like that."

"They were married shortly after?"

"No; my daughter-in-law worked for an airline as air hostess; she had to give reasonable notice of her intention to leave. And then, of course, there was a house or flat to be found and furnished. Altogether they were engaged for about six months, and during that time, as I got to know her better, I realized that my son had picked a fine gal. I was delighted. I bought them this house as a wedding present. They were married, let's see, yes, it was at the end of July; they flew to the South of France for a honeymoon. Since then one has had every reason to suppose that it was a successful marriage. I mean, there wasn't any doubt about it that those two were wrapped up in each other. I have no doubt that it has passed through your mind, Inspector, that my son led a double life; but, believe me, he didn't. He was one of the most candid, open, yes, *uncomplicated* people you could meet."

The inspector nodded thoughtfully. "That is the impression of your son that one has," he agreed, "but . . ."

"But he was murdered!"

CHAPTER V

Imprisoned in every fat man, we are told, is a thin one wildly signalling to be let out. But the thin man in Sir Jason Cragg, chairman of the Golden Fleece Shipping Company, worn out with wild signalling, had within recent years become a weary, attenuated creature, waving feebly, hope spent. Sir Jason, madly successful, had reached the top of his particular tree, or mast, at the early age of forty, after which he had nothing more for which to strive, and nothing to which he could look forward other than thirty years of being an extremely rich, successful man. Though he bustled about, flying to America and back by Pan American Airways, hurtling around Europe by BEA, playing golf at Gleneagles, the thin man in him felt lonely and frustrated.

In his large, cheerful and altogether successful face were two pale brown sad eyes, like the eyes of a small dog with a lovely nature but, through no fault of his own, an anomalous body.

By the natural law of things-as-they-are, Sir Jason's son should have turned out to be a wastrel, a minor poet or an unsuccessful artist; but nothing of the sort occurred. York seemed to be as perfect a son as any man could possibly wish. He studied law at Cambridge, got a good second-class degree and went straight into the firm where, with his great charm of manner, he made a splendid representative.

So well did his son turn out that Sir Jason began, almost unconsciously, to be slightly bored; he longed for his son to marry and to produce a son of his own. Secretly, Sir Jason fancied himself as the benevolent grandfather, getting his grandson out of innumerable scrapes, paying his debts and doling out sly advice as to the way to deal with women.

But what did it all add up to Sir Jason asked himself, lying back in the comfortable arms of a hired limousine as it purred back from the crematorium. *"Funeral private, no flowers and no letters, please."*

If only York could have been killed in that last exciting year of the war when he had been in the RAF and flown over the British Expeditionary Forces at the landing on the Normandy beaches on D-Day! How proudly he would have borne the memory of his hero son for the rest of his life!

He looked at his daughter-in-law, silent and forlorn, sitting unhappy beside him in the motor car, looking out through the steamy window, seeing nothing. One hand was lying limply by her side; Sir Jason picked it up and turned it over, looking thoughtfully into the pink, shell-like palm with the fingers curled over it like petals.

"What a useless little hand," he said tenderly. He studied her slender wrist upon which she wore four jingly silver bracelets. "Poor little Easter," he murmured.

"Don't, please don't be kind or I shall cry."

"Why not? You haven't cried at all, child. It would do you good." He was thinking: what a pity she's not going to have a baby, it would make all the difference, to us both; it would be something to live for.

He looked from her wrist to her slender ankles and neatly-shod feet, the long smooth legs, the brief tight skirt, the well-fitting jacket, her small set face, white and stern, her smooth unwaved hair, and her unlined brow, her closed eyes with the full childish lids. She had a faintly expensive smell.

Sir Jason turned his head away and closed his eyes. I could easily, he thought, marry her and have another son. Perhaps in time, when she has recovered from the shock . . . But the thin man wilted in sheer amazement. It would be like committing incest! To marry his own darling daughter-in-law! Sir Jason whipped out his clean pocket handkerchief and hastily passed it over his immaculate brow. What a lecherous old horror he was becoming; men of his age, he had heard, were sometimes taken with strangely uncouth, even lubricous ideas; he must take care.

"We'll have a bite of something to eat in Arlington Street and then I'll send you home."

"Thank you."

"That is, if you insist. But you know, Easter, what I feel about that. I am very much against your continuing to live in that house."

"If you could only understand."

"Understand what?"

"Understand just how much my home means to me. You know the sort of upbringing I had; the only home life I've ever known is since I've been married. I love my house, my furniture, my own bed. And I feel safe there . . . oddly enough," she added.

"To my mind, love, it's not the house that makes the home, it's the people in it, and the . . . let's say the affection and trust between those people. If you came to live with me in Arlington Street, for instance . . ."

Easter turned her heard sharply, frowning. "You can't be serious!"

"Why not?"

She fell silent for a full minute. "It wouldn't do," she said at last. "You're not exactly an elderly father-in-law, Jason."

"Indeed I am!"

"Fifty-seven?" she asked mockingly. "No wonder I've never been able to call you 'Dad.' I wonder why you married so young!"

"Because I met the right girl and because her father happened to be a successful ship-owner. I didn't marry her for money, though I must admit," he mused, "I did go where money was! I've been a widower for so long now," he said wistfully; "I felt myself an elderly man at twenty-five." He lapsed into thought.

"The chairman of the Golden Fleece Shipping Company and his young daughter-in-law . . . no, it wouldn't do. People are unkind. If you think it over you'll see that for me to go back to Putney and be on my own is the only thing. It isn't as though I mind being on my own . . ." she shrugged. "Since York had to be taken from me there's nobody else I *can* live with, is there?" There was a pause. "Is there?" she repeated.

"I suppose not."

"Well, then."

They were silent until they arrived at the entrance to Sir Jason's extremely luxurious flat.

"Wait to take Mrs. York back to Putney," Sir Jason told the chauffeur as he hoisted himself out of the car.

"I don't know why," he said later as he removed the wire and gold paper from the top of a champagne bottle, "I don't know why people always keep champagne for joyful occasions. I believe in opening a bottle of champagne when life's perfectly bloody." He poured the wine. "Well, Easter, here's to you and me! You and me! This terrible thing has happened to us and here we both are, getting around, keeping going, keeping up appearances, as they say. We could go mad, knock things about, scream and tear our hair, and I dare say if our juices were arranged differently, that's what we'd be doing. As it is . . ." He drained his glass and poured more wine into it. "You're wonderful, Easter. You're a woman in a million, my dear. I'm proud of you, and York would be proud of you." He wandered restlessly across to the window. "All this searching for the weapon! What a lot of rot it is; what a waste of the country's money. I actually told the inspector chap as much. I said: 'There's nothing easier to hide, or dispose of, than a dagger, knife or stiletto. A chap can clean the blade on some cotton wool, his pocket handkerchief, or, in fact, any rag of material, pull the plug on it and slip the knife into his trousers' pocket. Wrap something round the blade and you could slip a knife with a six-inch blade into a trousers' pocket easily. And as for final disposing of a knife, what could possibly be easier than the Thames? This chap that . . . this murderer of ours, Easter, could easily have stopped his car, let down the window and chucked it over Putney Bridge into the river. Or down a street drain. Or under floorboards in any house or flat. Or plunge it into the ground in any park, on Putney Heath, in Battersea Park, on Brighton Beach. Endless possibilities. Looking for the weapon! Hell!"

Easter was sitting in a chair, her long, lovely legs coiled sideways, holding her empty glass.

"The thing is," her father-in-law went on, "the police have their methods, their routine methods, I should say, and they've got to go through the whole boiling, in a murder of any kind. But seventy-five percent of their efforts are wasted in a lot of cases, this, for one. On the surface this murder looks so simple; every gangling youth these days has his dagger on him. Every Monday morning brings newspaper reports of the weekend's stabbing case. If York didn't happen to be who he was, I doubt if it would have raised any interest at all; a tiny paragraph in the national dailies and that's the lot! As it is, you will have noticed how the case has already been relegated to the smallest possible paragraph. There'll probably be a photograph in the cheaper press tomorrow, of you and me walking away from the crematorium, and that will be that. Yes, it is the simplest possible murder, on the face of it. The police, of course, don't believe for one moment that York was the golden-headed boy we make him out to be. I'm pretty sure they think that, once you were out of the house, York, having telephoned dutifully to his father, made off to some disreputable night-club or pub, got thoroughly drunk, got into some dispute with a thug who followed him back home and stabbed him then and there. There was a good deal of alcohol inside him, you'll remember."

"But that was accounted for by the celebration we'd just been having."

"Yes, Easter, and no doubt the Ramsgates' stomachs would have shown an equal amount."

"And mine."

"And yours. It was a cold night, a cold winter's night; even a thug would be wearing gloves to keep his hands warm, apart from the question of fingerprints. A pair of ordinary wool-lined brown leather gloves! You can stab quite as well in gloves as without them, I'm sure."

Easter turned her bracelets round and round her wrist. "Perhaps that's what did happen."

"Not it," Sir Jason said firmly. "People have to act in character. Can you see York slinking out to a club or pub the moment you and the Ramsgates had left the house?"

"I can't. But then, I can't see why York didn't come with us."

"Eh? what?"

Easter repeated what she had said.

"You can't. Why didn't you say that before?"

"Why should I? What good would it have done?"

"Do you really feel that, Easter?"

She nodded. "It was exactly six months since we were married. Just an excuse for a party; we'd booked four seats at the Windmill Theatre. John Ramsgate was to be host for the dinner and had already booked a table at the Hungaria. And then, as we're all starting out, what happens? York says he doesn't feel up to it; he's got a cold coming on! I ask you. An attack of flu."

"What did you have to drink?"

"Champagne cocktails only. I admit we had about three each, but we were only merry; John had no worry about driving, or anything like that. We had some of those little eats from Fortnum's with the wine."

"Were you surprised, Easter?"

"At what? At his not coming with us? I was astonished, and a bit worried too. I tried not to show it, but I had a hell of an evening worrying, wondering what was really wrong with him, wondering if he was going to be ill, or anything. And when I got home and found everything quiet, his light out and so on, I thought, well, perhaps he really did have a cold; anyway, everything seems all right now. I was thankful the Ramsgates didn't come in, though. I crept off to bed myself and didn't think any more about it." She paused. "Since you were talking about 'people acting in character' I had to mention that. It certainly wasn't acting in character for York to say he wasn't coming. You know how much he enjoyed everything. He loved an evening out. A cold!"

Sir Jason filled Easter's glass and his own. He raised it to her. "No, I can't make it a toast, but I solemnly swear that I shall not rest happily, nor allow my mind to be at ease, until I have discovered this murderer and brought him to justice. This crime *will not* go unavenged, Easter, this crime *will not* become just another *Unsolved* crime in the file at Scotland Yard. I shall use all the energy and all the initiative I can muster and, yes, all the money; if necessary, I'll employ a private eye, not your hole-and-corner Peeping Tom, your chappie paid to follow guilty wives or erring husbands. I'll get half the Secret Service on to it, I'll get the Quai des Orfèvres, Interpol . . ."

Suddenly he crumpled on to a chair, and, holding his empty glass between trembling fingers: "But what's the use? None of it will bring York back."

Easter uncoiled herself and, coming slowly across the room, she laid a hand on his stout shoulder for a moment, then walked swiftly to the door. With her hand on the knob, she turned to hear him say: "I'll be along tomorrow morning, if you don't mind, Easter; I'd like to go through his desk, his private papers, bank sheets, and so on . . ."

"Of course . . . Goodbye for now . . . Jason."

CHAPTER VI

To sort out the personal possessions of the dead is a dreary task, but Sir Jason was no procrastinator; when there was a particularly unpleasant job to be done, he did it as quickly and as soon as possible. Sitting at his son's large flat-topped, leather-covered desk in the small room they called the study, he scanned papers and letters, crumpling up those he thought irrelevant until there was a large pile of waste paper on the floor beside him. He kept photographs: prep-school groups, football teams, house groups, RAF groups, Cambridge rowing crews, amateur theatricals and, finally, photographs of York's wedding. He put these carefully aside, together with bank statements, the deeds of the house, cheque-book stubs and receipts. He made a separate pile of unpaid bills, but there were not many of these; on the whole York was methodical; his affairs were in as good order as those of anyone suddenly snuffed out were likely to be.

Why do people deliberately slip flat objects under the paper which lines the bottom of a drawer when they are not particularly anxious for them to be found? In some drawers, the lining paper invariably slides back, revealing the plain wooden drawer-bottom; and in other types of drawer, the lining paper stays firmly in place for generations. Why bother to slip treasured and private objects under the paper in a private drawer containing personal papers and always kept locked? There isn't a satisfactory answer. It is simply a trick of action or behaviour that occurs in people and is inexplicable; like fussiness about starting to eat a boiled egg at the blunt end, using a hanging chain on a motor car to prevent car-sickness, and passing the port round in a clockwise direction.

If a desk is being ransacked, there is not much chance of something hidden under the lining paper being overlooked; on the other hand, a document thus secreted has been known to turn up after a hundred years of concealment.

There was no earthly reason why Sir Jason should look under the paper of a certain drawer in his son's desk, but the grim fact remains that he did.

One thing is quite clear; the fact that it *was* pushed under the lining paper gave it an importance to which it might not otherwise have been entitled.

It was a shiny photograph of the publicity type, measuring eight by twelve inches. Some people might exclaim at the woman's beauty, others might be equally repelled, but it was certainly a striking photograph. At the bottom was written in stagey sort of writing: "To my darling York. Your Mavourneen."

Sir Jason held it at arm's length, as though he had found something extremely revolting: "Who the hell's this bitch?" he asked aloud.

It was the photograph of a woman of about thirty; she had the usual bust; it was her face that was striking. Her dark hair was drawn tightly upwards, away from her face, the heavy plait was worn like a coronet, her eyes and eyebrows were made up into an exaggerated upward slant and the mouth was a voluptuous monstrosity with an under-lip that never was on land nor sea. One ear only was visible and it was long and pointed, like that of a pixie. The whole was framed in a diaphanous, sari-like stole.

After studying it for some time with an inscrutable expression on his face, Sir Jason slipped it back under the paper where he had found it. He finished his task in the study and went heavily upstairs to sort out his son's clothes. Easter was out; shopping, she had said, but Sir Jason appreciated that she had preferred to leave him alone to his melancholy employment.

They had decided to send all York's clothes to the vicar of a poor East End parish, and with this in mind Sir Jason went through every one of his son's pockets, to make quite sure that no letters, addresses or anything of the kind went with the clothes. He was careful to look under the lining paper of each drawer as he emptied it. When he had finished, he went downstairs again, resolved upon destroying the photograph, tearing it into scraps and burning it on the drawing-room fire.

The police, he knew, had already been through all York's personal possessions, with the exception of the locked drawers of his desk, looking for letters which might be incriminating. Before the search, however, Easter had evidently taken the desk keys into her possession, and she had handed them over to her father-in-law at the funeral; it was understood that if anything relevant to the murder had turned up, Sir Jason would have told the police.

Was it possible, Sir Jason now wondered, that the photograph had
any bearing whatever on the murder? Once again he opened the
drawers, took out the photograph, propped it up on the chimneypiece
and sat down in an armchair.

The impeccable York's past, he thought bitterly. He remembered
the emphasis both he and Easter had laid upon their version of York's
blameless character to the police. Methinks he doth protest too much,
he thought wretchedly. And then: *Et tu, Brute?*

He could so easily tear the photograph into small scraps and burn
it along with the pile of irrelevant papers he had been through, and
nobody would ever know anything about it. But would he have a
happy and comfortable moment after it? To the end of his life he
would have to wonder, speculate, imagine . . . he would never
know.

A lot of fathers would not want to know, they would prefer to forget it. But Jason Cragg was not made like that. He had to know. And
so long as he kept the photograph there was a chance of finding out
who and what she was; if he destroyed it, he would never know.

He found an envelope large enough to take the photograph and,
with shaking fingers, he slipped it inside and put the envelope into his
despatch-case.

When Easter returned, he was squatting beside the drawing-room
fire, burning papers. He was no dissembler; the wistfulness in his pale
brown eyes was replaced by a stolid bewilderment which couldn't be
mistaken for anything else.

"You've found it," Easter said immediately. "I half hoped you
would. It will be a relief to share it; it's been getting me down." She
threw off her mink coat, untied her head-scarf and slipped to the floor
beside the fire. "Let's talk about it, Jason, shall we?"

"Who the hell is she?"

"She's somebody he called Mavourneen, possibly not a name, but
an Irish term of endearment."

"I know that much."

"She's either a minor, very minor actress, or a model-girl,
or . . . anyway, I'm sure she earns her living from her looks, one way
or another. York has known her for years; she's been The Woman in
His Life. No wonder he didn't fancy any of the pretty debs you were
so hopeful about, darling."

Sir Jason heard the darling and looked down at his hands, with her slim hand resting lightly on them, in amazement and with some pleasure.

"I'm not at all sure where she lives, the envelopes and the few letters I found had various postmarks and I hadn't time to study them. She puts 'Sat.' at the top of her letters, and that's all."

"Don't tell me there's a child, after all. That would be too, too ordinary."

"I'm quite sure there isn't. But then she was quite sure that York would marry her."

"And because he didn't, she had her revenge, coming along one night when he was alone and stabbing him, ha ha!" Sir Jason said mirthlessly.

"That sort of thing," Easter nodded unhappily.

"Which would account for his staying at home when you all went to the theatre. Possibly she had said she was coming and he arranged to be alone here at that time. Oh, crikey, what a thing!" he groaned.

"Why do men keep letters?" Easter asked. "I can't understand *why*. York hadn't kept all her letters, by any means, I'm sure. There were six, two of them only notes. And she couldn't write anyway. I mean, they were the letters of a house-maid! Notes, really, protesting undying love, begging him to see her."

"You destroyed them?"

"Yes, I did, Jason, I did. I don't want anybody to think that everything wasn't all right between York and me. It was. York had finished with her before he went to St. Anton. He was sick to death of her. He told he there 'had been a woman' but that it was 'all over,' and there was no need for me to ask any more. There were times, since we married, when I knew he was worried about something."

"Didn't you see the letters arriving?"

"There weren't many, Jason. There couldn't have been more than three or four in the last six months. I suppose I could have discovered something about her if I had studied the postmarks, but I was in such a hurry to get them destroyed. You ask if I did not see them arriving? Was I likely to look with suspicion at York's post? He had lots of mail every day, why should I notice particularly those few letters?"

"Why didn't you tear up the photograph too?"

Easter sat back upon her heels. "Ah, why? That's something I can't answer. Unless . . ."

"Unless what?"

"Don't you see? That she killed York."

"Weren't you a bit late in coming to that conclusion?" he asked irritably. "You destroyed the letters, which might have made it possible to track her down. "What can we do with this single photograph? There's nothing to go on. You were too hasty in destroying the letters, Easter."

"Perhaps. Maybe I had a sort of sympathy with her, temporary, of course. The same sort of feeling I had about that platinum blonde, years back, the last woman ever to be hanged, who shot her lover dead as he came out of a pub in Hampstead. Remember?"

"Of course I do. She wanted to be hanged, poor wretch."

"There you are, you see. You've got some sympathy for her, too."

"But Easter, my dear, you've compromised. You haven't done either one thing or the other. You destroyed the letters and kept the photograph. I've sworn that York's murderer will be 'brought to justice,' as they call it. There is nothing I can do other than hand it over to the police."

"And then all the world will know that I was a 'wronged woman,' " Easter said. "The sensational Sunday papers will simply ooze sympathy and point the finger of scorn, as they call it, at the wicked husband who deceived me, or else, the faithless lover who deserted his woman for another. It won't be: 'poor York Cragg, who was murdered,' it will be: 'that wretched York Cragg who had it coming to him.' "

"Go on."

"There's nothing more to it. If we want to damn York in the eyes of the world, all we have to do is give that photograph to the police. And anyway," Easter went on, after a pause, "do you really think a woman could do all that stabbing?"

"If you'd ever done bayonet-practice you'd say yes."

"Bayonet practice!" Easter cried. "A straw-stuffed uniform! York was over fifteen stone!"

"Of course a woman might have done it . . . " Jason said soberly. "Look at Charlotte Corday, for instance. There are ribs in the way, but if you have a sharp enough knife, Easter, and get between the ribs with the first shot. Oh, hell! What a bloody awful life!"

Easter was thoughtful, twisting her silver bracelets round and round her tiny wrist. "What are you going to do, then?"

"I must think it over," Jason said distractedly. "I will take that damn photograph away and, well, just think it over."

"Then you didn't mean what you said last night?"

"What did I say last night?"

"After the funeral, about finding out who the murderer was at all costs."

"I mean every word of it. Dammit, woman, give me a chance."

"Where is the photograph now?"

"In my despatch-case. I'm taking it away with anything else that has to be kept; bank sheets and so on."

"Then you are going to do something about it?"

"I don't know." Jason was in the hall, shrugging himself into his overcoat. "But I do know that I'm going to make sure there's a police watch kept on this house whilst you are alone here."

"That won't be the least necessary," Easter pointed out, "if who we think did it—*did it.*"

Standing in the hall, heavy despatch-case under his arm, hat in hand, Jason looked at his daughter-in-law. The large, brisk, confident, successful businessman seemed to have merged into something not inferior but different; though more careworn, he was younger, less self-confident, and perplexed.

"Did you really love York?" he asked quietly.

"I thought I did, at first."

"And then?"

Easter shook her head and said nothing.

"So you didn't love him?" he persisted.

"I thought he was something that he wasn't."

"How do you mean?"

"He was like you, Jason. He modelled himself on you, he had some of your mannerisms, he talked like you, behaved like you, up to a point; but there wasn't anything beyond that point. He was an ordinary, ordinary man."

"I've wondered," he said, "why you didn't cry."

"I'm crying now," Easter wept in astonishment, "I'm crying," she cried, "because I believe it's you I've loved all the time."

With his weighty despatch-case in one hand and his bowler hat in the other, he stood, as immobile and ineffectual as a scarecrow. Then her arms were round his neck, she was pressed against him and her face, wet with tears, was rubbing against his own astonished face. He tasted tears. He was quite silent, as though stricken dumb for life. It might have lasted hours, minutes or seconds, he never knew. Somehow, some time, it was over; she turned away from him, still weeping. He stood by the front door, wondering how on earth to get it open and then realizing, with surprise, that he could put his hat into the same hand that held the despatch-case and open the door with the other. It was as easy as that.

The chauffeur closed the door of the car and, as they drew away, Jason shook himself like a large wet bird.

It hadn't, of course, happened.

CHAPTER VII

"Mavourneen," he kept saying to himself. "Mavourneen." It was soft and round and satisfactory, like her breasts.

He went to the City, he had a committee, he interviewed the family solicitor, handing over all that he had taken from York's desk (except the photograph), he had drinks at the Savoy with two business acquaintances, he went to his club for dinner. And all the time he could not let his despatch-case out of his sight. All day he longed to take out the photograph and have another look at it, but not until after midnight, alone in his flat, did he do so.

What a strange, haunting face! The apparent fact York deserted her for the immature schoolgirl who was his wife was material for endless speculation. Easter was a clever girl; she made a fine wife; efficient, intelligent and self-reliant. And she was pretty, with her smooth, shining hair, her long slim legs, her tiny waist. But after the rich wine that was "Mavourneen," she seemed a draught of lime-juice and water.

Was it possible that Mavourneen had loved York so deeply that, rather than lose him to another woman, she stabbed him to death and thus lost him forever? If so, his father thought appraisingly, there must have been a lot more to York than one would think. Large, cheerful, athletic, a good dancer, an efficient skier, popular as a cocktail-party guest, a delightful escort; did York really rouse Mavourneen to extremes of primitive passion?

As the night wore on, Jason realized unhappily that his resolve to avenge his son's death was being undermined. It was being replaced by another, far less worthy, resolution. Somehow or other, he would have to find the woman and satisfy himself about her.

He pulled himself out of his armchair and went across to the window, drawing the curtain aside and peering out over the acres of slate roofs to the bare trees of the park. It was a stormy night, with black clouds racing out of the west and the moon playing a coy game of hide and seek. He had a stupid desire to go out and walk about, peering into the face of every woman he might meet.

His mind formed an eldritch advertisement, inserted in *The Times:* "If Mavourneen with the pointed ears and wonderful eyes will get in touch with the advertiser she will hear something to her advantage." There was precious little agony in that column of *The Times* these days, but his, at least, would be a cry from the heart. And, of course, Mavourneen would not see *The Times*.

The obvious, the only sensible thing, was to hand her photograph over to the police who would, in due course, deliver it to the more senational papers who would publish it on their front pages: "Friend of the murdered man who, it is believed, can help the police in their enquiries." "Have you seen this woman?" "Who is she?"

It was easy; someone, somewhere, would recognize her. Within a week of giving the photograph to the police, he was sure, he would meet her, see her for himself.

But he remembered the woman in Hampstead whom they had talked about, hanged for shooting her lover: a *crime passionel* which, in France, they virtually condoned. He had always condemned the old "eye for an eye" rule; how would the punishment, in one way or another, of Mavourneen help his son?

He looked at the long thin neck and shuddered at the thought of the rope round it, knotted below that pixie's ear. No, he mustn't risk that. He had a better idea.

CHAPTER VIII

He was worried about Easter. Though for some days he neither went to Putney to see her, nor did he telephone to her, nevertheless he was worried. Easter had become something of a problem.

The trouble was that, knowing her background, one's opinion of Easter was apt to be confused by a certain pity for her. She had been, as she was inclined to joke, "born an orphan." When she was only a few days old, somebody had left the infant girl in a London Roman Catholic Church before High Mass on Easter Sunday. She was handed over to a community of nuns who had brought her up.

There was really no need for much pity; Easter had had a happy childhood and youth. When she reached the requisite age, the nuns sent her to a smart and expensive boarding school run by a branch of their community and in due course she was sent to another branch in Brussels for "finishing." Seldom has a foundling been in less need of sympathy. But the fact remained that there was something infinitely appealing, and very nearly pathetic, about Easter now that she was a widow.

The police might be keeping a constant watch on the house, Jason thought, but there she was, all alone in her house with her possessions. The morning woman apparently had not come, not having recovered from the shock; Easter was going through the daily routine of dusting the house, shopping, cooking her own cutlet and going to bed. If she had had a mother or a sister who could have lived with her at this time, one would have felt happier. Nor did she seem to have a particular friend who could come to stay with her.

Perhaps he ought to send her away for a time, into the sunshine. He should insist that she fly to the Bahamas, away from it all, for the time being. Having considered it for a day or two, he rang her up.

"I can't bear the thought of your being down there all alone," he told her. "If you won't come here, will you let me arrange for you to fly to the Bahamas? We have an agent out there; I could cable him to get you fixed up in a first-rate hotel. The sunshine, Easter, the change of scene . . ." Sensing a lack of enthusiasm at the other end of the line he tailed off.

"Could you go too?"

Jason hesitated; after all she had primly said about the two of them together in the Arlington Street flat, this was a surprise.

"I would," he stammered at last, "I would if it weren't for business. It's not convenient at the moment, as a matter of fact. Whilst this Board of Trade new scheme is unsettled, I'd rather stay at the helm."

"Then I'd rather stay here and be near you."

"But you're not so near me."

Though he could not see it, he knew she was smiling her charming smile; there was a pause during which he could have imagined that she whispered: "Not so near as I would like to be."

"What?"

"At the end of a telephone line, Jason, which is better than nothing."

"Then you won't accept my offer?"

"It's lovely of you, but no, thank you. And by the way . . . that photograph. You said you were going to think about it."

"Yes, and I have been doing so."

"I don't know what you have decided, but you wouldn't do anything without talking to me first?"

Pause.

"Would you?"

"We can't possibly discuss it on the telephone, Easter."

"It's just that I'm worried about that photograph. I wish it were destroyed."

"Would you feel happier if it were?"

"Of course. It's something between you and me."

"And York."

"Jason, you're treating it like a scrape York got himself into. It matters terribly to me. Please, please may I have it back?"

"Of course you shall, Easter. I'll bring it back to you and you can do what you like with it."

"When?"

"In a day or two."

"Why a day or two?"

"Easter, if it would make you any happier I would tear it up now. But we've talked it over and I'm still thinking it over. It's been one hell of a shock; it takes time to recover. You are the more pressing worry. It is only under protest I'm leaving you alone down there. Understand, Easter? Under protest."

She went upstairs to York's dressing-room and stood there for a long time. The policewoman had cleaned up the bottom of the cupboard after the blood-sodden cases had been removed, but there were still darkish, scrubbed-looking patches on the white woodwork of the cupboard's base and on the close-fitting carpet. After a while she peered inside the empty wardrobe; she opened the drawers; they were all empty, but on the dressing table were York's silver-backed brushes, his leather stud-boxes, a photograph of his long-dead mother. And a photograph of herself in the smart uniform of the airline for which she had worked. She had asked him why he did not put out the photograph she had had specially taken on her engagement, but he said he preferred the one in uniform. "Though I'll have both if you like," he had said, kissing her.

Easter wandered round the room; she looked out of the window on to the forlorn-looking, as yet unmade garden and beyond to where the fog hung among the bare trees, tattered and untidy, like gipsies' washing. She went to her own room, sitting down before her dressing table and looking closely at her reflection. Her face showed little sign of the recent anguish. Always colourless, there were shadows under her eyes which gave them added depth. She put on some of the pale lipstick she had bought in Paris on their way back from the honeymoon. She picked up the photograph of York and, like her father-in-law some days previously, she studied it for a long time, as though she had never seen it before.

She went downstairs to the study and, taking a sheet of writing paper from the bureau, she wrote, "Mavourneen," and then she paused, biting the end of her pencil. Presently she wrote, as a sub-heading: *"What I think I know about her."*

(1) She was York's mistress for years. Months?

(2) York had broken with her, or so he believed, before the holiday in St. Anton at which we met.

(3) York had certainly spent some time with her in Paris.

(4) She was older than he.
 ? She was Irish.

(5) When exchanging confidences about our "pasts," there came a point when playfulness ended, beyond which York would not go.

(6) I think she was an actress. He always seemed knowledgeable about the stage and I do not know from what other source he could have picked up the odd scraps of information he sometimes produced.

(7) If I am right in thinking she was an actress this would account for the letters he received, from time to time, written, probably, from the provinces.

(8) I am almost certain that York saw her after we were married, though the letters did not say anything to confirm this, beyond asking him to meet her at "the usual place."

(9) I am almost certain that York gave her money.

Easter read through what she had written and, a few minutes later, she was again talking to her father-in-law on the telephone.

"I've been sorting out my thoughts about this woman," she said. "You said I might have that photograph back within the next day or so, but if I bring you the result of my thinking-back, could I have it?"

Jason hesitated. "I've been sorting out things, too."

"How do you mean?"

"I'll tell you when I see you. How about dining with me here? I could send the car for you tomorrow evening."

"Tomorrow? What about tonight?"

"I have an engagement."

Easter said nothing in answer to this.

"Tomorrow, then?"

"All right."

"And, Easter, dear. Is there a bobby outside the house now?"

"I don't know. The police car drives up from time to time."

"You won't go out after dark, to a cinema or—or anything, will you?"

"There is nowhere I want to go, except to you tomorrow night. But we can't go on like this indefinitely. If anyone wants to do me any harm, they can easily wait until your police-protection is over."

"By that time, please God, we shall have found the murderer."

CHAPTER IX

It was unusual for the father, or indeed for any relative, of a murderee to ask to interview the doctor who conducted the post-mortem examination. But being who he was, Sir Jason Cragg's request was treated with respect. The Home Office pathologist himself was too busy, but he instructed his assistant to call on the bereaved father.

"Poor chap," he said; "if it makes him feel better to get himself into a bustle about his son's murder, it isn't for us to criticize him."

So his young Chinese assistant called at Golden Fleece House in Throgmorton Street to be told that Sir Jason would see him at once.

"I want to ask you about my son's injuries, Doctor. I understand you were present at the autopsy?"

"That is right, sir."

"Will you tell me in your own words, not necessarily the words you used in your report, what sort of injuries these were?"

The young surgeon brought out his notebook in which he had made jottings. "Altogether there were seven stab wounds in the back, sir. They were in varying depth and degrees of violence. It is not easy to say in which order they were inflicted, but it is obvious that the first blow must have been successful in penetrating the chest above the first rib, and thus causing your son to be unable to turn to defend himself. This first blow probably brought him down and made him unconscious. The lungs and kidneys were severely injured. The heart was untouched."

"Could you penetrate as far as the heart from the back, with a long enough weapon?"

"With a long enough weapon, yes, provided the victim was thin. But your son . . ."

"Quite." Sir Jason tapped his paper-knife on his desk with the regularity of a woodpecker.

"Five of the wounds were successful, sir. That is, they were penetrating, two were not."

"You mean, they were surface wounds?"

"Not exactly. But they weren't mortal; he could have survived if he had only had these two."

"Would you regard the whole picture as being a very savage attack indeed?"

"Very much so. The photographs which the police have taken, if I may say so, are very good. I mean, sir, they'll make a good show at the murder trial. They won't leave any doubt in the minds of the jury."

"That there was malice aforethought and evil intent?"

"That the murderer certainly meant business. There is an excellent photograph taken as he lay, untouched, face down, half inside the cupboard. And then there are the photographs taken at the mortuary. Every member of the jury will have copies of those photographs before them for most of the trail; it will keep their minds on the job. The police have to go so carefully with the evidence, these days, they can let themselves go on the photographs."

"Thanks, I don't want to see them," Sir Jason said drily. "Now, what about the weapon?"

"A very sharp knife."

"The police have mentioned stilettos, daggers, jack-knives, double-edged knives."

"It doesn't do any harm to generalize when the search for a knife, or weapon of any kind, is going on. A dagger is a dagger." The young surgeon gave a very Eastern shrug. "The only thing that is certain is that it was sharp, otherwise it would not have penetrated so far."

"That would depend, surely, on the weight and strength behind the blow?"

"Oh, yes. And, if you have experience, it is easy to tell if a sharp knife was used."

"I see; I'm just trying to reconstruct this horrible scene in my mind, Doctor. Let us say my son opened his wardrobe, presumably to take something out. He kneeled down to reach his case or something and, as he did so, he was attacked from the back. One violent blow and he would fall forward, in, probably, the position in which he was finally found. After the first blow the assailant had it all his own way, he could go on stabbing for as long as he liked?"

"He had it all his own way, as you say, from the first. It was a cowardly and brutal attack."

"It must have been someone who hated my son very much to have gone on stabbing after the first damage was done."

"It certainly was not someone who loved him," the surgeon said, without the vestige of a smile.

"But isn't it mad to go on stabbing after it was unnecessary?"

"Isn't murder mad anyway?"

Sir Jason stirred restlessly in his chair. He had not yet brought himself to ask the question which burned him because he did not know how to make it light and casual enough.

"You think it could have been any sort of knife at all?"

"I didn't say that, sir," the surgeon protested. "There are a lot of knives it could not have been. But if you showed me a knife, I could say, roughly, whether that knife could have done it or not. The paper-knife that you are holding, for instance."

"Well?"

"That could not have done it. I dare say you could kill someone with it if you found the right spot and put enough strength behind it, but it would make a more jagged wound, if you understand me."

"Perfectly." Sir Jason looked at the weapon in hand in some surprise. "Well, thank you, Doctor, you have been most co-operative. I'm sorry to have bothered you."

With the intention of sending him a case of sherry, he noted down the visitor's name and address and walked him to the door.

He cleared his throat nervously: "You'd say, of course, that the assailant was roughly a man of my son's size?"

The little Chinese stopped and turned round. "Not at all, not at all!" he protested in his thin high voice. 'Did I give you that impression? I am sorry. I could have done it, even I, if I had had a sharp enough knife."

"A woman, perhaps, could have done it." Sir Jason employed, in his agitation, a slightly macabre jocularity.

"Certainly a woman could have done it. Oh, but no!" the little yellow man added, shocked. "No woman would perform such a violent act; once, perhaps, in anger, but seven times; I think not."

"It is curious that a police surgeon could say that."

"Only speaking non-professionally." The Chinese was becoming confused. "I did not mean from my experience professionally. From that I know that a woman can do everything, anything. A woman can be a monster. If you'll forgive me, sir, when you asked if a woman could have done the injuries to your son, I reacted personally, as it were. There are no unnatural women among my acquaintances, therefore I do not feel qualified to give an opinion."

"Perhaps you have been lucky in your experience of women," Sir Jason said wistfully. "Thank you for coming, Doctor. Good day to you."

One minute later he took the photograph out of his despatch-case and stared thoughtfully at it. "Monster?"

The buzzer sounded at his side and, when he pressed the button, the husky, canned voice of his secretary, Miss Blockley, was heard saying: "The representative of the Board of Trade to see you, Sir Jason."

"Bring him in," and wearily Sir Jason put away the photograph.

CHAPTER X

They dined at Scheherazade, a restaurant in the basement below the block of flats in which Sir Jason lived, and at which he was a frequent visitor. The decor was so exotic, the lighting so indefinite, and the atmosphere so unfresh, that one had the distinct feeling of being at the bottom of the sea, and a tropical sea at that. So oppressive was the environment that Easter had the feeling that she was a fish, incapable of crisp thought and inclined to open and shut her mouth without saying anything.

They ate pressed duck stuffed with *foie gras* and drank Château *Mouton Rothschild* and Jason observed unhappily that, though only nine days since his son's death, they were undoubtedly enjoying their meal. This, he comforted himself, was not indicative of the regard they had for York, but merely showed a healthy condition of their nerves.

During the meal he told Easter what provision he was making for her. Though York had had every intention of making a will, he had not done so at the time of his death. The amount of the company's shares, however, that he had possessed would bring in an income equal to the salary he had received from the firm during his lifetime. He was arranging to have the shares transferred to Easter. The house would be hers in any case, Sir Jason pointed out, as he had given it to them both on their marriage. He, Sir Jason, would be responsible for the death duties which they hoped might not be too high.

He patted Easter's hand and told her in a fatherly way that she had nothing to worry about. She could look round for another husband, he said magnanimously and, if she had any children, he would look after them as though they were his own.

Easter remained unenthusiastic about this proposal. She said gloomily that she was going to be just the job for some lazy twerp who wanted to be kept without having to do any work for the rest of his life.

They talked about the Ramsgates and Easter said she thought it might be nice to give John Ramsgate a sum of money as a present, as from York's will. "They've been so kind to me and with two children they can use it," Easter added thoughtfully. And Sir Jason patted her hand again and thought what a nice gal she was.

Relaxed, her cigarette smoke ascending in a straight line from between her fingers, Easter looked round her at the murals depicting scenes from the Arabian Nights.

"Scheherazade . . . what does it mean?"

"Don't you know? Scheherazade was the daughter of the Grand Vizier who married the King of Arabia whose habit it was to kill off each of his wives when he tired of them. When Scheherazade's time to be killed arrived she told the King a story every night, and, when she reached the most exciting part, said it would be continued in her next, that is the following evening, and thus she kept herself from being killed like the others. Clever, wasn't it? But all women are 'tellers of tales,' aren't they?"

"More so than men, do you think?"

"Much, much more." Yes, he thought, "Mavourneen" might be Scheherazade with her wild look and her fabulous mouth.

His brain was oddly divided; he appeared to be giving his whole attention to Easter and to what he had to tell her, but his eyes wandered to each woman in the restaurant and to everyone who entered or left. He could remember every small detail of the photograph and, if he saw her again, he would know her instantly. As an ornament in the front of the coronet of hair, he remembered, she was wearing a Turkish-looking brooch, a crescent of brilliants holding an octagonal star. It was only a matter of time, part of him thought with a thrill of excitement, before they would meet. With his money, with the powers he had, the tracking-down of this woman could be completed. Would be.

"Let's go up to the flat," Easter murmured. "I can't remember what I've come for; I feel like a fish."

"You've eaten too much, dear."

"No, it's not that. Everyone looks like a fish, look how slowly they are moving . . ."

"It must be the claret," Sir Jason signed the bill and they rose.

Everyone watched the good-looking couple leave; some nudged one another and whispered: "Sir Jason Cragg, you know, whose son . . ." There were a few unkind and furtive smiles. "That's his daughter-in-law, the widow . . ."

In his flat Easter drew aside the curtains and looked down over the wet slate roofs while Sir Jason fiddled about with the grog tray. "This should be called the Eagle's Nest!" she said, "High up above the streets of London."

"Easter, *dear,* we were fish a minute ago. In any case I'm not a bit like an eagle, much more like a whale. Moby Dick, the great white whale. Armagnac?" He handed her a moderately-sized globe-shaped glass.

Easter laughed. "Yes, perhaps you are like Moby Dick, but please, the real one and not the plastic one working by remote control that we saw in the film." She sipped her brandy dreamily. "Besides," she murmured, "Moby Dick had little piggy, knowing eyes."

"Perhaps I've little piggy, knowing eyes." Sir Jason looked anxiously at himself in the looking-glass.

"You haven't, darling, and you've the mind of an eagle, anyway." Through the glass he could see the shining top of Easter's head as she looked down into her drink. The thin man was wildly crying for help: "Help, Help!" but the voice was not of this world, it was higher than the cry of a bat and there was no one to hear.

Sir Jason lowered himself into his big wing chair as gingerly as though he were a bubble that he wanted to keep intact; he felt, in fact, rather like a bubble. But not for long. It is bad for a bubble to be sat on and no sooner had he sat down, his brandy on a small table at his side, than Easter sat on his knee.

He was shocked, of course, but you can be shocked and other things at the same time, and the pleasure he felt greatly exceeded any other feeling and that went for the shock, too.

There was no deep emotion in it because the thin man would have had to share in that and he, alas, had vanished. Jason felt exactly the same pleasure as he had felt at the times when his nurse tickled him as a small boy. It was all too degrading to stand thinking about; he abandoned thought and simply went on feeling delightful and when, finally, she slipped to the floor, they were both giggling like schoolchildren.

"That's the trouble," Easter said, continuing to sit where she was, between his knees, and sipping her brandy. "You've never been young. You married ridiculously early, before you could have any fun, and then you were left with a baby boy and all the cares in the world on your great hefty shoulders. And that is what was wrong with York; he, on the other hand, never grew up because *you* kept all his troubles, or nearly all. He never had to make his way in the world, build up a flourishing business and all the things you've done. He was born with a silver spoon in his mouth, as they say, and he was spoon-fed right up to the day he died!"

Nine nights ago, the thin man might have reminded them, had he not been in abeyance.

"There was always you between York and the hard cold world and so he never developed properly. In spite of being a huge man, he was a shadow, really. That is why he never dealt properly with . . . with this 'Mavourneen.' You wouldn't have treated her the way he did."

"How do you know how he treated her?"

"One can only guess," Easter shrugged. "It is clear that whatever way he treated her was the wrong way, isn't it?"

"You mean, if she killed him?"

"Yes, if she killed him. He must have bungled the affair horribly. Getting killed was a proof of failure, poor darling," she added. After a pause she went on: "He mucked things up, didn't he?"

"I don't think I want to talk about York, God rest his soul," Sir Jason said.

"We'll talk about you, and how young you feel," Easter smiled up at him. "Shall we, Jason? Shall we?"

Presently the buzzer went to tell them that the car was waiting and, as he carefully wrapped Easter in her mink coat:

"Thank you for the lovely evening," Easter whispered, holding up her face to be kissed. "I suppose it is naughty of us, but it's been quite a party!"

He held her small face between his hands: "Does it say anything in the prayer-book about not marrying your daughter-in-law?"

"The prayer-book doesn't say anything, I'm sure," she answered lightly, "but everyone else would, at the moment, anyway. You see now, darling, what I meant about me not coming to live here with you?"

"I see now," he murmured dreamily, "and I'm going to kiss you."

The buzzer went again.

Easter said: "Oh, bother. I really came to tell you things I've got written down here on a paper in my handbag."

"Never mind about that now."

"Jason, I must go."

"Yes, darling Easter, I suppose you must."

"That photograph?"

"What?"

"The photograph, darling."

"Easter, I can't let you go."

"Please, the photograph. Is it there, in your case?"

Holding it, she threw her arms round his neck and kissed him. She ran out, slamming the gates of the lift and blowing him a kiss through the iron grille.

As Sir Jason moved about his flat, preparing for bed, he was still using the old consolation: "It hasn't happened."

CHAPTER XI

It was easy not to see Easter for the next eight days. He had a great deal of work to do and the need for an urgent visit to Amsterdam occurred. He asked his secretary to telephone his daughter-in-law to tell her that he had to leave the country for a couple of nights and to ask if there was anything she wanted.

On his return he spoke to her himself. She asked him to dinner with her and, as it happened, the best evening for him was the one following his return.

"That would do," Easter said, "except that I'm having my hair done in Dover Street at four."

But there was no other evening available in the near future, so it was decided that Easter would leave dinner prepared, come to town and have her hair done, go to Throgmorton Street in a taxi and drive down to Putney with Sir Jason. This being one of the occasions when it was simpler not to use the chauffeur, Sir Jason would drive himself.

At the appointed time Easter arrived at Golden Fleece House. She sat in the luxurious waiting-room for a bare five minutes before being joined by Sir Jason. He apologized for keeping her waiting and asked if she would mind walking round to the car park with him, or whether she would prefer to wait until he got the car. It was a fine frosty evening and Easter said she would walk round with him. They left the impressive entrance, with its great bronze doors not yet shut for the night, the commissionaire saluting them as they passed.

It was a small square enclosure, almost pitch dark, a well between the immensely high walls of two new blocks of offices.

"I can't see a thing," Easter complained, wondering at the roughness underfoot.

"Wait a minute—stay where you are until I turn on the lights."

When the quiet little cul de sac was illuminated, Easter could see that there was barely room for the parking of three large cars.

"That's the back of Golden Fleece House," Sir Jason pointed. "Hop in. When they were rebuilding, this small enclosure was left because of an Ancient Lights rule, something to do with that building, which, by the way, they are going to pull down. It's a small fur factory, almost derelict. Two others and myself pay a small annual sum for the use of this little space, but when we have to give it up, it's going to be a nuisance."

They slid out into the bustle of the city's rush hour.

Sir Jason's old Rolls-Royce was a 40/50 drop-head coupé with a body specially built for him twenty-five years ago by Hooper.

"I'd love to drive it some time," Easter said wistfully.

"You can drive it now," Sir Jason said promptly.

"Better not, there's too much traffic and I don't really know my way about the City."

"Talking of cars," Sir Jason said, "what about York's Bentley, Easter?"

"It's in the garage. I've had no occasion to use it; it is such a nuisance trying to find somewhere to park that I find it is easier to come up to town by train."

"You're not going to want to keep it?"

"Definitely not," Easter said promptly.

"Well, I'll tell you what I've had in mind. I know I can get a good price for you if you let me sell the Bentley within the next month or so. And I propose giving you a little runabout."

"I would like that," Easter nodded enthusiastically, "something small that I can take into Harrods under my arm, or nearly."

"That sort of thing. An MG perhaps. And I'd like to give it to you; I was going to give you one, as it happens, for your birthday, that is some time in March, isn't it? Right, I'll see to that. And if you really want to drive this, you can drive me down to Southampton on Sunday." He mentioned some friends in the shipping world, who lived on the edge of the New Forest and with whom he was going to lunch. The trip would be fun, he said, if Easter would come with him, and so it was arranged; he would call for Easter and she could drive all the way, if she liked.

They glided out through the suburbs, taking a complicated route but one which Sir Jason was convinced was shorter, through Walham Green and Parson's Green, and finally, over Putney Bridge and home.

Easter's house was reached through the gateposts of what had once been the approach to a mansion. Four modern houses of luxurious type had been built in the space available. Though close together, they were cleverly arranged to give the impression of isolation. Big banks of rhododendrons and azaleas had been left separating the houses; the gardens had, in fact, been as little disturbed as was feasible. Each house had its own gravel approach and garage and yet was hidden from the others by pre-existing screens of evergreen.

Easter's house looked out across a small space which was to be planted as a lawn, over banks of dark-leaved rhododendrons to the bare trees beyond. There was, as yet, no independent lighting in the small estate, though the installation of lighting for the drives was under discussion with the local council. Each house was responsible for the lighting of its own drive and approach.

As there was no one at home, the house and garden were in darkness and the headlights of the car swung round, lighting up every corner.

"It's a damned awful house for you to be in alone," Jason grumbled. "The police may be giving you special protection but I can't see how it can be adequate. Anyone could lie concealed in those bloody great bushes."

"I don't feel like that about it," Easter told him. "I'm not more than fifty yards from the next house; look, that red glow is their kitchen window, with a red blind. I've only got to give a small scream and the people in all three houses could hear me. And that new block of flats positively overlooks the back of the house; if I gave a shout there would be a head out of every window, in no time. As it is, people spend ages simply staring out of their windows, down on to us, from the new flats. And as for the police protection, I hear the car crunching up three or four times during the night. I don't think there's a man there all the time now, there would be no point in it; anyone who wanted to break in would know all about a watchman by now."

But Sir Jason was not happy. While Easter made the final preparations for their meal he sat gloomily drinking his son's sherry under no illusion that this particular evening was going to be a happy one.

They dined at a low table beside the fire in the sitting room. Candles lit the table and the fire burned brightly.

During dinner he told Easter that he was sorry, but he must talk about the police and their investigations for a moment. "I'm not going to bother you," he said, "but you ought to know how things are going."

"Going? Are they going at all?"

"Of course. But I haven't let them bother you. I think you told them all they wanted to know. Anything else they've had to come to me for. You said you'd been making notes, or something, about that gal. What was it you had to tell me that night at Scheherazade?"

"It was about the mysterious Mavourneen. I tried to remember every little thing, in the light of my having found the photograph, that would tell me something about her. After I had finished and read it over, it looked as though I might have got something. But with the passage of time . . . I don't know. There's awfully little to go on."

"It doesn't matter a bit about the passage of time, as you call it. I'm a ruthless man, Easter. I know you think I'm an old dear, but I'm not. I wouldn't have got where I am if I'd been a woolly-minded-dodo."

Easter leaned across the table and put a cool hand on his.

"Don't get cross. And please try to see the thing from my point of view. I've told you how I feel about it, our private life dragged in the gutter. I'd much prefer, at this stage, to let the whole thing lie!"

"And the murderer of my son go . . . scot free?"

Easter shrugged.

"Or live to do it again? Show me the notes you made."

Easter did so and he read them through carefully. "May I take these with me?"

"To show the police?" she asked quickly.

"To brood over."

"All right." Easter rested her head on her hand, her newly-set hair falling forward, hiding her face.

"It's no good," he said, after a long pause, "I'm not comfortable in this damned house. And I don't know how you could be. I'll be only too happy the day you decide to move out finally. When is that going to be?"

"It depends on a lot of things . . ."

It may be that the atmosphere of the house was strangely oppressive, or it may be that their own minds pictured overvividly the scene of York's death; whatever it was, it was quite clear that they could not get back to the happy relationship of the dinner they had last had together.

"Don't let's talk about the police and whatever investigations they may be making. Nothing they can do will bring York back. You say you're a ruthless man; by that do you mean you're lacking in pity? Short of kindness? Because you aren't either of these things."

"I mean that when I say I'm going to do a thing, I generally do it. I don't let things stand in my way; I don't let sentiment clog the wheels."

"Don't you?" Easter was silent, thinking it over. "I don't either. Maybe I'm ruthless, too. But as I see it now, with the first horror and pity worn off, it might be that what happened was all for the best. Yes, you're shocked. You can be ruthless, but you don't like me to be. But let's face it, Jason: York's life came to a sudden end, he had no pain. If he had lived, there might have been a great deal of pain and unhappiness, because how could our marriage have stood up to the years?"

"Don't! I will not talk that way, or even allow myself to think that way. I loved York; you think I loved him too much, ruined him. Well, perhaps I did. But this I am decided about. I'm not going to let whoever killed him get away with it. I'm repeating that to you, Easter, to let you know I feel the same about it as I did at first. Now, I won't discuss it any more; I can see you'd rather not. I'm going and leaving you in this damn house only under the strongest protest, as I've said before. Repeat, strongest protest."

"All right," Easter murmured. "But I'm not too worried about the Mavourneen person. A woman couldn't have done that frightful damage."

"You're wrong there. I'm satisfied that a woman could have done it. An angry woman, a wronged woman, as they say. You won't remember the old song with the line in it: *'He was her man, he done her wrong.'* It's gone through my head often since I saw that photograph."

" 'He was her man, he done her wrong.' " Easter's arms were crossed and she rocked slightly to and fro in her chair as she repeated it. "Yes, could be. But she would have got another man to do the dirty for her."

"Very far-fetched indeed," Sir Jason snapped. " 'He was my man, he done me wrong,' so you go and stab him to death for me? Don't be silly!"

"It was far-fetched that York was stabbed to death at all," she argued.

The evening was not being a success, but how could it be?

Jason and Easter, Easter and Jason; he felt that it was no easy matter to slip out of the old relationship and into the new. "I always wanted a daughter," he remembered saying when York first presented his fiancée, and the curious situation that had developed made him feel vaguely incestuous, uncomfortably like the Dirty Old Man of debutantes' gossip. In the circumstances of everyday life it was not easy to change the habit of his regard for Easter.

He sat beside the cheerful fire, sipping his brandy and feeling a deep melancholy. Easter sat on the floor; she was wearing a red woollen dressing-gown affair, which she called a house coat, with a long satin collar and cuffs and with her hands clasped round her knees, she leaned against him slightly. She looked oddly childlike and charming.

"Deep-bosomed daughter of the ocean," Jason thought, and it was not Easter to whom his thoughts referred.

"You're a business-like little thing, aren't you?" he said dispassionately. "I mean—this document you've just handed to me—were you quietly thinking all these things over to yourself all the time you were married to York?"

"Don't you think most women are always quietly on the lookout for unfaithfulness in their husbands?"

"Do I? I dunno." He laughed shortly. "But I do know that, if I were in any doubt as to whether you had really loved York, this indictment, as you might call it, wouldn't leave me in any doubt."

Easter seemed surprised. "But it depends what you mean by love. There is affection which you could call love."

"It sounds trite, I suppose you'll say you felt affection for York," he returned irritably, "and that was as far as it went! I don't know the first thing about women; don't understand the species. There's a load of mischief here." He tapped the pocket into which he had put Easter's memo. "You've used a good bit of imagination, too. Such odd things you've remembered! And there's nothing really helpful, nothing that's going to help us to trace her," he grumbled. "Pure guesswork. And how do you know she was Irish? The name? It doesn't follow at all. And why did you want the photograph back?"

She put a hand on his knee. "Aren't you being a bit unfair? The photograph was York's most treasured possession; he evidently couldn't bring himself to destroy it. It seems a mean thing to bandy about something a dead man thought a lot of and wanted kept secret."

"Average decent behaviour flies out of the window when murder comes in at the door."

And, rather pleased with the phrase, he prepared to leave.

"Be sure you lock yourself in properly," he told her. "Promise me you won't forget?" And, giving her a hasty peck, he hurried away.

Unkissed Easter stood a minute, forlorn, in her brightly lit hall. There was not a sound, not even a clock ticked. Not a gurgle came from the perfectly-run central heating. Not a breath of wind stirred the stiff, brittle leaves of the rhododendrons in the drive.

It was the house, Sir Jason decided as he drove back to town. The house gave him the heebie jeebies; it was not possible to have a repetition of their happy evening of the previous week in a house which had known such violent happenings. He felt that the house, with its smooth perfection, was in league with the murderer against him. Through that sleek hall the killer had crept, he had stepped across the thick, cream-coloured rugs on the hall parquet, up the bare polished oak stair, past the deep window-recess filled with indoor plants and the thick interlined pale gold curtains of the landing. He, Jason, would not care to spend a night alone in that house and it irritated him that his daughter-in-law should be insensitive to its ambience.

It provoked him, too, that he and Easter did not agree in regard to what must be done about the photograph. It piqued him not to be able to discuss with her what exactly he intended to do about it; he had deliberately said that he did not let sentiment clog the wheels, with the idea of letting her know that he thought *she* did. But she hadn't seen it that way; she had retaliated by telling him that she, too, was ruthless. Of all the absurdities!

CHAPTER XII

In the gentlemen's cloakroom of the Piccadilly Hotel, Sir Jason put on his almost black sunglasses and peered anxiously at himself. It was a dull winter's day, with a sullen fog hanging over London; no day for sunglasses. Nor, Sir Jason observed, were the dark glasses in any way a disguise. They gave him, however, a confidence he needed. Behind them he felt more secure; he could pass an acquaintance without it appearing obvious that he had seen them and wished to pass unnoticed. No amount of disguise could, in fact, have concealed his identity. His figure was both distinguished and distinctive and he had a particularly individual way of walking, a bustling, sprightly walk; for a heavy man, he was singularly light on his feet.

Taking a last anxious look, Sir Jason wished himself luck, picked up his despatch-case, hurried up the stairs and out on to the crowded pavements. Taking his bearings, he steered north-north-east, straight into darkest Soho. He found the shop he had in mind exactly where he had expected to find it. The window was filled with shiny photographs. He went inside. The shop was empty but an assistant came out at once from behind a curtain at the back of the counter. Sir Jason felt unable to see any more of him than his moustache which was of an unusual kind, being waxed at the ends and moulded into a form that strongly resembled the handlebars of a racing bicycle.

"Er . . . " Sir Jason fumbled inside his despatch-case. "I wonder if you could help me? Could you shed any light on this photograph?"

"You want to know who it is, or what? Is it one of ours?" The young man held it up to the light. "No, it's not one of ours."

"It's a copy, taken from a photograph that might, originally have been one of yours. I had it done from the original at Harrods."

"Got the original?"

"Unfortunately not."

"We've got hundreds and hundreds of this sort of photograph. Tin files packed with them out the back."

"I realize that it must be so, but what about that file or reference number in white in the left-hand corner?" Sir Jason knew it by heart. "C.L. 1007. Ser.L.17."

The young man shook his moustache and his head behind it slowly from side to side. "It's not ours. It's like a laundry mark, see, sir? Could be any photographer."

"I've never seen a photograph with the serial or file number, or whatever you call it, on the front," Sir Jason protested, heartened by the "sir."

"Oh well . . . " the young man paused for the suitable words and then leaned confidentially across the counter. "It's a publicity photograph, this is; taken for a theatrical agent or some such. On this type of photograph you often find the serial mark; it's nearly always used by this class of photographer."

"Ah!" Sir Jason felt happily that he was really getting somewhere. "I see."

Co-operative to a degree, the young man flashed out a dozen or so photographs of a similar type: "That's our 'laundry mark,' " he said whimsically.

"Are there many of you?"

"This class of photographer? Coo, yes! Half a hundred in this district, shouldn't wonder."

"In this district? But perhaps this photograph wasn't taken in this district. It might not have been taken in London at all. It could have been taken in the provinces, on the Continent, South Africa, America, anywhere."

The young man was thoughtfully studying the photograph. "In that case," he remarked, "you've got your work cut out if you want to find out who this dame is. But it looks to me . . . " he said slowly.

"Yes?"

"It looks to me like this is a West End job. Could be wrong. Could be USA, as you suggest. Could be. But it's worth trying, if you're all that keen."

"Worth trying the other half-hundred, you mean?"

The young man nodded, handing the photograph back to Sir Jason with all the sympathy and understanding in the world in his warm look. "I suppose I can't tempt you with anything else?"

"You could," Sir Jason stated, "but, as you say, I've got my work cut out. And I've no doubt you can use this." He leaned across the counter and shook hands with the young man.

This . . . was a pound note.

Sir Jason took a taxicab in a north-north-westerly direction. A firm trading under the name of Any Questions Ltd. occupied rooms in a large house in Harley Street and existed for the purpose of answering any enquiries that might be put to them. The minimum charge was half a guinea for a simple question like: "Where can I find the Velasquez picture, 'The Water-Seller of Seville' "? and rose in proportion to the amount of work involved in finding the answer. It was their proud boast that, unless a question were leading or rhetorical, in which case it was disqualified, they never failed to find the answer.

Though they covered a wide field, they did not, of course, include personal questions. Sir Jason could not, for instance, produce the photograph, ask "Who is this?" and expect to be told. But what he was able to do was to ask them to make a list for him of all the photographers in the West End of London who took photographs "like this" with the file number in the left-hand corner written in tiny figures.

"Yes, sir," the young lady said briskly, pen poised ready to take down his particulars. "Your name and address, please?"

"I'll call in."

She looked doubtful. "I don't know how long it will take."

"It's very urgent."

"Yes, I'm sure it is. I'll see what we can do."

At the same time two days later Sir Jason was standing in the same place with the coveted list in his hand. There were twenty-two names and addresses, not half a hundred. Twenty-two. He smiled at the young lady. "Thank you very much indeed," he said cordially. "And now I think you can help me some more. Can you give me the address of an investigation agent who could go round to all these photographers and find out which one uses this particular type of identification mark?"

The young lady's eyebrows shot up. "You mean a private detective?"

Sir Jason looked uncomfortable. "Well, not really."

But that, of course, was what he did mean and before long he was speeding down Harley Street. But not more than a block and a half; the private detective also had an address in Harley Street. On either side of his lair, citadels of medical respectability stood, still unstormed. But in a steamy attic, in the upper air of Harley Street, the investigator sat, like a spider, and sent out busy little men all over London, spying, creeping, peering, asking, peeping, and then sending in enormous bills to his clients: "For Services Rendered."

This particular commission was simple but expensive. It was a matter of the men's time but, realizing almost at once that in this case the expenditure of money would be no objection, he became enthusiastic. Sir Jason left three copies of the photograph behind so that three men might function at the same time. He also left a large deposit in the form of five-pound notes as a security, arising from the fact that he did not wish to leave his name, address or telephone number. He arranged to return in three days' time and, when the three days were up, he had the name and address of the photographer where the original photograph had been taken. He paid the remainder of his bill most gratefully and was uncomfortably aware, as he slipped the three photographs back into his despatch-case, that his hands were trembling conspicuously.

Sir Jason felt almost homesick for the sympathetic young man with the odd moustache as he entered the new photographer's, which was not half a mile from the original shop.

This time everything was brisk and impersonal. He was attended to by a blonde whose mind was clearly not on her job. The photograph was taken, she said, last February, nearly a year ago. She supposed that if he wanted the address of the customer, there was no objection, but it was unusual, very. The look she gave him was inclined to be saucy, but as Sir Jason's eyes were hidden from her behind his glasses she was not sure of herself. The production of the wallet and the pound note brought her to the alert more quickly than anything.

Within a remarkably short time Sir Jason had the paper, with a name and address written on it, clutched in his hand and was hurrying down the street. He felt almost dizzy with excitement and went into a coffee bar which he happened to be passing. He sipped a *cappuccino* and smoked a cigarette before he felt calm enough to read what was written on the paper:

> Mrs. Valentine Millage
> Rosedale,
> Victory Avenue,
> Edgware, Middlesex.

How relentlessly disappointing!

"Mrs. Valentine Millage" didn't even tell him whether Valentine was her own name or that of her husband. "Rosedale, Victory Avenue, Edgware." Perhaps she had two little "kiddiz." If that was so, how dared she look like that?

Almost furtively Sir Jason slid one of the photographic copies out of his despatch-case and studied it.

"A 'Messalina of the Suburbs,'" he decided, with a heavy sigh, and ordered himself another *cappuccino*.

CHAPTER XIII

Much travelled though he was, Sir Jason made a journey he had
never yet undertaken; he took the Underground to Edgware. He did
not even know until now that beyond Hampstead the train took an
upward slope, emerged into the open air and ran along an embank-
ment some feet above the houses and gardens for several miles. Arriving at his destination, he emerged from the station feeling as
conspicuous and uncertain of himself as a camel on the shores of Loch
Lomond. There was no taxi-rank that he could see, nor was there a
policeman of whom he could ask the way. There was, however, a road
sweeper with a friendly eye who was able to send him in the right
direction.

It was a long walk. Sir Jason was wearing his black topcoat, his
Lock's bowler hat, a Paisley-patterned scarf in blue and red silk, and
carried a beautifully furled umbrella. He looked like someone who
was in Edgware on a special mission. There seemed to be no other
men walking the tree-lined roads; he met a great many women, some
carrying shopping baskets and others wheeling prams. It was a dark
and sullen-looking day, damp and raw, and as he tramped along he
began to feel the utmost depression.

He passed a row of shops and an Odeon cinema where he again
asked the way. He pressed on along a road of similar houses which
petered out and the road looked as though it might be going out into
the country, but it led simply past a sewage farm and a filling station,
up a slight slope and on to a double-track by-pass road.

What a fool he had been, he thought. What idiotic streak of quix-
otry had directed him to make these personal investigations into his
son's secrets? This was a job for the police, not for a middle-aged businessman; this was a sentimental journey, based on emotion rather
than on common sense. It was instigated mainly by his desire not to

have his son appear a fool, or worse, but also, and here he must be frank with himself, also because something about the face of the woman in the photograph compelled him to seek her out before, as he liked to put it this time, "throwing her to the wolves."

He trudged along wishing very much he was not on a by-pass; anyone in one of the cars zipping past might recognize him. Someone might stop to ask if they could give him a lift and he would have to pretend that his car had broken down, for what other excuse could he possibly make for being found where he was? It began to drizzle; he pressed on. He did not think of opening his umbrella; it had, in fact, never been opened. He passed a square concrete toffee-factory, whitewashed and tidy, and another filling station. Another row of shops. And then quite suddenly, out of the murk, he saw the words: "Victory Avenue."

Avondale, Ivycroft, Fernbank, The Lilacs, Wenlock. "Victory" evidently referred to the 1918 Victory rather than the more recent one; the houses were thirty years old and more; they were semi-detached and had small front gardens.

Rosecroft and Rosedale were joined, like Siamese twins, and approached by a single pathway which divided, one branching to the door of Rosedale and the other to the front door of Rosecroft.

He pressed the bell of Rosedale which buzzed angrily like a live thing immediately under his finger. He did not feel the least excitement such as he had felt in the coffee bar. The long dreary walk from the station had successfully quelled any anticipatory thrills and the cries as from innumerable children from within only confirmed his apprehensions.

She was as black as his own Lock's bowler hat and a great deal more shiny. She held a baby in her arms and three small round-eyed toddlers peeped round her skirts; no doubt, Jason thought, there were others concealed beneath her skirts.

He raised his hat and said absurdly: "Mrs. Valentine Millage?" because, of course, he knew perfectly well it was not she. Out of the *chile con carne* of words that she broke into, he was just able to make out that Mrs. Millage no longer lived here, and he was turning away, a broken man, when a brisk voice hailed him from the front downstairs window of Rosecroft.

"Bye bye!" The children were shouting and waving their small black hands at him. Jason shut his eyes; soon he would wake up and tell Miss Blockley of the absurdities of his dream and they would laugh together about it.

"If you're looking for the Millages I might be able to help you." The woman from Rosecroft leaned out of the window. She was a tortoiseshell cat of a woman, with thin lips and yellow eyes, but she had a pleasant enough expression on her face; at the moment, in fact, it was illuminated by something approaching delight.

"Do come in." She ran out to the front door and was ushering Jason inside out of the rain before he was quite aware of it. But once inside he stood firm, refusing to have his umbrella taken from him, and deliberately refraining from removing his gloves. In the dim recesses at the back of his mind lurked the thought that the job of salesman to lonely-hearts in the outer suburbs was not without its compensations, but he suppressed it for further investigation at a more suitable moment.

Now what he must do was to extract all the information about the Millages that he could from Mrs. Rosecroft, giving none whatever in return.

Out of a great deal of irrelevant detail, he was able to collect the salient facts: the Millages had lived for two years at Rosedale; Millage worked as a clerk at a well-known firm of instrument makers on the Great North Road; he was younger than Mrs. Millage, who had "been on the stage." They were not happily married; Mrs. Millage was "flighty"; the ménage broke up, Mr. Millage going home to his mother and Mrs. Millage "back to the stage." (There were no children.) The house had been let to West Indians since last August.

It could fit in, Jason thought, trying hard to make it so. Nothing had turned out to expectation but *it could fit*.

"Was her name Mavourneen?" he asked.

The woman shook her head. "Not that I know of, though it might have been her stage name. Val, he always called her. He was fond of her, mark you, and between ourselves, she treated him like dirt."

She would. Yes, that was Mavourneen!

"I don't know how he put up with it," the ginger-cat woman chatted on. "But one day the worm turned; he flung her out."

Or did she fling him?

"And no one's heard a word from her from that day to this."

Hadn't they? Jason hugged himself mentally, happy again.

"I saw Ernest Millage only a fortnight ago walking along, on Watford by-pass. My hubby had a word with him, but nothink was said about Val."

"You know Mr. Millage's address, perhaps?"

She shook her head. "No, but he's in the same job, that I do know."

Jason jotted the name of the firm down in his notebook.

"Do let me make you a cup of tea, Mr.—er—?"

"You've been very kind." Jason was at his most charming. He bowed slightly over her hand in a thoughtful way, as though he might kiss it in the Continental manner.

"You've had a long walk from the station!" But Jason was not to be drawn. Unctuously, he withdrew from the little house, giving nothing, not even a pound note, but leaving Mrs. Rosecroft with the feeling that she had had an exciting day.

He knew that she and Mrs. Rosedale, all the children and a number of neighbours were watching his withdrawal. Aware that it would never again achieve its furled perfection, he opened his umbrella. The way back to the station seemed to take less than half the time. He was trying to make up his mind what would be the best reason he could give to the husband for his enquiries as to the whereabouts of his errant wife. The most fanciful, but the one he liked best, was that of himself as talent-spotter, but he was sadly aware that the one which would occur to the husband would be the obvious one, that he was a "sugar-daddy."

He decided finally that he would call at the factory and ask to speak to Mr. Millage on a matter of urgent business. In these circumstances the husband would be taken by surprise and would be less likely to dwell on detail than if he were to call at his home address. Sir Jason could state briefly that he was a solicitor and unable to give any reason, for the present, as to why he wanted the wife's address. Ten to one, the husband would give it immediately.

One "prop," Sir Jason realized, that he must have, was his car.

Miss Blockley had no idea where he really was; he had made a variety of excuses for his recent absences from work; today it was Kempton Park races. His car was in the basement garage in Arlington Street; he could take it out, drive to the factory, and return to the city for an hour or two's work before evening.

He went back in the Underground to Leicester Square and had a snack luncheon at Fortnum and Mason's. He felt faintly unhappy about his deception of his faithful Miss Blockley. She had been so kind and understanding about his frivolous activities in the past few days. She knew how much work he had to do but she had smiled with the utmost forbearance when he had told her that he was going to Kempton Park. He knew that when he returned to the office at tea-time she would ask how he had "got on" and he would invent some picturesque lie about what he had lost or won.

It was curious, Sir Jason mused as he drove north, what a difference arriving at the factory on the Great North Road in his car would make to him. This afternoon he was a different being from the camel-like creature emerging from Edgware Station. He blew a great blast on the horn, which sent pedestrians scampering before him, almost flattered to be scattered by such a magnificent car.

CHAPTER XIV

Something, clearly, had to be done about the garden. Easter tied her hair up in a pretty yellow scarf, put on an old waterproof and went out to dig. It was drizzling dismally but she dug like a busy beaver, plunging the fork deeper into the soil with her foot on the tines as she had seen gardeners do. Presently she was sniffing frequently and was often obliged to remove a drop from the end of her nose with her pocket handkerchief, but her cheeks were a pretty pink and she felt delightfully healthy. The digging was no light work; the soil was heavy with moisture and the police had tramped it down hard, but she toiled happily all afternoon. The light was going when she finished the wide strip of soil they had planned to plant as an herbaceous border. She went round to the drying yard at the back and scraped the mud off her gumboots at the back door. As she was doing so the telephone rang.

"Is that you, Easter?" Jason's voice was high with excitement.

"Where are you talking from?"

"From the office, but on my private line. Can you hear me?"

Jason wanted to talk to her, could she possibly come up to town now, if he sent the car for her.

"What is it about, darling?" Easter asked.

Jason, choosing his words carefully so that they would not be understood by any chance listener, told her that he had been making certain enquiries; she might be able to guess in what direction.

She was quite wordless; shocked into silence.

He had been more successful than would have been thought possible. "Are you still there?"

"Yes, yes, I'm here."

"You're so quiet."

She ran a tired hand across her forehead.

"I've done nothing that you didn't want me to do. With regard to the police, I mean. I've been very, very discreet." There was a touch of pride in his voice. "But I must discuss with you what we are going to tell the police, in the light of what I have discovered."

"But, darling," Easter protested. "You couldn't do much without the photograph."

"Couldn't I? I could have copies made of it."

"But that was mean!" she cried.

"You won't think so when you hear what I've found out. But we must get on with things, Easter, and I must talk to you quick."

"I'm far too tired to be intelligent about anything tonight," she said. "Wouldn't tomorrow do?"

"I thought if you could come now . . . But I won't press it, dear. I'm dining with a friend at the club; fellow just home from the Middle East; haven't seen him for a couple of years; I wouldn't be happy about putting him off."

"Wait a minute." She sounded tired, as, indeed, she suddenly was. "I'm coming up to town to have my hair done tomorrow, and then I planned to have lunch and go to a movie with Jill Ramsgate. I could come to you after that."

"You mean, spend the evening together?"

"Here."

"There? Why not Arlington Street?"

"I don't like coming back home late alone, and I don't want to drag you out at that time of night. Do come here! We might meet in town and drive down together. I'll order some smoked salmon to be sent and we'll have dinner here, by the fire. How's that? I'll leave everything ready so it won't be any trouble."

"All right, if you prefer it that way."

"And, Jason . . . you won't do anything more until we've talked it over, will you, about the police or anything? I'm a bit frightened.

You've been barging about doing I don't know what. And we don't know what we're up against. I don't like it."

"I don't like it either. Are you really frightened, Easter?"

"Only in a way. I'm frightened for you. I'm afraid you've been stirring things up."

"I did warn you. And I'm not going to let you persuade me to drop this thing; we're on to something, I'm sure, and with every day that passes the clues are getting cold, as they say."

"What time shall we meet?"

"What time does your cinema end?"

"I'm not sure. Jill is staying up in town; she and John are dining with friends."

"Should we say six, then?"

"Yes, that would do nicely. What about meeting at Green Park Station and if you were held up I could shelter under the Ritz arches."

"I can't wait long at Green Park Station; it's a bus stop."

"Just by the Ritz main entrance, then? I won't keep you waiting, promise. I'll be there in good time."

"Right. I wish I could see you now, Easter, all the same. For God's sake, see the house is properly locked up, and don't hang about in the back yard in the dark, or anything."

"No, I won't. Promise, again. But do let me remind you; there are burglar catches on all the windows and double locks on the front and back doors. So don't worry. It's you I'm worried about."

"Hum. Well, see you tomorrow night."

"Good night—" Easter gently replaced the receiver—"darling," she whispered, her eyes shining.

CHAPTER XV

One can feel as exposed to the weather in the streets of London as on some Lancashire pike. As he left the little sheltered corner in which he parked his car and turned into the street, an icy-cruel wind threw itself against Jason and caused him to clutch his hat and bend forward with watering eyes. The sky lay, heavily grey, on the rooftops of the city. There's snow on the way, Jason thought; I must ring up Easter and tell her to stay at home.

But sitting in his warm office he changed his mind. He must let the poor kid have her outing if she wanted, however simple it might be. It would do her good to get away from that house even for an afternoon.

He lunched at the Savoy with two business friends and as he took a taxi back to the city he noticed that the weather had not improved, though it was still not snowing. At half past five he asked Miss Blockley for his letters for signature and, as he signed them, she reminded him that there was a report he ought to look through.

"It will have to wait till tomorrow," he said. "I'm meeting my daughter-in-law at six and we're dining in Putney."

"Oh, dear!" Miss Blockley said mildly.

"Yes." Jason signed his usual slow, laborious signature.

"It must be lonely for Mrs. York, poor little thing."

"It is, very." Jason took off his glasses and looked at Miss Blockley. "I'm worried about her," he said, "but I think I can understand her unwillingness to leave that house. She had an unusual childhood, as you know, and I think her determination to stay there is a craving for security. The only security she has ever known has been there, with York. It's the only home she's had. It will take time to persuade her that the right thing is to sell up and to live somewhere else. I'm leaving things as they are for the time being, but I don't intend to let her stay there indefinitely."

"It's such a horrible night." Miss Blockley shuddered.

"I know." Jason signed the last letter and got up. Miss Blockley helped him into his overcoat.

It was still dry as he walked round to the car park, but as he drove westwards along Piccadilly big blobs of sleet-like rain squashed themselves against the windscreen. It was just six o'clock as he slid past the top of Arlington Street. He scanned the Ritz arches, a few yards short of Green Park Station; Easter would almost certainly be sheltering. He stopped by the last arch and waited, looking back to see if she was coming. She was not.

Good, Jason thought. He was glad he had not kept her waiting. He watched the crowds pouring into the tube station; everyone looked preoccupied, frowning and red-nosed, in a hurry to get home.

A prostitute, wrapped like a parcel in mink, was doing her best to attract his attention from the pavement under the arches. Surely, Jason thought, he looked like a man waiting for a woman? He frowned at her and she answered with a good-natured wink.

Presently a policeman came up, He knew Jason well by sight. "Good evening, sir."

"I'm waiting for my daughter-in-law, Officer."

"You haven't chosen a very good place, sir."

"Good lord!" Jason looked at the clock on the dashboard in astonishment. "I'm supposed to meet her at six; it's six-fifteen now! She's not the sort of person who's ever late. Look, will you keep an eye on the car while I run back to my flat? She might possibly be there as the weather's so awful."

Jason trotted down Arlington Street but, according to the commissionaire of the block of flats, no one had called, and there were no messages. Jason used the commissionaire's telephone to dial the Putney number, and waited. "Ringing note, but no reply."

He went off up Arlington Street hoping to find Easter already in the car. But she wasn't and now he was really worried and told the policeman so. It was the fear of the unknown, Jason thought, as he sat gloomily at the wheel. What were they up against? If it were never to be discovered who killed York, the rest of his life would be spent in being uneasy. Whenever he thought of York's death, he would have the crawling uneasy feeling in the gut that was real fear. He remembered a line from *Henry V* which he had learnt at school: "Possess them not with fear; take from them now the sense of reckoning . . ."

And that was the heart of the matter, it was the result of his reasoning that was frightening him. So he must stop trying to think things out. A frightened fat man was no good to anyone, he thought.

And a frightened fat man, possessed by a thin one wildly signalling for help, is unseemly in theory. In fact, the prosperous businessman, wearing his Lock's bowler hat, sat in his elderly Rolls-Royce, frowning and biting the corner of a thumbnail.

A minute before half past six he started the engine, took a final look round, put the gear in and crept past the policeman, now standing at the entrance to the station, with an acknowledgement of his salute and went towards Putney as fast as he was able to drive.

He was driving over Putney Bridge just after a quarter to seven which, he thought, was surely a record in the rush hour. He had had York's keys in his pocket with his own ever since he had been through York's possessions and Easter knew he had them. If the house was in darkness he would let himself in; he did not quite know what he expected to find.

He turned off the busy main road, drove some few yards and then into the entrance to Silverdale. It was quite dark; though he could see cracks of light from behind closely drawn curtains in the other houses there was no light from Easter's house. He swept round the drive and stopped at the front door, his headlights illuminating the rhododendron bushes. He left the lights on and sat still for a moment. There was probably some perfectly simple reason for Easter's non-appearance. Her watch might have stopped, for instance. It was only a few minutes' walk from the cinema to the place they had arranged to meet, but she might have tried to get a taxi and failed, she might have fallen and sprained her ankle, she might have met an old friend. He should have waited a quarter of an hour longer.

But as he was here he might as well go inside and . . . Jason shied away from the thought . . . look round. He took York's bunch of keys out of his pocket. There were two mortice and two Yale keys, one of each for front and back doors. He did not know which was which so he left the door of the car open in order that the light should illuminate the entrance porch while he tried the keys. It didn't take a minute; the front door was opened and Jason put his hand inside and turned on the hall light. He was shaking. Just to show himself how normal he felt, he turned back to the car, switched out the lights, shut the heavy door carefully and went into the house, taking his ubiquitous despatch-case with him.

A wave of hot air met him. Perhaps the thermostat of the oil-fired boiler had gone wrong. It was certainly abnormally hot, but then, he remembered, Easter was inclined to overheat the house; he had noticed it before. The sittingroom door was closed. Jason opened it and went in, switching on the lights. It looked charming; the curtains were drawn close and the small fireside table was laid for dinner for two with a lace tablecloth, fish knives and forks, the silver candlesticks from the dining-room, wine glasses and a Sheffield plate wine coaster. The fire had died down in the grate, but a filled coal box and log basket stood on either side of the fireplace. On the grog tray were clean glasses and a dish of olives.

Jason sighed with relief; the dear gal! Though she had left the house during the morning she had thought of everything, even to leaving the curtains cosily drawn. He would ring up the Ramsgates to see whether Jill had returned, and then, with his hand on the telephone receiver, he remembered that Jill was to stay in town for dinner and would not be coming home until late.

Smiling, he looked round. Everything was prepared for a delightful evening *à deux*. In a minute or two the telephone would ring and he would hear Easter's worried voice telling him what mishap had occurred. He would probably have to jump into the car and go to Putney Bridge Station and meet her.

In the meantime, Jason returned to the hall, took off his hat and peeled off his coat and scarf. Back in the sitting-room he stood in front of the bottles and wondered what he would have. He would mix a cocktail for them both. Knowing his liking for a dry Martini, she had left a lemon and a small silver knife to cut the rind. Ice . . . in the fridge. He went across the hall and into the kitchen, switching on the light.

And then he stopped, his back tickling almost unbearably as though every small hair had come upright. He stood quite still, his hand on the switch, and listened. There was not a sound, not a creak. He shook himself irritably; this was the limit, he was becoming an hysterical old woman. He went across to the refrigerator, opened the heavy door and pulled out the ice tray, which he carried back into the sitting-room. He put several cubes of ice into the mixture and stirred it thoughtfully, round and round in the big glass beaker which York had used for mixing cocktails. Dear York, he thought, how fussy he was about detail. He had taken back to Fortnum and Mason the big cocktail shaker which a business friend had given him for a wedding present, and changed it for the glass beaker.

He poured a little of the cocktail into a glass and tasted it, added a little Vermouth, tasted it again, filled the glass, drank about half, went across to the fireplace, put the glass on the chimneypiece and knelt down in front of the fire. He put on a handful of small wood and taking the bellows he used them vigorously.

And when it happened he felt that he was having a *déjà vu*, the feeling that all this had happened before. He had always believed that time was a matter of relativity and this was now to be demonstrated in that it all seemed to happen so slowly. The first blow fell high, almost at the back of his neck, above the collar bone, and he thought: so that is where the first wound was! Unfortunately, that first blow was so violent that he crumpled forward, hitting his face on the logs he had put on the hot ashes and breaking two front teeth, which hurt a good deal more than the stab wound.

He was being stabbed again and again and he was not feeling any more pain but rushing down a long dark tunnel at the end of which was a bright light. He wanted very much to get to the light at the end of the tunnel but he knew that there was still something he must do.

He must turn round and see who was attacking him. But he was not able to. Only when he was nearly at the end of the tunnel was he able to look back over his shoulder and see, away back, a tiny, tiny thought, and it was: they are enjoying it, they like stabbing me, they like killing! But he did not feel surprise, or horror, or fear. He felt nothing but delight because he was so near the end of the tunnel now and nothing else mattered.

He left behind the fat man and the thin man and he was simply Jason as he went out into the light.

CHAPTER XVI

As Easter was stepping out of the train at East Putney Station, she caught the pencil heel of her shoes on the edge of the step. She succeeded in not falling and, looking round, she was dismayed to see the heel had become completely detached and was lying on the floor of the carriage from which she had alighted. A man picked it up and handed it to her politely and Easter, balancing on one leg, thanked him.

She proceeded towards the ticket collector at the station exit in a series of hops. She looked at the clock, which said twenty-five to eight. She waited until the crowd had passed through before handing him her ticket and saying: "Look what's happened! Do you think someone could telephone for a taxi for me?"

"Phone box there," he said gruffly, with a jerk of his head.

"Oh!" Easter opened her eyes very widely at him. "Could you ring up for me, please? I haven't any coppers."

"Bert," the ticket collector shouted. "Lady in trouble!"

Easter followed Bert to the office and stood on one leg while he telephoned for a cab. "Thank you so much," she said, and he was almost more grateful for the charming smile than for the half-crown she pressed into his hand. She sank heavily into a shabby small chair. "Oh, dear, I'm so tired!" And she looked it. "It's such a beastly day in town and I was going to meet someone who never turned up. I waited for ages!"

The exchange of pleasantries went on for a few minutes. Easter looked at the clock. "Ten to eight, nearly!" she said. "Do you think the taxi will have had time to get here?"

A porter accompanied her as she hobbled down the stairs and into the taxi.

When the taxi arrived at the house Easter cried: "Oh, thank goodness!" as she saw the lights on and the Rolls in the drive. Carrying her broken shoe in one hand, she paid the man, thanked him and turned to the front door, calling: "Co—oo—ee! I'm here!" She felt in her handbag for her keys. "Jason," she called as she fitted the Yale key into the lock. The taxi driver, unable to go right round the drive because of the Rolls, was having a little difficulty in reversing without running into the yard wall in the dark. He had several shots at it, revving up his engine noisily.

Easter went into the house. "Jason," she called again. "What on earth happened to you?"

She threw her black suede gloves on to the hall table and went towards the sitting-room. The door was wide open; she could see everything from where she stood, on the threshold.

The taxi driver had succeeded in getting his crate round without damaging either it or the Rolls and was about to drive away when he heard the screams.

He cringed in his seat, feeling several sizes smaller, remembering with horror that this was the house where that murder had happened. Easter appeared at the door, silhouetted against the light, and scream after scream tore up the darkness. The taxi driver was shocked stone cold, as he afterwards said, by the terrifying sound of her screams. He'd had three years of jungle warfare against the Japs but nothing had ever scared him like those screams. The one thing that seemed important was not to see what she was screaming about so much as to stop the noise, and with this in view he climbed heavily from his driving seat.

But by now the neighbours were on the scene, husbands torn from the dining table with food still in their mouths; there were half a dozen people.

"I've nothing to do with it," the taxi driver kept protesting after he had had one fearful peep into the sitting room. "Nothing to do with me; I only brought the lady up from the station. That's all I did, just brought the lady up from the station."

CHAPTER XVII

"If you ask me," Police Constable Bacon said (he always prefaced his dissertations with "if you ask me," possibly because nobody ever did), "this lot is a Special Branch job. International. That lot isn't murder, it's hashash—ashash—ashass—" he cleared his throat and started again, calmly—"assassination, that's what it is."

"What's the difference between murder and ash . . . what you said?" his wife asked dutifully.

"Murder's murder," he said profoundly, "but the other thing is done for a political cause, as it were. And it's not half as bad."

"How can you say that!" his wife reproached him. "When the son was murdered you wasn't half upset; you said you'd seen some sights in your time but nothing that got you like that job. Made you feel sick."

"Maybe I'm getting more yewsed to it," he suggested. "But I reckon there's a lot behind this that'll never come out. Mind you, there's a lot more clues in this last murder."

"A lot more? You reckoned there wasn't anything to go on last time."

"Nor there was. No weapon, no fingerprints. This time there's a mackintosh left laying on the floor not far from the corpse."

"Whoever would be so careless as to leave their mack?"

"It was left there on purpose. It was covered with blood. This Sir Jason Cragg was a bleeder, different to his son, York Cragg, who bled quietly to death. The blood spurted up out of his father. And the murderer didn't bother about cleaning himself up, he simply steps out of the mack and leaves it laying there on the floor."

"What else?"

"He got in through the cloakroom window. They have what they call a downstairs cloakroom in these posh houses. A lavatory, no less, and this one's divided up, like. There's the lavatory and hand basin, excetera, divided from the rest, and the rest's a small room with hooks round the walls where they keep the golf clubs, and umbrellas and coats and macks and scarves, very ar-la. And that's got quite a big window, but higher up than most. This particular one's got opaque glass you can't see through, like you get in bathroom windows. It's a sash window and looks like it was always kept fastened. There's a radiator under the window what the murderer could step on when he climbed through, and down on to the floor, see? Well!" Police Constable Bacon sat back, his thumbs in his waistcoat armholes. "Blow me if they ain't stuck two plasters like you get for backache on two panes outside the window. The window's made up of small panes of this size. They stuck two plasters, one under where the central catch is and the other to the left, next pane but one, where the burglar catch is, that's a kind of screw you screw in by hand. See?"

"No."

"So's they could break the pane and get their hands in and undo the screw without making a sound! It's a regular burglar's trick, that is."

"Then it was burglary?"

"No. That's the rum part of it. Unless the chap was out after some special document the police don't know nothing about, there's nothink he was out after. Nothink's been touched. No drawers opened, nothink."

"Well, I never!" Mrs. Bacon exclaimed. "What else? You said there was a lot more clues."

"I meant two. But if it had been snowing properly!"

"He wouldn't of done it."

"That's true." Sam Bacon was thoughtful. "It does seem fate has got it against that young Mrs. Cragg, I must say. They tell me she's all alone in the world. Makes your heart bleed to see her. Friends have taken her in for the present."

"I wouldn't go back there if I was her."

"It's her home, duck, when all's said and done. And there's people don't mind what's happened in a place just so's they've got somewhere to live. Ever heard of the housing shortage?"

But Police Constable Bacon was not feeling really flippant. "Dear me," he sighed, "this was a dirty job, if ever there was one. There wasn't much of a fire, smouldering wood, but they left him with his face in the fire and when we pulled the poor devil round his face was black and burned and his front teeth broken and blood all over. But I don't know. Those two, father and son, they must of been up to something, I reckon. There's international gangs at the back of this. A foreign power."

"Who, dear?" Mrs. Bacon asked mildly.

Police Constable Bacon looked to right and to left in a distinctly cloak-and-dagger manner. "Russia!" he hissed.

The Second Part

CHAPTER I

Nathaniel Sapperton lingered before the looking-glass on the dressing chest in front of the window of the bedroom in the flat he had taken furnished on the edge of Putney Heath. He was not really worried about getting bald but it had become a habit to smooth his hand over the top of his head and quite often, as he did so, he was startled to find how little hair he had on top.

Forty-two, he told himself now, as he adjusted his bow tie. Too old to be suspected of being Up To No Good, not old enough to be accused of being in his dotage; neither young wastrel nor elderly lecher; neither ne'er-do-well nor successful tycoon: what label could he wear? For a label was essential. Poet or writer? No, that would necessitate some evidence of achievement. Musician? He didn't know the first thing about music. Seafaring man? Captain in the Merchant Navy, perhaps? Soldier?

Leaning past the looking-glass, he peered once again through the net curtain down into the gardens of the recently-built houses called Silverdale below. The hose was still lying on the concrete of the yard but she had not yet returned from the house. She intended to come back, though, because she had left the water running; he could see it streaming down across the dry concrete to the central drain.

Drawing back into the room, he looked at himself in the glass; what did he look like? Dispassionately Mr. Sapperton studied his face which he considered to be ordinary. But what could be more ordinary than one's own face? Something one has to see day in and day out, over the years, for a lifetime?

Mr. Sapperton had two eyes, a nose and a mouth; "pofaced" he had always considered himself to be. He was neither tall nor short, dark nor fair, his jaw was neither "square" nor receding.

Dear me, he was so average that he had better stick to the truth, the plain, unglamorous truth. He was a civil servant attached to the Foreign Office and he was on leave after a special posting in the Persian Gulf.

There she was; she had evidently been into the house for a leather, for now she was vigorously wiping her car after the hosing.

He picked up his field-glasses from the dressing-chest and studied her through them. Her hair was tied round with a bright yellow scarf and she wore a mackintosh tightly gripped at the waist with a leather belt, and gumboots. She was energetically wiping her red MG over with wide vigorous strokes.

Lowering the field-glasses, Mr. Sapperton reached across for the telephone which he now placed on the dressing-chest; he dialled a number, Putney 0909. OK so far; she left the leather on the bonnet of the car and hurried into the house. The ringing tone stopped as the receiver was lifted. "Hallo?"

"Is that you, honey?" Mr. Sapperton cooed softly.

"Who is that?" the voice answered sharply.

"It's me, Nat."

"I'm afraid you've got the wrong number. This is Putney 0909."

"Putney! Why, I dialled Riverside. I'm sorry." Mr. Sapperton managed to put not only a laugh into his reply but a slightly American accent; his own voice reminded him strongly of Gary Cooper's as he fluted: "I'm saw-ry!"

"You've been mis-routed; you'd better replace your receiver and dial again."

"I've been wha-at?"

"Mis-routed," she repeated clearly.

"Have I, indeed? Mis-routed, well, well. Say, who are you, honey?"

"This is Mrs. York Cragg speaking, I'm Putney 0909. Please replace your receiver." There was a sharp click which came with the surprise of a small stab to Mr. Sapperton, who thought he had been getting on so nicely.

She came out of her house and, picking up her leather, she renewed her wiping of the car even more energetically than before.

Mr. Sapperton reconsidered the situation. It was important not to waste time and he might spend several days trying to get to know her. Her house was, for his particular requirements, so awkwardly placed; it was impossible to approach without a definite object in view. In fact, none of the ordinary methods of approach seemed feasible.

After a suitable pause he dialled again and watched her, once more, return to the house.

"Is that Mrs. York Cragg? This is the bloke who's just been annoying you with—er—mis-routing. I say, I must apologize. Will you please forgive me? The fact is, you sounded so like someone I know, used to know, rather. Your voice, that is . . ." he began to babble, chattering on about a young woman he used to know at Riverside 0909 and how he was feeling kind of lonesome, coming back to this country after so long and not knowing anyone, and now he had discovered that this particular young woman had gone away and her flat was let to some people who couldn't even speak English. He did hope, he babbled feverishly, that Mrs. Cragg would forgive his impertinence but just to hear a friendly voice meant a lot to him.

Not having the slightest idea as to what sort of person she was, made the essay a tremendous gamble. Some women would have slammed down the receiver in indignation, others, not. It would all depend on what sort of impression his voice made and to him his voice was as ordinary and unremarkable as was his face.

"Who are you?" she asked irritably when she was able to make herself heard.

"I'm Nathaniel Sapperton," he cried eagerly. "I've got a furnished apartment at Nero House, on Putney Heath; took it from a chap I know in the FO."

"The what?"

"The FO. Foreign Office." He burbled on.

He felt emanations of amusement from the end of the line and stopped abruptly. "What's the joke, honey?"

"It's only that you're a neighbour."

"Well, if that isn't a coincidence! What flat are you?"

"Not a flat. I live in one of those new houses you overlook, Silverdale, or perhaps you're on the other side of the block, facing the Heath, are you?"

"Why, I must be looking down on you right now! The sitting room faces the Heath, but the bedroom . . . I'm on the third floor, next to the top. You don't say!"

They both laughed.

"Well," she paused, "goodbye, for now." She put down the receiver, but gently this time.

But this time it was all right. Mr. Sapperton grinned cheerfully at himself in the looking-glass; not that there was really very much to smile about, but it is always delightful when deep-laid schemes come off.

There was a photograph of a woman on his dressing-chest; he gave her a copious wink before putting it away in a drawer under his clean shirts.

Clearly she was half expecting him; the car was now quite dried off, but she was polishing vigorously at the chromium with a dry duster. Nothing was said that was not entirely conventional but, behind the commonplace exchange of words, each was eyeing the other with the alertness of the unattached male and female meeting for the first time.

He thought: yes, she's pretty, but there is something more interesting there. Her manner was warm and friendly enough, he considered her distinctly charming, but there was a detachment about her comparable to that of a pretty hospital nurse. There was that something else about her, which, for the moment, he found indefinable.

He picked up a duster and for some minutes he helped her to polish. He stood back, finally, and remarked that it was a very pretty little car and split new, he felt sure. Yes, she told him, she had had it only a few weeks. It had been a present from her father-in-law who, as a matter of fact, had never seen it. It arrived after he had died.

Mr. Sapperton clicked his tongue. Wasn't it a pity, now, he observed.

Easter tossed the duster down and pulled off her cleaning gloves. "Thank you for helping me, Mr. Sapperton. Now, the least I can do is to ask you in for a drink. Do come; it's nearly six o'clock."

Protesting that it was not his habit to accept drinks from ladies, Mr. Sapperton followed her eagerly enough into the house. In silence she mixed a cocktail in the glass mixer and it was only when she raised her glass to him and met his puzzled look that she said: "Doesn't the name Cragg convey anything to you?"

Mr. Sapperton settled himself comfortably into an armchair. "Out there in the Persian Gulf, where I've come from, you get a bit out of touch," he explained chattily. "What with the heat, and all the drink one consumes; it's not that you feel so far from home as that you get things, and by things I mean the film and book reviews, the news of what's going on in Parliament, and so on, all a bit out of focus. They don't seem to matter much out there in the heat and you're too darned hot to understand them, anyway."

"But the ordinary news."

Mr. Sapperton's face appeared to undergo a series of convolutions before it more or less righted itself. "Isn't that, Cragg . . . do you mean the Golden Fleece Cragg . . . I mean to say . . . that is . . ."

He had the weirdest feeling about her; it seemed almost as though she were being deliberately modest, like a famous actress who has just allowed her real identity to slip out. He was shaken with a shudder, as though the small hairs on his spine were suddenly sprouting.

He watched her smile that was not a smile but a curious downwards turning of one side of the mouth, accompanied by a lowering of the eyelids. It was the look of slightly sneering modesty exactly similar to that which Mr. Sapperton had, from time to time, observed upon the face of the Mona Lisa: "Here I am, a famous character, through no fault of my own; look as much as you like, you clots, you won't be any the wiser." He had never been an admirer of Leonardo's heroine.

"Well—" she shrugged slightly—"you would have wondered where my husband was. Better to tell you straight away."

"Quite." He gulped down the rest of his drink. "Quite." And stood up to go.

Easter filled his glass. "Don't take fright," she said. "I'm enjoying having you here. I'm probably more lonely than you are. I've a daily woman who comes in the mornings, and my friends the Ramsgates live not far away, but still I am lonely. Horrible things happening to people seems to make them lonely. It singles them out, and if other people are sorry for them and are kind to them it still gives them the feeling of being isolated. One is the Kind of Person that Things Happen to. 'That poor Easter Cragg.' Do I sound sorry for myself? I am rather."

"Let me get this straight. Somebody killed both your husband and his father? Stabbing, was it?"

She nodded. "And the verdict was murder by person or persons unknown, which means the police can go on 'investigating,' that is, interviewing thousands of people, or rather, getting them to fill in forms stating where they were and when, and looking into the movements of every known criminal in the country . . . and out of it. 'Nationwide probe' they may call it. Every now and then the papers publish a small paragraph telling how busy the police are and at any moment now there's going to be an arrest. It'll go on just until there have been enough new murders to take people's minds off the stale ones, and then it'll be dropped. UNSOLVED, I suppose they'll write in their files."

Mr. Sapperton drank his second cocktail in one gulp, murmuring something a little unintelligible about not being surprised she felt embittered, it was a dreadful thing, really dreadful . . .

"Don't get me wrong," she said with a sharp little laugh, "I only want them to drop it *now*. Why can't they let sleeping dogs lie?"

"Don't you want them to discover the criminal?"

"Not at the expense of laying bare Jason and York's private lives for everyone to see, chew over, speculate upon."

He nodded sympathetically. "I think I understand."

"I don't believe in the eye-for-an-eye principle, it's out of date. Besides, people don't get murdered for nothing."

"How do you mean?"

"Well, I mean . . . somebody evidently thought both Jason and York needed to be murdered. And if they have done something that is so wrong and wicked . . . well, they're dead, let's not tell the whole world about it!"

For a long time Mr. Sapperton was quiet, leaning against the chimneypiece with his empty glass in his hand, idly kicking a log in the hearth with the toe of his shoe.

"Of course, you may take an exactly opposite view, like my friends John and Jill Ramsgate. They think the criminal should be discovered at all costs; they want me to offer a huge reward for information that may lead to the discovery of the murderer. What do you think?"

"I . . ." Mr. Sapperton was obliged to clear his throat. "I'm not sure what I think. I'd like to know a lot more about it."

"So would I."

"I mean, I'd like to know at least as much as everyone else," Mr. Sapperton corrected himself. "I did read about it, of course, but now that I've met you the whole thing looks different."

"It's taken on a more personal aspect, I expect. All at once you see that I'm a real person and not simply one of those newspaper characters whose relations, husbands, lovers, get murdered. I suppose that's what you mean."

"In a way. Do you mind if I look up the recent newspaper reports?"

"Are you one of those people who are passionately interested in murder, then, Mr. Sapperton?"

"By no means, but you asked my opinion just now."

There was the very slightest suggestion of a pout about her full, babyish mouth as she looked down into her empty glass. What lovely eyelids she has, Mr. Sapperton thought, so young!

"Are you here all alone?" he asked.

"I suppose you're thinking: 'How could she!' A lot of people do. The Ramsgates can't understand it. But it's my home. The only home I've ever had."

He looked down at the hearth.

She nodded. "Yes, Jason was killed right there, where you're standing." She added after a moment: "I haven't much imagination," as though in some surprise.

There seemed to be nothing adequate Mr. Sapperton could find to say.

"I'm sorry," she said at last and put out a small hand to touch his own. It was cold, like the touch of a dead mouse's claw. "When you left your flat and came out to find me, you probably felt gay and cheerful. We might have had lots of fun together . . . That is . . . if things had been different."

Now was the time to say: "You poor kid, etc., etc." But somehow or other Mr. Sapperton could not. He was too shocked or . . . something. He could not say it. He looked at her with an oddly helpless, where-do-we-go-from-here look.

"Don't think I mind talking about it," Easter went on. "Go away and look it all up at *The Times* office in the last few weeks' papers. Then we can talk it over, talk it out of the way, perhaps."

"And have fun after all," he suggested sadly.

CHAPTER II

In the movie there were two American businessmen shooting off their mouths at each other, and there was a gorgeous blonde, top-heavy with outsize breasts, teetering between them, firing off wisecracks with a babyish lisp but, though he did not take his eyes from the screen, Mr. Sapperton did not see or hear anything at all, he was entirely absorbed in his thoughts.

Going over the simple facts of the two murders there seemed to be not one single definite conclusion arising from them. Though it was probable, it was not safe to say that both the murders were done by one man, or that they were both done by one man unaided by someone else.

Was it a plot or a plan? A plot pre-supposes more than one person engaged, a plan would be the intended proceedings of one person. If the first murder had been either plotted or planned, it showed little signs of either. It could have been unpremeditated. In the second murder, there were distinct signs of plot or plan. There was the burglar's trick of the plaster on the cloakroom window which could have been arranged either before or *immediately after*. There was also the grey plastic mackintosh which did not necessarily prove either plot or plan. Snow clouds had been gathering the whole of that day, and early in the morning after the murder, snow had fallen heavily; anyone might have been wearing a plastic mackintosh over a warm coat.

On both occasions it appeared that the murdered man was alone in the house; Mr. Sapperton had a curiously strong impression arising from this fact; he could see a watcher outside the house, hands deep in the pockets of his coat, possibly already holding the knife, hat pulled down over the face. The house, almost buried up to the eaves in its banks of mournful evergreen, could be watched so easily by someone entirely concealed.

Someone who knew a good deal about the Cragg movements.

Someone, for instance, who knew that York was alone in the house when his wife and friends had left for London. Someone who knew that Jason Cragg was alone when he let himself into the house before Easter's return, with his dead son's key. Someone who found it a great deal more convenient to stab Jason Cragg in his daughter-in-law's house in Putney than in his own flat in Arlington Street, within eyeshot of the commissionaire. Understandable, that.

The first murder was done, undoubtedly, by someone whom York knew, or someone who had a password which caused York to let him into the house.

At the inquest on York Cragg, his friend, John Ramsgate, giving evidence, had said that he thought York was suffering from a perfectly ordinary cold and headache such as we all had from time to time. He had told him that he didn't feel well but that he did not want to spoil their evening; as they were starting out he had evidently not felt up to a dinner in the West End. His father had also said that, when he had had the telephone conversation with York, he had told him that he was not feeling too well, a cold, or something, but that he hoped to be all right for the business trip. The evidence thus showed that York's evening alone at home was not prearranged.

The second murder—for the moment Mr. Sapperton discounted the larks at the cloakroom window—could have been done in exactly the same way. The watcher could have waited until Sir Jason had opened the front door, returned to his car to put out the lights, gone into the house and shut the front door, before approaching. He could then have rung the front door bell; Sir Jason, having taken off his hat and coat, would open it and the visitor would say something which would cause Sir Jason to invite him inside on this cold night. Inside, and into the living room, where Sir Jason would mix a drink for them both, pouring some into his own glass and tasting it before stooping to attend to the fire. It was then that the visitor would strike, high up, as before. And when it was all over he would step out of his blood-drenched mackintosh and leave it lying on the floor. The plasters on the outside of the cloakroom window and the unfastening of the catches could be completed in three minutes; the murderer could slip away, out into the darkness and the wilds of South London and be lost forever.

The police enquiries into the plastic mackintosh could not lead anywhere; the manufacturers reported weekly sales of some ten thousand, all exactly similar; they were sold in their hundreds at the price of a guinea each at all big stores and a great many small ones all over the country.

Since the Craggs' public life allowed of as much concealment as the inside of a bird cage, the guiding principle of both the murders must lie in their private life, and about that, Mr. Sapperton was sure, Mrs. Easter Cragg must know something. Something.

The view she was taking about "letting sleeping dogs lie" was absurd and, moreover, primitive. Was there the suggestion of the wronged woman about the beautiful Easter? Like all women, Mr. Sapperton thought irritably, she confused the issue. Didn't she realize that it was far more dreadful to have your husband and your father-in-law revengefully stabbed to death than to have their private lives ripped wide open and exposed to public gaze? That the one must follow the other was a self-evident inference; if it turned out that there was nothing discreditable in their private lives, well and good, if not—not. It was an equal chance. And if it proved to be the case and there was something which would involve Easter in a loss of repute, she would have to put up with it. Murder was desperate and final, and finding the answer to it allowed for no consideration of the feelings of a sensitive and lady-like young woman.

And thus, having reached at least one definite conclusion by a process of careful reasoning, Mr. Sapperton was aware that he was looking into the eyes of the blonde in a head some three hundred or so times bigger than his own and in a tremendously loud, husky whisper she was saying: "You need me, darling, as much as I need you."

CHAPTER III

"And so you see," Mr. Sapperton said, "so long as these murders remain unexplained, you'll never really have a happy moment."

"Oh, I don't know." Easter, with lowered lids, pressed out the butt of her cigarette. "I'm happy now, for instance. I'm even having what you might call a lovely time." She looked round the little Chinese restaurant at which they were dining, and sipped her hot milk-less tea.

Mr. Sapperton shook his head. "It's nice of you to put it like that, but I know you're not really happy, you can't be. You're a nice girl, and a brave girl, if I may say so, and you don't believe in making a fuss. But you're never going to be really happy, inside, till you know who did the murders, and why."

"All right, if you say so." Easter smiled amiably. "But perhaps foundlings look at things differently."

"All this crap about foundlings, and by the way, it's a dreadfully out-of-date appellation. You've got a Victorian streak in you that positively revels in being what you insist on calling a 'foundling.' "

He flipped open his lighter as Easter helped herself to another cigarette. "You don't mind my saying these things, do you?"

"Not at all. Everybody likes talking about their fascinating selves."

"Well, as I say, all this crap about foundlings. Move with the time, girl. Every other home, these days, is a broken one."

Easter pursed her lips in a disbelieving hiss.

"Well, almost. The family as a unit doesn't amount to anything now. All the high-falutin' talk about security and happy-faces-round-the-fire—" Mr. Sapperton flicked his fingers in dismissal—"a lot of hoo-ey. Children are brought up to consider no one but themselves and I dare say it will turn out to be as good a generation as we've ever had."

"That's a matter of opinion, and you're slightly drunk," Easter observed.

"I don't think you've suffered in the least from being an orphan," Mr. Sapperton, undeflated, declared.

"I may not have suffered, exactly," Easter said slowly, "but I'm different."

"Everyone likes to think they're different. In what way are you different?"

"I'm an entity on my own, with no background. It does make a difference, you know. I live for the present. And that is why it is really true when I say I'm happy *now*. I haven't gradually emerged from my childhood as an integrated person. No one has ever been anything but kind and sweet to me but in an impersonal way, so that my character hasn't been formed out of *anything;* am I putting it clearly? I haven't evolved, opened out, developed, like a normal child. I'm merely a skin containing all the characteristics I was born with in adult form."

"So what?" Mr. Sapperton asked crudely.

"So—I'm different."

Mr. Sapperton took her small hand, which lay unemployed upon the tablecloth. "You're not all that different, as they say, but go on thinking so, if you want. And I'll go on thinking you're not happy. We don't have to think the same way about everything to get on fine, do we?" He forced her to smile back at him.

"If I'm not happy, I'm feeling extremely comfortable inside after all that exciting food. And this delicious jasmine tea—I could drink gallons of it." She helped herself to more.

"Now listen—" Mr. Sapperton took some more tea himself—"you foundling. I think you need some help; you're so awfully alone. And being a natural busy-body with a few weeks of idleness ahead of me, I think I'm the bloke to help you. Do you want me to?"

"Of course."

"Well, then, will you take my advice?"

"That depends."

"On what?"

"On whether I think it's good or not."

"Well, I'm damned! I want you to telephone to the press, the *Daily Gape* if you like, and tell them you're offering a reward for information leading to the arrest of the person, or persons, who murdered your husband and his father. And make it a good big one."

"Oughtn't it to be done through a solicitor?"

"If you like. Certainly, if you want. But it is important that the so-called cheap press should make a big thing of it."

"But the past few weeks have been one long struggle to avoid the reporter from the *Daily Gape* and some of the Sunday papers too. They've even offered me money to write an article about my life with York Cragg."

"All the better. All you have to do is to make the simple statement; you are offering a reward of so-and-so. It doesn't mean you have to throw open your doors to their sexi-rama boys."

"I'll have to think about it."

Mr. Sapperton stirred uneasily. "Nothing ages as rapidly as a murder case. There is at least one person in this world who at this moment is congratulating himself that it's 'all died down.' The police are busy on new murders now, and we've a limited police force, after all. There's got to come a time when investigation slackens, and that's the time for the reward. Five thousand pounds for information that leads directly to an arrest. Somebody, other than the murderer, must know something."

"What makes you say that?"

"Well, it's obvious."

Easter looked puzzled. "I don't see it at all."

"Look, there must be someone who knows something, or who has their suspicions."

"Give me an example of the sort of thing you mean."

"Use your imagination."

"I haven't any, I told you."

"Well, someone's *behaviour,* for instance. You don't walk in from stabbing a man, hang up your hat, eat a good supper and settle down to watching TV without showing some kind of stress."

"Don't you?"

"Then there's the odd bloodstain. Don't tell me that first murder took place without there being any blood anywhere on the assailant's clothes. And there's the knife. Someone must have bought or stolen a knife. Or even used the family carving knife which must have been missing for a while anyway. Oh, I sound too damn silly; I had no idea I had it in me. I ought to write thrillers!"

"You're absolutely sure, aren't you, that someone other than the murderer must know something?"

"Yes, I am."

"Well, I don't agree."

"Then that will have to be another point on which we disagree. You may be right, and if you are right, then your Five Thousand Pounds will remain intact, unclaimed," he ended triumphantly.

A full minute passed.

"All right," Easter agreed at last. "I'll do what you say. I must telephone to the family solicitor first and make sure that it's all right. The estate isn't anything like settled yet, and I dare say if that Five Thousand Pounds were to be awarded to an informant, he would get it put down on some expense account, and not let it be liable for Income Tax or Death Duties, or something." Easter smiled. "How's that?"

"Fine."

For once Easter had driven to London in her MG which she had parked nearby. They left the Chinese restaurant and walked arm in arm to the garage in Brewer Street.

"Sure you wouldn't like to go to a movie or anything?"

"Isn't it getting a bit late?"

"Late for a movie, perhaps, but too soon to go home."

"I'd like to see your flat."

"You would!" Mr. Sapperton looked down at her, delighted by the implication. She looked lovely and smelled lovely, was she going to *be* lovely?

CHAPTER IV

No, not quite that, but Mr. Sapperton was convinced that it was all due to carelessness on his part that their dinner at the Chinese restaurant did not culminate in a night of love. Sheer carelessness, for before leaving he forgot to put away his newly acquired vintage Rolls-Royce in the communal garage beneath the block of flats and when Easter swung round the gravel drive in front of Nero Court in her MG with Mr. Sapperton beside her, the old black-and-cream Rolls lay there, in the drive, as portly and dignified as ever.

She stopped in front of the lighted portico and Mr. Sapperton could see her face. She was staring at the Rolls as though at something obscene and her face was the colour of a mid-day December sky.

"What's wrong?" he asked sharply.

"My father-in-law's car," she choked.

"No, mine."

"They told me it had been sold through the solicitors!"

"And I bought it. It's only a coincidence, honey; no need to upset yourself."

"But it's a fantastic coincidence," Easter declared.

"All coincidences are fantastic. When I got home from the Middle East I stayed at the little hotel off St. James's Street I always use; I happened to go with a friend to collect his car from that big underground garage in Arlington Street and saw this job. Said I'd like to buy it if there was a chance and a few days later a car salesman rang me up and I had a trial run in it and it was fixed. Nobody told me the owner had been murdered. Thought it might put me off, I dare say."

"My father-in-law's name will be in the logbook," Easter exclaimed, a trifle wildly.

Mr. Sapperton took her hand, which was icy cold. "Your tiny hand is frozen," he murmured whimsically. "I dare say it will, but I don't read logbooks; I haven't even looked in it. But I have blown the bulb horn, boom! Sounds like the *Queen Liz* coming up Southampton Water, or a cow in labour."

"It's the most extraordinary coincidence I ever heard: I can't get over it."

"I could tell you of two or three even more extraordinary. It's a tiny world."

But Easter did not seem to want to hear them. She sat limply at the driving wheel as though all the strength had gone out of her. Mr. Sapperton leaned over and turned off the engine.

"Like to have a better look at her? I'm proud of her, you know."

"No, thanks. I know every inch of it. He let me drive it often."

"Then let's go in," Mr. Sapperton said brightly.

But the evening was shattered, there was no more fun to be had. She didn't want to see his flat now; all she wanted was to go home, to bring the evening to a close. He stayed with her until her car was put away and she had opened her own front door. It was obvious, after she had switched on the hall light, that she was trembling.

"You don't want me to come in, do you?"

She shook her head. "No, I'm tired."

He looked anxiously past her into the house. "Do you really not mind being here alone?"

"Not a bit," she murmured, "but I suppose everything has left me nervy. It is sudden shock I don't like. I've had so many lately. I never used to be like this. People with no imagination don't usually suffer from nerves."

"But look what you've been through." Mr. Sapperton wished very much they might go inside and continue this conversation in the warmth of the living room. But Easter had no such intention; she was withdrawing gradually so that now she was inside and he was not and she was gently but slowly and firmly shutting the door.

"And you won't forget," he reminded her urgently, "what you're going to do in the morning. The *Daily Gape*, remember . . ."

"Good night, and thank you for the evening," she said politely, and shut the door.

CHAPTER V

Police Constable Bacon had had a busy day. It was not until late in the evening that he got home from work and was able to relax in front of the telly. He picked up the *Daily Gape.*

"Cor, strike me dead!" he begged.

"There you are, Sam Bacon, there's your chance," his wife laughed.

But PC Bacon did not see the joke. "Five Thousand Pounds!" he muttered, more than once. "What couldn't we do with Five Thousand, eh, Doris, girl?"

"We could use it," Mrs. Bacon said temperately.

"And how, we could use it! A smallholding on Purley Downs, eh? A second-hand Austin pick-up to take the veg to market, eh? We'd be all right, you and me. No need to worry about our old age and not having no kids to keep us. Yes, we'd be all right." Police Constable Bacon was thoughtful.

"Have you got any ideas, then, Sam? I mean, could you supply any information leading to the arrest of the chap who done it?"

"Could I?" The Sam Bacon of a generation or so ago would have spat into the fire. Our Sam Bacon simply scratched himself. "Could I?" he asked the cat.

"Perhaps it don't apply to a member of the Force."

"Look, girl. How could I have any information on the QT? This is to tempt somebody who knows something. An accessory, maybe, another crook who'll turn Queen's Evidence."

"Five Thousand Pounds," Mrs. Bacon mused, "it's as good as winning a football pool. You was right on the spot, Sam. Up to the neck in it, you were."

"Too right," he snarled, "but I didn't see the bloomin' murders. I was just a few minutes too late!"

Mrs. Bacon enjoyed prodding Sam into angry sarcasm born of the

ingrained feeling of dissatisfaction with himself. It was her own peculiar way of reviving his far too latent ambitions.

"When your brain gets working, Sam, you never know. Do you,
Puss?" she asked in her turn the cat. "You never know what might
happen!"

"All right," Sam said bitingly, "I'll put on me thinking cap, you
never know . . . "

CHAPTER VI

Mr. Sapperton did nothing until the evening of the day that the news
of the reward was published. Then he telephoned.

"Well done! Now we shall see what we shall see."

"Nothing's happened so far," Easter returned.

"Don't expect somebody is going to rush round to the newspaper
office the minute he's read about the reward. He'll take time to think
it over. The police will be smothered under a whole heap of false
clues. There'll be some wonderful feats of imagination."

"The chief inspector called on me again today. I think, on the
whole, they're pleased. He didn't tell me anything, of course."

"He'd nothing to tell."

"He was very mysterious about their various 'lines of enquiry.' "

"He would be. What are you doing, Easter?"

"Nothing."

"Nothing?"

"Well, reading, actually."

"Reading! I couldn't be more surprised. May I come round?"

"Yes, do. I'll make some coffee."

She was wearing a long red woollen dressing gown affair, when he
arrived. The living room curtains were closely drawn and the fire was
blazing cheerfully.

"This is all very nice and cosy," he said appreciatively. "What are
you reading?" He picked up a glossy magazine. There was a large pile
of them on a small table.

Tonight Easter was all woman; she looked soft and warm and
friendly. But only friendly.

"What have you been doing today?"

"Jill and I went to a dress show. Hartnell's spring collection."

"Jill?"

"Jill Ramsgate."

"Tell me about your friends, the Ramsgates."

"I don't know what I should do without them," Easter said warmly. "They took me to stay with them after . . . after Jason. It was Jill whom I was with at the movies the day I had arranged to meet him."

The evening was going nicely. Mr. Sapperton had his own idea about how it would have ended had it not been, this time, for the fateful telephone call.

This particular evening, for the first time, he felt something for Easter that more nearly approached real concern and affection. He had thought her easy of approach but difficult to get to know, an odd anomaly. But this evening he told himself he had been unfair. How could one sum up fairly any young woman who had just emerged from the experiences that had befallen Easter?

With the coffee tray balanced on the pile of magazines on the low table in front of them, they sat side by side on the big sofa, close together, and Mr. Sapperton had a very real stab of remorse. Playing with her fragile-looking hand, he said sadly: "I'm old enough to be your father."

"Only just, surely. I like men a lot older than myself. York was nine years older than I. And Jason . . . "

"Did you like Jason?"

"Yes."

"How much?"

"I could have married him."

"Did he ask you to?"

"He didn't have time."

Mr. Sapperton was shocked into a full minute's silence. " I couldn't be more surprised," he said lightly.

"Jason *had* something. He was a fascinating man. So successful and yet so . . . so . . . "

"Humble?"

"That's it. Humble. How did you guess? Boyishly enthusiastic too, and almost uncertain of himself at times. So different from York. In fact, York seemed years older than his father. Jason had that youthful freshness you can't kill. I mean . . . " she paused. "I mean, he didn't

seem old. It was all such a pity, such a damn pity." She changed her
position, tucking her feet up into her long skirt. "Now you tell me
something," she begged comfortably.

"Are you going to turn out to be one of those tiresome women who
ask personal questions?" But the affectionate look he gave her took
away any sting from his words. "All right, I'll talk. But people who
ask personal questions don't expect to get the whole truth," he
laughed gently.

> "I remember, I remember,
> The house where I was born
> The little window where the sun
> Came peeping in at morn . . ." he began.

And then: "No, you only want to know if I'm married, don't you?
That's the only thing a woman ever really wants to know about a
man she meets, isn't it?"

Easter nodded.

The telephone stood on a little round Georgian wine table between
the fireplace and the sofa, within an arm's length. There was an ala-
baster lamp, softly shaded in pale peach with an ivory-silk fringe on
the same table, and a Sunderland saucer that was used as an ashtray.
The telephone sat, squat and brooding, the Villain of the Piece and
about to break up the evening so that nothing was ever the same
again.

Mr. Sapperton felt wildly silly, he might have been playing for
time: *"I was born one wet Whit Monday, in a studio near the Boltons,"* he
quoted.

" 'Airs on a Shoe-string,' darling," Easter reproached him. "It isn't
as though you'd had anything to drink, not here, anyway."

"As a matter of fact," Mr. Sapperton began, and when people start
a sentence with "as a matter of fact" it is always suspect, "I married at
twenty-four and was divorced at thirty. She divorced me, so now you
see what you're up against."

Being quite literally up against him, Easter laid her head on his
shoulder and at this crucial moment the telephone rang. "It'll be Jill,
about tomorrow. We're going to another dress show if she can get
Nannie to change her day." She picked up the receiver: "Putney
0909. Yes, this is Mrs. York Cragg. Who are you? *Who?*"

Quack, quack, quack! Mr. Sapperton heard. Quack, quack! Easter put her hand over the mouth-piece. "Oh, God!"

"Who is it?"

Easter shook her head, staring at him. "I don't know. A man, a common voice. He wants to come."

"Lord!" Mr. Sapperton leaped up, gesticulating wildly. "Tell him to come. Give us ten minutes to get the police," he whispered.

Easter spoke back into the mouth-piece. "Are you there? One minute, please." Her voice was husky with fear. Once more all the colour and vitality had drained out of her face with the rapidity of water running out of a hand-basin. "It's him! It's the murderer. That must be how he phoned first York and then Jason, *and now me!*" she whispered. "He says he's in the phone box at Putney Bridge Station."

Mr. Sapperton pressed his fist against his front teeth in an effort to think clearly. "Tell him to come along."

"You can get the bus from near the station to the corner of the road," Easter said into the mouthpiece, evidently in reply to a question. "But please give us a quarter of an hour. We . . ."

"We're just finishing our meal," Mr. Sapperton hissed.

Easter repeated his words into the mouthpiece and replaced it.

"What are we going to do?"

"You're going up to change out of that dressing-gown affair and I'm going to fix us both a stiff whisky. Hurry!"

But Mr. Sapperton was in a state of indecision. Whisky in one hand, he paused with the other hand on the receiver. Should he or should he not ring up the police? They would arrive in their car, blocking the drive and scaring the visitor away. Was it, in fact, the murderer, returning inevitably, or was it . . . of course, it was, someone who wanted to claim the Five Thousand reward!

He said as much when she came down. He smiled, calm now, and reassuring. "This will be the first of many. Here, drink this. Why didn't we think of it? You'll be snowed under with mysterious phone calls, letters, callers. All they've got to do is to look you up in the telephone directory. You'll have all the crackpots and cranks in England after you, proposing marriage and heaven knows what else."

"That reward was a shocking mistake."

"Wait and see. Let's wait and see."

"Oh, Nat! Hadn't you better get the police?"

"I've been thinking, better not. You said *us*, Easter, you wise child.

Did you do it purposely? He knows you're not alone."

Easter had drunk her whisky and soda; she was feeling much better. "But isn't it wonderful that you happen to be here?" she said. "I'd have been scared out of my wits if I'd been alone."

"Perhaps that'll teach you," he murmured.

"What?"

"Not to be alone."

Easter wandered nervously about the room. "He said his name was Ernest Millage. He had a thin cockney voice. He was nervous, he called me Miss."

Easter stopped in front of him and looked at him with that particularly wide-eyed candid look which he knew was something to be careful of, in a woman. "Have you ever heard of Ernest Millage?"

"No," he said, looking equally directly at her. "Give me a sheet of writing paper, Easter. I'm going to do something very amateurish and schoolboyish. A Precaution. I'm certain this is only a visitor about the reward, but this house has had one too many mysterious visitors coming here out of the night."

With his fountain-pen Mr. Sapperton wrote:

8.50 p.m. A mysterious cockney voice has just telephoned to Mrs. York Cragg, asking to see her. He states that he is at Putney Bridge Station and is now on his way to the house. I am with her and we are awaiting his arrival.

He made a hieroglyphic at the bottom of the paper.

"Why don't you sign it?"

"This is in case he takes out a gun and shoots us both; they'll know who is meant by *I*."

Mr. Sapperton went out of the room and Easter helped herself to another whisky from the grog tray.

"Where have you put it?" she asked on his return.

"I've slipped it inside the kitchen table drawer, where you keep all your cooking knives and things. He'll be unlikely to look there, if he ever gets round to ransacking the house. But the police look everywhere. It's all right, dearest girl, nothing is going to happen. It's simply a silly little man called Ernest Millage with a bit of useless information. Here he is . . ."

Mr. Sapperton had shattered the intimate atmosphere of the sitting room by switching on the brilliant ceiling light before opening the front door. Ernest Millage stood pale and blinking, a little dirty and ill-looking in the ruthless light. He was clearly very nervous, jerking forward like a puppet and holding out his hand to Easter. "Mrs. Cragg? Pleased to meet you."

"This is Mr. Sapperton, a friend of the family," Easter indicated.

"Pleased to meet you." Mr. Millage shook hands spasmodically.

Easter looked completely mystified. "I'm afraid I've no idea who you are, Mr. Millage." She did not look frightened now, nor particularly worried; Ernest Millage did not have the appearance of any sort of monster. He was short and good looking in a white-mouse-faced way. He had a large nose and a slightly receding chin and his eyes were faintly pink-rimmed. He was wearing an exaggeratedly smart and inexpensive overcoat and a coloured silk muffler and would clearly have looked more comfortable in a grubby raincoat.

When he said that his attention had been caught by the announcement of the reward that was being offered for information leading to the arrest of the murderer of the Craggs, father and son, the tension was relaxed. Mr. Sapperton asked him to sit down and Easter offered him the open cigarette-box. There was an exchange of pleasantries about how far Mr. Millage had come, the frequency of the buses and the cold wind that had sprung up. And then an awkward pause.

Looking tensely at the glowing end of his cigarette, Ernest Millage said that it was about his wife. He had only been married a couple of years and realized that his wife had never done what you might call settle down, if they understood his meaning. But he'd read all about these enticement cases, as they called them, and he understood full well that he was the victim of some such case. His wife had never been *allowed* to settle down, and now she'd been enticed away altogether and Mr. Millage was not going to rest until he'd found her. The poor girl wasn't herself, it was like she was hypnotized. "She always did have ideas above her station," Mr. Millage said gloomily.

It was such a surprising outlook that Easter and Nat exchanged amused glances.

"You must have a drink, Mr. Millage," Nat said, going across to the grog tray.

"No, thanks, I'm a teetotaller," he returned aggressively, and lapsed into a savage brooding. Easter raised her eyebrows to Nat, and shrugged her shoulders slightly, and Nat, who had taken the opportunity of giving himself another drink, stood glass in hand before the fire, waiting, with a receptive look on his face, for Mr. Millage to continue. Which, presently, he did.

His Valentine, he said, was an actress and his mother had warned him, many a time and oft, of the danger of marrying an actress. But she was so sweet, so sweet . . .

Easter and Nat both looked away from the pitiful sight of Mr. Millage struggling with tears. He pulled himself together and went on. He knew full well, when he married her, that she'd a past, but then, so had he, neither of them were exactly chickens. But they had each agreed to ignore the other's past. Valentine was ready, even eager, to settle down and have a kiddie or two. They'd found a nice little house in Edgware and he'd gone off to work every day, leaving her as happy, as he thought, as a cricket, with her chores. But oh dear me no! She'd been up to all sorts of larks behind his back. Lunches in the West End . . . all sorts.

Easter and Nat again exchanged amused glances as words failed Mr. Millage as to the precise form of the larks.

There were no kiddies, that was the trouble, no kiddies. If there'd been a baby she'd have given Mr. York Cragg and all the rest of them the bird.

"Just a minute, not so fast," Mr. Sapperton exclaimed. "You can't make statements like that. Mr. York Cragg spent this last year in getting engaged and marrying."

Ernest Millage put his hand inside his coat and brought out a large envelope.

"This is a copy which his father Sir Jason Cragg had made of a photograph he found among his son's possessions, of my wife. He had three made in all, so there's two others somewhere. A photograph taken, mind you, without my knowledge only a bit above a year ago. Last February, to be precise. There was some writing on the photograph, great big actressy writing (as though she was *somebody*) and that has come out on the copy, large as life. Like to see it?" Millage's voice trembled under the weight of his bitterness and his hands shook perceptibly as he drew it out of the envelope.

"Mavourneen," he sneered, as he handed it over. "She would give herself a fancy name! And she knows full well I can't stand her with her eyes done up like a tart. Must have taken hours, tricking herself up. And the brooch I gave her! Chose it herself and it cost me all of ten pounds at that pawnbrokers in Oxford Street. 'What do you want a fancy thing like that for?' I says . . ." Once again Millage nearly wept.

"I don't want to discourage you, Mr. Millage," Nat remarked as he studied the photograph, "but you're asking for trouble when you take on a wife who looks like that."

He sprang to his feet and thrust his face close to Nat's. "You're wrong. You don't know my Val, she's a good girl at heart."

"Don't let's argue," Nat returned, "but I really cannot see how the fact of the name York on a photograph can lead you to think that you have any clue as to the murderer of York Cragg."

"Look, I want my wife back a lot more than I want this here reward, but I reckon if I had this five thou she'd come back a lot quicker. I'd give her a good hiding, I'd sweeten her up with the money, and we'd start afresh. Women like a good hiding; if I'd done it sooner I reckon I'd have been all right."

Nat was getting a little tired of Mr. Millage's matrimonial troubles. Briskly he swept them aside and asked for details of the meeting with Sir Jason Cragg.

And so they learned that Jason had driven to the factory on the Great North Road in his Rolls-Royce and had asked to see Ernest Millage in the middle of the afternoon, and he and Ernest had talked together for half an hour, outside, standing by the old car in full view of all the office. And he, Ernest, had been so upset he'd packed up the afternoon's work and gone home to talk it over with his mother, who had advised him to do nothing for the moment. Leave it to father Cragg, she had said. He's got all the money behind him, he'll find her. He was a big businessman, used to getting things done; Mrs. Millage senior was in no doubt at all that the wretched Valentine would soon be brought home repenting.

"But what could you think York Cragg had to do with her? He was a happily married man, living here."

Ernest Millage shook his head firmly. "He led a double life is my guess. He enticed my Valentine and he's set her up in a little establishment."

"Look, you've been reading some cheap fiction, Mr. Millage. Things don't happen like that nowadays. But suppose he had . . . what would it have to do with his murder, unless, of course, you killed him?"

"Me?" Millage's mouth all but dropped open. "Me?"

"Surely you can see what you've presented us with this evening? One great big motive; motive, Mr. Millage. Motive is one of the things the police are looking for."

"Police!"

"Ever heard of them?"

Millage looked as though someone had stamped on him.

"One big omission, however . . . you haven't given us a motive for killing Sir Jason, so far. Perhaps you could tell us a little more, Mr. Millage?"

A curious metamorphosis had crept over Nat, an air of firm authority that caused Mr. Millage to quail.

"There's a lot you haven't told us, Mr. Millage. I should like to know, word for word, what exactly passed between you and Sir Jason that day outside the factory. Come now, we've only got half the story."

"On my honour . . . !" he began to protest and then, under Nat's firm look, he changed into a lower gear. He slumped down with his hands hanging between his knees and went into a long narrative full of "he says to me" and "I says to him" and "he says" and "I says, I says," from which a fairly accurate picture emerged.

Sir Jason had wasted no time but had at once brought out several copies of a photograph. "Is this your wife?" he had asked. And "Is this her handwriting?" And Millage had said that it was neither his wife as he knew her nor her handwriting as he knew it. He was exceedingly angry, to begin with. Sir Jason had told him to calm down, nothing was to be gained by spluttering with anger. It was, was it not, in fact, a photograph of his wife and the loving message was one which his wife would be capable of writing? Yes, Millage had reluctantly admitted it. The name "Mavourneen" was not one by which her husband knew her, but it was at least within the bounds of possibility that she would give herself such a name for the exclusive use of a lover. Millage had to admit this, too.

Then Sir Jason had asked a lot of questions the half of which Millage couldn't for the life of him remember. He had asked what sort of acting parts had she had, and here Millage had been forced to admit that she wasn't so much an actress as a singer and dancer. "In the chorus, in fact?" Sir Jason had summed up. He also made Millage admit that she had not, in actual fact, ever appeared on any London stage; her appearances had been mainly in the provinces, the smaller towns: Grimsby, Ashby-de-la-Zouche, Wigan. "A touring company?" Yes, touring companies, when she was doing well, but she didn't always do well, she spent a lot of time in the agencies. The stage was a very poorly paid profession when you reckoned how much time they spent unemployed.

How long had Millage known her before marriage? Four weeks, to be precise. That wasn't very long, was it? How was Millage to be sure that she had broken with all her old connections? Alas, he wasn't. He only knew he loved her, and she loved him, and he had believed that she wanted security. Then she might have been York Cragg's mistress for years before Millage knew her? Quite so. Could it be that York Cragg had tired of her and she continued to love him? No, Millage was quite definite there; that was absolutely out of the question. But still, Sir Jason had persisted, she had run away from him. Had Millage been expecting that? He had not; it was the shock of his life when he found she'd gone, gone without a word, without a trace.

"Perhaps she's dead. Murdered too," Sir Jason had said.

Millage had been deeply shocked at that; he also considered it completely impossible until Sir Jason reminded him that his own son, York, had been murdered most foully and that such things did happen, almost every day. His wife had vanished without leaving any hint as to where she was going, and from then, last November was it, until now he had had no sign at all that she still existed. How could he state definitely that she was not dead?

And then: "Did you report her disappearance, Millage?"

No, he had not.

"Why?"

Why? Why? WHY?

Because he, Millage, did not want everybody to know that his wife had run away from him.

"What a putrid reason!" Sir Jason had said.

But it wasn't really. Respectability, the step-sister and a poor relation of pride, was something that Millage and his like treasured more than any other thing. In his halting way Millage had tried to explain this, but it was something Sir Jason was quite unable to understand. He, Jason, did not give a damn what anyone thought of him, and he couldn't understand that anyone else could.

It was obvious at this stage, to Nat, and possibly to Easter, that Sir Jason was convinced that Ernest Millage had killed his wife and either hidden, or disposed of, the body, and, as a natural corollary had also stabbed York, whose suspicions with regard to the husband of his late mistress had been thoroughly aroused.

"And so I says to him: 'What are you going to do, sir?' " Millage went on. "And he says: 'Find your wife, Millage, either dead or alive.' And I says: 'Can I have one of these photos?' and he says: 'Take it, by all means.' I wanted to show it to Mum; she'd never have believed it if she hadn't seen it with her own eyes. 'I'll get in touch with you,' he says, 'possibly tomorrow. I want to think this thing over.' He thanked me and says ta ta! and that was the last I saw of him. Next day but one I read about him being found, here, it would be." Millage stared in some horror at the comfortable-looking hearth. "In this very room," he repeated in wonder.

CHAPTER VII

For an hour Millage "chewed the rag" as Nat put it; ruminating, speculating, reminiscing, discoursing, debating; the fire burned low and it was only when Easter rose to make it up that he showed signs of leaving.

"What was your wife's stage name?"

Millage looked even more unhappy. "That's just it! She's had half a dozen that I know of. She went on the stage as a kiddy of twelve in pantomime and I reckon that was what spoiled her; she got the idea that she was good and that one day, if she tried hard enough, she'd have her name in lights across Piccadilly Circus for certain. She started as 'Kitty Valentine,' that I do know, and when we met she was—" Mr. Millage cleared his throat in slight embarrassment—"she was one of these here stationary nudes at Collin's Music Hall, in Islington. Lucy de Lacy, she called herself then, but she'd no pride in it, a stop-gap, she called it, and when she packed it up there she stepped out of the name."

"Like she stepped out of her clothes," Nat murmured.

"Pardon?"

"Where did she get her stage names?"

"Thought them up—" Mr. Millage smiled—"talk about imagination! That's why it didn't surprise me when I saw the loving message: 'To my darling York; your Mavourneen.' " The smile dissolved in bitterness. "Sloppy . . ." In exasperation, Millage jumped to his feet, wrapping his gaudy coat around him and tying the sash belt.

Nat was still holding the photograph. "One thing," he said, "I must ask you. Don't waste any more time before informing the police that your wife is missing. You've made a big mistake in not getting in touch with them up to now. And if I were you, I'd keep quiet about your York Cragg ideas."

Millage's eyes narrowed suspiciously. "You would, would you? I'll see about that."

"Just as you please, of course." Nat shrugged. "But one thing I must ask you, as a favour. May I keep this photograph for a day or two?"

"If I'm to go to the police to tell them my wife's missing, I'd best take it, that stands to reason."

"Haven't you any others?"

"Dozens of 'em, literally dozens. She was always having them took, for agents and managers and so on."

"Well, take as many as you like to the police; but remember, if you take this particular one, they will want to know all about that inscription, 'to my darling York,' whether you've made up your mind to tell them or not. I only want to help you, Millage. And I don't want to raise your hopes, in any way, and have to disappoint you; but if you could lend me this photograph for a day or so, I'd be grateful."

Easter held out her hand for it and studied it as Mr. Millage collected himself for departure.

Out in the hall, Millage whispered something to Nat, who showed him into the cloakroom; when he came out, Nat was staring out into the dark of the drive; he had turned out the hall light and the threshold was now illuminated only from the light of the sitting room.

"Well, good night," Millage managed a "Sir" at last. He shook hands. "Thanks for . . . thanks . . ." he stumbled out into the dark.

"Haven't you a torch?"

Millage said no.

"Well, look, over there are the lights of the main road; there are buses up to midnight so you'll be all right. Turn right round that clump of bushes and you'll see the lights ahead. So long."

"You've got my address OK?"

"Yes, I have. Good night, Millage."

"G'night, sir."

Nat waited, listening to the sound of his receding footsteps before closing the door. He returned to the sitting room where the fire was now burning brightly.

"I didn't turn on the outside light and his step was a bit uncertain. I may be wrong, of course, but one didn't get the impression that he'd been here before and knew his way about. And his handshake was firm and warm, unlike that of a dead fish. And did he ask to go to the lavatory for purely natural reasons or . . . ? What are you burning, Easter, what the hell are you burning? Oh, you bloody little silly fool. Oh, damn you, damn you!"

"I had to."

He took her by the shoulders and shook her, shouting angrily: "You utter fool!" But he might as well have tried to shake a female puma; she fought back, scratching and biting and making vicious jabs with her knee until, in self-defence, he took a Japanese hold of her and flipped her face downwards on to the sofa. After which he was as emptied of anger as the top half of an hour-glass is emptied of sand and, feeling slightly foolish, he adjusted his tie and collar and pulled down his cuffs to a nice proportion below his sleeves.

For some minutes she lay, as she had fallen, vibrating. Nat took the empty tumblers into the kitchen, where he rinsed them under the hot tap and dried them carefully. He opened the table drawer where some of Easter's *batterie de cuisine* lay in a tidy row, and took out the sheet of paper, tearing it into small pieces which he put into his pocket. He took the tumblers back into the sitting-room and laid them on the tray.

Fragments of burnt photograph were wafting lightly about in a black corner of the fire; a faintish green flame flickered in and out on the surface where the photograph had been. But the picture of the woman was etched deeply upon his mind's eye.

Easter uncoiled herself slowly, pushed her hair out of her eyes, and blew her nose.

"Why did you burn it?"

"You know perfectly well why."

"Self-respect," he said derisively, "exactly like Ernest Millage. You don't want the world to know you're a wronged woman. You little bourgeois!"

"Take that view if you want. It could have been altruistic. I took the two copies out of Jason's case, after he was dead. His despatch case was on the hall table for hours and the photographs were in it, together with the negative he had made. He gave me back the original photograph, so I burned the lot. It's much better so. That photograph has done, I mean might do, endless harm."

There was nothing unusual in her composure. Women, Nathaniel knew, were like that. Fighting like wild cats, screaming, hysterical, beyond themselves one moment . . . and the next . . . powdering their noses and applying lipstick as though nothing had happened. Feeling, in fact, a lot better, while their pulverized males could only gape in an astonishment which was in no way mitigated by the number of times it was experienced.

She was like a small Siamese kitten which, having ripped a pair of Dior nylons to mere threads, sits back on its haunches and looks up wide-eyed; infinitely, deliciously, free from moral wrong.

"You look absolute heaven like that," Nathaniel said disapprovingly, and, gathering her up into a silken armful, he kissed her crushingly. "I loathe you," he murmured passionately, "you horrid, common, screaming little hellcat."

CHAPTER VIII

"But nevertheless . . ." Nathaniel scraped away at his face with his cut-throat razor, the use of which he took some pride in. "Be that as it may . . ." and "However . . ."

All that had been parenthesis and had nothing to do with the matter in hand. Besides, it hadn't come to anything. He had carried her upstairs and had tossed her down on her bed and left her there. He had turned out the lights before leaving and had locked the front door after him, putting the mortice key back into the house through the letter-box.

And now he was going to get into the old Rolls Royce and drive madly about until he found "Mavourneen" and he was going to leave Easter to think it over. Because he was seriously annoyed with her. It was all very well, but to destroy so finally something which might have shed some light at least upon York Cragg's private life, and thus, possibly, upon his murder, seemed quixotic to the point of sheer insanity. Furthermore, he did not trust Easter as a pursuant of lofty but impracticable ideas; she was as likely to have done it from self-interest as from devotion to her dead husband's reputation.

She didn't know anything about Nathaniel Sapperton if she thought that mere destruction of the photographs was going to discourage him. On the contrary, it only hardened his resolve to find "Mavourneen" with the pixie ears and the lovely pouting mouth. If, of course, she was still alive.

Ernest Millage could have murdered her and buried her in the small back garden at Rosedale, Edgware, in the county of Middlesex. Anyone could be a murderer and, unless one knew without a shadow of doubt, it was impossible to say for certain: he is a murderer; *or:* he is not a murderer. And moreover, Nathaniel reminded himself, how much nearer to being a murderer was he himself when he wished somebody out of the way, than the man who raised his fist and, knocking down this same somebody, accidentally killed him. The term *murderer* needed revising; it was losing its meaning.

Nathaniel dabbed his face with shaving lotion.

Ernest Millage might have murdered all three but, if he had, he was pretty sure of himself; he would keep until Nathaniel had made some further investigations. One thing Nat was certain of was that Millage wouldn't shoot himself to avoid punishment; he was the type who would face it, cocky and self-confident to the last. The tears which had so nearly overflowed down Millage's face had been those of sympathy for his own heart-breaking situation, rather than any sign of remorse.

And another thing. Mrs. Valentine Millage would read at least one newspaper, provided she was alive. Would she be able to resist the dangling bait of Five Thousand Pounds? From what he had heard of her, she would leap at the reward like a trout at a piece of orange-peel, only too eager to come over with excessive detail about her love-affair with York Cragg. Would she take the unusual step of getting in touch with the widow? No, that was something that Ernest Millage did for special, personal reasons. Mrs. Valentine Millage would communicate with the police. Or not. And if not—she was dead.

CHAPTER IX

Having ascertained at a police station which was the right directory in which to look up the information he required, he made a list of the theatrical agents in London. There was a surprising number of them and there was nothing to indicate which were the reputable ones and which were not. In any case, what did it matter?

It was slow, tiring work; most of them seemed to be situated on top floors, requiring the mounting of innumerable steep narrow stairways. There were others in basements and some over shops with obscure entrances round the back. If he had pictured himself picking his way through a galaxy of glamorous starlets, reality fell far short of his hopes.

At the bigger, better agents, there were small groups of people waiting who, from their appearance, might well have been people waiting in an out-patients' waiting hall. Occasionally, someone outstanding would catch the eye: a couple of tiny gnomes, waiting for a circus engagement; a coloured girl six feet tall with measurements 50-23-39, dressed in tight tartan slacks and a sequin-encrusted sweater; an elderly Negro with snow-white hair, like white icing on a chocolate cake; a child of ten with white-blonde, candy-floss hair and huge black eyes, like an illustration out of *The Wide, Wide World*. But they all wore the dull, uniform expression of people who wait, without much hope.

Nearly always Mr. Sticklebaum, Mr. Pfui and Mr. Glamer and their brethren were out, leaving the office in charge of a single woman, elderly more often than not.

Each time Nathaniel trotted out his piece, it seemed to him more phoney: "I'm looking for someone called Valentine Millage, or you may know her as Lucy de Lacy or Kitty Valentine. Would you be good enough to see if she is on your files?"

He suffered considerably from his sympathetic manner which

nearly always involved the need to appear to listen attentively to chatter about last week's influenza which kept her at home in bed so that she still wasn't feeling up to the mark; the misfortune which had occurred to a pair of glasses that morning as she left the house; the annoyance of not being able to have her luncheon hour from twelve to one at the same time as her boy-friend; the peculiarities of the office cat!

But the time wasted was repaid because, when nothing turned up under any of the three names he mentioned, he asked if he might look through the photograph files and, having shown himself to be pleasant, he received co-operation in return.

At the eleventh visit he had some success. Under the heading "Miscellaneous," Lucy de Lacy (nude) was filed, the form being pinned to two others which described her as "Kitty Valentine" (song and dance) and "Veronica Valentine" (show girl). There were also three photographs of an extra-ordinary variety: full-length, she was wearing a bikini of sequins, her hair fluffed out into a dark cloud; in the second she was in some sort of Russian outfit, her hair hanging in two plaits on either side of her face, and in the third she stood in a haughty pose in a skin-tight evening frock, but in each it was the unmistakable face of "Mavourneen."

What an old-fashioned type York Cragg must have been at heart, Nathaniel mused: in these days, when any number of young women could be had for a few cocktails and the asking, why complicate one's life with a woman of this sort, like a roguish Edwardian masher? It was incredible but, as Nathaniel's Lancashire grandmother so often said in the dialect: "There's nowt so queer as folk!"

"When did you last see her?"

"It was last September she was in. As a matter of fact she got herself fixed up through another agent." The clerk shuffled the papers about for a minute before saying: "Yes, I thought so. I've made a note of it. There was a postcard from her on the seventh of the tenth of last fall, asking us to keep her name on our books; she'd got fixed up temporary."

"Where?"

"Ah, there you're asking me!"

"Do you mean to say you don't know!" Nathaniel exclaimed, incredulous with frustration.

The clerk, too, was disappointed; he had seemed so nice, very much a gentleman.

"As a matter of fact," she said coldly, "I do. Or rather, I happen to know the agents who fixed her up: Obergurgle in Long Acre."

"How clever of you to remember," Nathaniel gushed a little retardedly.

"A little birdie told me," she said severely. "Shut the door on your way out!"

"Music hall's done for," Mr. Obergurgle lisped nostalgically. "The young folk have no time for it; the only audience they collect is a handful of old grampars. They don't want a good laugh, when they go out, this generation don't; they're a lot of culture cretins in their drains and drapes . . . ah me!" He explored the inside of his nose thoughtfully. "This lot is touring the provinces under Wulfie Lyon; it's a re-hash of the show he had on Clacton Pier last summer, only not near so good. And this 'ere, what's her name?" He peered through the lower-half of his steamy bi-focals, at the engagement book: "Wanda Valentine . . ."

"Veronica Valentine," Nat murmured. "Have you seen her?" His voice took on a hoarse note arising from excitement.

"Yes, I've seen her," Mr. Obergurgle said dully, but he was more interested in his nose; he made no comment whatever. "I can't say where you'll find them now but here's a list of places with theatres that put on shows like Wulfie Lyon's." After some rummaging in drawers and files he produced a copy of a typewritten list. "It's all there. Rochdale, Halifax, Huddersfield, Newcastle . . . Happy landings," he said sarcastically. "If I had a break, I'd prefer Majorca meself."

So would Nat, but at the moment there was, unfortunately, no choice.

The Third Part

CHAPTER I

He did not telephone to Easter before leaving. To do so would mean that he would be obliged to say when he would be back; he might be back in twenty-four hours, and he might be back in ten days. He did not want to have to say. Nor did he want to give any explanation for his absence; it would do Easter good, after her exhibition of temper, to cool off slowly; it might make her realize that she had behaved, to say the least of it, foolishly.

Nathaniel was delighted with his newly-purchased car. Up to the present he had had little time to fuss over her, but the mere fact of possession gave him infinite satisfaction. She was not yet a veteran but she had the dignity that a veteran did not possess; she engendered admiration rather than ribaldry. A drop-head coupé, she had a leather hood which worked on the principle of a perambulator hood; Jason had had it kept supple with repeated dressings of saddle soap. Two butterfly screws secured it to the windscreen and, when they were loosened, the hood could be pushed upright, slipping back and collapsing with slow dignity, fold on fold, above the boot.

On the door was a coat of arms, a paschal-lamb, inappropriately enough, with crossed oars behind it: the badge of the Golden Fleece Shipping Company. The radiator cap had the Rolls's silver lady fixed to it, that derivation from the Winged Victory of Samothrace, standing, as in all the old models, and on the front of the radiator the overlapping capital R's were red, showing that it was built before the death of Sir Henry Royce.

A weighty T-shaped carriage key for the boot was kept in one of the door pockets, and over each keyhole, on either side of the boot, heavy metal caps clipped down to prevent rain entering. The lid of the boot opened upwards into a great rubber-lined cave; it was kept open by two metal elbows. Nathaniel slung his canvas grip containing his night things inside and re-locked the boot, though this was hardly necessary as the lid kept down by its own weight. The number plate was a solid metal job and hung, like a dangling petticoat, below the boot, stating its owner to be "PP3." The only tribute to progress that had been made was the electrification of the cut-glass oil lamps used as parking lights on either side of the windscreen, and the two automatic rear lights fixed to the great swooping mudguards at the rear.

"To the North," the road signs said, giving Nathaniel a small thrill that was wholly unconnected with reality. But Dick Turpin made better time; hours later, having achieved Doncaster, half asphixiated, Nathaniel told himself that he had had enough, for the moment, of the stinking alley that was the Great North Road; he went to bed at the first likely hostelry he could find.

CHAPTER II

A telephone call between the Ramsgates and Easter Cragg was an almost daily occurrence. Often for as long as a quarter of an hour, the
two women chatted about their plans for the day and the events of
the previous day. Easter had made slightly amused references to a
"boy-friend" with whom she had dined several times of late.

Jill had said to her husband: "You know, I believe Easter's beginning to get over everything; there's a man of sorts about."

"Good," her husband had answered, "it's the very best thing that
could happen from everybody's point of view. Easter could become
quite a liability."

"I'll be very tactful; I won't ask her about it."

"No, don't. We'll be asked to meet him if there's anything in it."

Consequently, Jill chattered on about her own affairs and did not
ask Easter questions. She talked about the children, one of whom was
in his first term at a kindergarten school; her new suit; the film they
had seen the previous evening at the Curzon; their plans for the summer holidays abroad. And then she said:

"Oh, by the way. John saw Jason's old car yesterday. He was
lunching at the Traveller's Club and he saw it parked outside in the
square when he went in. When he came out two hours later it was still
there, but, while John was backing out our own car, the new owner of
the Rolls came to collect it. And who do you think has bought it?"

Silence.

"Ian Wainwright."

Still silence.

"Of course, you've never met him. He's been in the Middle East for
the last two years, but you've heard York and Jason speak of him.
He's a very bright lad indeed. He was decorated for some terrific
thing he did in the Secret Service during the War, and now he's at-

tached to the Foreign Office on the very hush-hush side. Are you still there, Easter?"

"Yes." Pause. "I'm still here."

"Are you getting a cold, darling? Your voice sounds awfully hoarse."

"Perhaps I am. This Ian Wainwright—of course, Jason and York often spoke of him. He sent us a cheque for a wedding present."

"Well, he's home for a bit now, waiting for a new posting. He was in England and saw Jason just before . . . he's been in Sweden since then; his family are on holiday there with his wife's people. My dear, he's got the most glamorous Swedish wife! What did you say, Easter?"

"He has children?"

"Two! They look absolute popsies, John says, from their photographs. Both very fair. Well, it isn't quite a coincidence Ian's buying Jason's old car. He wrote to the solicitor and asked if he could. We're so pleased about it; I don't like to think of Jason's dear old car knocking about, belonging to anyone, do you?"

"Jill . . ."

"Yes, darling?"

"What's this Ian Wainwright like, to look at, I mean?"

"You must meet him. John asked him to dine but he's away on business for the next few weeks. He'll let us know when he's back."

"But what does he *look* like?"

"Nothing much to look at. But you'd like him. He's amusing."

"Where's he *living?*"

"They haven't a permanent home. He's probably in a hotel. Now, what are you doing today? It's going to be heavenly. It's Nanny's day out; come over after lunch and go for a walk with us on the Heath. No? Well, perhaps you ought to look after that cold."

Easter put down the receiver and went to look at her reflection in the looking-glass. She stared at herself in astonishment as though she was surprised to see the same creature she had been some quarter of an hour earlier.

She sat down and turned over the pages of the new magazine which had been delivered that morning. It was one of her favourite magazines but she was not interested. She jumped up and went out into the yard, looking up at the block of flats and in particular at the

window she knew to be Nathaniel Sapperton's bedroom. It was
closed. She went to the telephone and dialled the number of his flat.
"Is that Mr. Ian Wainwright?" she would ask.

Prr-prr, pause, prr-prr, pause, prr-prr, prr-prr.

It was like toothache, each ringing sound stabbing deep into her
nerves. There was a certain grim satisfaction in the self-torture, which
helped to make bearable the agonizing doubt and uncertainty into
which Jill's scrap of gossip had plunged her.

At hourly intervals throughout the day and most of the night she
dialled and listened for several minutes to the bell ringing in the
empty flat before replacing the receiver. Sooner or later he would answer; he could hardly have gone away without saying a word to her.

But no light appeared in his room nor was there any change in the
position of the curtains.

He had come into her life like a great moth, blundering in at dusk;
he had beaten up the settling dust of her life as the big moth disturbs
the fluff on the electric light bulb. And Easter, because she was lonely,
had accepted him, believed everything he told her, trusted him. She
had not questioned his obvious desire to help and comfort her. As an
attractive, solitary young woman, what was more natural than that
he should seek her out? Oh, the vanity of it! If Easter was angry it was
with herself, that clever, detached self upon whom she relied utterly.
If that safe self could fail her, what else might not fail? This so-called
Nathaniel Sapperton might murder her; Easter winced when she
thought of the hours they had spent together, and alone.

She looked in the looking-glass, reproachfully seeking, in her own
well-known, well-beloved face, the answer to the question: how could
she have forgotten herself to such an extent? But there was no sly
pixie looking from her eyes; her face was smooth and kitten-innocent,
slightly puffy and expressionless, showing nothing of the troubles
through which she had recently come. A baby-face with wide guile-
less eyes and the mouth that seemed to pout for kisses; it told her
nothing but looked back at her in mild surprise.

To dial, to press the receiver to her ear and listen to the monotonous *prr-prr* became a habit; there was nothing else she could do.

CHAPTER III

Mrs. Sam Bacon was far more excited about the Five Thousand Pounds reward than she would have cared to admit; though she went about her housework as usual, she was seething with sensationalism inside. She hung the front page of the *Daily Gape,* with its tall headlines proclaiming the reward, from the chimneypiece, and throughout the following day her eyes turned to it again and again.

Doris Bacon was a great go-er-in for competitions; upon one occasion she had won a musquash coat for her selection of coats in order of merit in a Sunday paper. Once she had won a cake for guessing its weight, and another time she had gained a bottle of whisky for guessing the correct number of beans in a jar. It was, of course, over-ambitious to the point of farce to imagine that she could win the Five Thousand Pounds reward but someone could. Some quite ordinary person would win it. Someone, possibly, like themselves. Because, of course, there was an answer.

It might be that the answer would never be discovered and that the Five Thousand would lie unclaimed but that didn't mean that no answer existed. Sir Jason Cragg and his son York had been killed, there was no denying that, and therefore someone had killed them, since they had neither killed themselves nor been killed by accident.

Sam had been right in on the whole thing from as early a moment as possible, but somehow, Mrs. Bacon sighed heavily, Sam's mind, somehow . . . but Mrs. Bacon would not allow herself to think disloyally. There was nothing wrong with Sam's mind; he was a good, reliable policeman and she was proud of him. It wouldn't do for a policeman to go off at a tangent, wondering . . .

But there was no harm in a policeman's wife doing a bit of thinking. In the dresser drawer lay the copies of the *Daily Gape* in which had appeared the reports of the police-court proceedings to date, of both murders. Mrs. Bacon, leaning across the table, studied them carefully. They told you nothing, really, she speculated. Little bits of sensationalism and sentimentalism were picked out and enlarged upon by the *Daily Gape*'s own reporter, who was like someone picking up the roasted almonds off the top of a rich fruit cake. On an old postcard she jotted down the dates upon which the reports appeared and on her way back from the shops, armed with her laden shopping basket, she turned in at the public library.

In the reading-room she whispered to the attendant: "Could I please see the back numbers of—" having been told, by way of several large posters that: "Top People Read *The Times*," Mrs. Bacon felt she could go no higher—"*The Times!*" she hissed and, putting her shopping basket down carefully, so that she would not break the eggs, Mrs. Bacon brought her reading-glasses out of her pocket and gave them a good polish with her pocket handkerchief and breath.

CHAPTER IV

People were kind, and ready to be helpful. Nowhere in Asia, or, for that matter, in Southern Europe, would it be possible to go about asking for a theatrical company travelling under the aegis of someone with a ridiculous zoological name without giving some explanation. But in the North of England, at least, they answered his queries with grave courtesy, and if they felt eaten up with curiosity they did not show it. Mr. Sapperton discovered that by telephoning to an office in Manchester he would be told exactly where the Wulfie Lyon show was playing. And this he did.

Having been born and brought up in the County Palatine of Lancaster he was pleased to learn that they were at present playing the Pier Pavilion at Liverton-upon-Sands under the name of "Yours Cheerfully."

It was early afternoon when he arrived there and, having had no difficulty in getting a room at the Empire Hotel, he left his bag and the car and sauntered out on to the "Front."

An icy wind from the northwest seemed to have blown most human beings from the tarmac, but there were people huddled in the landward sides of the shelters. As far as it was possible to see, one saw grey sand, stretching out, flat and uneventful, into infinity, beyond which, Nathaniel knew, the sea was coming in at the rate of something like five miles per hour. It was a busy sea, covering miles upon miles of grey sand twice a day, a sea so worn out by activity that, when it arrived at the "Front," it would have lost its sea-savour and would both taste and look like icy-cold, diluted pea soup.

The pier strode out across the sands, its long iron legs looking strangely bare from a distance. The Pavilion was at the entrance to the pier; the box office was open and, with his heart beginning to thud a little from excitement, Mr. Sapperton stepped into the foyer and looked eagerly round for the photographs of the cast. But there were none, only a notice-board bearing the names of the performers which he studied, with increasing disappointment, for several minutes.

"Wulfie Lyon," he read, "offers something for everybody."

"YOURS CHEERFULLY!"
"New Faces—New Ideas—New Acts."

It was all rather puzzling; among some thirty or so names on the bill that of Veronica Valentine did not appear. She might, of course, be one of *The Tophole Trio,* or part of *Gloria Gagg and her Girlies,* one of the pawns in *The Crooning Checks.* Was it possible that she was a unit in *Moon and Son?*

Deeply reflective he became aware that the young lady in the box office was regarding him with as much curiosity as he was devoting to the notices.

"One stall for the first house," he said, putting down ten shillings.

"Twice nightly on Wednesdays and Saturdays only," she said firmly. "Tonight at seven."

"One stall," he repeated.

"One . . ." she pronounced it to rhyme with on, "three and six, please."

"Do you happen to know if there is someone called Veronica Valentine playing?" he asked politely.

She shook her head. "I wouldn't know. They're only here for a week. They're good, though. That Tommy Raffles is a scream!"

Thoughtfully, Nathaniel paced the damp boards of the pier. In the season, the pier was a seething mass of people, all, apparently, enjoying themselves. But at the moment he had it to himself. When he was a small boy, he remembered, he had had a tremendous thrill from looking down between the cracks of the boards, at the sea miles and miles below. But today his diversion held neither thrill nor attraction. The Ghost Train was closed down, the Amusement Palace was closed, and even the kiosk selling rock, toffee apples and Phulnana cachous was shrouded in tarpaulin. When he was young, there had been machines all along the pier in which one could, by inserting a penny, have exciting competitions with oneself, trying to catch worthless articles with giant clippers, playing a football match and enjoying What the Butler Saw. But all these attractions had been either banished altogether or were now gathered under the roof of the Amusement Palace where an attendant could keep a watchful eye to see that young toughs did not bust them wide open.

It was eight degrees below dull.

He returned to tea at the Empire Hotel, where he sat suffering acutely under the curious glances of old ladies who tried to look as though they were engrossed in their library books. Dinner, he noticed, was at seven, the same time as "Yours Cheerfully" began, making it quite evident that those who dined at seven did not go to variety shows on the pier. So he would have to go without dinner. But if the entertainment started at seven it would be over by ten, at the latest, more likely by nine-thirty. He might find a chop house open to which he could take "Veronica Valentine" to eat "after the show."

He had a definite plan of action; he would send round a note and ask her to meet him afterwards; he would be the Unknown Admirer, struck all of a heap. He did not anticipate much trouble in persuading her at least to have supper with him. What happened after that would depend upon what he was able to discover during the meal. So far everything had gone splendidly; he had had marvellous luck. It had been only a fifty-fifty chance that Mr. Millage's runaway wife had returned to the stage; Nathaniel quailed at the thought of the time he might have spent ascertaining this; two days of traipsing round the agents had been more than enough. And now, he was going to see her at last; the fabulous *Mavourneen,* that seducer of strong men and breaker-up of the happiest of homes . . . he looked at his watch: still two hours to go. He drifted out into the grey evening and sought cheerful companionship at the Dun Cow.

CHAPTER V

There was nothing bucolic about the clientele of the Dun Cow. By the time he had absorbed three pints of mild and bitter, for one only of which he was allowed to pay, he began almost to feel for the straws in his own hair. Their comment upon current affairs was voluble and astringent. They were much-travelled, too. The man in the cloth cap, a leather worker, had just returned with his wife and two "kiddies" from an Easter holiday in Taormina; the man who was clearly a bookie had spent his Easter in Paris and from the smacking of his lips one gathered that he had split Montmartre wide open; the man with the beautifully-cut trousers and the suede short boots, to which he proudly referred as "brothel-creepers," was planning a holiday in Jugoslavia on the proceeds of property sales, and the tiny man who had nipped in from the greengrocer's next door squeaked that he was off to Le Touquet for a golfing weekend.

Far from being the back o'beyond, Liverton-upon-Sands was clearly only a little short of the centre of the universe; Nathaniel felt proud to be there and sure of the success of his venture. He stood everybody a round of drinks, including the landlord.

" 'Ere's your very good 'ealth." Down south the landlord would undoubtedly have added, with the utmost casualness: "Staying long?" It may, of course, have been in part due to the flat vowels with which Nathaniel lightly larded his speech that he was accepted as one of themselves.

At ten to seven, when he made known that it was time for him to go, he told them he was on his way to the Pier Pavilion; the announcement was accepted as normal, no one even smiled. Each made his own particular casual gesture of farewell.

Outside it was not yet dark, the time having been recently advanced an hour. The sky was a lowering grey and the lights of the Pier Pavilion stood out with weird effect. Nathaniel bought his programme and subsided into his seat with a thrill of excitement that had more to do with the overture which the small orchestra was playing than with the beer he had consumed. There was a certain quality about the playing of the orchestra which engendered an excitement which he had not felt for many years. He studied the screen, plastered with advertisements and peculiar to variety shows from time immemorial; he looked round; the auditorium was filling up rapidly and for the most part, he noticed, with men.

When the curtain went up he realized, almost at once, that variety was not, as Mr. Obergurgle appeared to believe, on the way out. It was, in fact, very much alive. There was nothing whatever that was "new," as the poster declared; it was as old as music hall itself: the same old thing, the mixture as before, but each item was received with a storm of clapping and after particular favourites there were shrill whistles and cat-calls.

There were no less than six comedians, ranging from the arch-face-puller down through the smile-less lunatic, the drunken Irishman, the comic who fired off jokes like a tommy-gun, the lewd-looking fellow in the top hat who left almost everything to the minds of his audience, to the last, lowest and best of all, the coster's own comic, a delightful individual with no talent whatever but with a tremendous personality. His appearance was greeted with a thunder of applause; he wore a cloth cap and short dress trousers showing red and white striped football stockings, and a tailcoat several sizes too large for him with a red button which wouldn't keep buttoned for as long as you could count three. The lights went green as he came on and, when he stated gloomily that he was going mouldy, the women in the audience screamed with the same delight they might feel on the giant racer in the amusement park. He brought the genuine antiques out of the joke box, one after another: "Are you 'andcuffed?" he asked, suggesting that the applause was below standard. "Ladies and gentlemen, you will observe that during this wonderful dance I am now doing, my feet have not once left my body!" and Nathaniel, along with everyone else, roared with laughter.

It was all rather a long way from Jason and York Cragg and his pleasure had, of course, a lot to do with the alcohol now coursing round in his bloodstream, but for the moment Nathaniel abandoned himself to pleasure.

It was only during the equilibrium act at the end, which was done

by three young people obviously under fifteen, that Nathaniel realized there had been no chorus, no nudes and no display of rhythmic
legs. Fed on *Reveille* and the *Daily Mirror,* people no longer needed to
go to the theatre to see glorious bodies. During "God Save the
Queen" he studied the programme feverishly: *the woman lassoist, Big
Chief, the Human Candelabra, the Sixteen Singing Schoolboys* . . .

With something like a feeling of panic, he realized that Mr. Millage's Val did not appear in the programme under any of her stage
names. Who was he looking for? he thought dizzily. But what did it
matter? He would know that fabulous face anywhere.

"Is this the face that launched a thousand ships?" he asked himself
as he went round the back to the stage door, wavering very slightly.
His watch said nine-fifteen, so there was still time to go back to his
friends at the Dun Cow. Something had gone wrong somewhere: he
had never thought seriously that she existed, Nathaniel now told
himself. Tomorrow there would be time enough to think everything
out.

There wasn't a porter at the stage door; peering inside he heard a
good deal of noise; talking, even shouting. He retreated hastily and
walked some yards to the railing at the side of the pier, against which
he leaned, hands stuffed deeply into the pockets of his British warm.
The sea had come in and was making no great fuss on the sands
below, the wind was whining through the ornamental ironwork of the
pier; he waited until the first member of the cast came out, but he
waited impatiently, sure, now, that he would be unsuccessful and
only anxious to see if the landlord of the Dun Cow could produce
some food.

"Do you happen to know if there is a Veronica Valentine in the
show?" he asked. *The Sixteen Schoolboys* had come tumbling out as noisily uninhibited as a pack of choirboys out of church. None of them
had the least idea until a small one piped: "Miss Valentine, that's
Minnehaha; I had to take somepin to the "Forty-Eight-Hour" cleaners for her this morning."

"Tell her there's someone to see her, there's a good lad." Nathaniel
pressed half a crown into his hand and, taking the programme out of
his pocket, he tried to study it once again, in the poor light from the
stage door.

"Big Chief, the Human Candelabra," and below, in much smaller print:
"and Minnehaha."

Minnehaha being the squaw who had handed the great Big Chief his torches of burning petrol to swallow! She had had straight black hair and a reddish brown face and she had worn trousers edged with feathers and a hair-band straight across her brow in which one feather was standing upright.

The small boy returned, looking at him for a moment oddly, as though sizing him up. Apparently he liked what he saw, for he approached and said in a low voice: "She's not having any."

"What do you mean?"

"Big Chief scares the lights out of her. She's hopping it out the main entrance."

She was, was she?

The front entrance of the Pavilion was flush with the pier entrance but the whole edifice was situated inside the pier; it would be impossible for anyone to leave without coming out either by the pier turnstile or by the Pavilion foyer. Nathaniel, sprinting round to the front and out on to the promenade, stood a little to one side and watched. He hadn't been there half a minute before she emerged, like a late-leaving member of the audience, from the main doors. She was wearing a camel-hair coat and a headscarf knotted below her chin.

It was all going to be difficult, Nathaniel realized. Nobody in their right senses would believe that Big Chief's little assistant had attracted any specific attention for herself. He would have no ready excuse for waylaying her but, acting on impulse, he did so. So excited was he and so unlike his usual self that he actually put a finger under her chin and raised her face to a better light.

"Yes," he mused thoughtfully.

She was extremely nervous but she was also clearly not unused to casual meetings with men. She was not formally polite but stated at once that he must be a detective sent after her by Ernest Millage. He did not contradict her but allowed her to believe so until he had thought up a better explanation. They walked slowly away from the pier along the almost deserted promenade from circle of light to circle of light cast on the pavement by the tall standards.

Her nervousness subsided. The conversation prospered, an understanding was reached. Ernest must understand, she said, that he didn't need her. It wasn't that she didn't love Ernest, she wouldn't go into that now, but his life was complete without her. After all, she had her life to live; Ernest couldn't expect to keep her cooped up with nothing to do indefinitely. He was selfish, and he was jealous. But how, Nathaniel asked, could he both be complete without her and jealous? No, there was more wrong than that. But, in the meantime, would she come out to supper with him? Great strength was added to his request by the purely fortuitous fact that they were now passing the Empire Hotel and that the old Rolls was still standing suave and gallant where he had left her.

"I've got my car there," he said casually.

No, she didn't think she ought to. Doxie Lee would expect to find her in bed when he got back and there would be trouble if she were not. "That's Big Chief," she said simply, "he gets ever so fierce."

He dismissed Big Chief in a few words of one syllable.

"You don't understand. I'm living with him. His wife's died, her that was Minnehaha. He was desperate three months back. I met him in Obergurgle's, that's the agents; he got himself fixed up with Wulfie Lyon, and he pays me. He was all cut up about his wife and I . . . well," she said modestly, "I've been able to cheer him up."

It was maddening not to be able to see her face properly, the face that had haunted him, and had dwelt with Jason Cragg so that it had driven him to God knew what indiscretions. Notwithstanding her ready admission of adultery, she was as respectable as a church hymnal; shocked at the idea that the man with whom she was living should know she was out with An Other.

"Look," he said urgently, "there's Tom's Chop House at Saxon, nine miles up the coast. They're open till all hours. I'm ravenous; I don't know about you but I guess it will do you good to have a steak and chips."

He had edged her over towards the car and it was that stately automobile that decided her. She'd be tickled pink, she stated, to go out in that. She'd go, she said, if he'd make it snappy.

CHAPTER VI

He had only been able to look away from her lovely face long enough to feed himself. Now, after several large glasses of Pimm's No. 1, he relaxed over the black coffee and did some curious remembering.

There was Jason's voice remembered: "Would you say that was the face of a murderess, Ian?"

"There is no typical murderer's face."

"But a woman could have killed York. I have made certain of that. Does she look what you might call a psychotic personality?"

"What exactly do you mean by a psychotic personality?"

"I don't know, but that's what they say a murderer is if he isn't either a mental defective or a split personality."

"I think you'll find 'psychotic personality' is a very loose term. And people generally show signs of being psychotics before they commit anything so drastic as murder."

He remembered that.

And he remembered that hand-written memorandum which Jason had showed him. "York's little wife, bless her, has taken this business marvellously, on top of the murder itself. She's doing her poor best to help me and she's been scraping her memory. Read this—it's a bit thin in places—but I did ask her to do all she could to help and this is the result."

He remembered reading it through most carefully and, after he had handed it back, Jason had said: "I don't say anything is exactly untrue, but it's a lot of hooey. There's only one solid fact, only one thing young Easter says she *knows.*"

"That York spent some time with her in Paris?"

"Yes." Jason was tearing the "memorandum" into fragments. "Useless," he declared.

Nathaniel looked at her thoughtfully. There was a marked diversity in the way she did her hair.

"Did you wear a wig during your act?"

She nodded. "Big Chief's marvellous, isn't he? He's never looking for work for long. He gives the public something. And it's dangerous! Lots of people think it's a trick, but not it! It's no trick, believe me."

She leaned forward earnestly. "There's real petrol in that bowl he dips the torch into. The cotton in the top of the torch soaks it up. It scared me silly the first time I saw it, I can tell you. But he's been doing it all his life and his father did it before him. He's a real, genuine, honest-to-goodness fire-eater. He's modest about it, too; he says it's all a matter of the angle you hold the torch at and the way you breathe. He deliberately breathes petrol fumes in and sets light to the puffs as he jerks them out. He's upset inside sometimes, gets frightful indigestion and it makes him irritable. And he has burns round his mouth now and again."

She stabbed out her cigarette thoughtfully. "You see, he really needs someone to look after him, and even though he gets in a paddy and gets a bit rough, too, at times, I'm fond of him."

"Are you Irish?"

"No." She looked directly at him with her wide-open eyes.

"Are you?"

"No. I just wondered. Have you ever been to Paris?"

"Yes, often. Look, duck, I've had a lovely time but I must be getting back. He's gone off with the comedians to the billiards hall and I don't think he'll be back before midnight, but I must get back first. And it's rather late at night to begin a discussion about Ernest, don't you think?"

In the car on the way back she remarked thoughtfully: "Ernest must be using the money he's put on one side for a car. To think he's throwing away money like that, all over getting me back. I mean to say, it don't cost him nothing to get a posh guy like you."

At the present moment she seemed bitterly disappointing, Nathaniel thought, as he must have known she would be. Psychotic personality? Maybe, but he didn't think so, somehow.

It was Doxie Lee the fire-eater he wanted to meet now, because if Doxie hadn't got much else, he had a Motive.

Fantastic character though the fire-eater appeared to be, he fitted into the motive all right. There was now a complete set of circumstances: York and his actress-mistress, then York marrying and the mistress-habit not quite leaving him; Valentine Millage, trying to make a successful marriage, yet yearning after her past state; Valentine leaving her husband and returning to the stage where she becomes the mistress of the recently widowed music-hall performer; York jealous; the fire-eater jealous of York; jealousy the basis of three-quarters of the premeditated murders. QED.

Fictional? Yes. But Nathaniel returned to his theme-song, that ran like nerve-fibre through all his reckonings: murder must have a plan, a blue-print. The blue-print had to be planned and, if it were planned and the murder did not take place, it was fiction; if the murder did take place, then it was no longer fiction but plain bitter fact.

That, then, could be the blue-print for York's murder.

Jason's murder followed because Jason was too inquisitive and too successful in his enquiries.

Under the heading of jealousy, suspicion lay equally heavily upon Millage. And opportunity, possibly, even more heavily.

And now, driving along the main road to Liverton-upon-Sands from Saxon under the livid sodium lighting, Nathaniel glanced sideways at his companion. She was nodding, on the verge of sleep. Her face appeared a ghastly colour, her lips black, she looked like the plate of her own photograph.

But she knew Nathaniel was looking at her. "You're very quiet," she murmured.

Inwardly he cursed. If he could have produced the photograph now and challenged her with it, how simplified the situation would be. She would know instantly that he knew—well, almost everything. No doubt Easter had acted from the best of motives, poor kid; a kind of desperate loyalty to her dead husband had blinded her to the overwhelming advantage that possession of the photograph gave them. With the photograph as a fulcrum, he could lever a confession out of someone. Without it, he had to creep about on the thinnest of ice. One thing, however, was quite certain; he must get to know Valentine and the fire-eater a great deal better and with this end in view he turned the car up a side-turning and came to a stop among the sand-hills with the tufts of sharp grass sprouting here and there.

She turned towards him automatically and wound herself round him like an affectionate spring. He kissed her passionately, loving her directness and loving, too, her warm, soft lips. It was very, very nice and he went on for a long time.

"It's all wrong," he said at last, "to say that a happily married man with an affectionate, beautiful wife, cannot enjoy making love to someone else. In fact," he enlarged, "if you stop to think it out, it's a compliment to the aforesaid wife."

"Well I never!" she chuckled. "That's a new one on me!"

He kissed her until he exclaimed: "God, I'm seeing stars!"

"Yes." She wriggled herself off his knee and back into her seat. "We'd best be getting along."

More than slightly intoxicated, he pursued a dog-eared theme: "Why don't you go back to your husband? Why do you racket about with this gipsy-guy? You know how you'll end up if you go on like this, don't you?"

"Why should I tell you?" she asked primly.

"After all that kissing, I think you might," Nathaniel observed, aggrieved.

She chuckled, then said: "Marriage is one thing and making love's another. It don't surprise me at all that Ernest's got one of these private detectives . . ."

"Meaning me?"

"Meaning you. It don't surprise me at all. But that don't mean I've got to talk to you about my marriage. That's my business."

He was beginning to like her very much. "You're right," he said thoughtfully. "Nothing is more personal, yet nothing excites other people's interest quite so much. Only the protagonists know what goes on behind its smooth face."

She was applying lipstick by the light from the dashboard. "What's that, when it's at home?"

Nathaniel laughed lightly as he backed the car. "I must meet your human candelabra."

"You'd better not! He's got a temper, I can tell you. He's told me more than once he'd give me a black eye if I carried on with anyone else and there's one of the comedians in the show . . . Well, never mind that."

They were back on the main road now. "If you ask me," Nathaniel observed, "that's just what you need. If Ernest Millage had given you a few black eyes we wouldn't be where we are now."

And York: where did he come in?

"Ernest has never laid a finger on me in anger," she said soberly.

"More fool he. Now, where am I to take you?"

"We've rooms in Southsea Road, off the prom. But you'd best drop me at the pier. I'll tell him I've been with some of the other girls, if he's back before me."

Liverton-upon-Sands had gone to bed; it lay like a sleeping turtle under its greenish lights. The clock on the plain face of the Baptist church showed it to be a few minutes to midnight. A turning off the main road led straight down to the promenade, the pier and the sea, and it was as they were gliding silently between the closed shop fronts of this street that they passed a gaggle of men, straggling down the streets in ones and twos, shouting and laughing. At the red lights of a crossing they were obliged to stop and the group of men caught up with the car.

Though Big Chief was now wearing a cloth cap and a turtle-necked sweater, Nathaniel recognized him from his hawk-like profile from which the remains of kohl markings and greasepaint had been but poorly removed. He thrust his fierce face against the window with such suddenness that Nathaniel felt he had been hit by a tomahawk.

"Now then, now then!"

Valentine fumbled with the window handle, while he stood with his face terrifyingly close and made noises like a growling dog. She got it lowered at last. "This gentleman took us out to supper at Saxon," she said breathlessly, "me and two others. We've dropped the others and he's just taking me back."

Why tell a lie that could be so easily proved? Nat leaned over and drew back the door catch. "Care for a lift?"

The traffic lights had turned from green to red again. "Thanks." Yet undeflated he stepped inside with some dignity. The front seat was so wide that it was scarcely necessary to move closer to Nat, but she did. They glided past Big Chief's erstwhile companions, who all looked tactfully ahead, and in a ghastly silence they reached the pier. Out of the side of his mouth, Big Chief dropped instructions and presently they drew up at the lodgings.

"Go on in," he ordered, jerking his thumb at Valentine. In his present state of mind, Nat felt it wiser to say nothing. He nodded briskly at the two of them, his foot on the clutch ready to depart.

But Valentine was not one to forget her manners. "Thank you for the pleasant evening." She leaned across in front of the gipsy and gave her hand formally. She also gave Nat a slow, delightful wink.

"Cut along," the fire-eater barked impatiently, and then he put his extraordinary face inside the car rather unpleasantly close to Nat's own face. He smelled strongly of stale beer but so did Nat.

"If you've got'ny sense, you'll keep off. Get me?"

"I get you." Nat smiled, managing with some difficulty not to laugh. The look Big Chief gave him and the sound he made were remarkably like that of Captain Hook in *Peter Pan* when he creeps in and shakes his hook at the audience with a fantastic leer and a "Grr . . . rr" that sends shivers of apprehension down the spine.

CHAPTER VII

"I'll swear," the fire-eater boasted, amid general laughter, "that I've never struck a woman with anything bigger than half a brick." Though he could not be said to expand exactly, under the influence of an admiring audience, he certainly intensified, became more so, as it were.

In Nat's experience there was almost no situation which could not be clarified by the liberal application of alcohol; he made it his business the following day to get as much drink as possible inside Big Chief in the short time available. And now he had the pleasure of sitting quietly in the background, watching the result of his expenditure.

As a fire-eater it was the fire that impressed rather than the man; without his flaming petrol torches, he was as ineffectual as a gas-cooker without the gas. But off the stage, now that one saw him in the round, the man made an impact. There was something of the mystic about him, something of the brooding, introverted "outsider." His dark hair and skin, his curiously high voice and strange intonation, the high cheekbones and beetling frown made him something of a phenomenon. There was a refinement about him deriving from his Hindu blood and Yoga-practising progenitors, upon which his present boastful, pub-crawling manner lay incongruously.

"So she's been warned. She knows where she gets off. One woman at a time, that's my motto." Loud laughter and a burst of lubricous wit greeted this sally.

There's a rake-hell for you, Nat thought, but did he stab first York and then Jason because he was jealous of the woman of the moment? Prematurely aged (he was twenty-nine and looked fifty), there was a faint air of desperation about him. Undoubtedly the hazards of his occupation predestined him for an early death; did these same hazards also affect his mind? The lining of his stomach must be in a ghastly state, Nat thought, and the lines on his face were caused, no doubt, by constant pain.

If the fire-eater had been an ordinary person, guilt could have been proved, or disproved, by the process of going backwards through time, week after week, to the two relevant dates. Where was he when first York was murdered, and then Jason?

Nat had gone into this with him as far as it was possible without causing annoyance and it appeared that shortly after the day in the autumn when he had met Valentine Millage at the agents, they had been touring the North of England. And that was as far as it would go.

The fire-eater and Minnehaha travelled in a not very plain van, rather reminiscent of a henhouse on wheels, known affectionately in the profession as "the privy." It had a good old Austin engine in front of the amateurishly-built body and was painted a bright yellow. "Big Chief" was splashed in large red lettering across the yellow, "and Minnehaha" appeared below in much smaller letters of a sober black, on either side of the van. It was an almost farcical thought that any-one should set off on a murder-trip in such a vehicle.

Both the Craggs had been murdered on a weekday; could the gipsy have made an involved journey from the North of England to Lon-don and thence to Putney by trains and Underground without being absent from his work longer than twenty-four hours? Yes, he could, and with time to spare.

But *would* he?

That was something which Nat intended to find out.

Unfortunately, the clarity of his mind was clouded by the insane desire to see Valentine alone. It was madness to allow personal feel-ings to enter into an investigation of this kind, but there it was . . .

Nat considered his vulnerability to women a handicap; it was more than time he grew out of it, but at the same time he made no great effort to overcome it. I'm nearly middle-aged, he used to think, and then it will be all over. But now he really was middle-aged, and it wasn't over, not nearly.

Though he had been with the gipsy all day he had not been able to see Valentine other than on the stage at the evening performance in her ridiculous disguise of Minnehaha, and he was now planning to get Big Chief so drunk that he could slip away from the Dun Cow and see her for a few moments, at least, at her lodgings in Southsea Road.

The gipsy was drunk now, but only up to a point, and it was already closing-time.

"The privy" and the Rolls were parked side by side on a piece of spare ground at the side of the public house; neither of them being in the least class-conscious, they waited with dignity for their owners who presently approached a trifle uncertainly. Big Chief suggested, with a bellow of laughter, that they exchange vehicles. Nathaniel looked at him closely. If he had been to the house in Putney on that cold January night that Jason Cragg was murdered, Big Chief could not have failed to see the old car parked in the drive, immediately outside the house. If he had, then he must know that Nathaniel's meeting with him was not a chance one. If he had murdered Jason for knowing too much, then he would now murder Nat, and probably using the same successful method as before. What was going on behind those hooded eyes, that insolent, drunken expression?

It being closing time, a dozen or so drinkers from the bar had followed them out and now stood about in a shouting, laughing group after the manner of men at closing time.

Nathaniel, proud of his car, was perfectly determined not to let Big Chief, or anyone else, drive it, but he was also anxious to continue in the role of jolly-good-fellow that he had spent the day in building up so carefully. He laughed good-naturedly, murmuring that he was sure the "privy" could knock spots off the Rolls for speed.

At once a marathon was planned and someone offered to make a book. "Two to one, bar one" and tick-tack movements confused the situation. Fierce argument as to the relative accomplishments of each vehicle broke out.

With the watchful bobby no longer on the beat, minor rioting broke out. The two vehicles were pushed out on to the now empty High Street and there was a general scramble for seats. It was now quite an impossibility to retain his popularity and not agree to the race.

"But no passengers," Nathaniel said firmly. "If I crash there's only me," he shouted. "I don't want to have to keep any of your families for the rest of my life." This seemed reasonable enough and most people fell back. A fat man appointed himself official starter and the route was described to Nat. They were to race along the promenade as far as the amusement park, up the sandy track on to the main road and back along the main road and down the High Street to the Dun Cow. Roughly two miles. The fat man took out his stopwatch.

There was a great deal of fooling and bets were actually made. Big Chief cleared everyone out of his van and, hitching up his trousers with a gesture of determination, he climbed in and grimly started up his engine. A coin was tossed for position on the road and the Rolls was brought level with the van.

It's madness, Nat thought, but he had no intention of racing. He would let Big Chief careen ahead, so far ahead that there would be no need for him to drive recklessly, and they would return to the pub unimpaired, having appeared to be a couple of daredevils, no bones broken, honour and sportsmanship intact.

The fat man stood on the edge of the kerb with a handkerchief held ludicrously, limply from its extreme corner. "Have you got your engine running, mister?" he asked Nat incredulously. "Can't hear a bloomin' thing!"

No one could fail to hear the engine of the "privy" which Big Chief was revving-up importantly. "Are you ready now, gennelmen?" the fat man asked. "OFF!"

It was a false start; shouts of laughter and warning cries stopped them. One humorist had climbed into the boot and pulled the lid down on top of himself; when the Rolls started he had been unable to keep the joke to himself, had raised the lid and waved farewell to the watching crowd. He was pulled out and the lid thumped back into place; Nathaniel cursed himself for not locking it.

"There is no one else in there, is there?" he asked with comic good humour.

On being assured that there was not, he signalled to the fat man, who again got himself into position with the handkerchief.

"One," he puffed, "two, three and OFF!"

With an impressive roar from its Brooklands silencer the "privy" was off, rocking and rolling down the High Street towards the pier and round the left-hand corner on to the promenade at a terrifying angle, on two of its wooden-spoked wheels. Nathaniel caught him up on the straight, but a glance at the grim face at the driving wheel told him that the gipsy was in dead earnest.

All right, Nat thought with a stab of excitement, and pressed the accelerator down. Fifty, sixty, sixty-five, seventy . . . the "privy" was still ahead, but so was the fun fair, shuttered and closed down now, but undoubtedly there. Nat slowed down, ready for the second left-hand turn onto the cinder track.

He yelled: "Slow down, you fool!" and pressed the horn continuously in warning, but incredibly the "privy" went forging on with the inexorability of a satellite, ploughing its way through the wooden fence; staying miraculously upright, it bumped its way right into the heart of the group of light wooden kiosks with all the abandon of an old Ford in a custard-pie comedy film in the early days. It came to a standstill only because at last it toppled over sideways. It was not more than twenty yards into the fun fair but that twenty yards was now a very depressed area indeed.

As Nat picked his way over the debris, Big Chief, the Human Candelabra, emerged from the upward door of the van like a wounded and furious wasp.

"Are you hurt?" Nat cried.

"No," was the answer, "but you're going to be!" As the angry man advanced upon him, Nat had a grateful thought for the Japanese he met in Burma who had taught him the two useful ju-jitsu throws he knew.

"It was a trick," Big Chief shouted, "a big bloody, mean trick! And it came off, yes, it came off . . . but you'll pay for it." He was standing only a couple of yards away now and his anger was as tangible as the flames which at other times he blasted from his mouth. Involuntarily Nat stepped back.

"I'll bash you to pulp," Big Chief shouted drunkenly, "and I don't care if I swing for it, you bleedin' little swindlin' toff. I know your sort; take a fancy to another man's girl and you've got to have her. You inherit the world, eh? Take that, you stuffed swank, and that, you rotten little pimp."

Though he had had time to prepare, Nat was not ready for a fight, he wasn't feeling like fighting, he seldom did. He was suffering from drink and shock and a certain lassitude. The first blow woke him up, the second hurt very much indeed and the pain roused him to violent anger. Stepping back for momentum, he darted forward, butted his head into Big Chief's crutch and took hold of his legs in the way he had been taught. Up went Big Chief, as though he had been tossed in a blanket, up and over Nat's head and through the air like an autumn leaf; he landed, grunting with pain, on the corner of the overturned fortune-teller's tent. A wealth of fascinating appellations flowed from his lips but Nat did not stay to listen.

CHAPTER VIII

Now, Nat realized as he drove slowly back along the promenade, past the Empire Hotel, was the time for the evening to be brought to a close. He ought to go into his hotel, go to bed and leave things to sort themselves out. But he seldom chose the path of discretion.

The return to the Dun Cow was a shocking anti-climax.

The race, which only a few minutes before had seemed amusing, a subject for laughter and re-telling with more laughter, now appeared the most childish and puerile of pranks. For a man of Nat's standing (and, indeed, age) it was unbelievably silly. It just goes to show, Nat thought in a highly unsatisfactory extenuation, how alcohol cripples judgment.

Everyone was looking up the High Street for the first appearance of the victor. Nat drew up almost silently behind the riotous crowd before he was noticed. "I don't know what happened," he told everyone. "He went crashing on into the middle of the fun fair instead of turning off up the cinder track. It was poorly lighted. I don't think he's badly hurt."

It was a little difficult to state satisfactorily why he had not brought Big Chief back with him. "He's fighting mad," he tried to explain. "Somebody had better take a doctor along, he's concussed, perhaps. Couldn't keep his hands off me." He was determined not to return to the fun fair. "Look, I'll go and find a doctor, and if somebody could telephone for an ambulance . . . he'd better be taken to hospital for a check-up. The van's wrecked."

One or two of them had cars and motorcycle combinations of their own; the accident had a sobering effect; they quickly organized themselves into a helpful unit. Some of them went off to the hospital to collect an ambulance, and the rest, anxious not to miss anything, set off for the scene of the accident.

Nobody had mentioned the woman and she must certainly be told.

Nat had spent most of the day in Big Chief's company. The only opportunity the gipsy could have had of finding out exactly which girls were *not* with Nat and his Valentine the previous evening was during the evening performance at the Pavilion. Why, then, had he not at once challenged Nat? Why had he agreed to come to drink at the Dun Cow after the show and appeared reasonably friendly? Whatever the reason, it told Nat that Big Chief had more than his share of low cunning. Perhaps he had planned to murder Nat, to stab him in the back that evening, given a suitable opportunity.

The more he thought of it the more convincing it seemed. They would all have said goodnight and dispersed, Big Chief climbing into his van and leaving with the rest. Then Big Chief leaving his van, possibly outside the pier, where it so often stood, and going swiftly to the Empire Hotel, waylaying Nat as he closed up his car for the night, strolling with him along the promenade, a pretext for talking things over and then, up some quiet turning, the stabbing . . . that skilful, deadly successful stabbing. Perhaps the stupid race had saved Nat's life.

There would have been no suspicions directed at Big Chief, for had they not been seen together all day, in and out of the public houses of Liverton-upon-Sands, and again after the evening performance, the best of friends?

Nat felt his palms wet with sweat on the steering wheel.

All this seemed very far from being mere fancy when he met Valentine in the dark, narrow little hall of her stuffy lodging house. He told her, quickly, everything that had happened.

"I knew it," she declared, "I knew something was going to happen! He found out from the girls that no one had been to Saxon with us last night. I could tell, when we was doing the act . . . he was shaking with rage and he snatched the torches off me. He would have beaten you up and then come back and beaten me up!" She said it almost proudly.

Nat gazed at her incredulously. "How can you stand it?"

"It makes a change after Ernest," she said. "I could shake Ernest, he is that tame." Nat took heart from the use of the present tense.

"I'd leave the bruiser," he advised urgently. "He's had a good shaking up, I'm sure they'll keep him in hospital a day or so, you won't have the act tomorrow."

She clicked her tongue: "Tt—tt! And it's matinee day, too, Saturday!"

She's so superficial, Nat thought, that she's mentally unapproachable, she doesn't seem to feel. It is only when you have her in your arms that she's anything at all and, to add verisimilitude to his thesis, he did that, winding her round him, in the narrow, dark hall, and kissing her passionately.

She's not a tart, he thought, exactly, but she's a splendid vehicle for kissing et cetera, and laughed at his own ambiguity, focalized in the et cetera.

"Look," he said, setting her upright. "You'll never do any good with this man, and you know it, at the bottom of your heart. You're just a good-time gal, and you aren't getting any younger. Why not drop it before you get badly hurt? You'll end up as a frowsty old tart and then you won't even be that, you'll be a bent, crippled, lined old woman creeping out into the Edgware Road, clutching your shabby purse with the remains of your weekly old-age allowance in it, off to buy yourself half a pint of milk . . . or bitter."

He was holding her gently now, whispering into the pixie ear which he could not see but knew to be there.

"You've got a good man there in London who adores you and wants you back. Why not go back to him and settle down and have children to love and to look after you in your old age? Youth doesn't last for ever, you know." He pulled the ear gently. "You haven't all the time in the world left to have children. They're worth having, believe me . . ."

Nat put everything he had into his plea. Though he had no proof against the fire-eater as yet, he had resolved to put his suspicions before the CID and if Big Chief were ever to be arrested, it was going to be extremely unpleasant for his female assistant. Nat did not give a damn about Ernest Millage but he was certainly the answer to his lawful wife's present predicament.

"You're so lucky," Nat hissed, "to have that man devoted to you, ready to forgive, because when all's said and done, you have let him down, done the dirty . . ."

Somewhere upstairs in the smelly little house a thin door banged; somebody had clearly been doing their best to overhear, and that same person had possibly gone back into their room to look out of the window and examine the Rolls by the light of the nearby lamp-post.

"Come now," Nat pressed her. "Drive back to London with me now. It will save a lot of trouble."

"He'd be after us, don't you worry!"

"What in? The van's smashed up!"

"No . . ." Valentine said uncertainly.

"Don't tell me you love him! Just don't tell me that because I'll never believe it."

"No, I don't exactly love him but I don't want to go back and live my old life in Edgware. Rosedale . . ."

"You can't do that," Nat said wildly, carried away by his own verbosity, "you'll not do that; it's let to a West African woman with a lot of black kids," and then cursed himself inwardly for his indiscretion.

"How do you know?" she asked, turning her great eyes round to his own alarmed ones. "Well, that settles it! If Ernest has gone back to his mother that settles it!" And, tearing herself from Nat's arms, she ran upstairs.

But he knew she was crying and he was not without hope as he let himself out quietly.

CHAPTER IX

"Sam," Mrs. Bacon addressed as much of her husband as she could see beneath the extended evening paper, his uniform trousers and his feet in thick grey socks. A tray holding cups of cocoa and a plate of sandwiches between them, they were watching television, Sam reading his newspaper and Mrs. Bacon darning a clean pair of Sam's grey socks.

"Yes, love?"

"About those Cragg murders . . ."

"Coo, what a morbid mind!"

"Well, somebody's going to win that Five Thousand."

"Not necessary-ly."

"I bin thinkin'."

"Don't do it," Sam advised. "It's only nuts and crackpots that gets thinking. You should see some of the folk who've bin thinking about that money . . . cranky, nothink less! It's giving us some work, I can tell you. The ole man says: 'You never know,' he says, 'the one you think is the biggest dud of the lot may turn out to be the one that's got the answer.' Dozens of people have turned up with bits of damn silly information. But you mark my words, it's nobody in this country done it; it's an international crook, like I've said all along, cooling his heels in the Kremlin now, shouldn't wonder."

Mrs. Bacon looked crushed but still puzzled. "What, exactly, does it mean by *information leading to the arrest?*"

"Just what it says. The trouble is that folk bring you along information that leads nowhere."

"Would a vital clue be *information leading to the arrest?*"

Sam Bacon lowered his paper and looked with interest at his wife, exhaling breath through his front teeth as he did so. "Vital clue!" He gave a great belly laugh. "You and your *vital clues.* Doris, the Richmond sleuth, eh?"

But Doris did not join in the laughter. "Who would you take your vital clue to?" she asked.

"My old man, of course." Sam's laughter over, he returned to the newspaper, but was overtaken by a further attack of wit. "If I see you coming, I'll say to the inspector, I'll say: 'Here comes my old woman with a vital clue!' " He became convulsed. "He'll get me to go out and tell you what you can do with it!"

Mrs. Sam looked thoughtfully at her husband over the top of her glasses. She was not amused.

CHAPTER X

He awoke at eight with less of a hangover than he deserved. There was a painful area in the vicinity of his gallbladder and he had a stiff neck, but he was able to eat a good breakfast and about ten o'clock he strolled out of the dining room with the daily paper under his arm.

She was just paying off a taxi and the doorman was carrying in a variety of gaudy and unsuitable luggage. Nat stared in some horror at the galaxy of zip-fasteners, plaid material and imitation light-weight pigskin, but more in terror of what they represented than their actual appearance.

"Yes," she stated unnecessarily, as the doorman withdrew some yards with a discreet cough, "I've come. I haven't slept a wink all night, thinking over what you said. So here I am."

"That's fine!" Nat smiled brightly, acting as ever, on impulse. He examined closely her charming, upturned face, full of trust. It is always difficult to read accurately the thoughts of a woman who gives her body generously but has nothing else to offer. Did she mean she had decided to return to Ernest or . . . ?

"Where can we talk?" she asked, looking round.

"Out in the car is the safer place."

"Shall I bring out the luggage?" the doorman asked officiously.

Yes, of course. Nat raised the lid of the boot whilst the porter piled the luggage into its vast interior. Of course, it was the only way.

"Listen—" she grasped his arm with warm strong fingers, when they were inside the car—"the police have been round this morning. Doxie wasn't injured, like you said. He's been discharged from hospital this morning and he's round at the police station now. They came to tell me. There's going to be a lot of trouble about last night's affair; over the insurance, see? Doxie's making all kinds of wild statements about you and the police'll be coming round here to get your side of the story."

"That's all right. Everything is perfectly straightforward as far as I'm concerned."

"I guess so, but you was an eye-witness of the accident; the insurance people will want your story too."

"Is that all?"

"Look," she said nervously. "Don't waste time. Let's beat it. Doxie's going to half kill you if he sees you. He says he'll give you the biggest thrashing of your life, that you planned the race and all the rest of it. He's reckless, that one, he doesn't give a fig for going to gaol for a few weeks for assault; it gives his insides a bit of a rest from fire-eating. He always comes out feeling better. It'll hurt if he gets at you, believe you me!"

"I'm sure it will," Nat said, uneasily feeling his sore ribs.

"It's this bloomin' great car," she complained, "so conspicuous, be seen all over the place."

Nat thought. He thought about the new modern house in Putney in its garden of rhododendrons. He saw Easter sitting by the log fire in her charming sitting-room; pale and withdrawn and lonely, awaiting his return. Waiting . . . perhaps reading one of her innumerable rag mags to pass away the time, perhaps idly turning on the radiogram; listening for the door bell, listening for the telephone and jumping nervously at the sound of either. Easter.

He saw the outline of a diabolical plan. A plan of which the details must be filled in by circumstance, but nonetheless . . . devilish.

"Just one sec," he said. "I'll get my bag and pay my bill and I'll be with you."

"All right, dear," she agreed cheerfully, following him back to the hotel, "but give me time to brighten myself up in the 'Ladies.'"

CHAPTER XI

After paying his bill, Nat handed the receptionist a slip of paper on which he had written: N. Sapperton, 2 Silverdale, Putney, S.W.

"Look," he said, "the police will be here today about that accident along at the fun fair last night; I was an eyewitness. But I've got to rush back to London and they'll have to get in touch with me there. Give them this address, will you? Now don't lose it; if they try to get hold of me through the registration number of my car they'll find it's in another name and address. But don't panic, there's a good girl. Everything's okey dokey!" Wishing very much that it were, Nat gave her one of his most charming smiles and departed.

With deep interest Nat watched Valentine Millage step into the car while the doorman held the door open for her; she settled herself with the ease of a regular Rolls traveller, giving the doorman a curt nod. His face was a study.

So that, Nat thought, as they slid away from the Empire Hotel, and from Liverton-upon-Sands, is how she slips out of the lives of her lovers, without a backward look. *Le roi est mort, vive le roi . . .*

Ernest Millage, Doxie Lee . . . and York Cragg? Did she leave York or did he leave her? Seen in the whole, Valentine was an unlikely mistress for York; for one thing, she did not dress well and York had been fussy about women's clothes. In the arms, however, she was better than most, and possibly York never saw her dressed. That, in crude fact, was the only way in which Nat could see York in love with Valentine, and he sympathized. How secret was York's secret life and how bitterly unfair it was that it had to be exposed in all its cheapness. And yet, if a man knew that his most foolish peccadillo would be laid open to universal judgement after his death, would it make him any more careful? Was it, perhaps, worth it?

"You're very quiet, dear," Valentine obs   "I'm thinking about penny for them."

"I'm thinking about York Cragg." Perhaps it was unwise to mention his name when he was driving and therefore unable to observe the result.

"Who's he, when he's at home?"

The edges of Nat's teeth felt as uncomfortable as though someone had scraped the blade of a knife against china.

"He was the son of a very old friend. He's dead."

"Tt . . . tt . . . tt."

Nat drew to the side of the road and stopped the car rather hurriedly. He turned to Valentine, looking at her directly and with a serious face.

"York Cragg," he said clearly and slowly, "the son of Sir Jason Cragg, the shipping magnate." Had she, in fact, gone slightly red? She had certainly not paled. Perhaps it was his own behaviour which was embarrassing her.

Nat re-started the car. She was by way of being an actress, he must remember. He also reminded himself that she could not have known York under an assumed name; he could see now the actressy scribble at the bottom of her photograph: "To my darling York . . ."

"You are acting queer," she remarked. "What's up? Getting cold feet, are you? Worrying about the wife and kiddies?"

"No. They are the last thing I am worrying about. My wife is in Sweden for two months' holiday with her parents. The children are with her. And, by the way, I love my wife."

"Why aren't you with her, then?"

"Business," he said shortly.

"Oh, you businessmen! You beat me!"

"We don't, that's the trouble!"

She giggled. "Where are we off to now?"

"To London. It is Saturday, by the way. Haven't you let down Doxie Lee's act rather badly?"

"He'll get someone to do my job, never fear. I've left the clothes and the wig and all at the Pavilion; he'll get one of the other girls for today's performances, anyway."

"What would have happened if he'd been badly hurt last night? What would Mr. Wulfie Lyon have had to say?"

She shrugged. "There's a notice in the programme that the management aren't responsible for anyone failing to go on."

"I always thought 'the show must go on' was the most important thing in an actor's life."

"Well, dear, it's not quite the same in this sort of show."

"I see. Then Doxie Lee, the Human Candelabra, can simply walk out, can he?"

"It's not as easy as that. We're playing Huddersfield next week; Doxie'll have to get himself fixed up with someone before Monday."

"You know damn well he won't! He'll be after you, Valentine."

"What would be the use? He doesn't even know your name. And I've got no address at the moment, so how can he find me? Besides, the van's smashed up."

"There are always trains to London."

She was quiet for a long time and then she said: "He'd kill me, you know. Not that he loves me all that much, it's just his temperment. He's a real gipsy and gipsy women are faithful; he gave me a long jaw about that when he took me on. I was as good as a wife, he said. It was after I'd left Ernest and was on the road with Doxie he came up with all that. Quite shook up, I was."

"You don't give yourself time to think, do you? Well, I sympathize, I'm rather like that myself."

"It was a bit of a school kid he had helping him after his wife died. There was nothing whatever between them; she was one of these stage-struck kids. He sent her home to her mum when he caught up with me." She was quiet again for some time. "Yes," she went on gloomily, "gipsies are, what do you call it, mono . . . mono what's its."

"Monogamists. Married to only one at a time."

She nodded. "That's right. Regular old-fashioned. I took no notice," she said comfortably. "I thought, when I've had enough of Doxie, I thought, that'll be it."

I bet you did, Nat agreed.

"Well, the world's a big place, he'll have a job finding me, unless he traces us through your car number! This bloomin' car!"

"You could hardly be more conspicuous if you had ridden off on a white charger."

After which sobering thought they drove for many miles in silence.

Nat was pleased that he was able to pick out his own patient way, down, as he called it, through the rural heart of England, after his years abroad. They stopped for lunch at an excellent hotel at Bake-well in Derbyshire.

Though he had no cocktails himself he gave her two martinis before the wine which they had with lunch, and when he had got her in what he considered to be the right state of mind he said: "I expect you'll be very surprised to hear that I'm going to put you into an hotel tonight. Don't worry, I'll pay the bill but I won't be there myself. There are certain things to be attended to. It isn't that I don't want to sleep with you but you'll be surprised to hear that there are more pressing things I have to do."

"I'm not fussy."

No, you're not, he thought. Very far from it.

"I trust you absolutely!"

You would!

"I know a gentleman when I see one."

"I'm not impressed with your judgement, all the same. Your husband is a good little chap; you made a big mistake walking out on him."

Her face took on a curiously puffy, almost stupid look.

"Come on, out with it. You may as well tell me the lot!"

"I don't know how much you know Ernest. Look," she said, suddenly and somewhat retardedly anxious. "If Ernest sent you up to Liverton to get me to go back to him, this wouldn't be quite the way he'd think of your doing it, would it?"

"It was entirely your own idea that Ernest sent me. At least you thought Ernest cared for you enough to do something of the kind. You live for the moment, don't you, Val? What went before, what comes after . . . you couldn't care less . . . could you?" He put his hand affectionately over hers. "But seriously, Ernest has a case. He took you on as he found you, and I bet that wasn't exactly as a virgin, was it? I mean, to put it mildly. He took you on, for better, for worse. And then, because life isn't madly exciting, you pack your bags and walk out. I'm sorry for Ernest. I'm on his side, if you want to know."

"Poor Ernest," she mused, "and he puts his savings into tracing me. Shows he's keen. Oh, it's such a mix-up."

"You may as well spill it all to your old uncle. I'm sure to find out sooner or later, so you may as well tell me now."

Silence. Such beautiful eyes, he thought; with so little behind them, how is it they have any expression at all? Or had they? Was it not simply the way they were made up?

"What was it about Ernest? Is he a pervert, or what?"

"A what?" she gobbled innocently. "No, dear. It was his mum."

And so the trite little story came out, the perfect example of the letter asking the advice of "Uncle Nat" in *Women Only:* how to deal with the over-possessive mother-in-law.

As she became more and more emotional, Nat looked nervously round at his fellow lunchers, most of whom were now on the point of departure. "She hates me; for all her smarmy welcome, she meant to get me away from Ernest right from the start. And she's not one you can have a real set-to with; she thinks herself a bit upper-class and she's sarcastic and mean . . . Oh, she's mean! Every evening, on his way home from work, Ernest went in to see her and then home to me with the things that woman had said to him against me written all over his face!"

She wept.

What a very, very rum thing, Nat thought, if she didn't care so very much about Ernest, she cared passionately about her marriage.

"Well, strike a light!" he exclaimed flippantly, but he was moved.

CHAPTER XII

Easter went on living her life: she made a fourth at bridge after dining with the Ramsgates; she lunched the following day with Jill at Scheherazade; she went to a movie in the afternoon; she had her hair done and a manicure at her hairdresser in Dover Street; she went to an art exhibition in Bruton Street. On the Saturday morning she shopped in her car, in Putney High Street. It was dull buying weekend food for one; she bought a small roasting fowl, fruit, bread, a walnut cake. She bought an armful of the newest glossy magazines. She ordered sherry and some half bottles of white wine. She drove back home. She cleaned the car; she dug in the garden; she toasted herself crumpets for tea; she listened to Elvis Presley on the gramophone; she telephoned to Jill; she did a little ironing on the kitchen table.

She made up the sitting room fire and lay on the sofa reading her magazines; she slept a little; she got up to prepare her supper. She brought her supper into the living room and ate it upon the low table by the fire. She sat for a long time, thinking. She cleared away and washed up the supper things. She returned to the sitting room and, turning on the gramophone again, she danced a little, by herself. She turned on the radio and lay on the sofa, one foot swinging, listening to the Saturday night programme. She went upstairs to her bedroom, drew the curtains, turned on the electric fire, changed into a dressing-gown and came downstairs again. She went into the kitchen to make herself a hot drink. As she stood at the sink, mixing the Horlicks, she moved aside the curtain, out of sheer habit, and looked up at the window in the block of flats.

There was a light!

The shock of seeing the window lighted again, at last, after looking so many times, caused her almost to drop the cup and spoon. She looked at the clock—eleven!

She made her hot drink and returned to the living room where, suddenly, the telephone had taken on a presence; impersonal, it was very much there, black and crouching and full of foreboding. As she sipped her hot drink she stared at it over the rim of her cup.

Everything that she may have been going to say to Mr. Sapperton, né Wainwright, in her earlier fury and bewilderment, had now deserted her. Anger equipped one with ability; in anger one could act constructively, or the reverse. But, at least, one could act. Without it, one could be left wondering miserably what to do, what to say; whether, indeed, to do or to say anything.

Easter clasped her arms round her knees and, sitting on the floor beside the dying fire, she rocked herself slightly to and fro and the telephone leered at her across the hearth in the gentle light from the lamps.

At one o'clock she rose, stiff and chilly, and returned to the kitchen. The light was out in the bedroom. So, for the moment, the question was shelved, there was nothing she need do. Easter crept thankfully to bed.

CHAPTER XIII

Sunday morning has a special character of its own; Easter lay in bed and enjoyed it. York was always fearfully active on a Sunday morning; he would disappear into the boiler room and spend much time working out oil consumption and testing the thermostat; he would potter about with a spanner, tightening things up; he would oil hinges and stop dripping taps. Before lunch they would have friends in for tumblers of Black Velvet and in the early evening, if they were not going out to other friends, they would drive to the West End to see a movie and have a late supper at a restaurant.

Easter lay luxuriously with her creamy arms behind her head and enjoyed doing nothing. How long would it be before Nat came, she wondered? After the fierce frustration of not being able to see him at once, she felt a comfortable patience; he could take his time.

He came at teatime; Easter's sitting-room was flooded with sunlight and heavy with the scent of hyacinths. "Darling Easter," he said, after the conventional greetings. "Will you ever forgive me? I could not have let you know I was going. You'd never have put up with it, or, I should say, there'd have had to be a lot of explanation which, at that time, I was not prepared to give. May I have a piece of this delicious-looking walnut cake?"

She went for another cup and saucer and Nat sat down; he was tired.

"I'm going to tell you all about it, everything. My God!" he exclaimed. "Your good husband let himself in for something over that dame."

Her face tightened. "I'll never forgive you if you've been meddling in that affair."

"Of course you'll forgive me. I may as well tell you that the Craggs were my friends as well as being your husband and father-in-law. They were my good friends. I hate to mention my shock and wretchedness when your own must have been so much greater, but, nevertheless, their deaths were a terrible shock."

"What was the point in keeping your name secret? What was the idea in getting a flat overlooking this house? To spy on me?"

"It was my method, that's all. I wanted to get to know you. I'd heard a lot about you and I didn't want to crash in as a ready-made friend of yours. As it happens, that flat belongs to a chap in the FO and I heard by the grapevine that he wanted to let it for two years, as he's been posted to Bogotà. A married couple I happen to know have taken it, but they agreed to let me have it for a few weeks while they're on holiday in Juan. Simple."

"But why the assumed name?"

"I see." Nat was thoughtful. "The Ramsgates. I knew it was bound to come out, just as the Ramsgates, one day, would certainly walk in here. But as it happens it is not an assumed name. Ian Nathaniel Sapperton Wainwright . . . that's me. Nathaniel after a Lancashire grandfather who left me some shares for it, and Sapperton was my mother's name. Still simple, isn't it?"

"I still don't see the point," Easter said coldly.

"Don't try to, just accept it. I'm one of whom my mother dotingly said: 'Boys will be boys.' Madcap Ian, the pickled schoolboy, one of those Englishmen who never grow up, if you like. York and Jason would be among the first to appreciate the fun I'm having."

Easter was giving him some curious looks, almost as though she suspected him of being not quite sane.

"Only I'm beginning to wonder," Nat went on, "whether I know anything about my friend York. His amours are unlikely in the extreme."

"You're absolutely exasperating," Easter exclaimed, her voice only just avoiding shrillness.

"It is now that things become far from simple," Nat said, finishing his tea and replacing the cup and saucer carefully on the tray. "I have managed to run his Valentine, or Mr. Millage's Mrs. Millage, to earth. She has, in fact, flung herself upon my breast; in other words, got herself into my hair. She is living, or was until yesterday, with a real live (live is the word, he's probably lousy) gipsy, Doxie Lee, or Big Chief, the Human Candelabra. A crazy-mixed-up gipsy." Nat paused. "Or is he? And whether this gipsy did or did not murder first York, out of jealousy, and then Jason, because he Knew Too Much, is a simple question of dates. *Where* he was and *when*. And it's so easy—the police are busy on that now—it's so easy to find out where a Human Candelabra is, and when; specially when he goes about in a fearfully conspicuous yellow-painted van with his name in large letters on the side. By tonight the police will know just where he was billed on the night York was killed, and ditto Jason. If he was playing at Brixton, for instance, he could have done it. But if it was Tynemouth, or Swansea . . . not."

Easter was standing in front of the fire, one arm along the chimneypiece, her head bent towards the fire and her hair falling across her face. "I see."

"I think there's a very big chance that he did it, Easter. He's the sort of person who becomes heavily involved."

"In what way?"

"In life, I mean. Thoroughly old-fashioned. He lives his life right up to the brim and he feels things so passionately that you can sense his oscillations a mile off. Probably it's partly indigestion. The lining of his stomach is burnt to ribbons, it gives him hell."

"You're mad!"

"You can see him for yourself. He'll probably be here tonight and you'll meet him. The police are also going to be here, Easter, dear. I hope you don't mind."

"Not at all," Easter returned, feebly sarcastic. "I'll have coffee and sandwiches ready."

"It will be quite a party," Nat said thoughtfully. "But I may be all wrong. Never having met a gipsy before, I may have got him wrong. He may *not* be arriving at Euston this afternoon and be coming straight here to 'knock my block off.' On the other hand, if I have got him correctly typed, he will. With your permission I am also going to fetch Valentine herself."

Easter put her hand to her long slim throat. "Oh, Nat!"

Nat was serious now. "It's horrible for you, darling," he said, standing up beside her and putting his arm round her. "But there's got to be a show-down. It's the only way. If we can *show* the police who murdered the Craggs it's a lot better than simply telling them what we think."

He looked round. "We must have them in this room. Do you think we could have that Spanish leather screen you've got in the dining-room, across that corner? We can put the inspector and his mate behind it."

Easter crumpled down on to the hearth. "Are we going to have a rough-house?"

"Not for long, if at all. There are going to be police cars in Putney tonight, on the look out for Doxie Lee. You see, he *may* not come to the house."

"You said he would."

"I said I *thought* he would. I think he'll come after me because he thinks I've stolen his girl, which, for the sake of argument, I have. Almost certainly his first act on Saturday morning would be to go to my hotel in Liverton-upon-Sands, so I left this address there for him. He couldn't come yesterday as he was playing Liverton, but he could come today, by a slowish Sunday train from the North. When he sees the address Silverdale Number 2, he'll know that I know a lot more than I should. He won't be able to rest or sleep until he's spoken to me and he knows exactly how much I know. And, you know, that old saw about the dog and its vomit isn't altogether an empty cliché. The place where they murdered has an irresistible attraction for some murderers; they've got a compulsion to go back and look at the place where they did it. He's had two good murders, good successful murders, right here. And third time lucky . . ." Easter was sitting on the sofa now, her eyes closed, her head back, her face a deathly white.

"Do I have to be here?" she asked, through a dry mouth.

He used whisky and kindness and a few kisses before he got her back to normal. He made up the fire and he rubbed her cold hands and kissed her cold face. The sun had left the room and now a chilly spring light was filling it. He lighted the lamps and cleared away the tea things and carried in the embossed screen.

"That was one of Jason's wedding presents to us," Easter murmured as she watched him arranging it across the corner beside the far window. "It won't be damaged, will it?"

"I hope not." Nat looked at the clock and at his watch. "Doxie can't possibly be here before six. I think he'll wait till dusk, somehow. He'll want a meal when he arrives at Euston, too. If he has murder on his mind, he'll wait until it's dark. Blast that daylight saving hour."

He sat down again beside Easter and took her hand.

"But my best work," he said, "has been on Ernest Millage. I'd make a fine patcher-up of bust marriages. I spent the morning with Ernest Millage pointing out to him the folly of his ways, the folly, that is, of letting his mother have such an influence over him. I've cracked up his Valentine so that he can hardly wait to get her back and start afresh. I haven't lost sight of the idea that he might possibly be a murderer. A simple character on the surface, there are those who would say that he was a far more likely murderer than my flamboyant Doxie. We shall see. We are creating a situation full of possibilities for collisions of temperament. He may give himself away under the stress of emotion. If he does the police will be there to witness it."

"Where is this Valentine now?"

"She spent the morning in a respectable hotel, the most respectable she has ever stayed in, in Bloomsbury. After my interview in Finchley with Ernest Millage we, that is, Valentine and myself, lunched together in town, and now she is here."

"Here?"

"Resting in my flat," Nat said, very slightly smug. "I shall ring through and tell her to come when I want her. She knows exactly where to come." Nat cleared his throat. "Valentine and I understand each other perfectly."

"How nice," Easter remarked coldly.

"Valentine," Nat stated sententiously, "has her points." And in order to dissipate any ill-feeling, he took Easter in his arms and buried his face in her sweet-smelling hair.

"Why do you lie to me, Nat? What was the point in telling me that you were divorced?"

"It is perfectly true. My first wife divorced me, our marriage was a flop. Never heard of a man marrying again?"

"Do you love your Swedish wife?"

"Very, very much."

"Then why do you want to maul me about?"

Nathaniel was not often shocked, but he was shocked now. As he told his wife later his blood ran cold. He disentangled himself and moved across the sofa.

"Because you're a pretty girl."

"Do you kiss every pretty girl you meet?"

"Nothing like it," Nat replied cheerfully, "but that doesn't mean I don't want to. I thought you enjoyed it."

"Well, I don't," Easter returned curtly.

"You mean," Nat said nastily, "you don't if it's not going to lead anywhere." He thought for a minute. "And I don't mean to bed; I mean to the altar, to the registry office." He looked at her thoughtfully. "You're respectable, aren't you, Easter?"

"I'm not a tart, if that's what you mean."

"A nice respectable girl," Nat said dreamily. At last light was dawning, at last he was beginning to understand Easter. At last he was beginning to see the marriage of his friend York and Easter in the whole. It needed a big effort of imagination, but he could now see York's thoughts turning to his old love, his thoroughly unsuitable, third-rate, superficial, but nevertheless warm-hearted Valentine. He had a glimmer of understanding as to why York could not bring himself to tear up her photograph. Only a glimmer.

CHAPTER XIV

If the inspector and his assistant had accepted drinks the waiting period might have been easier. But the inspector was wondering if some practical joke were being played upon him, and, it being a Sunday evening, he was in no mood to be trifled with and he showed it.

His men were deployed among the dark bushes of Silverdale, some of which were now breaking into gaudy flower, the whole division was on the alert and a cordon could be thrown round the house within a few seconds. It was nerve-racking to sit in the sitting room of the murder house, making desultory conversation and waiting for something which might not happen.

"If Millage comes too soon," Nat said nervously, "he'll have to go into the dining room, and wait, as though waiting his turn at the dentist's. I'd better attend to the front door, Easter. And, Inspector, will you both disappear behind the screen when the bell rings? Oh hell!" Nat exclaimed. "I'm beginning to wonder now whether I haven't been a complete fool and this extraordinary gipsy chap hasn't upset my judgement."

The inspector is his well-cut light tweed overcoat was as non-committal as someone who had come to talk about an insurance policy. There was nothing whatever in his manner to show whether he had, or had not, discovered anything significant about Doxie Lee's recent movements. Nat guessed he was probably longing to be back home at his own fireside.

After an hour or so Nat began to sweat with anxiety. Easter sat in a corner of the sofa, making no attempt at conversation, idly turning over the pages of a magazine she must now know by heart. The inspector and his assistant sat, simply sat, not even smoking, taking up space and breathing air but otherwise adding nothing to the gathering. Nat wandered about, in and out, fidgeting with the curtains, attending to the fire and finally, almost defiantly, mixing himself a scotch-on-the-rocks. And another. And almost another, but there was a noise outside like a helicopter arriving in the driveway.

Doxie Lee had come, but by this time Nat's nervous tension was such that he could not produce a smile or a quip; he went, stiffly unsmiling, to the front door.

Yes, Doxie Lee had arrived, but not the way Nat had expected. One of the comedians, whose face Nat vaguely remembered as the drunken Irishman, had brought him in his ancient but distinguished Jaguar. In spite of Sunday's licensing hours they had both had plenty to drink. Both were noisy, blustering and pugnacious and, though they were clearly out for trouble, Nat felt some relief; it was so obviously not the arrival of a man intent upon murder.

The first struggle was to get Doxie to leave his friend outside in the car. Why not get his friend to come back for him later on, Nat suggested. But no, that wouldn't do. He was the only friend Doxie had left in this hard, cold world, he must come in too. Besides, he might come in useful when it came to getting Valentine out, because get Valentine they would, that's what they'd come for. Doxie, pressed, refused to cross the threshold unless his friend came too so he, Nat, could darn well go and tell that girl to pack her traps and come, otherwise they would wreck the place, and when he said wreck, he meant wreck.

"And make it snappy," he roared. "We've been on the go since mid-day and we're driving back to Huddersfield tonight with the woman, so we've no time to stand here jawing. Minnehaha'll be playing Huddersfield tomorrow night—or else."

"Those sort of tactics don't work these days," Nat tried to argue, with an uncomfortable feeling that they did. "She doesn't want to come back to you."

"She's thrown in her lot with me and it's me she'll stick with, you—you . . ." Doxie thrust his face up, and Nat felt his odoriferous breath upon his own.

"Watch out now, watch out," came the shrill voice of his friend who had now retreated into his car in an excess of caution.

Doxie knew better now than to start a fight with Nat. He pushed impatiently past him, through the hall and into the lighted sitting room where Easter sat, the image of domestic felicity, beside the fire. Nat shut the front door and followed him in.

"Now, Mr. Lee," he said briskly, "shall we let bygones be bygones?

This is Mrs. Cragg, Mrs. York Cragg, Mr. Doxie Lee, Easter. How about a drink? Horse's neck? I'm having scotch-on-the-rocks myself."

If this were the room in which he had committed murder, he seemed hardly interested. Merely uncomfortable. He accepted a drink with alacrity, his manner subtly altered in the presence of the lady. He looked like a cart-horse finding itself in the paddock at Ascot.

He snatched off his cloth cap, he begged pardon, he fumbled with his spotted made-up bow-tie, he cleared his throat, he glared angrily at Nat.

"Let me explain," Nat said, when he had supplied him with a tumbler of brandy and ginger ale. And in a kindly manner, like a family doctor explaining the situation to the relatives, he accounted for his subversive presence in Liverton-upon-Sands by saying that Ernest Millage had sent him to try to get his wife back, that he had persuaded her to return to her husband and that they were on the point of being reunited. How much Doxie Lee believed him was neither here nor there.

Nat was thinking, with sinking heart: this is the most awful anticlimax; I've made the most shocking fool of myself. For whereas he had arranged everything so that Doxie Lee would prove himself to be the murderer, here he was, showing quite clearly that he was not.

He sat, with bowed head, sipping daintily at his drink, more in sorrow now than in anger.

Nat looked at his watch; he had told Millage to arrive "about seven-thirty" and it was now after that. "Would you like Valentine herself to confirm what I've told you?" he asked.

Yes, he would.

Nat dialled. "She'll be here in less than five minutes," he said.

And then Ernest Millage arrived and the sight of him caused Doxie to become as intractable as a bull.

Millage was still aggressively teetotal; he stood uncomfortably beside the door, twisting his hat round and round. He seemed unable to look directly at the gipsy but darted glances at him from time to time. Doxie stared angrily at the little man, muttering in an audible voice subversive remarks like: "What the bloomin' hell does she see in him? Of all the . . . !"

Then Valentine arrived. She took her cue from Nat and with the movement of a homing bird and a cry of the Millage to its mate, she flew into her husband's arms. She played it perfectly.

Then, suddenly, everything became extremely confused. Everyone was talking at once and no one was listening to anybody else. Easter sat in the corner of the sofa, looking shrivelled, the magazine still open across her knees. She was the only one who said nothing.

And then the front door bell rang. For a moment Nat could not believe it; had he heard it? It rang again. He ran his fingers distractedly through his hair. It would be Doxie's friend getting impatient.

As if he hadn't enough on hand!

But it was not Doxie's friend. He was waiting in the car, ostentatiously keeping out of trouble's way.

It was a shortish, fair-haired woman dressed in a neat grey coat and skirt, with trim ankles and tidy feet and a worried expression on her face.

"Could I speak to Mrs. Cragg, please?"

A lady-help? A dressmaker?

"I'm afraid she's busy at the moment." This was upheld by the sound of angry voices coming from the half-open door of the sitting-room.

"Can I give her a message?"

"Who are you?"

"I'm a friend of the Cragg family. I. N. S. Wainwright by name."

"A friend of Sir Jason Cragg?"

"Yes. I'm afraid . . . we're awfully busy at the moment, Mrs. . . . er . . ."

"Bacon is my name. I would like to speak to you but I can see you're busy. I've written down my name, in case I couldn't talk to anyone. And I've written down what I've come about." She dug about in her handbag and brought out a folded sheet of paper. "Best have these things in black and white. You see, sir, my husband is a constable in the Metropolitan Police, Putney Division. He's been telling me about this Cragg case and I bin thinking. He's no idea I'm doing this and it would make things very awkward if he knew. So would you mind . . . that is . . . if you could . . ."

"The reward!" Nat exclaimed impatiently. It sounded now as though at any moment fighting would break out behind him.

"Certainly, Mrs. Bacon, I'll hand it to the right quarter."

"No, no!" she exclaimed. "That's why I brought it here, to show to young Mrs. Cragg. Not to the right quarter, please, Mr. Wainwright. It's only an idea I had. I don't mind making a fool of myself but I don't want to make a fool of my Sam. I'd never forgive myself if it got out I'd done this. Sam thinks I'm seeing my mum tonight, and I'm off there now . . . Oh, dear, whatever is happening?"

"You'd better move or you'll be mixed up in another murder," Nat hissed, thrusting the note into his pocket.

Mrs. Bacon didn't need to be told twice. She rounded the car parked in the drive and sped out of sight.

So Nat's carefully planned locality of events was used for a common brawl such as could take place outside any public house any Sunday night with the police taking names and addresses and charging both the men to appear at Putney Police Court the following morning.

Doxie shouted a great deal, pointing out that he was billed to appear in Huddersfield the following night and the inspector telling him that he could still do so and Ernest Millage bleating plaintively that he was a teetotaller and had nothing to do with the brawling, that Doxie was an enticer and a so-and-so.

Valentine wrung her hands in the tradition of a woman for whom men are fighting and Easter wrung her hands in anxiety about her wallpaper and the paint round the door.

Finally Doxie flung off angrily with his now considerably sobered friend.

Valentine and Ernest Millage walked away, each supporting the other, to an hotel where Ernest had arranged to stay until he could find somewhere, other than with his mother, for them to live.

The CID were the last to leave, more in sorrow than in anger. The inspector's manner was only faintly reproachful.

CHAPTER XV

Nat slumped in an armchair and held his head in his hands. The fire had died down; the silence in the room after the recent noise was almost palpable.

"Honestly," Easter said at last, "I don't know what to make of you. As the only Cragg left I ought to be angry with you. You come crashing in, behaving like some ridiculous amateur detective, under a footling alias, and rip poor York's wretched little private life to shreds. And where does it get you? Exactly nowhere. You've simply made a fool of yourself, and of everybody else."

"Yes," Nat agreed, "I have made a fool of myself, you're right. But not just for amusement, Easter. Listen, the night before Jason died, we dined at his club; I'd just got back from the Middle East and hadn't seen either of the Craggs for a couple of years. Naturally I'd been terribly shocked to hear of York's death and, of course, poor Jason couldn't talk about anything else. Do you blame him? He talked about York's whole life and upbringing, his University career, his business career, his bachelor life, his marriage, you, yes, you at length, and finally, when dinner was over and we were back at his flat in Arlington Street and having a last drink, he took out the photograph of 'Mavourneen.' He told me about having had copies made and the steps he had taken to trace her and how he'd actually seen the husband that afternoon. He told me about having interviewed the pathologist's assistant and got out of him that a woman could have done the stabbing. In short, he told me everything that was in his mind, and we sat up late discussing the whole thing, with the photograph propped up on the chimneypiece in front of us."

Nat got up and walked restlessly about the room.

"Well, twenty-four hours later he was dead! It was like a nightmare, Easter. But you know . . . you must know how ghastly the shock was. Probably a lot less bad for me than for you. And once the shock was over, I started wondering . . . what must I do? Well, I couldn't simply go to the police with everything Jason and I had talked over. There was nothing definite, nothing to go on. It was all just talk and . . . supposition . . . surmise . . . guesswork. But all the same, I couldn't leave things like that. I joined my wife and the children in Sweden for a few days and talked everything over with her. We decided that I must go further into things so I left them there with my wife's parents, having rather a good holiday, and I came back here and started snooping. I had luck to begin with, getting the flat in Nero Court. That was a marvellous bit of luck. But if I hadn't done that I should have thought of some other way of getting to know you, probably through the Ramsgates. Buying Jason's old car had nothing to do with it; I had always coveted the dear old thing. I should have tried to buy that anyway. So now you know everything, Easter. It doesn't seem so fantastic and silly now, does it?"

"Then where do we go from here?"

"That's just it. Nowhere, as far as I can see. Dead end. It could be a dismissed employee, someone with a grudge, an unsuspected lunatic, somebody that no one other than Jason and York know anything about."

Easter got up and shook herself, like a little crumpled cat.

"Let's have some supper," she said. "All those awful people about, all that quarrelling. Ugh, it's been beastly! I'm sure the inspector was annoyed, Nat."

"I'm sure he was. But I'm not worried about that."

Nat stared broodingly at the dying fire. Easter started to get supper. She put the low table near the fire, arranged the chairs beside it and went into the kitchen, where Nat could hear her rattling plates and dishes.

He remembered Mrs. Bacon and took the folded sheet of paper out of his pocket.

He read:

Evidence at the inquest of Sir Jason Cragg

Police Constable No. . . . Metropolitan Police, Vine Street Division, said in evidence that he had seen and talked to Sir Jason Cragg who had been at the Ritz Arches at about 6.10 p.m., who had told him he was meeting "Someone" at 6.0 who had not turned up.

Porter in block of flats stated in evidence that Sir Jason Cragg had arranged to meet his daughter-in-law at 6.0; he, Sir Jason, had used his telephone to ring through to the house in Silverdale, Putney, to see if she was there. There had been no answer.

Mrs. Cragg said in her evidence that she had arranged to meet Sir Jason at *6.30* at the Ritz Arches.

Did Sir Jason arrange to meet *the murderer* in his car in Piccadilly at 6.0? Did he intend to drive to Putney with his daughter-in-law and *the murderer?* Did *the murderer* drive down to Putney with him and murder him when they entered the house? Where was Mrs. Cragg between 6 and 6:30?

Nat, his mind full of the recent happenings, did not grasp the significance at the first reading. He read it again.

"What a very curious thing," he said as Easter spread a lace-edged supper cloth on the low table. "Listen . . ." He read it to her.

"Who brought this?" she asked.

Nat told her. "But is it so, Easter? What time did you arrange to meet Jason?"

"Six-thirty."

"Are you sure?"

"Of course I'm sure."

"Couldn't you be mistaken?"

"I could, but I'm not."

"What exactly did you do in the afternoon?"

"Jill and I had lunch and went to a movie."

"Where?"

"At the Curzon."

"Did you have tea after?"

"No . . . yes . . . no . . . I mean . . ."

"It is only a very few minutes' walk from the Curzon cinema to the Ritz. What were you doing between the time the movie came out and meeting Jason? A good hour and a half."

"I told Jill I was meeting him . . ."

"Yes, but at what time?"

Her eyes were vagrant, roving round the room; she was trying to remember.

"Look, I'll ring through to Jill Ramsgate and ask her. She'll remind you."

"Wait . . . wait . . ." She was worried, thoughful. "I . . . we came out of the cinema at . . . about five . . . Jill was going to meet John at his club and they were dining with friends. I told her I was meeting Jason . . ."

"At six . . . or six-thirty?"

"Oh, what does it matter?"

"It does matter, Easter. Because it means that about half an hour of Jason's time is unaccounted for. He could have met anyone in that half-hour, anyone . . . who could, as Mrs. Bacon points out, have driven down to Putney *with him*. Do try and remember. It might be frightfully important. It's the tiny things that matter in a show like this."

"We came out of the cinema at five," Easter repeated woodenly.

"Yes. You said goodbye to Jill, and then what? An hour and a half before you had to meet Jason, at a point about three minutes' walk away . . . What did you do till six-thirty? If you could only remember it would help us, you know."

"I went into a coffee bar."

"Ah! Now we're getting somewhere. Which one?"

"Really, Nat. You're carrying this ridiculous detective stuff too far. As a matter of fact I don't remember the name; it was that coffee bar almost opposite the Curzon, in that street turning off Curzon Street up to Charles Street."

"You were there for an hour and a half, until a few minutes before half past six? Oh, Easter, are you sure? Look, I'll ring Jill, just to get everything straight."

"Wait . . ." She ran her hand across her now-furrowed brow. "Oh, Nat! That was an agonizing night. What happened afterwards put everything else out of my mind. I may have sat in the coffee bar for an hour and a half. I don't remember. Can't you understand how awful everything was? You've just told me what a shock you had over Jason's death. How do you think it was for me? I *found* him, lying there. I came into the house and *found* him." She buried her face in her hands for a moment. "And now you expect me to account for every moment before the beastly murder. Have a heart."

"I'm sorry, Easter. Believe me, I'm sorry. But I must get this thing straight. There's something here that isn't right somehow. I can't be satisfied until I've got it straight."

She looked at him sadly.

She went round the room restlessly. "There's a smell of people in here," she grumbled, "unclean people. That lousy gipsy stank of drink."

It was now quite dark outside. Easter threw up the sash of one of the windows and drew the curtains across. She drew all the curtains. "What a ghastly scene," she murmured, "if anyone had been looking in!" She looked at Nat again. He sat in the position of Rodin's "Penseur," his thoughts very far from her and his surroundings.

"An hour and a half," he muttered, "one and a half hours. Miss Blockley, Jason's secretary, would know what time he left the office. What time he had to meet you. Yes, Miss Blockley will know."

Easter went back into the kitchen where, on the table, was the tray already laid with cutlery, plates, glasses. She turned back and called, from the kitchen door: "Please make up the fire, Nat."

An uncarved cold roasted chicken stood on its dish on the table. She went slowly towards the table and thoughtfully opened the table drawer. She looked at her row of knives lying neatly in the drawer. She chose a steel knife, a French meat knife, wide at the hilt and narrowing at the point. There was no need to test it, she knew it was sharp. It was the sign of a good cook to keep efficiently sharp knives in her *batterie de cuisine*.

She put the knife on the tray among the table cutlery and carried the tray into the sitting room.

"An hour and a half," Nat was still muttering as he rose to make up the fire. With the tongs he reached for a piece of coal and put it on, then for another; supporting himself with his left hand on the edge of the chimneypiece he stretched out for a third lump.

"An hour and a half, but listen . . ." he turned slightly and as he did so the first blow misfired. Aimed at the back of his neck it sliced through the material of his jacket across the top of his shoulder, braking on the shoulder blade. The tongs clattered on to the hearth.

He caught hold of her and stared full into her face, her face of pleasure, of delight, of fiendish, unearthly gladness.

"So it was you." He forced her arms down into the position he had learned. The knife dropped on to the hearthrug. She laughed wildly. He had to use all his force to get her hands behind her back, but he succeeded, though waves of nausea were weakening him. When they both fell to the floor he was still within reach of the blessed telephone.

"You're hurting me, you're hurting me. You brute!" Kicking forward was no good, she tried kicking backwards, she could not see him now, he was behind her, putting every remaining scrap of strength into holding her with one hand whilst he dialled with the other.

They lay panting together on the floor, like two exhausted animals. "It's murder," Nat told the telephone, "at Two Silverdale. They'll have to ram the front door; no, a downstairs window is wide open! Hurry, for God's sake hurry!"

He dropped the receiver because he could no longer spare the hand to hold it. "You opened the window so that Doxie Lee could return, or Ernest Millage, or Valentine . . . or so that the police would think they had. Third time unlucky, though. How did you do the impossible? How did you kill Jason? Tell me, tell me . . ."

She was screaming with laughter now; he had never heard her laugh before. A blackness was stealing up and a dizziness was seizing him. Quickly . . . quickly . . .

، Nat looked at his own large hands clasping the tiny wrists with their four silver bracelets. He was pressing the bracelets into the skin. Her wrists were like small branches, but willow branches, the strongest, springiest wood known. Willow branches . . .

There was a great deal of darkness and very little reality left when they burst in between the heavy curtains.

"Here's your murderer, Inspector," she screamed. "He was going to kill me, but I was too quick for him. Look, there's the knife . . ."

Nat felt a stream as of warm milk flowing round his neck; there was blood on the pale hearthrug, and down below his sleeve blood poured over his hand and over Easter's small hands.

"I think not," he heard the inspector say, before he became unconscious, "I think not . . ."

CHAPTER XVI

It was three days before the inspector called at the private wing of St. Thomas's Hospital. Nat was lying in extreme comfort with the pleased look of one who has escaped death by millimetres.

"Well, Inspector, have you got everything tied up?"

The inspector looked a little grim. "What about you?"

"I'm sewn up; twenty-four blessed little stitches have been hemmed into me. It's hard to believe in the strength of those fairy-like wrists, unless you'd like to see my wound!"

"No, thanks," the inspector said hurriedly. "I'll believe anything you like to tell me about the strength in those tiny wrists!" He sat down beside the bed. "When do you think you'll be well enough for the police court proceedings?"

"A week, perhaps? You'll have to ask the house surgeon."

"Well—" the inspector looked weary—"we've got our statement. We always do, of course. The murderer's vanity always comes out over the statement. They're all proud of themselves, at heart, they like making their statement. It gives them no end of a kick. If they'd only keep their ruddy mouths shut it would be a lot better for them."

"How do you mean?"

"I mean, if they'd only refuse to make a statement until they were legally represented . . . it's always the same; when they do, finally, get a lawyer, he groans over the statement and they try to retract, say they want to make another statement, or say that the statement was made under duress. This dame said at first she wouldn't make a statement. Then she thought better of it. She asked for pen and paper and said she'd write it. Well, that didn't do at all. It read like pure fiction. She'd got a wonderful imagination."

"Funny; she always says she's got none."

"Believe me, it's marvellous. The imagination she's shown over the planning of the two murders! Just listen to this. That first murder, her husband; it seems it is quite true, he wasn't feeling well that night. It was the six months' anniversary of their wedding, you may remember, there was a small celebration. She says that at that time the marriage had never been consummated; she'd never been in bed with the husband because, her own words: 'she didn't want to,' she 'hated all that sort of thing.' When she got back from the theatre with her friends, and let herself into the house, she found her husband had been dosing himself with aspirin and rum, to keep off the flu he thought he was getting. According to her he 'started a row' downstairs in the kitchen, where he was boiling the kettle to make himself some more hot grog. He said that if she wouldn't go to bed with him their marriage was a failure, he was going to sue her for restitution and what was more, he wasn't going to spend another night under the roof. He said the position was undignified, he'd rather break up the whole thing, let the world see that his marriage was a failure, than continue to live with her in the circumstances. He went upstairs. She followed him, with the kitchen knife, and as he was getting his travelling-bag out of the wardrobe, she . . . well, you know the rest. After that she turned the central heating up as high as it would go, to keep the body reasonably warm, and went off to bed for a good night's sleep . . ."

"Surely she didn't write all this!"

"She started writing a kind of novelette, like a magazine story, leading up to it. Of course, I couldn't let her. I got everything out of her in one long stream, in the end. All in her own words, not drawn from her sentence by sentence by any means."

"I can tell you from experience," Nat put in, "it wasn't done in a fit of anger. It was done in the coldest of cold deliberation."

"I believe that. Wait, wait till you hear . . . she began to think, after that, began to be a bit afraid of all the investigation and so on. Afraid that someone might start to think. So what does she do? Provides a first-class red herring. She goes to that photograph shop on the corner of Brewer Street and Sparrow Lane, in Soho, where they sell photographs of stage people; know it? She goes there and buys that glossy photograph for four shillings and sixpence, writes her message on it, and slips it under the paper in her late husband's desk. There's imagination for you," the inspector said, almost proudly.

"She says she hadn't the slightest intention of murdering her father-in-law, but it seems in the end she 'had to.' Sir Jason wasn't content to leave things as they were, he insisted on finding out something about the photograph. Apparently actresses can go and have their photographs taken for a nominal sum, at a photographer's of that kind, on condition that the photographer can do what he likes with it. It is good publicity and they can have as many copies as they like for themselves at a low cost. Sir Jason put some thought, care and money into discovering who this woman in the photograph was; it was only a matter of time before he would find out that the hiding of the photograph where he found it was a trick. Everything about his son's death would have been, suddenly, only too clear. So she had to plan Sir Jason's death with some care."

"In that," Nat said, "She did the impossible. I can't think up the answer to that one."

"Can't you? It is so simple. The boot of that old Rolls-Royce car came in useful."

Nat remembered the joker at Liverton-upon-Sands who had got himself into the boot.

"But there were several things she had to do first," the inspector went on. "She had to buy plasters and break the cloakroom window, to make it look like forced entry; she had to buy a man's grey plastic mackintosh; she had to prepare the room for a nice little supper party for two; she had to loosen the heel of her shoe; she had to build up an alibi for herself in town. It was that alibi that let her down. It was rotten, rotten! She relied too much on her own perfection, on the fact that no one would ever suspect her. She said at the inquest on Sir Jason that she had arranged to meet him at six-thirty, but, in fact, she told him six, and that I have been able to confirm with the secretary. Between coming out of the cinema about five with Mrs. Ramsgate and parting from Mrs. Ramsgate, the young lady was very busy. She knew all about Sir Jason's little private car park in the city, and she used it for her own advantage. This murder grew out of existing circumstances, that's where it's so darn clever. She parted from Mrs. Ramsgate about five, casually, as people who meet frequently will. First she went to Green Park Station and bought herself a ticket to East Putney. Then she went to the city in a taxi, which she left somewhere near the Royal Exchange. Then she walked to the private car park. She knew damn well that Sir Jason locked his engine, but not necessarily the car itself, unless he had anything in it, an overcoat, a rug or something of the kind, that might be pinched. But in any case, the left-hand window was divided, you will know, so that a slight pressure of the arm would make it open outwards for hand signalling. She knew that by exerting pressure inwards on the chromium at the top of that slip window, on the outside, she could make it swing open outwards and could easily get her hand inside and unlock the door. As it happened she didn't need to; the car was unlocked. She took the T-shaped key out of the leather door pocket, unlocked the boot, put the key back into the pocket, *put on the grey plastic mackintosh* and got into the boot of the car, keeping the lid open a small fraction in order to have fresh air. She did all that in the dark. What a nerve, eh? Things could have gone very wrong. Sir Jason might have opened the boot for some reason. But he didn't. No, sir, he didn't. She says she knew he wouldn't, there wouldn't be any reason to. No, Sir Jason did exactly what she expected him to do. He arrived at the car park about twenty to six, climbed in, drove out, waited for her at the Ritz Arches, got worried about her non-appearance and drove down to Putney at top speed."

The inspector paused.

"Go on," Nat urged.

"It's so damned simple that I feel almost ashamed I didn't think of it myself. But it is all built on premise, that premise being that nobody was going to suspect *her*. Now that we know she's guilty, it seems impossible that we didn't. But the fact remains, we didn't. And we never should have. Well, Sir Jason arrived at Two Silverdale, in a minor panic. Jumps out of the car, opens the front door with the keys she knew he had, goes inside and looks round. Finds nothing wrong, comes out and turns out the headlights of the car, goes back into the house. Our heroine climbs stiffly out of the boot, runs round to the back yard, lets herself into the kitchen with the back-door key, picks up the knife she has left ready, the same knife that you know so well, and waits, concealed behind the back lobby door. She knows he's getting ice to fix a drink, and she waits, watching him from the darkness of the kitchen, until he makes up the fire in the sitting room. She's been successful with stabbing in the back before, she must keep to the pattern. She's kicked off her shoes, now she swoops in as he's making up the fire . . . you know the rest."

"Far from it."

"Very well . . . after that neat bit of butchery she steps out of the mackintosh, leaving it on the floor; she washes the knife in her own spotlessly clean sink, and puts it away in the kitchen drawer with the other knives. Leaving everything as she found it, she lets herself out of the back door, which she locks behind her, hares off to the main road, catches a bus to Putney Bridge, the stop *before* East Putney on the London side. She's already got a ticket from Green Park to East Putney in her purse. She attracts no attention at Putney Bridge Station, buying a ticket to Wimbledon which she destroys later. She steps out of the train at East Putney, along with other rush-hour commuters, *remembering* to wrench off the heel of her shoe so that she imprints herself upon the memory of the railway staff if ever it should come to a show-down, which, of course, it never would. But just in case . . . Incidentally, she's given up the ticket she bought at Green Park Station. Then into a taxi and up to Silverdale and the body found with the taxi-driver as a witness. And it all worked out exactly as per schedule. I think she thought that was positively her last murder. And it probably would have been if you hadn't come barging in."

"Oh, no! No . . . no . . . you're wrong there! It was Mrs. Constable Bacon, your Constable Bacon's missus. It was she who pointed the finger of doubt. I don't think," Nat said slowly, "I would ever, ever have suspected her if it hadn't been for Mrs. Bacon; and incidentally, Inspector, she must get that Five Thousand Pounds reward. And she deserves it, she's a woman of parts."

"I will get on to the Craggs' solicitor about that straight away. I'm delighted for Bacon and his missus to have that. Bacon is a good chap, though he lacks inspiration."

"His wife more than makes up for that."

"By the way, the family solicitor has been knocked practically out by all this. Mrs. Cragg asked him to represent her but when he'd heard a few of the facts he flatly refused. We've got another solicitor now, for her legal aid. He knows that all the Cragg money is at his disposal, he'll get the best counsel there is, Mr. L—, I have no doubt. It creates a very curious anomaly, doesn't it? Cragg money used to get her off!"

"But she won't get off!" Nat exclaimed, startled.

"I wouldn't like to say," the inspector murmured. "She'll make a lovely show in the witness box. The mourning widow, the sorrowing daughter-in-law."

The inspector paused, walking over to the window.

"And then there's always the vexed question of insanity. With all that money at the disposal of the defence they may decide to go all out for acquittal on the grounds of insanity and they'll probably get the best psychiatrist for their purpose. He'll stand up there in the witness box and declare she was a psychotic personality. Nobody knows exactly what that is but the magic words will make the jury sit up and take notice, letting the photographs of the stabbed men fall from their fingers."

He smiled a little wanly. "I've experienced it so often; I know the form. There'll be a long argument as to the exact definition of psychotic personality, of responsibility, and oblique references to the MacNaughton Rules, and the judge will look his wisest."

"But she's not 'unfit to plead,' nor anything like it!" Nat exclaimed.

"No, but what about all that laughter when she was having a go at you? And she's not shown one scrap of remorse. Nor fear of the consequences. Of course, they may decide not to go for the madness plea. They can wipe up her statement and lay stress on her first explanation, when we found her with the knife on the floor between you. You're a sex maniac, they can say, and the minute you were left alone with her you tried to rape her and, in self-defence, she snatched the knife from the supper tray and stabbed you."

But the inspector laughed at the expression on Nat's face.

"No, I'm pulling your leg; there's too much that goes before in this particular case. The defence will have to decide what line they are going to adopt after the charge is decided upon; she won't be charged with the attempted murder of you, but the murder, accomplished, of either her husband or Sir Jason Cragg and that will depend upon the evidence available. The weakness lies in the motive and you may be sure the defence will stress that. 'What motive had she?' Mr. L— will ask. 'Why kill her husband?' or 'Why kill her father-in-law?' The motive is wispy to say the least of it."

"You and I don't find it so, Inspector," Nat declared, "because we know her. She's a frigid woman all right; marvellously acquiescent up to a point and after that . . . nothing. She's out for material gain only. She didn't kill York because he was going to insist upon his conjugal rights . . . oh, no! She could have done that any time during the past six months. She killed him because he was going to leave her, and she found there was nothing she could do to stop him other than . . . what she did. She thought she'd got him and the house and her position as a married woman all tied up and when she found that he really meant to abandon her, and possibly to sue her for restitution, she killed him. There was no planning about that first murder; she did it and then relied upon her own integrity, her acting ability, her iron nerves and her imagination. She knew no one would suspect her, and no one did; did they now?"

"Quite frankly, I didn't."

"Nor anyone else."

"And Sir Jason was killed because he stuck his neck out."

"Yes. He couldn't leave bad alone. And I'm sure she enjoyed that, too. You know, I saw her face when she was attacking me. It is something I shall never forget; I hope I shall never be nearer to Hell. But I believe there is a deep psychological flaw there, shown by the undoubted fact that she liked doing it. Enjoyed it. And when she'd finished she was pleased and stimulated because she'd saved her face in the sight of the world, she was still the respectable and infinitely pathetic widow. If you want the psychological significance you'll have to go to Freud or some other 'investigator of the Id by the Odd.' "

CHAPTER XVII

Police Constable Bacon beamed at his wife over the top of *Huggett's Weekly Home Finder*. His manner resembled that of a husband who has just been informed that his wife has had triplets: he was proud, pleased and yet slightly puzzled and bewildered.

"When did you really start to suspect?"

"I've known all along," Mrs. Bacon lied. "Right from the start!"

"Fancy!" PC Bacon was thoughtful.

"Trust a woman's instinct."

"But you never even saw her! It was only what I told you. I've said all along what a nice little thing she was."

"Well, it just goes to show."

"Exactly what?"

"She was a bit too pathetic for my liking," she extemporized. "I thought and I thought. And when I read the report I couldn't believe my eyes. Half an hour out, I thought, and not a soul has noticed it! She's got them all eating out of her hand, I thought. Just like men: a pretty face and good measurements, that's all you think about."

"She's not all that beautiful," he argued, "but she was every inch a lady!"

THE END

WITCHROCK

BY

BILL KNOX

Published by special arrangement with Doubleday & Co., Inc.

PRELUDE

George MacKenzie came back to reality slowly, feeling sick and confused, not knowing where he was or how he'd got there. But his fingers told him that he was lying on cold, hard, strangely damp rock. He could hear the steady rhythm of breaking waves somewhere very near, and the air had a salty tang.

He stirred, giving a soft moan at the effort it cost him. The movement brought a raucous, indignant screech followed by a quick flapping of wings. Startled, he forced his eyes open and raised his head.

It was night. The moon was almost obscured by cloud but there was enough light to show the white shape of a large herring gull circling watchfully a few feet above him. He was lying on black, smooth-worn rock close to the sea and a lighthouse was flashing steadily somewhere out across the water.

A tall man but thin, with greying hair and a leathery skin, MacKenzie let his face fall against the cold rock again and lay still, breathing in short gasps while he began to remember.

It had been close to midnight, with the tide well on the ebb, and he'd taken his boat out into the Brannan Sound for a couple of hours of line-fishing.

Low tide and slack water was the best time for fishing in the Sound—and fishing has always been his favourite method of getting away from the rest of the world when he had to think his way through a problem.

From there, suddenly, he remembered the rest with a frightening clarity. The other, bigger boat that had loomed out of the night and come alongside. The two men who had jumped aboard, the gun that had been pointed at him, the flicker of movement he'd caught out of the corner of his eye, a prelude to oblivion as something blunt and hard had been brought down on his head. His head still ached and throbbed.

Forcing his body to obey, George MacKenzie managed to get to his hands and knees. He stayed that way for a minute, shivering despite the heavy fisherman-knit wool sweater he wore with old blue serge trousers, thick socks and the down-at-heel seaboots he'd cut to ankle length.

Inquisitive, the gull swooped down. Its wings almost brushed him as it passed and the big, cruel beak opened in another shrill cry. He swore at it, heaved himself upright, and stood swaying on his feet. Head thumping, he looked around, saw why the waves were breaking so close to him, and knew raw, clutching fear.

He was on a low, time-worn natural platform of rock which had the sea all around it. Pock-marked here and there by tiny tidal pools, totally flat and empty, a black, wet gleam in the faint moonlight, the rock wasn't more than thirty feet across at its widest point. And the distant lighthouse with its steady flashing stood on a dark mass of headland which made everything else unmistakable.

He was on the Witchrock, the most dreaded spot in the Brannan Sound, a finger of black basalt rock covered by a full seven feet of water when the tide was full, only drying out and visible when the sea retreated to the half-tide mark or less. Five miles away across the Sound, the flashing light on Broch Point marked the nearest land.

Little things suddenly and irrationally mattered to George Mac-Kenzie. He discovered his clothes were only damp, not wet, that his wristwatch had gone but that his cigarettes and lighter were still in his hip pocket. He noticed the way a long strand of dark kelp-weed had been left snagged to a crack in the rock near his feet. The realization came home to him again.

God, he was on Witchrock. He brought out his cigarettes, lit one with hands that quivered, and tried to work out time and tide.

At most, he reckoned, he had a couple of hours.

Wings fluttered and he looked round again. The gull had landed nearby and was eyeing him insolently, no longer afraid. But it rose again as a wave larger than the rest broke white and came swirling in, to lap against MacKenzie's feet.

Moistening his salt-dried lips, he dropped the stub of his cigarette. The red tip died with a hiss, then the tiny stub was drawn away as the water retreated.

And MacKenzie tensed as a new sound reached his ears, the faint murmur of an engine. The murmur grew until, straining his eyes against the night, he picked out the silhouette of an approaching boat. It came on slowly, without lights, the soft, thudding beat of its engine a monotonous rhythm, a mere wisp of phosphorescent wake showing astern as it started to circle the gradually shrinking patch of black rock.

George MacKenzie shouted and waved and dragged out his cigarette lighter, sparking it to life and moving the tiny flame frantically above his head.

The boat came nearer, still circling. But suddenly MacKenzie knew it for what it was and let his arms fall despairingly to his sides.

They had come back to make sure. As if to confirm it, the boat began to widen the circle again, her engine beat now reduced to a point where it could be giving little more than steerage way.

The next wave to foam in across the rock snatched at MacKenzie's ankles and the next did the same, while he cursed the men who were out there, watching and waiting.

The darkened boat kept to its slow, wide circles while the tide crept in. The wavecrests were slapping at his knees and the entire black hump of the Witchrock had been swallowed by the sea when George MacKenzie decided he had had enough.

He was no swimmer, but he had no choice,—unless he wanted to just stand and wait for death.

He had already kicked off his seaboots. Now he pulled off his heavy sweater, threw it aside, and deliberately began walking into the waves. When he reached chest-height he stopped and saw the boat murmuring in a little closer, as if the crew's curiosity had been roused.

"Damn you all to hell," he shouted, and began swimming.

It was five miles to the headland, against the tidal stream. George MacKenzie was tired after ten minutes, exhausted after fifteen. He struggled on a little longer, using a clumsy breast stroke. Then he simply sank from sight.

The boat nosed in near to where he'd gone down. Men hustled briefly on deck and George MacKenzie's dinghy was dumped over the side, overturned. A boothook shoved it clear, then the boat gathered speed and turned away. To the east, the sky beyond Broch Point was beginning to grey with the first hint of early dawn.

Far below, a school of young mullet scattered in the underwater darkness as the strange, lifeless shape sank down, limbs still twitching occasionally in the pull of an unseen current.

Lower down, where the bottom weed waited, the dead man's body snagged briefly on a ridge of rock. The current pressed impatiently and he came free again, rolling grotesquely.

In the process, a slip of plastic fell from his pocket. It drifted down and landed on soft sand, sending a started fiddler crab scuttling away.

The plastic card said that Constable George MacKenzie was an officer of the Scottish Northern Constabulary and showed his photograph. The little fiddler crab crawled over the warrant card a moment later, then the first grains of sand began to settle in.

I

The pale January sun shone down on a cold, grey Edinburgh which was shivering under a wind from the north. Snow was forecast, most of the population seemed to have gone into hibernation, and the few off-season tourists bravely exploring Princes Street were discovering why their package tours had been low-cost.

It was even colder up on Calton Hill, where the wind whipped the flags which flew above the austere frontage of St. Andrews House, central government administration headquarters for Scotland. Outside the building, sitting behind the wheel of a parked station wagon, Chief Officer Webb Carrick of Her Majesty's fishery protection cruiser *Marlin* kept his feet under the stream of lukewarm air being churned out by the heater fan and watched the rear view mirror. He had it angled so that he could see the massive bronze doors of the main entrance without turning round.

His broad, weather-bronzed face shaped a grin as a girl in a sheepskin coat and knee-length boots scurried out, crossed the parking lot, and tumbled into one of the cars as if frostbite was nipping at her high heels. Then, behind her, another figure emerged from the building, the one he'd been waiting on.

Small, plump and bearded, like an elderly teddy bear in a duffel coat, Captain James Shannon stumped his way across to the station wagon, got in on the passenger side, and slammed the door shut with a grunt.

"Blasted bureaucratic beehive," said Shannon bitterly. Hunched in the seat, he chewed a stray tendril of beard for a moment. "Ever notice what's carved on the doors, mister?"

Carrick merely nodded while his gaze strayed back to the rear view mirror. The Biblical quotation "Follow Me and Ye shall be Fishers of Men" was heavily embossed on the metal doors, the pious whim of an earlier, Calvinistic generation. It certainly had nothing to do with

Fishery Protection—their headquarters base was on the other side of the city, at Leith Docks.

"I'll tell you what that mob in there are really saying," said Shannon. "Hard luck, everybody—but we've got you on the hook." He glared at the world outside the station wagon. "The next patrol is cancelled. We're being detached for special duty, floating errand boys—when all they need for the job is any damned overgrown rowing boat."

Carrick raised an eyebrow, but the way the summons had come meant he wasn't totally surprised. Four hundred tons of fast patrol cruiser and built like a miniature destroyer, *Marlin* was in harbour at Greenock, on the Clyde, which was over fifty miles away. Her crew had straggled back from a week's leave that morning and she was due to sail for the Outer Hebrides on the evening tide.

But Captain Shannon had had to drop everything when the message from St. Andrews House had arrived. Then they'd come charging through, Carrick being brought along to chauffeur their borrowed Fishery Protection transport. Shannon would tackle any hazard afloat, but he was a nervous wreck on four wheels.

"What kind of special duty?" asked Carrick, realizing that the information wasn't going to be volunteered.

"Servants of democracy," answered Shannon. "They're voting in the Lochard constituency Parliamentary by-election at the end of the week. It happens to include a whole damned clutch of off-shore islands."

"And we've to ferry in the ballot boxes?" Carrick winced at the thought. Fishery cruisers got landed with that kind of job now and again. It meant dealing with fussy local officials, fussier party agents, and all the other fringe awkwardnesses of a political circus. "Where will we base, sir?"

"Feanport—it's a fishing village on the mainland, near the head of the Brannon Sound." Shannon glanced at his wristwatch, sucked his lips thoughtfully, then asked, "Did you get that spares list problem sorted out?"

"Yes, sir." Carrick nodded solemnly. The spares list problem was the kind created by Shannon for Shannon—an excuse to get Carrick along as driver. "I saw our Department people. It's straightened out." He paused, then added tentatively, "If we're finished here, maybe we could eat before we head back west. I know a place—."

"Here, in Edinburgh?" Shannon looked startled at the thought. "Mister, I haven't that kind of time to waste. More important, I know what they charge for a drink. No, just get moving—we'll eat aboard *Marlin*."

"Aboard *Marlin*," agreed Carrick sadly. He key-started the station wagon, began backing it out, and asked over his shoulder, "Why did we draw the ballot-box run?"

"Simple," grated Shannon. "Every other fishery protection captain on the West coast has gone into hiding, has engine trouble aboard or has dreamed up an excuse. They wouldn't have caught me if we hadn't been coming back from leave." He paused, watching nervously as they left the parking lot and slipped smoothly into the main road's traffic stream. Then, relaxing with a sigh, he asked, "Ever been to Feanport, mister?"

Carrick shook his head, keeping his attention ahead.

"The average fisherman around Feanport could give a mule lessons on being stubborn." Shannon kept silent for a moment as they passed a perfectly harmless truck then drew a relieved breath. "Still, there's one particular claim it has to fame. Ever met a real, live witch, mister?"

"There's a few of them around," said Carrick mildly. "Blonde, brunette and redhead—I'm not prejudiced."

"Very funny," said Shannon. "But don't expect a laugh from it around Feanport. There's a woman up there called the Witch of the Isles and the average skipper around the Brannan Sound still makes sure he keeps on her good side. A few even ask her blessing on their boats at the start of a season."

"Suppose the by-election candidates get the same idea?" asked Carrick, the hungry drive ahead still annoying him. "Sort of play Cinderella and say they want to go to Parliament."

"Turn pumpkins into politicians? I think somebody's been doing it for a long time." Then he settled deeper in his seat and half-closed his eyes. "I'm going to catch some sleep, mister. So stop yapping and watch your driving. I'm getting too near pension age to take risks."

The weather forecast had been right. The first flecks of snow began falling almost as he spoke.

*   *   *

By dawn the next morning the fishery cruiser *Marlin* had travelled a long way from the Clyde. Her lean grey hull was thrusting through lumping seas in the Passage of Tiree, the five-mile wide channel that cuts a reef fringed track towards the Outer Isles.

But it had been a long, hard night. She had sailed from Greenock on the evening tide straight into a blinding snowstorm, the kind that reduced visibility to a swirling obscurity. The snow had stayed with her, on and off, until almost three A.M. with Captain Shannon constantly in the command chair and refusing to compromise with the weather. While most other craft had been heading for shelter he had navigated by instinct as much as the radar screen—and *Marlin* had stayed on course and schedule.

"He's a stubborn old sod," declared Petty Officer William 'Clapper' Bell with a wry admiration. Massive paws wrapped around a mug of galley coffee, newly relieved from the helm, he gave a tired-edged grin towards Webb Carrick, who had draped himself against one of the bridge heaters. "You look the way I feel—knackered."

"Who's arguing?" Carrick yawned and braced himself as the fishery cruiser rolled and a new curtain of spray drenched her hundred and eighty foot length.

Shannon had left them only minutes before, heading below to his cabin. The sky had cleared overhead. To starboard, the high hills of Mull were a startling white with a red rim of watery sun gradually rising behind them. On ahead, twin pinpricks of light still stabbed a pale challenge at the dawn from the northern end of the Passage. But, as it had all night, the rest of the world seemed compounded of the steady, underfoot vibration of the fishery cruiser's twin diesels and the high pitched singing of the wind through her aerial rigging.

"So what's the rush?" Clapper Bell, *Marlin*'s bo'sun and six feet of brawny, ginger-haired Irishman, ambled across to join him. "Somebody stand on the old man's tail?"

"Something like that," agreed Carrick mildly. Clapper Bell was his partner in the fishery cruiser's scuba diving team and that kind of mutual reliance created its own kind of discipline. "Don't expect too many happy smiles till we've collected those ballot boxes."

"Playin' at ferry-boats for a few days won't harm him." Bell's eyes were heavy from lack of sleep and he needed a shave badly. "Anyway, there are worse places than Feanport."

"If you know where the action is?" asked Carrick dryly.

"They've never even heard o' the word," admitted Bell sadly.

"There's a stone-faced village cop called MacKenzie who makes sure o' that. But he's all right off duty—I got pretty friendly wi' him." He fought back a yawn. "Still, I'm wi' the Old Man on one thing. Stuff all politicians—an' I'm off to my pit while I still know how to get there."

He left, clattering down the companionway stair that led aft. The new helmsman, a ruddy faced native of Barra, was humming under his breath as he eased the wheel a fraction. The relief lookouts on the bridge wings were already slapping their arms and stamping their feet as they got used to the temperature, and Carrick was left as the last of the overnight watch still on duty.

Some tiny, moving dots caught his eye on the Mull shoreline. He lifted the bridge glasses, and the dots came into focus through the powerful lenses. They were deer, forced down from the hills by the ferocity of the overnight blizzard—and at that, they were probably the lucky ones.

"Picture postcard stuff," said a cheerful young voice unexpectedly. "That's what I call a view, Webb."

"You're late." Carrick lowered the glasses and scowled at the chubby, freckle-faced arrival. Jumbo Wills, the second mate, showed all the benefits of a few hours' sleep but Carrick was in no mood for bright-eyed vigour. "Where the hell have you been?"

"Checking the weather forecast." Wills looked slightly hurt. "Wind decreasing, occasional light showers, moderate sea—and the temperature rising soon. No problems."

"Right." Thankfully, Carrick dumped the bridge glasses on their shelf. "We're on zero-zero-nine magnetic and you have the watch."

"Zero-zero-nine," repeated Wills dutifully with a glance at the helmsman, who nodded. "Anything else?"

"You've to call the Old Man when you clear Ardnamurchan Point," Carrick told him.

"Why?" the last of Wills's smile faded.

"Ask him," suggested Carrick, wooden-faced. Jumbo Wills had a sad record of minor disasters on most patrols and Captain Shannon tended to treat their second mate like a juvenile delinquent. "But do it when he's in a happier mood."

Flushing, Wills levered himself up into the command chair while another lumping sea sent *Marlin* rolling and fresh spume spattered against the bridge. Then he faced Carrick again.

"I'll tell you something people keep forgetting," said Wills frostily. "If you and the Old Man were both washed overboard or something equally beneficial, then I'd be left in command of this ship."

"You'd want a band playing that day," said Carrick. "One like they had on the *Titanic* when she went down."

Wills spluttered. The helmsman made a choking noise and kept his eyes glued to the compass—and, satisfied, Carrick headed aft, past the tiny chartroom and down the first flight of companionway stairs.

He paused there, then from sheer habit opened a door and stepped out onto the lee side of the main deck to look around.

Even there, sheltered from the worst of the wind and spume, the cold cut like a knife. But *Marlin*'s duty watch were already settling into their day-time routine. Two oilskin clad ratings were methodically checking their way along the lashings on the deck gear. He could hear the coughing rasp of a launch engine being started on test and further aft, past the pulsing shimmer of exhaust throbbing from *Marlin*'s squat funnel, a figure was dumping trash from the galley over the side while the usual attendant gulls swooped in.

Tired as he was, Carrick stayed a moment longer watching the gulls, then the way that the Blue Ensign of the fishery protection squadron flapped and crackled at *Marlin*'s stern. But he was still glad to step back into the warmth, close the door, and head 'tween decks and aft.

*   *   *

Andy Shaw, their chief engineer, was finishing breakfast alone in the wardroom. A lanky, middle-aged individual who always looked grimy, Shaw gave him a yawning nod but left it at that. Like Carrick, he'd been on watch throughout the night.

"Coffee and a bacon sandwich—I'll take them with me," Carrick told the hovering steward. While he waited, he turned to Shaw. "Good leave?"

"What I can remember of it," said Shaw. "Want to buy what's left of a hangover? Last night was one hell of a way to try to cure it."

Carrick grinned in sympathy, collected his mug of coffee and the thick slab of sandwich, and went along the narrow passage which led to his cabin. Going in, he heeled the door shut behind him, sat down on the edge of the narrow bunk with a sigh of relief, and chewed on the sandwich without really tasting it.

Thirty-one years of age, a stocky, five-foot-ten in height with the kind of muscular shoulders which came from keeping in constant scuba diving trim, Webb Carrick had been Chief Officer aboard *Marlin* for a shade more than two years. He had dark brown eyes, darker brown hair and a broad-boned face with lips a little too thin to allow any idea that an easy-going manner meant he could be pushed around—as even Captain Shannon had learned.

Most of the tiny crow's-feet lines around his eyes had been acquired in those last two years while *Marlin* patrolled the treacherous, island-studded Scottish west coast. There had been plenty to learn, from a new, fine-honed brand of seamanship to the realities of keeping the peace and maintaining the law in the multi-million pound Scottish fishing industry.

Marlin rolled again. Carrick swore to himself as some of the coffee slopped from the mug. Then he gulped down the rest and abandoned the bacon sandwich, realising he'd been almost asleep.

All he really wanted to do was get his head down. Stripping off his uniform jacket and the white roll-neck sweater he wore under it, he kicked off his short-length sea-boots and crossed the cabin to splash some water on his face at the tiny washbasin. Drying off with a towel which caught at his dark beard stubble, he finished undressing, flopped down on the bunk, and considered the cabin through heavy eyes.

It was small and sparsely furnished, the single porthole close to the waterline, any extras he'd added were bachelor style, from the few books crammed into a shelf to a framed photograph of his last ship, a deep-sea oil tanker.

That seemed another life away, one that had ended when, a newly won master's ticket in his pocket but no ship available, he'd been called to a Fisheries Department interview on the strength of a lone forgotten application. The same day he'd been appointed Chief Officer under Shannon and had been handed the black warrant card which declared Webster Carrick an assistant Superintendent of Fisheries.

A hybrid mixture of sea-going policeman and civil servant with, from the average fisherman's viewpoint, the worst features of both.

Fishermen were supposed to work within rules and quotas, seasonal bans, net sizes, zones and limits, even Common Market regulations in the modern mood. Boats of a dozen nationalities could be found fishing off the Scottish coastline—and German or Dutch, French, Russian or native Scot, they shared a stubborn, independent streak and a basic code.

Get the fish, and you get the money. The local Scottish boats on their own landed a regular £60 million worth of catch at Scottish ports. With maybe a quarter of it caught illegally, according to some market men.

Lying back, Carrick listened to the steady throb of *Marlin*'s engines and the sound of the seas which met her hull.

Like the rest of the protection flotilla, she covered an average of 17,000 sea miles a year on her beat from the Butt of Lewis in the north to the southern limits of the Solway.

Her job was keeping the lid on things. Chasing poachers through all weathers and among a maze of islands, reefs and currents which had few parallels anywhere. Or, suddenly, having to switch to any one of a score of other roles from rescue to settling local fishing wars or plain law enforcement.

He yawned, eyes almost closed, thinking of Shannon and the other protection cruiser skippers who had to outwit and outsail the fishermen at their own game among the islands.

That needed a tight, efficient ship—the way Shannon ran *Marlin*. No guns broke the line of her distinctive silhouette of high-raked bow and square cut stern. What she had instead was the thirty knot speed of her twin 2,000 horsepower diesels, the Blue Ensign with the gold Fisheries badge, and her go-anywhere capability.

Which came back to Shannon again, with his crew of twenty, three watch-keeping officers and an armoury of cunning.

The kind of cunning learned the hard way that Carrick knew Shannon was now trying to pass on to him—pass on in the short time left before Captain James Shannon reached compulsory retirement age and was pensioned off like some old, abandoned horse.

Which in itself was a hell of a thought and a hell of a waste. Except, decided Carrick as his eyes finally closed, Shannon would fight that day off as long as he could—with the same kind of cunning.

*   *   *

The sea had moderated. It was the first thing that registered with Webb Carrick when he wakened. The fishery cruiser's pitching roll had become an easy, gentle sway and though her engine beat was un-changed there was no longer spray washing across his cabin porthole.

Even better, the sky outside was a bright, cloudless blue. It was noon by his wrist-watch, which surprised him and meant he'd been asleep for almost six hours. Yawning, he got out of the bunk and reached for the shelf where he kept his cigarettes.

Then he remembered and swore sadly. The last pack of cigarettes he'd bought was firmly taped above the washbasin mirror still un-opened. He'd promised himself this trip was the one on which he was going to kick the habit.

Try anyway. Gloomily, he washed and shaved, finished dressing, then ambled back to the porthole. The weather had certainly cleared and from the distant coastline's shape *Marlin* had come another long way while he'd slept.

A few minutes later he went up to the bridge. It was bathed in bright sunlight, the helmsman was wearing sun glasses to cut down the glare, and the officer of the watch was now Ferguson, a thin, grey-haired figure who grunted a greeting.

"Who bribed the weather man?" asked Carrick cheerfully, looking around. They were about three miles off the mainland, a long line of low green hills untouched by white. Ahead, a small cluster of islands basked in the sunlight on the port bow and he could just make out a string of tiny line-fishing boats working close in to their rock-fringed shores. "Whatever it cost, I'll pay my share."

"If you mean what happened to the snow, we left that behind when we cleared Skye," said Ferguson in a flat, disinterested voice.

Ferguson was middle-aged, *Marlin*'s third watch-keeping officer, and a withdrawn man. He rated junior second mate and had re-turned to sea after a long interval ashore—though exactly why he'd returned was a reason he kept to himself. As he spoke, he strode across to the compass binnacle, frowned suspiciously, then sniffed.

"Starboard a point, helmsman," he ordered. "You're damned well daydreaming again."

"Starboard, sir." The helmsman obeyed then added something softly under his breath as Ferguson turned away. *Marlin*'s junior sec-ond didn't top the ship's popularity poll. There was a big basking shark travelling almost parallel with them to port, its tall black, sail-like fin cutting through the swell—but the helmsman reckoned it wouldn't have liked Ferguson either.

"Tell me something," said Ferguson, as he came back to join Carrick beside the command chair. "Do you reckon we're on a fishery cruiser or is this really the Royal yacht in disguise?"

"If I see a woman wandering around wearing a crown I'll let you know," said Carrick. "What's your problem?"

Ferguson glanced round at the helmsman and lowered his voice. "Our Captain. I thought we were only going to ferry ballot boxes this trip—"

"Right," agreed Carrick.

"Well, while you were in dreamland he announced a surprise ship's inspection," said Ferguson. "It's going on now—he's checking everywhere, with Jumbo Wills trotting at his heels."

"Hard luck, Jumbo," mused Carrick. "So?"

"So why?" persisted Ferguson. "I heard him. 'Clean this, paint that'—and every second thing is 'a damned disgrace!' " He made it a passable copy of Shannon's snarl, then puzzled. "You're Chief Officer. Could there be something else going on we don't know about?"

"This trip?" Carrick shook his head. "No, politicians just worry him."

"They worry everybody," said Ferguson, still suspicious. "We'll berth at Feanport in another couple of hours. Maybe we'll know then."

Leaving him still muttering, Carrick left the bridge and headed aft. Keeping to the open deck as the best way to avoid Shannon's inspection tour, he paused and narrowed his eyes against the sunlight. An old black-funnelled interisland cargo ship was passing them to starboard, making her slow way south. She had cattle penned on her open foredeck and he could even hear their faint bellowing across the water as if the luckless animals knew their next stop would be a mainland market.

A different kind of bellowing was coming from the scuba compartment near the stern. Petty Officer Clapper Bell was singing. The door lay open and as Carrick entered the big Glasgow-Irish bo'sun broke off and beamed a greeting.

"Safe enough in here, sir," said Bell with a wink. "The Old Man's been an' gone."

"Good." Carrick sat on a crate of diving spares while Bell finished an adjustment he was making to one of their aqualung harnesses. "How was it?"

"The usual—you filthy sailor, get the place cleaned up. An' our Mister Wills lookin' like he'd already received the full wrath o' God, marked 'Personal.'" Bell set the harness aside, straddled another crate, and produced his cigarettes. "Smoke?"

"You filthy sailor, it's a filthy habit," said Carrick.

"Stopped again?" Bell made a deliberate performance of lighting a cigarette for himself and sucked the smoke happily. "Eh . . . how about a wee side bet on it, like the last time?"

"No way," said Carrick grimly.

"Feelin' touchy already?" Bell enjoyed himself. "A pity. I could have used the money, after a week's leave an' that—"

"I'll believe it," said Carrick.

Clapper Bell's leave usually revolved around some mammoth poker game. He grinned a little. His own seven days had ended up differently this time. Conscience had sent him visiting his parents, who ran a small farm. He'd ended up mending fences and working harder than he ever did aboard *Marlin*.

"I remember the last time we were at Feanport," said Bell suddenly. "The locals were havin' a little war all their own wi' some Norwegian shark boats. Three years ago, that was—right before you joined us." He considered the racks of scuba gear around the small compartment. "We should be comin' into the Brannan Sound about now, the approach channel. You know, if we've a chance, there's one or two good wrecks worth a dive around here."

"Maybe." Carrick was doubtful. "It depends on a few things, Clapper—like those ballot boxes."

"Stuff them," grumbled Bell. "I'll tell you who'll win any kind of election up here—the first idiot who promises to cut taxes more than anyone else."

Carrick grinned. The previous Member of Parliament for the Lochard constituency had been a tearaway Scottish Nationalist who had held the seat by a knife-edge majority. His death in a car crash had put four candidates in the ring and they were all making promises. But even the press and TV pundits were refusing to guess which way the votes would go.

He glanced around the scuba compartment for a moment, his sympathies with Bell. They hadn't had much diving practice on the last couple of patrols and that was never a good situation. Then another thought struck him.

"The last time you were up this way, did you come across an old hag called the Witch of the Isles?"

"Aye, we did." Bell drew irritatingly on his cigarette. "Uh—who told you about her?"

"Shannon."

"Did he give her a name?" asked Bell.

Carrick shook his head.

"Her married name's Vullan—Dorothy Vullan," said Bell with a soft chuckle. "She's not young, but she's no old hag. She's a rich witch too. That village cop MacKenzie I tol' you about says she owns a dam' great chunk of Feanport."

"And a golden broomstick too?" Carrick raised a caustic eyebrow. "What's the witch bit all about, Clapper?"

"It just runs in the family," shrugged Bell. "They drowned one o' her ancestors for puttin' the hex on a local preacher an' her family's been stuck with the reputation ever since." He paused and winked. "They've found it useful. Even today the Feanport locals avoid a quarrel wi' the Witch o' the Isles—just in case things start goin' wrong around them."

Carrick wasn't particularly surprised. People in the islands were hard-headed, intellignet and had their deep freezes and TV sets like anyone else. But deep down they still had the tendril remnants of an older way of life—remnants that came to the surface from time to time in the most surprising ways.

"Look, I still think we should talk about those wrecks," said Bell earnestly. "I've got them marked an' if you've got a bit o' time to spare—"

"Show me," invited Carrick.

Beaming, the bo'sun produced a creased, much-stained Admiralty chart, unfolded it, and began explaining.

*   *   *

Half an hour later they'd more or less agreed that the best of the selection of sunken ships available on Clapper Bell's chart was probably an old destroyer which had been wrecked in World War One and was supposed to be lying in about forty fathoms of water close to the reef which had finished her. But as Bell made enthusiastic noises about what was involved he stopped suddenly and gave a surprised glance at Carrick.

There had been a change in the note from *Marlin*'s diesels. A moment passed then a new shudder ran through her hull, her engine revolutions began climbing and her deck began to heel. The fishery cruiser was going somewhere new, and in a hurry.

They reached the door of the scuba compartment together and Bell gave an interested grunt. The creaming white wash now building from *Marlin*'s stern showed they were curving away from the shoreline.

"Trouble?" asked Bell hopefully.

"Could be," said Carrick as the thunder of air being sucked down to feed the diesels kept increasing. "I'll let you know."

He hurried along the deck, grabbing a rail for a handhold as spray drenched aboard, silver in the bright sunlight. All the signs were that Bell was right. Some seamen were readying one of *Marlin*'s boats, extra lookouts were in position on the bridge wings, and the shuddering note of power underfoot was still growing. As Carrick reached the foot of the companionway steps leading to the bridge Ferguson came galloping down and shoved past him, heading aft.

Carrick went on up. He found Captain Shannon already in the command chair with Jumbo Wills in position beside the bridge intercom and a petty officer standing by the helmsman. Shannon rasped an order and a moment later a signal rocket soared up, to burst high and white.

"Dead ahead, mister," said Shannon, greeting him with a nod. "Three miles, maybe. See for yourself."

Carrick took the bridge glasses from the bearded, moonfaced figure and deftly adjusted the focus a fraction. Shannon's eyes weren't as good as they'd been a few years back. Then, as he stared through them, his lips puckered in a silent whistle of understanding.

A thin pillar of smoke showed ahead, rising from a fishing boat which lay beam-on to the waves, rolling sluggishly and low in the water. As Carrick kept the glasses trained, *Marlin* vibrating on, he saw the tiny yellow blob of a life raft tossing in the sea beside the helpless craft and the way her wheelhouse was a broken mess.

"She's drifting west," said Shannon. "Better look there too."

Carrick did, and understood. A long, white line of broken water lay waiting there, an occasional black fang of rock showing, then disappearing again.

"Any radio contact, sir?" he asked, lowering the powerful glasses.

"We can't raise her," frowned Shannon. "Ferguson saw her first, on radar, and wondered what the hell she was doing so close to those rocks. Then she fired two distress flares and we spotted the smoke." He swung round in the command chair. "Mr. Wills—"

"Sir?" Jumbo Wills practically sprang to his side.

"Don't damned well do that," snarled Shannon. "You make me nervous. Pass the word I want a tow-line readied. Then let them have another rocket—they can probably use the encouragement." He faced Carrick again while Wills turned to the intercom 'phone. "As soon as we've closed, take a boat over to her, mister. Do what you can to help. But her people come first. If she's sinking, she's sinking—I want no fancy risks. Understood?"

Carrick nodded, looking out again to where the thin plume of smoke was now visible to the naked eye. Even at full power, it was going to take *Marlin* another seven or eight minutes to get within hailing distance of the crippled fishing boat. Presuming she stayed afloat that long.

The signal rocket Shannon had ordered roared up from *Marlin* a moment later and burst high in the clear blue sky. Carrick said nothing, but he had an idea that for once he and Shannon were probably sharing the same puzzled thought.

The weather was good and the sea was calm. Exactly how and when had the boat ahead got herself into this kind of trouble—and why?

*   *   *

Ten minutes later *Marlin*'s launch nosed in to touch the wallowing hull of the drifting fishing boat. As the two craft grated, Webb Carrick made a scrambling jump across—and a big, bearded fisherman waiting on the fishing boat's foam-washed deck grabbed his arm and hauled him firmly aboard.

"Never thought I'd be glad to see a Fishery man," said the fisherman hoarsely. His face, beak-nosed and weathered like granite, twisted a weary grin. "But I'd welcome the devil himself right now. Glad to see you, mister."

Carrick nodded, eased the small two-way radio he had on a sling over one shoulder, and glanced round. The launch was already edging clear again, waiting for orders, with Clapper Bell and three of *Marlin*'s hands aboard. A cable's distance out, almost as near as Shannon dared because of outlying rocks, the fishery cruiser lay with her diesels cut back to a slow, pulsing exhaust.

"Any injured aboard?" he asked as a first priority.

"One man—not too badly," said the bearded man. "We're the *Rachel*, out of Feanport. I'm Angus Grant, skipper and owner, for what that's worth now."

The hull gave a sullen roll in the swell and fresh foam lapped across the wet decking, emphasising how low in the water the *Rachel* was lying.

"Better show me how things are," said Carrick, knowing he had decisions ahead and little time in which to make them.

"Come to the wheelhouse," said Grant. "The others are there anyway."

They went across the deck to the shattered wheelhouse where the other four members of the *Rachel*'s crew were waiting. Two were fishing hands, both in their early thirties, and they greeted Carrick with relieved grins as they stood back to let him enter. Another man about the same age lay inside, propped against what had been a doorway, in an old blanket. Most of the hair had been scorched from his head and he was moaning a little, his eyes half-closed.

But the remaining member of the *Rachel*'s crew was a small, slim girl with long chestnut hair which was soaked and bedraggled. Kneeling beside the injured man, holding a flask of water to his lips, she looked round at Carrick with calm grey eyes and a serious face. She wore a blue jersey, slacks and seaboots like the others.

"My daughter, Shona," said Grant. "She came out with us for a pleasure trip."

Carrick bent over the injured man then glanced at the girl.

"How is he?" he asked.

"Lucky," she said quietly. "Burns and shock, maybe a fractured rib—but that's all. He could have been killed."

"Aye, he was lucky," said Grant, then, as Carrick rose, he glanced at the others as if for support before he went on. "Things are maybe the same way with the *Rachel* . . . . not as bad as they look, mister. She isn't sinking and we've been riding like this for a good while now. Maybe if your ship got a line aboard us and we tried a tow—"

He stopped there, eyeing Carrick, waiting.

Squeezing past, Carrick crossed to the little companionway hatch at the front of the wheelhouse and peered down into the dark interior of what had been a cabin below. Almost all he could see was a swirl of water topped by a scum of debris.

"It's worth trying," persisted Grant.

Still Carrick didn't answer. He left the hatchway, went to the wheelhouse door, and frowned out at the broken line of water to starboard which marked the fangs of the main reef. The distance between the *Rachel* and those hungry rocks was still shrinking as the boat drifted with the current.

But it might still be worth a try, as Grant claimed. The *Rachel* was a standard sixty-foot motor fishing vessel with a wooden hull, a kind that possessed plenty of built-in buoyancy. Damage on her deck area seemed restricted to the wheelhouse and the smoke seen by *Marlin*'s lookouts was explained by the few last wisps still rising from a smouldering pile of nets on the for'ard fish hatch cover.

"We used the last two flares when we saw you," said Shona Grant, as if reading his mind. "Then we grabbed anything left that might burn to make a smoke signal."

Carrick nodded and turned to Grant. "Skipper, what's your damage below?"

"We're holed badly on the waterline, starboard side." Grant's bearded, beak-nosed face tightened at the thought. "A gas cylinder blew up in the galley, like a dam' bomb going off, and punched straight through the hull. The wheelhouse took the rest o' the blast through the hatch and our radio was wrecked like everything else."

"And what happened to him?" asked Carrick, pointing to the injured man.

"He was in the galley when it happened. I'd sent him down to light the gas stove an' brew some tea." Grant shook his head. "Don't ask me why he wasn't killed down there. His brother was in the wheelhouse and got blown out through the door."

"His brother?" Carrick glanced at the two fishing hands.

"That's me." It was the taller of the two, lanky, with long, dark hair, who spoke, He had a gash on his forehead. "I'm Donnie Mac-Lean and that's my brother Willie over there. Och, but he'll be fine—" he gave a deliberate wink towards the injured man, who managed to shape a faint, painful grin "—an' that blowtorch hairstyle suits him, eh?" Hardly pausing, he gestured at his companion. "This is our cousin Lachie MacLean."

"Cousin Willie will be fine," agreed Lachie MacLean, a chunky fair-haired individual with a wispy straggle of moustache. He nodded seriously. "It takes more than a wee accident to kill a MacLean."

"Shut up, both of you," said Grant. He turned impatiently to Carrick and chewed hard on his lip for a moment. "It's up to you. Will you ask your captain to try a tow?"

For a long moment the steady wash of the sea and the throb of the idling launch, back almost alongside again, were the only sounds. They all watched him, even the injured Willie MacLean. Carrick glanced at Shona Grant, saw the silent pleading in her grey eyes, but still made up his mind in terms of a practical gamble.

"I'll suggest it," he agreed.

"Good." It came like a sigh of relief from Grant, then a sudden caution showed on the bearded skipper's face. "Mind you, it's only a tow I'm wanting. My crew stay aboard—"

"We're not hunting salvage money, skipper," said Carrick patiently. "But we'll move Willie—and your daughter better go with him. She can give Captain Shannon the story."

Grant relaxed and nodded. Bringing the little walkie-talkie to his lips, Carrick thumbed the transmitter button and called *Marlin*. Shannon's voice answered immediately.

"You've taken long enough, mister. Well, report."

"She's the *Rachel* out of Feanport, badly holed and one crewman injured," replied Carrick, unruffled. "The skipper wants to try a tow."

There was a pause, then a burst of louder static. "What's your opinion, mister?"

"That we haven't much time," said Carrick.

"Understood." Shannon's manner was suddenly and totally professional. "Let's get started. I'll try and shade nearer to you. But it's your feet that get wet if you're wrong."

Grinning, Carrick lowered the walkie-talkie and beckoned the launch in. She came alongside in seconds, rubbing the *Rachel*'s old motor tyre fenders, being held against them as Clapper Bell fed quick, short bursts of power to the engine. Two of her crew scrambled aboard the fishing boat and helped move Willie MacLean as gently as possible from one craft to the other.

While that was happening, Carrick took the chance to give Clapper Bell a quick rundown on the situation and what they'd need. Then, seeing MacLean settled in the launch, he looked round for Shona Grant just as she came over from the wheelhouse.

"Ready?" Carrick looked at her and marvelled. Somehow, she'd found a moment to comb her wet, straggling hair into order.

"Yes." She stopped beside him. "My father—he's stubborn, like a mule. But he loves this boat, so—"

"We'll cope with him," promised Carrick.

Clapper Bell edged the launch closer again. Shona Grant swung down into it, settled at the stern thwarts, and the little craft moved away in a haze of blue exhaust.

II

It remained a close-run race against the current and the reef. Passing the tow-line across to the fishing boat and securing it was a struggle on its own, and Shannon sent extra help to assist, headed by Ferguson. Then Clapper Bell returned while that was still in progress and dragged a load of big plastic flotation bags aboard the *Rachel*.

Carrick left Ferguson to worry about the tow-line and joined Bell. With Angus Grant assisting from the deck the two men plunged into the cold, water-filled darkness of the fishing boat's hull and began the laborious task of placing the flotation bags and triggering the CO_2 cartridges which inflated them.

Each bag meant extra buoyancy, slightly better odds for later. But it was a dirty, dangerous business of wading chest-high, sometimes ducking totally under, regularly colliding with unseen obstacles and bobbing fitments. There was even the hazard of getting clear as each flotation bag mushroomed out. Their fingers numbed, their feet soon had lost all feeling.

They were in the cramped space of the engine-room, struggling to jam an inflated bag under a metal beam, when the whole hull suddenly shuddered and rolled. Thrown off his feet, banging his head on something hard as he went down, Carrick came up spluttering. Clapper Bell had gone under too and surfaced cursing—then as the hull's shudder changed and the roll became a slow pitch they splashed and clawed their way back to the deck.

Then Clapper Bell's cursing changed to a bellow of delight. The *Rachel* was moving, the tow-line connecting her to *Marlin* already stretched taut and water pouring from its length. Gradually, still lurching and quivering, the fishing boat came round as the long grey shape of the fishery cruiser kept up the delicate manoeuvre.

Together, they stumbled over to the wheelhouse where Ferguson was standing with Angus Grant beside him. A little way aft, the two

MacLeans and the little group of *Marlin*'s hands were standing grinning.

"Finished down there?" asked Ferguson politely. Then the grey-haired junior second's habitually sour expression thawed and he thumbed towards the stern. "There's your safety margin."

Carrick winced. While he'd been below they'd drifted until the line of the reef was only about a boat-length away. Dark, individual fangs of rock were clearly visible among the white of the breaking swell.

The radio in Ferguson's hand crackled. He murmured an answer into it and a moment later *Marlin*'s siren bellowed. As the throb of her diesels began to deepen, the black diamond towing signal rose to her masthead. Then the tow-line creaked to a new strain and the fishing boat began moving ahead, slowly at first then the crawl gradually increasing as she was hauled away from what should have been her grave.

"I owe a debt to all your people," said Angus Grant. "I—"

"Skipper, I'd keep my thanks till you're back in Feanport," said Ferguson, cutting him short. He saw Carrick's raised eyebrow and nodded. "Captain Shannon reckons on a three-hour haul, but it's still the nearest harbour."

"Aye," said Grant. "And once I get back, once I've seen this boat safe on a slipway and Willie MacLean on his way to hospital, I've a few things to sort out." He stopped there, his face granite-hard for a moment, then cleared his throat and produced a flask from his hip pocket. "Carrick, you and the bo'sun look like you could both use a dram. Medicinal, I'd call it."

Bell took first gulp from the flask. Then it was Carrick's turn and once he'd felt the raw spirit burn its way down he glanced at Bell and grinned. Their faces were streaked with oil, water was dribbling from their sodden clothing, and they looked more like rescued than rescuers. He took another swallow from the flask, then passed it back to Bell.

The men aft hauled the yellow liferaft back aboard, working with a new relaxed air. The mood was infectious—the little fishing boat was wallowing along at a steady three knots, her bow meeting the low green swell in a steady, chunking rhythm as she followed *Marlin*'s wake.

"This captain of yours," said Angus Grant in a slightly worried voice. He paused, frowning, and rubbed a hand across his beard.

"How much does he know about towing? There's some advice I'd maybe give him—"

Carrick kept a stony face at the thought, but Ferguson, who had been listening to a new message coming over the radio, saved him from having to reply.

"Your boat, but our tow, skipper," he said. "I wouldn't recommend it—though Captain Shannon wants to talk with you." He glanced at Carrick and nodded. "You and Bell are ordered back—and you've to bring Skipper Grant."

"Leave the *Rachel*—now?" Grant hesitated.

"The MacLeans are here, so you've a crew aboard," said Carrick, guessing Grant was thinking of salvage law again. "You'd better come. Anyway, meeting Captain Shannon is an experience."

"People say that about bein' hit by a truck," muttered Clapper Bell, and ignored the glare it brought from Ferguson.

*   *   *

They made the transfer by *Marlin*'s launch a few minutes later, scrambled from there up a ladder to the fishery cruiser's main deck, and discovered Captain James Shannon had come down from the bridge to meet them. He had Shona Grant with him and her father hugged her for a moment.

"Ah—welcome aboard, skipper," said Shannon, shaking hands with Grant. He gave a faint smile at the way Grant kept one arm round his daughter. "I've already got to know the other half of your partnership."

The two bearded men, Shannon small and plump, Grant large and raw-boned, faced each other for a moment and then Grant nodded.

"I'm in your debt, Captain Shannon," he said formally, then glanced at Shona. "How's Willie MacLean?"

"Resting now, in the sickbay," she assured him. Snug in a borrowed change of clothing topped by one of Shannon's duffel-coats, she smiled at her father while her long hair was teased by the breeze. "They've radioed to Feanport for an ambulance to meet us."

"Now I want to know what happened—your version, skipper," said Shannon briskly. "We'll talk in my day-cabin." He paused, switching his attention to Carrick. "Mister, you and the bo'sun both look like you fell off a garbage scow. Do something about it."

Then he turned on his heel, leading Grant and the girl away. A deckhand standing near chuckled, then quickly froze any expression from his face as Clapper Bell glared at him.

"Easy, Clapper," murmured Carrick. "That's his idea of a compliment. You know how he works—never give a pat on the back if you can manage a kick up the tail."

"An' he's good at it," admitted Bell. "None better."

They parted, and Carrick went down to his cabin. It was another half hour before he came back on deck, having managed to scrub clean, change into dry clothes, and snatch something to eat in the wardroom.

Pausing beside a deckhouse, he looked aft. The *Rachel* was still riding along steadily at the end of her tow-line and he reckoned *Marlin* was now nursing the disabled fishing boat along at about five knots through the continued light swell.

"Aye, she's taking it well," said Angus Grant, surprising him by emerging from the lee of the deckhouse. The bearded fisherman gave a slightly sheepish grimace. "I came along here to hide from your Captain Shannon. That man asks more questions than an Admiralty Board."

Carrick nodded and leaned his hands on the rail. The mainland was about four miles to starboard, a jutting headland of rock topped by the slim white pillar of a lighthouse. To port and slightly astern a low black patch of rock broke the water about a mile away.

"Another ten miles, no more, and we're at Feanport," declared Grant, joining him. "We're well into the Brannan Sound now—we call that headland Broch Point." A bleaker note entered his voice. "There's a name for that patch of rock to port. We call it the Witchrock around here."

"The Witchrock." Carrick's interest stirred a little. "I've heard that Feanport has its own resident witch."

"Aye." Grant's hands tightened on the rail. "And the first damned witch in that family gave the Witchrock its name six or so generations back—she was marooned out there to drown." He snorted. "Some of the old ideas were good ones."

"Meaning you've a problem with the present generation?" asked Carrick.

"I never said that." Grant's eyes were still on the wet black hump of rock. "But I'll give you one piece of advice, Carrick. While you're in

Feanport, treat the Brannan Sound and all it contains with care—so-called witches included."

"I'll do that." Carrick knew better than to smile. "How about your own troubles, skipper? Does Willie MacLean have any idea why that gas cylinder exploded?"

"He's in no state to talk about it," said Grant. "And I'm tired of answering questions. I told Shannon that before I left him—do I have to say the same to you?"

Then, before Carrick could answer, the fisherman had spun on his heel and was striding off along the deck. Carrick stared after him till he'd gone through a companionway door. Whatever was wrong, he'd somehow scraped a ragged nerve-ending as far as Angus Grant was concerned.

Deciding that finding out more would have to wait, he headed for the bridge. Jumbo Wills had the watch with the duty helmsman and a leading seaman was keeping a permanent eye on their tow. When Carrick arrived, Wills was lounging in the command chair with his hands clasped behind his head.

"Good afternoon, Admiral," said Carrick. "Sorry to disturb you."

Wills jerked in surprise then grinned and climbed down from the chair.

"The gentleman from the garbage scow," he retorted. "You came at a good time. Out to starboard, Webb—what do you make of these two?"

Carrick looked and then reached for the bridge glasses. Two big, dark-hulled Norwegian shark-boats swam into focus through the lenses. They were pairing their way down the Brannan Sound from the north, heading for some new catching ground. And like Wills, he knew them instantly—on *Marlin*'s last patrol she had caught both boats hunting inside the limits.

"Log the sighting, Jumbo," he ordered, lowering the bridge glasses. "Leave it at that."

Wills nodded. Gradually the two Norwegian boats came closer, obviously curious about the black diamond towing signal at the fishery cruiser's masthead. Men appeared on the deck of both shark-boats, staring, then a signal lamp blinked a greeting from the leading boat's wheelhouse.

"Answer it?" asked Wills.

"Thank them," said Carrick, knowing the greeting was genuine.

There were no nationality barriers among the fishing fleets when it came to a "men against the sea" situation.

Wills took a signal lamp out on the bridge wing, triggered a reply in his ragged Morse, then returned. As the shark boats headed away, swinging back on their original course, he eyed Carrick cautiously.

"Webb, you know the Old Man didn't get to finish ship's rounds because of the *Rachel* panic." He paused, saw Carrick's expression, and nodded. "That's right, he wants you to finish it. He's in the radio room if you want to check—"

Carrick shook his head, took the clipboard hanging from a hook below the bridge intercom, and scanned the scribbled notes. He'd been left with the lower deck and engineroom.

*   *   *

Completing what remained of Shannon's inspection tour took about an hour. It was dull, it was routine and it was necessary—but at the end of it the lower deck problems came down to little more than a jammed sea-water intake while for once Andy Shaw, as chief engineer, could produce only one item that mattered. He had a worry about *Marlin's* main generator, suspected a bearing, and wanted Shannon to know he intended tackling the job as soon as they were berthed in Feanport.

Finished, Carrick climbed his way back up to the bridge—then stopped as he reached it and swore under his breath. One or two things seemed to have changed while he'd been below.

The first surprise was that Shona Grant was at the helm, her hands resting lightly on the polished wheel-spokes, while Jumbo Wills more or less breathed down her neck. *Marlin* was nosing her way up a mile-wide channel between the mainland and a collection of low, barren islands and weed-covered rocks.

"Signed on an extra hand?" he asked, going past them and returning the clipboard to its hook.

"Uh—Shona was keen to have a look around," said Wills. He grinned uneasily at the regular helmsman, who was watching from one side with a wary, not totally happy expression. "Right, Tam, back to work."

Shona Grant let the helmsman take over again, a slight twinkle in her grey eyes.

"No need to worry, Chief Officer," she said. "My father had me steering a fishing boat before I started school—standing on an orange box to reach the controls."

"You're promoted to navigator." Carrick's gaze strayed briefly towards the coastline. "And you're not far from home now."

"Another couple of miles to go, round the next headland. It's a deep water approach with a marked channel." She looked round the bridge with a genuine interest. "I like your *Marlin*."

"Captain Shannon's *Marlin*," corrected Carrick. He turned to Wills. "Where is he, anyway?"

"Talking to Angus Grant again—but he says everything is arranged for us at Feanport." Wills thumbed towards the empty command chair. "Give him another few minutes and he'll be back. Ever known the Old Man let anyone else take us into port when there's an audience?"

"This time he's welcome to it," said Carrick. "Start checking our readiness status. Get Clapper Bell to muster some extra hands aft, call Ferguson and make sure everything's happy on the *Rachel*. You know the rest of it."

Shrugging, Jumbo Wills crossed to the intercom, lifted the handset, and went to work. While the freckle-faced second mate punched buttons and talked, Shona Grant moved over towards the port bridge wing and looked over towards the dark line of little islands.

Carrick studied her. Slim, a fraction under medium height, certainly in her mid-twenties, she was the kind of girl whom men usually called attractive rather than pretty—and tended to remember. The long chestnut hair framed a delicately boned, lightly tanned face which had a slightly snubbed nose, and like most girls from the lonely North-West coast every movement she made held a supple, natural grace.

Shona Grant turned, beckoned him nearer, and pointed to a dilapidated old boat which was coming into sight, moored in the lee of the nearest islet.

"There's your welcome to Feanport," she said. "We haven't much in the way of tourist attractions. That's the *Piddock*, out gathering seaweed. She feeds a processing plant north of the harbour."

An old, converted herring drifter, brown paint badly weathered and faded, most of the *Piddock*'s deckworks had been removed. In their place she had a bucket-grab installed near the bow. As they watched, a low rumble came across the water and the long-toothed grab swung out, to plunge into the sea. In a few moments the workboat's winch gear rumbled again and the grab was hauled up, a mass of dripping wrack and kelp weed clutched between its teeth.

"Local enterprise or outsiders?" asked Carrick, curious.

"Local, strictly Feanport." Shona Grant waited while the grab swung in and two men with rakes appeared on the *Piddock*'s deck, guiding their catch into her hold. "Or the Vullan family, which is pretty much the same thing. Have you heard about them?"

"I've been told they have a share in most things here." He kept his eyes on the workboat. Seaweed was an old island harvest, one which had been almost abandoned for a time but now mattered again. Modern industry had new techniques for using the weed in everything from chemical manufacture to food production. "And about the Witch of the Isles—she sounds formidable."

"I happen to like her, like her a lot," said Shona Grant firmly. "I won't pretend everybody does—Dorothy Vullan just happens to be that kind of person."

"Who runs the weed operation?" asked Carrick.

"Her husband, Milne Vullan—at least he started it, then brought in a man called John Marsh to manage things." She hesitated slightly, then added, "Marsh isn't local, but he does a reasonable enough job."

The fishery cruiser and her tow began to leave the old workboat astern. Carrick stayed silent for a moment, puzzled.

"You say you like Dorothy Vullan. When I talked to your father, he made it plain he felt differently about her. Why?"

"It's a quarrel that goes a long way back—I told you he was mule-tempered at times. Right now, he's in a new rage about her but he just won't talk to me about it. All I've got out of him is a mutter that he won't let any damned woman, witch or not, give him orders."

A grunted plea for attention from the helmsman brought Carrick round. The man eased the wheel's spokes a fraction and nodded ahead. The fishery cruiser was approaching a low, heather-covered headland and behind it a large bay was opening up.

"That's Feanport," agreed Shona Grant. She flicked a loose strand of hair back from her forehead and rested a hand for a moment on the bridge rail. "I'd better go and find my father—and look in on Willie MacLean, make sure they've got him ready to move."

Behind them, Jumbo Wills finished hastily on the intercom, hung up, and came over.

"We'll see you ashore later, won't we?" he asked.

"In a place the size of Feanport you don't see people, you trip over them," she said cheerfully, and left them.

Jumbo Wills waited till she'd gone then gave a long, sad sigh.

"What's wrong with me?" he asked plaintively. "The only people I ever got to save from a watery grave were a bunch of hairy fishermen."

The helmsman treated them both to a gap-toothed grin, a souvenir of a boarding party *Marlin* had once put aboard a Polish trawler off Barra Head. Then he looked past them, switched to a quick, warning frown, and turned his full attention to *Marlin*'s heading as Captain Shannon erupted from the direction of the chartroom like a small, menacing nautical gnome.

"Am I interrupting anything?" he asked Carrick, totally ignoring Wills.

"No, sir." Carrick met the glare with a wooden calm which he knew annoyed Shannon more than anything short of mutiny. "We're at full readiness to enter harbour—tow included."

"Then let's get on with it." Shannon hauled himself up into the command chair. "Till it's done, keep that damned skipper of the *Rachel* away from me. He's as close-mouthed and stubborn as—as—"

"As a mule?" suggested Carrick.

"Yes." Shannon's mouth tightened and for a moment the scowl gave way to a more pensive look. "But he could be a worried mule, an angry mule—or both. I'm going to find out why, because I've a feeling it could matter."

*   *   *

Fean Bay, a bite out of the land almost two miles wide and about a mile deep, was a place where the sea met a series of sheer rock faces backed by hills. But from the moment *Marlin* rounded the headland the bay's benefits as a natural anchorage were immediately obvious. Feanport itself, a straggle of a village with a big stone breakwater enclosing the harbour, lay at the head of the bay—and about half a mile out from the shore a long, narrow island, low and a fertile shade of

green, offered the fishing village an additional, natural shelter from
the open sea.

An escort was waiting. Two broad-beamed fishing boats, idling
close beside the island, moved out and took up station astern as the
fishery cruiser and her tow crept on. Their skippers talked briefly by
radio to Captain Shannon, then kept their boats in the same positions, professionals who knew what they had to do and how to do it.

The little convoy slowly passed the long island. People lived there.
Carrick saw a scatter of small buildings, then a large white house
close by the shore with steps leading down to a small pier. A dark blue
launch, big and with the lines of a one-time naval boat, had just left
the pier and was heading for Feanport. But she gave the convoy a
wide berth and vanished inside the harbour.

Marlin stopped engines about five hundred yards from the outer
breakwater. As she rode gently in the slight swell, the tow-line sag-
ging, a boat was lowered and took Angus Grant back to the *Rachel*.
When it returned, it brought Ferguson and fishery cruiser men who
had been with him. At the same time, Angus Grant cast off his end of
the tow-line.

The fishermen were on their own. Smoothly and neatly the two
Feanport boats came in on either side of the *Rachel* and in moments
she was cradled between them, secured tightly fore and aft.

The black towing diamond had come down from *Marlin*'s foremast.
A klaxon horn sounded from one of the Feanport boats then, their
propellers churning busily, nursing the damaged *Rachel* between
them, they headed in through the breakwater entrance.

"One worry less." Captain Shannon delivered his verdict with relief from the bridge wing, where he'd watched the operation. He
turned, beckoned to Carrick, then glanced past him at Jumbo Wills.
"We'll lie here till the harbour tower signals they're clear. Stretcher
party ready to take that fishing hand ashore?"

"Ready, sir," agreed Wills. "Skipper Grant's daughter is with him
too."

"Right." Shannon looked out across the water at the island, then
switched his attention to Carrick. "That's Fean Island over there—
deep water on three sides, but a rock and foul ground to the north.
Don't try to take anything bigger than a rowing boat out that way."
He paused and scratched at his beard. "The big house on the island is
Fean House, Dorothy Vullan's family home. I've more than a notion

she'll be inviting some of us over—it's almost a tradition when a fishery cruiser comes to Feanport."

"I hope she does," said Carrick evenly. "I talked to Angus Grant, like you did."

Shannon stiffened, faced Carrick for a moment in silence, then nodded. He said softly, "The chartroom, mister. Not here."

Carrick followed him across the bridge, conscious of Jumbo Wills's curious glance, and into the little chartroom. Shannon heeled the door shut behind them.

"How much did you get out of Grant?" he demanded.

"Next to nothing," admitted Carrick. "It was what he wouldn't say that mattered."

Shannon sighed, leaned his hands on the chartroom table, and scowled at the scarred surface of the wood.

"That makes two of us." He paused, as if still trying to make up his mind. "I met him briefly, last time I was here—he's a widower, and the girl is all the family he has. She doesn't live in Feanport now, she's just home for a couple of weeks leave."

"Sir?" Carrick raised a surprised eyebrow.

"That's one thing he will talk about," agreed Shannon. "Grant's proud as hell about her. His Shona seems to have brains as well as looks. She works for one of the North Sea oil outfits, Anglo-Norge, on the research side. Probably earns twice what you do."

"That wouldn't be hard," said Carrick.

Shannon made a show of tidying away a couple of charts. Carrick waited, the deck vibrating gently underfoot as the twin diesels idled. Through the chartroom window he could see a solitary gull had perched on the starboard searchlight mounting. Other gulls, at least a score, were circling and crying overhead while they probably wondered about this new arrival and what kind of food it might provide.

"Do something for me, mister," said Shannon suddenly. "Once we've berthed, explore your way around that harbour. Sniff the air, get the atmosphere of the place. I've got a feeling I don't like, a feeling there's something wrong."

"Involving Grant, sir?"

Shannon shrugged. "Maybe, maybe more than that—I don't know." He took a pack of cigarettes from his pocket, stuck one in his mouth, and lit it with a battered gun-metal lighter. He took a long draw of the smoke, let it filter out again through his beard, then asked, "Notice anything unusual about the two Feanport boats who collected the *Rachel*?"

"No." Carrick stared at him, puzzled.

"Each of them had a rowan tree branch tied to the foremast with red cord. Rowan and red cord—that's the old island way of fending off witchcraft."

"In case helping Angus Grant got them on a witchcraft black list?" Carrick couldn't hide his sheer disbelief. "Hell, we're talking about people who have TV sets and deep freezes, sir. They send their kids to college, they're clever enough to make monkeys out of the Inland Revenue, they—"

"If they're worried, what's wrong with a little old-fashioned insurance?" interrupted Shannon. "And if they are worried, what's going on? Dorothy Vullan always made a joke of this Witch of the Isles business." He tapped the chart table with his stubby fingertips. "I don't think the girl knows anything, and it's probably the same with his crew. Grant won't talk—but see him, tell him we want to inspect what's left of the gas cylinder that exploded. Keep it casual, make some kind of a noise about a routine report. Understood?"

Carrick nodded. Over on the breakwater wall a signal lamp had begun winking in their direction. Shannon had seen it too, the all clear signal.

"One last thing," he said. "I got it from the girl, when we were down in sickbay seeing how that injured fishing hand was making out. The Feanport constable, a man named MacKenzie, got himself drowned about ten days ago—he went fishing one night and his body was washed up three days later. When I talked to Grant, he didn't even mention it." He paused. "I'm not saying there has to be any connection, mister."

"No," agreed Carrick. "But Clapper Bell will want to know. MacKenzie was a friend of his."

"I'll tell him." Shannon nodded unemotionally. "All right, I've a ship to berth. Let's do it sweetly—whether you see them or not, we're going to have plenty of spectators."

*   *   *

Ten minutes later, after an impeccable piece of ship-handling on Shannon's part, *Marlin* tied up at a vacant berth on the south quay of

Feanport harbour. Her nearest neighbour was a coaster unloading cement, beyond that was a small oil tanker which was getting ready to sail, and the rest of the harbour was a clutter of fishing boats of every shape and size. Most were Feanport boats by their registration letters, all had landed their day's catch, and the usual bustle of buyers were moving from one small mountain of overflowing fish boxes to the next.

An ambulance threaded its way through the confusion and reached *Marlin* almost at the same time as her gangway was run out. Another moment then, as the ambulance doors opened, Willie MacLean was carried down the gangway on a stretcher. Shona Grant was with him, waited until MacLean had been put aboard the ambulance, and stayed for a moment to thank the stretcher party once the vehicle had driven off again.

Carrick came back from checking the bow mooring lines in time to see her walking away, heading along the quayside towards the village. He noticed she was still wearing the duffel-coat she'd borrowed from Shannon, then his view was blocked as another load of cement was swung ashore from the coaster.

He headed aft. There was one thing he wanted to make sure about before he went ashore.

As usual, Clapper Bell was in the scuba compartment. He was spruced up, obviously ready to go ashore, but instead he was leaning in the doorway, staring out at the harbour with an odd frown on his rugged face.

"You've heard?" asked Carrick.

"Aye. The Old Man just told me." Bell spoke softly, a puzzled note in his voice. He sighed and tapped a clenched fist aimlessly against the bulkhead metal for a moment. "It's dam' hard to believe, though."

"Why?"

Bell grimaced, "George MacKenzie didn't take chances. An' even if he got into trouble, he was a fair to middlin' swimmer." He shrugged. "Still, if your number comes up—"

"You could ask around, find out what maybe did happen," suggested Carrick.

Bell nodded. "I will. An' raise a glass or two for him at the same time. Uh—fancy comin' along, sir?"

Carrick made his answer a vague half-promise. A little later, clear of the last of berthing duties, he went ashore. Once he had passed the coaster the quayside quickly became the usual maze of stacked fish boxes and drying nets, of container trucks being loaded and other trucks replenishing boats with fuel oil and crushed ice.

There was prosperity in the air—mixed in with the inevitable odour compounded of fish offal, diesel exhaust and rotting seaweed. Even the big black-backed gulls stalking arrogantly around were as plump as any he'd seen, and the overflowing fish boxes were crammed. Cod and haddock, blue-skinned mackerel, brown-skinned flat fish and the inevitable undersea oddities that came with them were piled along the quay, while the auctioning and price-haggling process went on around them.

But he noticed one other thing as he went along, keeping his pace to a casual stroll, evesdropping on bargainings between skippers and buyers, occasionally stopping to show an apparent interest in another newly landed catch. Fishery Protection uniform could produce different reactions from fishermen, from a friendly nod to blank-faced hostility. Somehow, in a way hard to label, Feanport was different. He was conscious of eyes following him as he passed, of conversations dying. It wasn't hostility.

It was something else, something close to apprehension and yet a couple of times he caught a man looking at him with what could almost have been hope—before the individual concerned turned quickly away and vanished among his companions. Captain Shannon had asked him to smell the air—and the Feanport air reeked of tension.

Rounding the head of the harbour, he slowed again. The dark blue ex-navy launch he'd seen earlier was tied up beside a cluster of line-fishing boats. Her name was the *Sea Whip*. She looked fast and bristled with sophisticated equipment, but he kept going, because something more important had caught his eye ahead, the tide-stained, barnacled edge of a repair slipway.

When he got there and looked down from the edge, the *Rachel* was lying high and dry out of the water with the hole in her port side—a hole big enough to thread a man through—clearly visible. Other spectators, mostly fishermen, were gathered around solemnly inspecting the damage, then he saw Angus Grant climbing the stone steps that led out of the slipway. A man in overalls was with him, they stopped and exchanged a final word at the top, then Grant turned to leave.

As he did, one of the spectators, a fisherman about Grant's age who had a patch over one eye, laid a hand on his arm and spoke to him in a low voice. Bleakly, tightlipped, Grant brushed him aside and strode on—then saw Carrick and seemed to hesitate before he came over.

"What's the verdict?" asked Carrick, thumbing down towards the fishing boat.

"It could be worse," said Grant carefully. "Two weeks, they say, then I'll be back fishing. The insurance will pay most of the bill." He glanced round at their audience and raised his voice. "Aye, two weeks—and I'll be back."

"I want to talk to you, skipper," said Carrick quietly. "Privately."

"Then you can walk with me." Grant's bearded, beak-nosed face didn't alter in expression. As they set off, he spoke again, in a slightly friendlier voice. "Lachie MacLean has my car over at the road beyond the harbourmaster's office—he drove Shona home so she could change her clothes. We're going back to get her, then we'll visit the hospital and see how Willie is."

They reached the car in a couple of minutes. It was an old Ford station wagon parked near the foot of a steep curve of road which led up to Feanport village. Lachie MacLean lounged against the driver's door, drinking a can of beer but broke off for a moment to give Carrick a grin. Behind him, a line of empty container trucks were parked on the slope, waiting their turn to come down and load at the quay.

"What is it you want?" asked Grant, stopping.

"Permission for one of our people to have a look at the damage on the *Rachel*," said Carrick, keeping his manner to a mild disinterest. "Captain Shannon has the usual routine report to file to Department—what we did, why we did it."

"He's welcome," agreed Grant with a minimal nod. "Anything else?"

"No." Carrick paused. "Should there be?"

Grant's eyes flickered. But whatever he'd been going to reply was lost as a hoarse, warning shout rang out from somewhere near. They swung round and saw the squat bulk of the leading container truck rolling silently and driverless down the steep slope above them, heading straight for the parked Ford.

Lachie MacLean had heard the warning too. The fair-haired young fishing hand stared open-mouthed for an instant while the truck, a big Volvo unit, silently gathered speed. Then he dropped the beer can and jumped clear for his life.

In almost slow-motion style the massive container truck struck the little station wagon side-on. Sheer weight and momentum carried it on, pushing the Ford ahead, while glass shattered and metal tore and twisted. Then the Ford, still being shoved sideways, hit a large mooring bollard on the quayside. Both vehicles came to a locked halt in a final crunch of metal.

Stunned into silence, Angus Grant stared at the wreckage. The Volvo truck had embedded its nose into what was left of his Ford but still seemed almost undamaged. White-faced at his escape, Lachie MacLean was picking himself up from the ground again while men came hurrying over from several directions. The first to arrive, a slim, middle-aged man wearing a sheepskin jacket and black beret, stopped beside Grant and shook his head.

"All I could do was shout," he said. "Sorry, skipper—I saw it start rolling, but all I could do was yell."

"Thank God you did," said Grant hoarsely.

"At least no one was hurt," said the other man. He eyed Carrick. "I'm John Marsh, from the seaweed plant. You're from the fishery cruiser?"

Carrick nodded, considering Marsh with a new interest. The man who ran the seaweed processing plant for the Vullan family had dark hair, a lined, sallow face and bright, calculating eyes. His accent was far removed from Scotland but was hard to place.

"You saw it happen?" asked Carrick.

"Yes. It just started rolling." Marsh turned to Angus Grant and shook his head sympathetically. "You're having a real run of bad luck, skipper."

"It would have been worse, but for you," said Grant in a tight voice.

A knot of onlookers had gathered. A fair-haired man in driving overalls pushed his way through them and moistened his lips.

"That's my truck," he said unhappily. "But hell, I left the handbrake tight on, so help me." Then seeing the expression on Grant's face, he took a wary half-step back. "Look, mister I'm just trying to say I'm sorry."

"Where were you?" demanded Grant.

"Talking wi' some of my mates," said the man defensively. "That's no crime, is it? The handbrake must have jumped loose—just one o' those things, right?"

Carrick went past them, eased through the onlookers, opened the truck door, and swung himself up into the Volvo's driving cab. As he located the handbrake lever John Marsh arrived at the cab door and peered in.

"Go ahead, try it," invited Marsh. "You've got a witness."

Carrick reached down and gave the lever a tug. It tightened a full inch before the ratchet clicked to a halt.

"Bad luck or damned carelessness," said Marsh. "Either way, his insurance company won't argue so Skipper Grant is all right."

Carrick returned the brake lever to its original position and climbed out of the cab again.

"Where were you when the truck started moving?" he asked.

"Over there." Marsh thumbed towards the quayside then nodded wisely. "I'm ahead of you, Chief Officer, but you're wrong. There was no one anywhere near it."

"Accidents happen," agreed Carrick.

"Right." Marsh slammed the truck cab door shut for him. "But don't count on Angus Grant seeing it that way. He gets some strange ideas."

"I'll remember," promised Carrick, and left him.

The same cluster of onlookers were still around Angus Grant and the luckless truck driver but Carrick deliberately skirted past them, heading back towards *Marlin*. Then he saw Lachie MacLean ahead, standing at the edge of the quay, staring out across the harbour. His face was strained, his eyes were on the dark blue hull of the *Sea Whip*.

"Feel all right now?" asked Carrick.

MacLean nodded.

"Nice lines," said Carrick, nodding towards the *Sea Whip*. "Who owns her?"

"Dorothy Vullan," said MacLean.

Carrick blinked. "Did she come over on it?"

"No, but her husband did," grated the fishing hand. "He went to see your captain—Marsh brought him over from the island."

"Lucky for you," mused Carrick. "Marsh probably saved your life."

"Marsh is all right," said MacLean. "A man has to earn a living." He turned and walked away.

III

The petty officer on gangway watch intercepted Webb Carrick as he stepped aboard *Marlin*. Captain Shannon wanted him to report immediately.

He headed for'ard, to the day cabin below the bridge. On the way, a difference in the fishery cruiser's normal background lifepulse registered and made him smile. The normal purr of the main generator was missing and the slightly higher whine of the auxiliary had taken its place—Andy Shaw was using a Chief Engineer's prerogative and wasting no time in carrying out the maintenance he'd programmed.

Carrick knocked on the door of the day cabin, heard the usual muffled bark which meant he could enter, and went in. Shannon and a stranger were seated in the cabin's two armchairs, a bottle of Shannon's prized single-malt whisky and two emptied glasses between them on a small table.

"Well timed, mister," said Shannon, welcoming him with a nod. "We've a visitor who wanted to meet you."

"I'm Milne Vullan." The other man, a tall, lantern-jawed figure who looked in his early fifties, rose with athletic ease and held out his hand. "From what I've heard, Carrick, you did a good job on the *Rachel*."

Vullan's handshake was a powerful squeeze. He had dark, wavy hair flecked with grey, a rugged, still good-looking face, and wore an open-necked shirt under an old tweed suit which was patched with leather at the elbows.

"It depends on the version you heard," said Carrick, noticing one thing more—Vullan wore a waterproof diving watch on his left wrist.

"I talked to Shona Grant," said Vullan. "I'd say she was pretty unbiased."

"We've been talking about ballot boxes, mister," Shannon said. "Collecting them, how and when—Mr. Vullan is local Returning Officer in this damned by-election."

"Which means being on the sharp end of any complaints," said Vullan wryly. "There are votes to gather from half a dozen islands, Carrick. Maybe no more than a couple of hundred votes altogether—but they could be enough to swing the result, so they matter."

"But we've sorted out a timetable," shrugged Shannon. His eyes flickered a warning. "How was your—ah—walk around, mister?"

"Ask Angus Grant," said Carrick. "A runaway truck thumped his car while it was lying empty."

"Grant again?" Vullan winced.

"But nobody hurt," said Carrick. "Your plant manager, John Marsh, was there—he'll tell you about it."

"No doubt." Vullan sighed and glanced at his watch. "Still, that man Grant is having his share of woe." He turned to Shannon and grinned. "Captain, it's time I got back. I've some fish tanks to tend, or that Witch wife of mine will give me hell."

"You and I have an invitation, Mister Carrick," said Shannon, getting to his feet. "We're invited to Fean House tonight for a meal, if you can find a clean shirt."

"I'd like that," agreed Carrick. "And I'll borrow the shirt."

Vullan chuckled a little. "It'll just be family, Carrick. I'll expect you both around eight—will I send a boat over, captain?"

Shannon seemed to consider for a moment, then shook his head. "We'll just arrive."

Vullan shook hands with them both again, and left.

"And I'm glad that's over," said Shannon once the cabin door had closed. He flopped back into his chair, topped up his glass from the bottle, then remembered Carrick. "Get a glass of your own, mister. Then sit down—make the place look tidier."

Carrick fetched a spare glass from a locker beside Shannon's old leather-topped desk. Twice as big as Carrick's cramped quarters, the day cabin had one startling feature—bright chintz curtains at the portholes, contributed by Captain Shannon's wife. *Marlin*'s commander loathed them almost as much as her other contribution, a rubber plant which moped in a corner and refused to die, but he seemed to lack the courage to get rid of them.

The rest, from spotless white paintwork to gleaming brass, was practical and comfortable. A roll pendulum and repeater compass hung above the desk. A bookshelf was crammed with Fishery Department handbooks and most of one bulkhead was occupied by a taped-up spread of Admiralty chart on which Shannon had outlined the new British two hundred mile exclusive fishing limits with a black felt-tip pen.

Black for mourning, decided Carrick. The new fishing limits had been decreed by the politicians, but the fishery cruiser captains were still waiting for the politicians to explain how, without major air support, you kept tabs on all that went on within that two hundred mile limit in anything more than pretend style.

Pouring himself a drink from the bottle, he kept it modest in size and didn't look for water. James Shannon regarded adding water to whisky as a sacrilege to be compared with being rude about the Queen or being seasick on his bridge.

"All right," said Shannon brusquely as soon as Carrick was seated. "Let's have it. I asked you to sniff the air. It sounds like your nose got you into trouble."

"If you mean Grant's car being wrecked it had all the look of an accident," said Carrick carefully. "The rest of it—well, it's hard to label. A smell, like you said. But—" he shrugged, then, flatly and factually, told what had happened.

When he'd finished, Shannon gave a slow nod then sat silent for a spell, nursing his glass between his stubby fingers.

"Doesn't help much, does it?" He scowled at the blacklined chart, a handy focus for his thoughts. "Seen Clapper Bell?"

"Not since he went ashore."

"He may pick up something," said Shannon. "But now we've got Vullan—the way he came aboard, almost as soon as we'd berthed, could be straightforward. He brought the blank voting papers and the sealed ballot boxes for delivery to the islands. But on the other hand he tried hard to find out if there was any other reason for us coming to Feanport."

"What about tonight's invitation?" asked Carrick.

"It's the tradition when a fishery cruiser arrives, like I told you." Shannon sipped a modicum of whisky and rinsed it around his mouth before he swallowed. "Still, whatever's going on, get one thing straight. Vullan is no fool—even if his wife usually overshadows him. He ended up commanding a destroyer in World War Two. Now he does high-powered consultant work in marine biology." His eyes strayed to the limits chart again. "That includes having advised half a dozen Government commissions on fish stock breeding areas. Don't jump to any wrong conclusions about him."

"But we go tonight?" pressed Carrick.

"I wouldn't miss the chance," said Shannon. A wisp of a smile crossed his round, bearded face. "Mister, we may learn something, we may not—but they keep a damned good whisky at Fean House. That's one kind of witchcraft I'll always respect."

*   *   *

It was about an hour later when Carrick went ashore again and the scene around the harbour had changed considerably.

Dusk was edging in from the sea. The sky had acquired a dull edge of grey cloud to the northwest, which might mean rain or snow before morning, and the wind seemed to have freshened. A few fishing boats were murmuring out for a night's work, pitching a little in the swell as they cleared the breakwater, but the rest lay deserted at their berths. The fish buyers and the container trucks had gone, and the harbour had a sleepy air as if it was resting.

He had two good reasons for going ashore. One was to locate Clapper Bell, who still hadn't returned from his wanderings and the other was to escape from Jumbo Wills, who was moaning about being stuck aboard as duty officer.

At the end of the harbour he reached the place where Angus Grant's station wagon had been demolished by the runaway truck. Everything had been cleared and only a powdering of glass remained to hint at what had happened. Going on, Carrick toiled up the gradient to the start of the village, and had his first real close-up view of Feanport.

Clinging to the rising ground, it amounted to a few tight, narrow streets of old stone cottages, with black slate roofs. Here and there naked granite rock jutted out between the buildings and broke the pattern. Occasionally there was a larger structure and higher up the hill, not much more than a silhouette in the fading light, he saw a church and a small graveyard.

He walked along, the scent of peat-smoke in his nostrils, the contrast of the TV aerials which cluttered the cottage roofs and the sight of a brightly-lit shop window filled with refrigerators and washing machines bringing a slight smile to his lips. The only signs of the coming by-election were a few political posters peeling from walls.

A voice hailed him and he stopped as another figure in Fishery Protection uniform crossed the street to join him. It was Ferguson, and *Marlin*'s junior second mate looked even more pinch-faced than usual in the greying dusk.

"Doing the town?" asked Ferguson. "I found a notice that says the British Legion pipe band have a practice in the village hall tonight. Add a couple of bars and a fishermen's co-operative store with a liquor licence, and you've heard it all."

"Rent a kilt somewhere," said Carrick. "You'd look good in a pipe band—the drum major could twirl you or something." He glanced up and down the little street, which was almost deserted. "Seen Clapper Bell?"

Ferguson scowled. "Yes, damn his insolence."

"Meaning?"

"You know him," said Ferguson. "One day I'll have him on report before the Old Man. But if you want him, he was in the Anchor Watch—it's a bar in the next street on your left."

Ferguson stalked off, and Carrick moved on past a small single-storey building which had a sign which said Cottage Hospital. Just ahead, an old truck clattered out of a side street and turned down towards the harbour.

"Fishery snoop," yelled the driver from the open cab window, then made a grating gear-change as he pulled away.

Unperturbed, Carrick glanced after the truck then paused. On the other side of the street a man had just slipped quickly into the shelter of a shop doorway. It was the little man with an eyepatch he'd seen trying to talk to Angus Grant at the harbour. Deliberately, casually, Carrick stuck his hands in his pockets and turned up the side street.

Once he'd rounded the next corner he stopped and made a pretence of studying another collection of neglected election posters, waiting. After a moment, the little man with the eye-patch hurried round, saw him, and kept going. But he stopped again, further along the street, apparently interested in another shop-window.

Casually, Carrick walked on, reached him, and stopped. The man kept his attention on the window display, though he'd chosen badly. It was a women's hairdressing salon, and as Carrick didn't move the man suddenly turned, almost dived away, and headed back the way he had come. For a moment Carrick thought of reversing the process and following him, but the Anchor Watch bar was just a little way along the street and he settled for that.

The Anchor Watch was small, the ceiling low, the woodwork dark with age and varnish, and the air was stale with tobacco smoke. Carrick paused inside the door, where the linoleum floor covering was so old the pattern had almost vanished, saw a cluster of fishermen playing darts in a corner, glanced round the rest of the customers, then spotted Clapper Bell elbowed up at the bar.

"I'm orderin'," said Bell with a slight grin as Carrick joined him. "Name it."

"Whisky," Carrick told the wizened barman, who had just dumped two pint mugs of beer in front of the red-haired bo'sun. "All right, Clapper, since when did you buy drinks for anyone?"

"It happens sometimes," said Bell. As the barman turned for the whisky, he added quietly, "An' I'd call this lubrication. I'm drinkin' with the harbourmaster, an old josser called Morrison. He's talkative, sir."

"Then I'll do the buying." Carrick paid for the drinks as the whisky arrived. But as Bell lifted the beer mugs, he stopped him. "What about your pal the village constable? Heard anything?"

Bell shook his head, his eyes bleak for a moment. "Not much more than that he went fishin' an' didn't come back. His body an' the boat were washed up near Broch Point."

"Talked to his replacement?" asked Carrick.

"He hasn't arrived yet," said Bell. "The cop in the next village is coverin', but that means he's on the end of a telephone twenty miles away." He glanced past Carrick. "My punter's gettin' restive, sir."

They took the drinks across to a table where a red-cheeked, elderly man wearing a dark blue donkey jacket sat with a peaked cap and a couple of empty beer glasses in front of him. Clapper Bell kept the introductions brief—Shuggy Morrison was a naval pensioner who regarded being harbourmaster at Feanport as a suitably non-strenuous way of picking up some extra money.

"Though there's a wee bit excitement now and again," he admitted, surfacing from his new drink and wiping the beer suds from his upper lip. "Like the *Rachel* coming in today."

"Tricky for you," said Bell solemnly and gave Carrick a cautionary glance. "But you were sayin' some of the boats are in the money, right?"

Morrison nodded. "The boats wi' sensible skippers, who know where to fish." He paused and winked slyly. "Or maybe I mean wi' skippers who'll do what they're told. It can be the same thing, eh?"

"Would Angus Grant agree?" asked Carrick.

"Him?" Shuggy Morrison hesitated and shrugged. "You won't find heather growing out o' my ears—I'm from Glasgow, like your bo'sun. But I still won't go feuding wi' the Witch of the Isles the way he does."

"That began a long time ago," mused Carrick.

"Before I came," agreed Morrison. He wheezed a wary chuckle. "I'm not saying she scares me. I haven't been scared of a woman since my wife ran off with a window-cleaner. But there's good luck and bad luck, and Grant's boat is out there wi' a damned great hole in it."

Carrick caught himself wishing for a cigarette, sighed for the pack taped to his cabin mirror, and fought down the momentary craving.

"What started their quarrel?" he asked.

"Domestic, something to do wi' Grant's wife when she was alive," shrugged Morrison. "Don't ask me why it flared up again, except he hasn't had much fishing luck lately. But even so—"

"Even so, what?" said Carrick.

Morrison looked around the bar cautiously, then lowered his voice. "Like I said, I'm no' one of your superstitious hairy Highlanders, right? But if I was, then I'd have gone a damned sight more carefully than Grant did. Because I'd have thought about what happened to the last man to start a feud wi' that woman." He grimaced. "That was the village constable, and he drowned."

"George MacKenzie?" Clapper Bell stared at him. "You didn't tell me that!"

"Did you ask me?" Morrison scowled, finished his beer in a quick series of gulps, and pushed back his chair. "I'm going—thanks for the drink."

"Not yet." Clapper Bell grabbed him by the arm.

"I'm not lookin' for trouble," protested Morrison, then gave a low yelp as Bell's grip tightened.

"Trouble just found you," said Carrick. "You're staying, till we hear the rest."

Licking his lips, the elderly harbourmaster glanced around. But the darts match was still in full swing and no one else in the bar seemed in the slightest way interested in what was happening to him.

"All right," he surrendered with a wheeze. "The gossip around the harbour is that MacKenzie got mad because the Vullan woman complained to his bosses about somethin' he'd done and landed him in trouble. Then—well, he began asking questions around the harbour. Questions about her boat, the *Sea Whip* and where people had seen it. He said he was going to get his own back." The man paused and looked at them earnestly. "So help me, that's all I know."

"And before MacKenzie?" grated Clapper Bell.

"You mean—others? A few idiots aroun' the harbour are blaming her for every damned thing from the odd storm at sea to their girl friends going sour. But that's only started now."

"Let him go, Clapper," said Carrick.

"I just do my job," said Morrison, scrambling to his feet as Bell released his grip. "Do it, and keep my nose clean. Remember that."

"I'll arrange a vote of thanks," said Carrick.

Barely managing a muttered goodbye, the man hurried to the Anchor Watch's door and left. As the door slammed shut Clapper Bell scratched his chin and didn't try to hide his bewilderment.

"What the hell did George MacKenzie get himself into?" he asked in a note of disbelief.

"Maybe I can ask Dorothy Vullan," said Carrick. "The Old Man's taking me to meet her tonight."

"A little bit o' witchcraft wouldn't do our captain any harm," said Bell. "But that business about the *Sea Whip*—"

"Could mean anything or nothing, so don't start building fancy theories." Finishing his drink, Carrick pointed a finger. "Why is Ferguson making complaining noises about you?"

"That?" Bell's rugged face twisted into an expression of innocence. "I just exchanged a private opinion or two with him, sir. If an officer starts accusin' you of runnin' a poker school in the galley, but agrees he can't prove it—"

"Then a wise man closes the game down, fast," said Carrick wearily. "Or he moves it on. Either way, I don't want to know. I've more to worry about."

"Sir." Bell gave a penitent nod, then winked. "But there's no harm in me thinkin' he's an old woman, is there?"

Carrick gave up, thumbed him to his feet, and they headed for the door. Several of the Anchor Watch's customers watched them go, a couple gave a brief, half-friendly nod of greeting, but none said a word.

Dusk had given way to dark outside, the sky had completely clouded over, and the temperature seemed to have fallen several degrees. But Feanport had a peaceful, tranquil air. Only an occasional car passed the two Fishery Protection men as they headed in the direction of the harbour through the quiet streets.

A dog was barking somewhere in the distance. Music and laughter came from one of the cottages, a baby was crying in another. The whole atmosphere was soothing and Clapper Bell began humming a tune under his breath.

But as they came near to the cottage hospital there was a sudden shout and the sound of running feet. A moment later a figure shot out of a lane just ahead and hesitated under the glare of a street lamp. It was Donnie MacLean, the third of the *Rachel*'s fishing hands—and as he tried to start running again two other figures pounced out of the lane and grabbed him. Something swung under the light, MacLean went limp, and the two men began dragging him back into the lane.

Clapper Bell charged forward, Carrick pounding along beside him. A third man appeared at the mouth of the lane, saw them, called a warning, and MacLean was abandoned, falling to the ground.

Tackling the figure nearest him, Carrick dodged a kick, slammed a fist into the man's middle, and heard a howl and a thud. Clapper Bell had grabbed his first choice and had literally picked him up and thrown him against the nearest wall.

While Bell swung round to challenge the third figure, Carrick's man came in again, cursing. This time Carrick circled warily as he saw the beer can ring-pulls which his opponent wore on each fist like knuckle-dusters—the kind of knuckle-dusters which could rip open a man's face.

Feinting, he faked a stumble, lured the man on, then catapulted forward. His shoulder took his opponent hard in the chest, they went down together, rolled, and he felt the cloth of his jacket tear as a slashing blow from the ring-pulls grazed his side. Carrick countered with a flat-edged hand-jab which smashed across the man's mouth—then as the man squealed and scrambled clear, another shout rang out.

Suddenly, as suddenly as they'd appeared, all three men ran back up the lane and disappeared into the darkness. As Carrick got up, Clapper Bell joined him, panting a little but grinning, and thumbed at the lane.

"Do we go after them?" he asked.

"No chance. We'd be chasing our tails." Carrick turned and stooped over Donnie MacLean who was lying groaning. "Help me get him up."

Between them, they got the fishing hand to his feet and he managed to stay that way, leaning against a wall.

"You'll live, son," said Clapper Bell cheerfully. "You took a thump on the head an' a kick in the slats, that's all."

"All?" MacLean grimaced, clung to the wall, and took a deep, painful breath. "Thanks for—well, being around."

"Recognise them?" asked Carrick.

"No." MacLean took a step away from the wall, swayed on his feet, but stayed upright. "They—they jumped me in the lane. I'd been to see my brother at the cottage hospital."

"You nearly booked the bed next to him," said Clapper Bell. "They were ready to make it a ring-pull job—the doctor who patched you would have needed a sewing machine."

"But why?" demanded Carrick. He didn't get an answer and tried again. "You must have an idea, Donnie."

"Drunks," said MacLean vaguely, and shook his head. "Drunks, or headbangers off one o' the outside boats in the harbour. Let's just forget it, right?"

"Forget it?" Clapper Bell asked incredulously.

"Easier, always is." The fishing hand nodded earnestly. "I'm okay, an' I live just at the top of the lane—my cousin Lachie is in the house, so no problems."

"If that's the way you want it," agreed Carrick neutrally. "How is brother Willie getting on?"

"Fine—bandaged up, but fine," said Donnie MacLean quickly. "They say he can get out tomorrow. Uh—I'll get home now."

"But we'll make sure you get there," said Carrick.

They went with him, ignoring his protesting noises. The lane snaked its way up through the village and the MacLean cottage, last in a row, overlooked bare hillside. The fishing hand opened the door and looked embarrassed.

"Thanks again," he said. "Thanks and—well, forget it, like I asked."

He'd gone inside and the door was closed before they could reply.

"Gratitude, sheer gratitude," said Clapper Bell. "Take a look at what one o' his little pals dropped."

The home-made cosh he handed Carrick was a crude affair made from lead piping bound with electrical flex and swinging from a piece of knotted rope.

"Primitive," said Carrick, swinging it speculatively. "But the weight's right."

"Spot on," said Bell. Then he realised Carrick was staring at something above the cottage door, took a half-step nearer, peered up, and swore softly.

"Rowan," agreed Carrick.

A fresh branch of rowan was nailed above the doorway. Donnie MacLean might say he didn't know who had attacked him or why, but he'd already taken out insurance of a different kind.

*   *   *

Ninety minutes later—ninety minutes that passed quickly—Webb Carrick stepped ashore on Fean Island for the first time.

Earlier, when he had returned to *Marlin* at the harbour, he had again brought Captain Shannon up to date with Clapper Bell beside him to give the occasional growl of confirmation. None of it had improved Shannon's mood and at the end they'd learned why.

Dragged away from repairing the main generator, Andy Shaw had visited the *Rachel* on the harbour slipway. But the fishery cruiser's chief engineer had returned empty-handed.

"He'll take bets that someone got there ahead of him," snarled Shannon. "There's just that damned hole in her side—and one or two bits of broken metal that don't matter a damn. The valve head, even the feed pipes to the galley stove have gone. Destroyed in the explosion or gone overboard—like hell they were."

Carrick knew that Shannon's real wrath was that he hadn't anticipated it. But later, once he'd washed and changed for their visit to Fean Island, he returned on deck to find *Marlin*'s commander in a more amiable mood and a minor surprise waiting. The fishery cruiser's brand new patrol launch had been lowered and was ready to take them on the short trip across to the island.

"I was going to use one of the small boats, then I decided to put on a show," said Shannon. "Just you and I, mister—call it a little bit of bluff for general benefit."

They climbed down a ladder, got aboard, and Shannon took the controls while Carrick cast off. Twenty-five feet long and with a high performance engine, the patrol launch rated as Shannon's newest toy and he guarded it like a secret weapon. Twin screws gave the slim-lined hull a speed well in excess of *Marlin*'s thrusting thirty knots—but when she went snarling out of the harbour a few minutes later she made a lot of noise and wash but was still throttled well back from maximum.

Shannon kept things that way, even once they were clear of the harbour breakwater. Standing beside him in the cockpit, Carrick decided it was a foxy move—plenty of eyes would have watched them leave, plenty of experienced fishermen would have been very interested in the patrol launch's performance. But he could guess their verdict, that the patrol launch was just another moderately fast boat that could be matched and probably beaten by quite a few local craft.

Including Vullan's *Sea Whip*. The thought was in his mind as the short trip to the island was completed and the patrol launch slowed, coming in towards the jetty below Fean House. The *Sea Whip* was there, tied up for the night beside a couple of smaller boats, and as the patrol launch murmured in beside her two figures appeared on the jetty alongside and hailed a greeting.

They were Milne Vullan and John Marsh, and they took the mooring lines, then waited in the darkness until Shannon and Carrick joined them.

From the jetty, they were led up the flight of worn stone steps that led to the dark silhouette of Fean House then round and across a patch of overgrown garden to the front of the house, where several of the windows were brightly lit. The door lay open and a moment later they were in the warmth of the house.

"Good evening, Captain Shannon," said a woman's husky voice. "It's good to see you again. Introduce me to your friend."

Mrs. Dorothy Mary Fergus MacDonald Vullan, hereditary Witch of the Isles, stood in the big hall of Fean House, her back to a stone fireplace where enough driftwood blazed to roast any self-respecting ox and smiled at her guests.

"You look well, Mrs. Vullan," said Captain Shannon awkwardly.

It was probably as much of a compliment as he'd paid a woman in years, but in Dorothy Vullan's case, it was justified. As Shannon muttered an introduction, Carrick adjusted to his initial surprise.

The Witch of the Isles was a woman in her early fifties, but that was incidental. Tall and straight-shouldered, with short, copper-bronze hair which glinted like flame in the firelight, she had a figure most women half her age would have been proud to possess. Her eyes were green, her face had a quality about it which ignored the first tiny lines of age, and she wore an ankle-length green velvet skirt with a simple white shirt-blouse and a chunky gold link necklace. Her only other jewellery was her wedding ring.

"I'm glad you could come too, Chief Officer," she said with a twinkle as they shook hands. Then she glanced past him. "Stop hiding back there, Shona."

"Who's hiding?" protested Shona Grant.

Carrick hadn't seen her till then. She came over to join them from behind a leather-topped cocktail bar, where she'd been laying out glasses. Her hair was caught back by a silver clasp and she wore a tailored suede jacket over black velvet slacks and a flame-coloured blouse. Dorothy Vullan turned her attention back to Shannon, leaving them alone for a moment.

"Don't look quite so surprised," murmured Shona. "I got invited, the same way you did."

"I'll bet that made your father happy," said Carrick.

"He's having to learn I make my own decisions." Her grey eyes clouded for a moment, then brightened again. "Well, what do you think of our Witch of the Isles?"

"She's—well, not what I expected," admitted Carrick. "I'm impressed."

"Go on," urged Dorothy Vullan's voice unexpectedly. She had come up behind him and looked amused. A wary-faced Captain Shannon was by her side. "How do you feel about witches, Chief Officer?"

"Right now I feel I must have read the wrong comic books at school," he said solemnly.

She liked that and gave a husky chuckle.

"Being a witch can be fun—sometimes," she said. "But it can have its disadvantages too—ask my ancestors. Most of them met some kind of nasty end."

"Most of them deserved it. But I've no complaints," said Milne Vullan, who had overheard. Coming over from where he'd been standing with Marsh, he laid a hand on her shoulder and gave her a look of genuine affection. "No complaints at all—not yet, anyway."

"He's the tolerant kind," explained Dorothy Vullan. "That's why I married him. Milne, while you're in that kind of mood how about pouring some drinks?"

The talk became general for a bit. Marsh helped Vullan with the drinks while Dorothy Vullan took Shannon and Carrick on a guided tour round the collection of old banners, glinting weaponry and paintings which decorated the stone walls of the hall.

"You've seen most of this before, captain, I know," she said almost apologetically. "But I enjoy doing it—when a house has been lived in for over three hundred years it collects history like cobwebs."

"Except for Bonnie Prince Charlie," murmured Shona Grant.

"Yes, we missed out there," admitted Dorothy Vullan sadly. "The Witch of that time had the kind of reputation that frightened him off."

"It wouldn't happen now," said John Marsh, offering her a drink.

"I wouldn't be too sure." Her mouth tightened for a moment, then she took the glass from him, sipped, returned to her theme. "Take a good look at those broadswords above the fireplace, Mr. Carrick. They were used at Culloden—on the losing side."

*　　*　　*

They ate a little later, at an oval oak table in a wood-panelled dining room, the walls decorated with heavily framed paintings of old sailing ship scenes. The table sparkled with crystal and silver but Dorothy Vullan served the food from a heated trolley—Fean House's domestic help came from the village by day and were back there by nightfall.

It was a meal in the Highland tradition, from game soup to grilled venison and finishing with a selection of island cheeses and tiny oatmeal bannocks. Placed next to Shona Grant and facing Shannon across the table, Carrick learned several things about their hosts and Marsh from the general conversation.

Milne Vullan and the Witch of the Isles had met and married while he'd been a young naval officer. Now he used Fean House as a base for his marine consultancy work and also helped Dorothy Vullan run a hotch-potch of family business interests around the Feanport area—most of them, he claimed ruefully, anything but profit-making. John Marsh, who stayed quiet most of the meal, listening, smiling, but seldom joining in the conversation, lived alone in a cottage at the south end of Fean Island.

His coming to Feanport was recent though, as Vullan explained, he and Marsh had known each other since wartime days. Marsh had come north on a visit after returning to Britain after a spell of working abroad and had ended up staying on to manage the seaweed plant.

"Strange things happen up here." With slight smile on his lips, Marsh glanced along the table at Dorothy Vullan. "Maybe somebody heaved a spell in my direction."

An odd look passed between Dorothy Vullan and her husband and her manner held an underlying touch of frost when she answered.

"I certainly wasn't involved," she said.

A flush showed on Marsh's lined, sallow face. Making a throat-clearing noise, Captain Shannon bridged the awkward silence that followed.

"As election campaigns go, I wouldn't call the one around here a fireball affair," he said. "What's wrong? Did we arrive too late—or too early?"

"Nobody cares," suggested Milne Vullan, looking relieved at the switch in conversation. "Well—" his glance switched to Shona Grant, who gave him a mock scowl, "—hardly anyone. You'll always find a few of the political faithful around. Shona for one."

"If you mean one of the reasons I'm home is so I can vote on Friday, that's right," said the girl with an unexpected vigour. "It's not my fault most of Feanport and the islands, in fact the whole Lochard constituency, would vote for a stuffed haggis if it wore the right party label."

"There speaks a bright-eyed, bushy-tailed Scottish Nationalist—home rule for Feanport, but don't ask her to stay there," said Dorothy Vullan good-naturedly. "Still Shona's speaking the truth. Bringing a political bandwagon up here is a waste of time. Even the candidates know it—about the most they've done is pass through quickly."

"You mean none of them have come wooing the Witch of the Isles?" Shannon helped himself to more wine and looked surprised. "I'd have done it, then put you to work drumming up support."

"I wouldn't do them much good." Dorothy Vullan gave a slight grimace. "Don't confuse inherited notoriety with popularity, captain.

Though I'm afraid I'm even a disappointment as a witch." She saw Carrick raise a quizzical eyebrow and shook her head. "I used to try very hard casting spells when I was a child, just to see if it worked. It never did."

"From what I can make out, the old Witches in Dorothy's family really used a mixture of folk medicine and psychology," said Milne Vullan. "Slip a man something that will purge his bowels and you're all set to scare the hell out of him."

"What about today?" asked Carrick. He saw Shannon give the faintest of nods and went on. "Some of the fishermen around Feanport still seem to reckon the Witch of the Isles can guide a man to a good catch—if she wishes."

Dorothy Vullan had a coffee cup half-way to her lips. She set it down slowly.

"Who told you that?" she asked, the expression in her green eyes hard to read.

"Sounds like some of your crew have been drinking ashore, Carrick," said John Marsh with a grunt that wasn't quite a laugh.

"Gossip," agreed Carrick. "But it wasn't about the old days—it was about now."

"I know about it," said Dorothy Vullan almost curtly. "I—"

"I think maybe Milne is the one who should explain it," Marsh cut in. He glanced at Milne Vullan. "I warned you about those stories, didn't I?"

"Yes." Vullan gave a resigned sigh and ran a hand through his dark hair. "I'd planned to tell you a little about it anyway, Captain Shannon. In fact, I can do better than that—I can show you the basics. All that has been happening is that I've been playing around with a few fishing ideas and occasionally getting one or two of the local skippers to co-operate." He turned to his wife. "We could do it right now."

"If you wish." She nodded. "I'll stay here and clear up."

"And I'll make that my cue to say goodnight," said Marsh. Pushing back his chair, he added, "I've some paperwork lying at the cottage, Milne. You don't mind?"

"No, go ahead," agreed Vullan. "Shona, you'll come along?"
She nodded.

"Good," he said, and gave a slight smile. "You've seen some of it before, but not everything."

They rose from the table and, once Marsh had gone, Dorothy Vullan began tidying while her husband led the others out of the room. They went along a corridor and down a flight of stairs, then stopped while Vullan opened a door and flicked on some lights.

"My workshop," he said, beckoning them to enter.

It was a long, narrow basement filled with fish tanks, equipment racks and laboratory benches. The neon tube lights shone down on a large table in the middle of it all where there was a three-dimensional undersea contour map of the waters around Feanport. A web of electrical cabling linked a series of control panels to some of the fish tanks and in the tanks, disturbed by the lights, scores of fish of all sizes were darting around.

Looking around, Carrick gave a silent whistle of appreciation. It was like being shown a Noah's Ark of the marine life of the Scottish west coast—from cod and dogfish to herring and tiny sprats, the collection was about as comprehensive as any he'd seen.

"Don't ask me for a population figure. It keeps changing." Vullan gave a tank a tap with his fingers and a large crab stalked across the gravel bottom to investigate then turned away. "I've got the usual pumps and filters to keep the sea water environment stabilized."

"I knew you had a laboratory," said Shannon, "but I didn't expect this."

"I don't bring many people down here." Vullan couldn't keep the pride from his voice. "This was old, empty cellarage when I started—though I'm afraid it had other uses too. Some of my wife's ancestors seem to have had nasty habits. When I knocked down one wall I found an old, bricked-up dungeon and a full set of chains and manacles."

"No skeletons?" asked Carrick.

The tall, dark-haired man grinned. "No. But the other thing I did find in another corner was a dump of Victorian liquor bottles. Dorothy's great-grandmother was inclined that way. Remember I showed you them, Shona?"

"Will I ever forget?" She laughed. "Yet the story is that everyone thought she was teetotal."

"They're the worst kind," said Shannon. He strode forward, inspected the contour map for a moment, then faced Vullan, his manner friendly but business-like. "So—how much help have you been giving the Feanport boats?"

Vullan frowned. "You make it seem like a regular arrangement. It isn't."

"But?"

"It'll sound like a lecture," warned Vullan.

"Go on," nodded Shannon. "I'm interested enough."

"All right." Vullan gestured towards the tanks. "My speciality is studying the behaviour patterns of fish stock. That means taking any number of factors into account—sea temperature, seasonal feeding, migratory spawning patterns, the rest. Then—well, it's possible to examine what happens if you add outside, artificial factors."

"Around Feanport?" asked Carrick.

Vullan nodded. "In the ordinary way, the local skippers know the fishing grounds around here well enough without any advice from me. What happens is I occasionally suggest where and when a skipper should try his nets—to help me." He smiled slightly. "They usually find it profitable."

Crossing to one of the control panels, he fingered a switch. A large flatfish suddenly exploded up from the sandy bottom of the nearest tank and swam around furiously before gradually settling again.

"Party tricks," said Vullan. "Here's another one."

He touched switches again and a bright red light appeared at the far end of a long tank. Immediately a score of silvery mackerel rushed towards the spot—but as they arrived, a cold blue beam took the place of the red and the fish scattered away from it.

"Basic stuff." Vullan switched off almost apologetically. "A very small electrical charge will bring any fish off the bottom in a hurry. Different coloured lighting can attract or repel, suggest food or discomfort—and, of course, these are laboratory fish, educated fish. I can build up laboratory theory here, I can go out with the *Sea Whip* and take things a stage further. But if I want any kind of practical small-scale trial I need outside help—fishing skippers."

Carrick and Shannon exchanged a glance. Science had been moving into fishing for some time—there were already forecasts that in a few years the old, relatively haphazard techniques of trawling and netting could be wiped away.

Almost every civilized country with a fishing industry was involved. Shrimp boats over in the Gulf of Mexico had been experimenting for years with electrical fishing—using electrically charged gear to tickle the shrimps out of their sand holes into the nets. French scientists had developed a system for stunning sardine shoals, then suction-pumping them aboard catcher boats. The West Germans were working on electrified trawling for eels, the Dutch and Belgians had sea farming projects, the Russians, Poles and East Germans all had their own programmes.

"You know the main research patterns, I imagine," said Vullan, as if reading their minds. "What I'm working on is a possible next-stage development. Call it fish-herding if you like—trying to get them to go where the nets are waiting."

"That has been tried," said Shannon slowly.

"I'm not saying it's totally original," said Vullan. "But I can go out in *Sea Whip*, pay out a line of fairly simple electrical packs astern, and know that I'm going to move a lot of fish in a certain direction."

"How much of this have you explained to the Feanport skippers?" asked Carrick, frowning.

"I've tried. Some seem to understand, but the others—" Vullan stopped there and shrugged. "How far would your own belief stretch, Chief Officer? Suppose I told you of a man who can train haddock to swim in races, a dozen at a time, as if they were track stars? Or of someone else who can ring a bell at the stern of a boat and have cod come queuing to feed from his hand?"

"I'd believe you—I've seen you do both," said Shona softly. She faced Carrick and Shannon. "It was years ago, when I was a child—I thought it was magic."

"Maybe some people still think that way," said Shannon.

"It's possible," conceded Vullan. Then, suddenly he seemed to deliberately brush the problem aside. "Captain, there's more I'd like you to see."

They spent another half-hour in the basement "workshop" while Vullan invited them to admire everything from a giant lobster called Fred to scale models of experimental trawling gear. There was no chance to get him talking about the fish herding trials again and at last they were led back upstairs and rejoined Dorothy Vullan.

Shannon shook his head at the offer of another drink and glanced at his wristwatch.

"It's time Carrick and I were getting back." He turned to Shona. "Miss Grant, did you bring a boat over?"

She shook her head. "John Marsh came over with a dinghy and collected me."

"Then we'll give you a lift back to the harbour—if you want that."

"Please." She smiled her thanks.

Milne Vullan brought her coat, a white coloured waterproof, then as they went towards the door of the house Dorothy Vullan suddenly laid a hand on Shannon's arm and stopped him.

"Captain, I want to ask you something," she said, a glint of determination in her eyes. "You've talked about collecting those ballot-boxes from the islands. But is there any other reason why your ship has come to Feanport?"

"No." Shannon eyed her gravely. "Should there be?"

"Gossip." The Witch of the Isles ignored her husband's mutter of protest. "Well, captain?"

Shannon's round, plump face reddened beneath his beard. Then he scowled at Milne Vullan.

"Your wife is a damned attractive woman," he said. "Tell her not to be a damned fool."

There was silence in the hallway for a moment, then Dorothy Vullan gave a sigh.

"Thank you, captain," she said quietly. "We'll walk down to the jetty with you."

Still looking concerned, Milne Vullan nodded and opened the front door. They left the house, went out into the dark, chill night, and started towards the steps that led down to the jetty.

Something moved in the shadows ahead of them, beside a patch of bush, and became the shape of a man.

"Who's there?" called Milne Vullan, halting.

The blast of a shotgun answered him. The charge snarled over their heads, smashing into the stonework of Fean House, then the figure had spun round and was running off into the darkness.

The common twelve-bore shotgun fires a load that can cut a man in half at fifteen yards, kill him less messily at up to forty yards, and still blind or maim for life at seventy yards. The three inch cartridge carries an ounce of lead shot, with a killing "spread" of about a yard.

Usually, too, it is either a double-barreled weapon or a five-shot pump action repeater. The last thought had been the one which had sent Carrick flat on the ground, pulling Shona with him, as the shot lashed over their heads. He'd seen Milne Vullan practically throw his wife behind a cement flower trough and drop down after her while Shannon took a speedy, totally undignified dive in the opposite direction.

But there hadn't been a second shot. Instead, Carrick listened for a moment to the sound of the gunman crashing through the bushes as he ran away. Then, taking a deep breath of relief, he scrambled to his feet again and helped Shona up.

The others were up again too. Unbelievably, they were unhurt if he discounted a graze on Dorothy Vullan's arm where she'd fallen. Shannon was cursing in a voice that would have subdued a hurricane, Shona kept a grip on Carrick's arm, and it was Vullan, staring into the darkness where the figure had vanished, who made the first move.

"Let's get after the maniac," he said hoarsely, starting forward.

"No." Shannon stopped him. "Get your wife and the girl in the house. He could change his mind and come back." The small, bearded figure turned to Carrick, rasped a quick, curt order. "Look around, mister. But carefully—don't get your head blown off."

Carrick nodded, gave Shona Grant a quick grimace that was meant to be reassuring, and set off.

There was a well-worn pathway beyond the bushes and he followed it at a cautious lope through more bush and scrub, every sense alert for the slightest sight or sound of the man he was pursuing, not at all certain what he'd do if he met him. Then, as the path almost petered out at a jagged stretch of rock, he saw something glint on the ground just ahead and picked up a used shotgun cartridge.

So the man had stopped to reload. Stomach tightening at the thought, he shoved the cartridge in his pocket and went on.

The path went through more scrub, then took a sudden dip and he realized it was heading towards the shore. A moment later, he heard pebbles rattle somewhere not far ahead, reached the end of the scrub, and looked down a bare slope.

A figure was scrambling along the slope, heading for the beach below. Carrick paused, and suddenly, his quarry stopped, turned, and seemed to be looking straight up towards him.

Then Carrick heard the snap of a twig behind him, started to swing round, and felt something hard explode against the side of his head.

The next thing he was vaguely aware of was that he was lying on the path, that a figure bent over him, and that he heard a chuckle. The figure stepped away, gave a soft, two-note whistle which was some kind of signal, then more pebbles rattled.

At least another minute passed before he had strength enough to struggle upright again. Head throbbing, still dazed, he looked down the dark slope again. All he could see was the faint outline of the rocks beside the shore and the white line of surf where the waves broke against them.

He gave up and made a weary, stumbling return to Fean House. On the way, a rabbit scurried in front of him, stopped, then scampered off again. He was glad it hadn't stopped to fight—the way he felt, the rabbit might have won.

*   *   *

"Two of them," said Captain James Shannon a few minutes later with minimal satisfaction and considerable sarcasm. "Well, at least you found out something."

"It always helps," said Carrick defensively.

He was sitting in a chair in a downstairs room at Fean House, clutching a cloth soaked in cold water against the aching bruise on the side of his head, holding a glass of whisky in his other hand, and the whisky seemed the more effective of the two.

Shannon was standing over him, scowling in frustration. Across the room, Dorothy Vullan sat on a couch smoking a cigarette while Shona bandaged the graze on her arm. The room curtains were tightly closed, Shannon had moved the chairs clear of the window, and Milne Vullan was prowling in the background nursing an old deer-stalking rifle.

"Milne, put that thing down," said the Witch of the Isles wearily. "All you're doing is making me nervous. Anyway if they stuck to that path they've gone now—probably the same way they came."

Shona Grant stopped bandaging, looked puzzled, then nodded agreement.

"It would take them to the north end of the island," she said. "The tide is out. They could make it on foot back to the mainland, if they didn't mind wading a couple of stretches."

"You're right." Vullan sighed and dumped the rifle on a vacant chair. "Well, I've 'phoned John Marsh at the cottage. He's coming over."

"Does anyone else live on the island?" asked Carrick.

"No."

"Tradition," said Dorothy Vullan, drawing on her cigarette. "Even the ones who work here prefer to get home before dark." Her mouth tightened. "These two who came over must have felt quite brave."

"They didn't mean to do more than scare you—this time, anyway," said Shannon.

"Firing a shotgun at that range?" protested Shona.

"At that range, he couldn't miss unless he wanted to," said Shannon. He put a hand in his jacket pocket, drew it out again, but kept his fingers closed around whatever he was holding. "I took a look outside, where the shotgun pellets should have hit the stonework. Here's what I found."

His hand flicked and three small, twisted, blackened silver coins rattled on to the low coffee table in front of Dorothy Vullan. She leaned forward, stared at them, then carefully stubbed out her cigarette, green eyes showing neither anger nor fear but something close to disbelief.

"You know what they are, captain?" she asked softly. "And why?"

Shannon nodded

"Old-fashioned silver sixpences." She gave a small, tight laugh. "There is only one way you can shoot a witch. You should load the gun with a silver bullet—but a crooked silver sixpence will do."

"What kind of sick mind plays a fool trick like this?" asked Milne Vullan.

Shannon didn't answer. There was a knock at the front door and Vullan hesitated, then picked up the rifle again and went out of the room. A moment later they heard him talking to Marsh in the hallway.

"I didn't think I'd ever be glad John Marsh was around," said Dorothy Vullan with a grimace, listening. "He tries, but we don't get on. Still—" she paused, looked again at the blackened coins, and shook her head. "Malicious, superstitious gossip—and it leads to this. Can you understand it, Chief Officer?"

Carrick hesitated. Shona Grant was close beside the Witch of the Isles and had a hand on her shoulder. With his face devoid of expression, Shannon obviously wasn't going to give him any help.

"I know plenty of city people who won't walk under ladders, and not just because something might fall on their heads." Carrick finished his drink in a gulp while choosing the rest of his words. "The fishing crews don't totally understand what your husband is doing."

"But his wife is the Witch of the Isles, and that's enough?" she suggested.

"For a few of them," agreed Carrick. "Particularly if other things they don't understand start happening, if it begins to look as though it is dangerous to quarrel with the Witch."

"George MacKenzie." The village constable's name came from her lips like a sigh.

"But they can't blame you," protested Shona. "He had an accident, he drowned—"

"Somebody broke an arm, somebody else's car crashed—" Dorothy Vullan grimaced "—people remember things, Shona. I'm probably being blamed for what happened to your father's boat."

"What was your quarrel with MacKenzie?" asked Shannon.

"A stupid thing. A few months ago the office at the seaweed plant was vandalised by a couple of juveniles from the village. MacKenzie didn't do anything about it because he knew their parents—and I complained to the Chief Constable, who had him on the carpet." She shrugged. "It just grew from there."

Shannon left it at that as Marsh and Vullan came into the room. Marsh was wearing a duffel coat over old slacks and a sweater and went straight to Dorothy.

"I was halfway to bed when Milne called," he said, with a concerned frown at the bandage on her arm. "You're all right?"

"I'll survive," she said dryly, lighting a fresh cigarette.

"Good." He faced Shannon and Carrick. "Milne is worried about calling in the police. I'm—well inclined to agree with him."

Shannon raised a surprised eyebrow.

"I overheard some of what Carrick said," Vullan told him, and shifted his feet awkwardly. "If this has anything to do with the fishing trials, they've almost finished. I—yes, I only need another couple of days at most." He paused. "Once they've stopped, maybe that'll finish any trouble. But it might make things even worse if the police were tramping around."

"It's worth trying," said Dorothy Vullan. "Captain?"

"One of my officers was attacked," said Shannon. "It's just lucky he has a thick skull. But if that's what you want—" he stopped there and shrugged.

*   *   *

John Marsh elected to stay at Fean House for the rest of the night and there was no opposition from the Vullans. A little later Milne and his rifle escorted Shannon, Carrick and Shona down to the jetty and as the patrol launch creamed away from the island they caught a last glimpse of him, a tall, sombre figure standing in the darkness with Fean House silhouetted above against the night sky.

Shannon had the helm, and hardly spoke until he had steered across the channel and they were back inside the Feanport breakwater. Then, as he throttled back and crawled the launch past the black shapes of the moored fishing fleet, heading towards *Marlin*'s berth, he gave a familiar throat-clearing noise.

"I'll land you two first, mister," he told Carrick. "We can talk in the morning. But it'll be an early start—we've those damned voting papers to deliver around the islands, and the sooner that's done the better. We'll treat it as a dummy run for the ballot box collections— and that's going to be done fast."

Moments later, he let the launch drift alongside a flight of stone steps that led up to the quay. Carrick and Shona stepped out, Shannon growled a goodnight, and the launch murmured along towards

Marlin, where an eagle-eyed petty officer was already waiting with some deck hands to hoist it back aboard.

Feanport's inhabitants were mainly early to bed, early to rise people. Only a few lights showed in the village and the harbour was deserted as Carrick and Shona Grant walked the length of the quay past the silent lines of fishing boats.

Outside the harbour, she turned to the right along a pathway which stayed close to the shore. Carrick took her hand and she smiled at him as her fingers laced in his. Then they walked on, listening to countless, unseen seabirds piping and crying in the darkness, feeding along the tideline. For a background, there was the steady, rhythmic wash of the sea and the murmur of a solitary fishing boat coming in.

The beacon lights on the breakwater were there to guide it. Out across the water, another glint of light marked Fean House. Slowing, Shona Grant looked towards the glint.

"I wish—" she began, then stopped and faced him. "No, I'm not going to talk about it. Not right now."

"Good." Quietly, Carrick brought her close to him and their lips met. For a moment, he felt the warmth of her body against his own and she pressed against him while they kissed again. Then she smiled, stood back, still holding his hand.

"I've an old-fashioned father waiting at home," she said wryly. "He's already peeved enough about where I've been."

"There's tomorrow," said Carrick. "I can fix the evening ashore if—"

She nodded and looked pleased. "I'd like that. Collect me from the cottage?"

"If it's still safe," he said wryly. "Is there any place we could go for a meal?"

"The nearest is well outside Feanport," she admitted. "But I can borrow a car." She paused and looked at him thoughtfully. "Webb, how long will *Marlin* be here?"

"Today is Tuesday, the election is Thursday. We'll probably resume patrol on Friday, unless—" he stopped it there.

"Unless there's more trouble?" she asked quietly, glancing out across the water towards the dark shape of Fean Island.

Carrick nodded. "You've known them a long time, haven't you?"

"Yes." Then she surprised him. "Dorothy Vullan and my mother were cousins."

They began walking along the path again, slowly.

"Then it's a family quarrel," said Carrick, frowning. "I knew it went far back, but—"

"My mother died soon after I was born," said Shona unemotionally. "Dorothy and Milne wanted to adopt me—they knew by then they couldn't have children. My father said no, they persisted, he told them to go to hell—and it smouldered on that way. He didn't involve me in it, and I could visit them all I wanted. But he'd have nothing to do with them." She shook her head. "They even helped pay my way through university when I left Feanport and he knew it—but he'll never admit it."

"But you didn't come back to Feanport," mused Carrick. "He's proud of the job you've got with Anglo-Norge. How do you feel about it?"

"Being part of the oil game?" She chewed her lip for a moment. "It's the same for most girls who grow up in Feanport. Either you marry a fisherman, or you leave the place—there's not much else. I move around with Anglo-Norge, I work on their North Sea production forward planning team, I like it—and they pay well. But sometimes I still miss what's here."

They kept on along the path for another moment or two in silence, the sea and the piping terns a tranquil background. Ahead of them, almost at the end of the village, a small cottage sat a little way back from the path with a light burning above the porch.

"I knew it," she said with an affectionate irritation. "He's waiting." Then her manner changed. "Webb, I'm worried about what's going on. Mainly because I can't understand it. Whatever else my father said about Dorothy Vullan, he always scoffed at this Witch of the Isles business. But now—"

"Does he go along with it?"

"He'll take anyone's side against her." Shona's fingers tightened against Carrick's as she spoke. "Even the way those damned fool MacLeans, all three of them, are blaming her for that gas cylinder exploding on the *Rachel*—he doesn't stop them."

"How many others maybe feel the same way?" asked Carrick bluntly.

"A few," she shrugged. "Not many, but enough to make trouble."

"The MacLeans have their own problems," he mused. "Donnie was in a small punch-up in the village tonight. Three men jumped him—he says he doesn't know who they were, or why."

She winced. "I didn't know."

They had almost reached the cottage. Looking at the light burning above the porch again, Shona hesitated then glanced at Carrick apologetically.

"I won't ask you in," she told him. "I—well, I think I'd better tell him myself what happened over there."

Carrick nodded, released her hand, then had a thought.

"Help me with one thing," he said slowly. "There's a little man with an eyepatch I've seen around the harbour. He was talking to your father. Do you know him?"

"That's Lampeye." She showed slight surprise at the question. "Harry Duggan, but everybody calls him Lampeye. He used to crew on the *Rachel*."

"Till?"

"Till he came aboard drunk once too often." Shona frowned. "Now he sometimes helps Milne Vullan on the *Sea Whip*. Poor old Lampeye—he was the last of the old crew on the *Rachel*."

"Then the MacLeans moved in?" Carrick felt puzzled. "When did that happen?"

"Three or four months ago. At least, that's when Donnie and Willie moved in. Cousin Lachie arrived a little later, after Lampeye got the boot." She shrugged. "They work well, even though they're not Feanport men."

"Outsiders?" queried Carrick.

She laughed. "From Stornoway—around here, you're a foreigner if you can't go back ten generations among the headstones in the churchyard." She paused and glanced towards the cottage. "Webb, I'll bet that father of mine is watching round the edge of a curtain. So—goodnight."

She had gone before he could answer. Carrick waited until she'd opened the cottage door which, West Highland style, wasn't locked and probably hadn't been for years. Then, hands in his pockets, he headed back along the shoreside path. Shona Grant was occupying a lot of his thoughts, but not all of them—and his destination wasn't the harbour.

Two men had been involved in the shotgun episode at Fean Island. Donnie MacLean and his cousin Lachie were gradually strengthening as possible candidates and it would do no harm to see if they were home.

Five minutes brisk walking took him through the streets of the sleeping village to the little cottage with the rowan branch above the door. The front of the cottage was in darkness but he circled round the small patch of garden, cursing under his breath as his clothes snagged an unseen thorn bush, then stopped as he saw a chink of light showing at one of the rear windows.

The only sound he could hear was the low murmur of the wind yet for a moment he looked around with a vague, uneasy feeling that he wasn't alone. Something moved in a patch of shadow, he tensed, then relaxed again as a small owl rose and flapped silently away with the limp body of a vole in its claws.

Relieved, he crossed to the window on tip-toe, pressed his nose against the glass, and looked round the edge of a piece of ragged curtaining into the kitchen of the cottage.

Both MacLeans were in the room, eating in their shirt-sleeves at the kitchen table. As he watched, Donnie MacLean rose, took his plate over towards a trash bucket, scraped what was left of his meal into the bucket, and dumped the plate into the nearby sink. When he came back to the table he brought two cans of beer with him and dumped one in front of Lachie MacLean.

The two men grinned, Lachie MacLean said something in a low voice which made his cousin laugh, then they raised the cans in a toast of some kind before they drank. But something else in the room interested Carrick more than the MacLeans' eating habits. The inevitable peat fire was smouldering in the kitchen's old-fashioned fireplace and laid out to dry on the hearth in front of it, visibly steaming, was a jumble of damp clothing.

Dorothy Vullan had said anyone could cross on foot to the north end of the island from the mainland at low tide, if they didn't mind wading a couple of stretches—having seen enough, Carrick drew back.

He was easing round to the front of the cottage again when a rustle of sound reached his ears. It came from almost the same place as before, but this time it was no owl.

Without giving any indication of haste, he altered his route so that he skirted a patch of gorse bush. Then, at the last minute, he pounced round the side of the bush on the figure who was crouching there. He heard a low yelp of fear but the figure didn't even try to struggle—and he found himself face to face with the little man with the eyepatch.

"Out of there," said Carrick softly, shifting his grip to the neck of the cringing Lampeye's thick wool sweater. "Move."

Trembling but silent, the little man allowed himself to be dragged several yards away from the cottage till they were behind what looked like a toolshed. Carrick stopped him there.

"Following me again?" he asked icily. "That's getting to be a habit with you."

"I wasn't—honest, I wasn't." Lampeye had a piping voice, accentuated by a note of panic, and there was liquor on his breath.

"Don't try to tell me you were meditating under that bush," said Carrick and shook his head. "You're not the type, Lampeye. You're just a nasty little nuisance."

"I came after you earlier, right," said the little man with a quivering earnestness. "I—well I was curious, that's all." He swallowed and straightened his narrow shoulders with an attempt at dignity. "An' it's not my fault you came along an' started snooping at the MacLeans' window. I was there first, followed them all the way from the harbour—"

"When?" Startled, Carrick eased his grip a little.

"About an hour back." Lampeye's one good eye blinked at him in sudden, faint moonlight as the clouds overhead thinned for a moment. "But they didn't come off a boat, more likely from the north shore."

"All right." Carrick drew a deep breath. "You followed them to the cottage. After that, why hang around behind that bush?"

The little man scowled and shrugged, saying nothing.

"Try," suggested Carrick softly. "Otherwise, I'll march you back to the MacLeans, heave you in their door, and tell them where I caught you—your word against mine."

"No, don't." Lampeye quivered at the thought. "Look, it was the way they went sneakin' along, like they didn't want anyone to see them. Their clothes were wet, drippin' wet, as if they'd been swimming in them. I stayed because I wondered what the hell they'd been up to, that's all."

"Were either of them carrying anything?" asked Carrick. The

question drew only a puzzled headshake and he'd expected that. If the MacLeans had been the shotgun heroes, they wouldn't want to risk advertising it. The gun could be hidden anywhere from a rabbit hole onward. "Tell me something different, Lampeye. Angus Grant fired you from the *Rachel* for being drunk, correct?"

"I'd had a drink, but I wasn't drunk," protested Lampeye. "The skipper just wanted rid o' me, to make room for the last o' those damned MacLeans. He wanted younger hands, thought he'd get more work out o' them."

"That's life," said Carrick. "How big a grudge does that leave you holding?"

"Me?" Lampeye inched closer, his stale breath unpleasantly near, and moistened his lips. "Well, I'll tell you—"

Suddenly, unexpectedly, he kicked Carrick hard on the shin. The pain was enough to loosen Carrick's grip on the wool sweater for an instant, and an instant was enough for the little man to wrench free and start running.

Swearing, Carrick stayed where he was and ruefully rubbed his leg. Lampeye had already disappeared among the cottages and he had a feeling the little man would prove very hard to find again. Sighing, he caught himself reaching for the non-existent cigarettes in his pocket, remembered, swore sadly this time, and, still limping a little, started walking back towards the harbour and *Marlin*.

Whatever else might happen that night, he'd had enough.

*   *   *

The snow which had threatened began falling just before dawn. It came lightly and briefly, just enough to leave a dusting of white on the hills above Feanport and a thin coating of puddled slush around the wakening harbour area, then the sky cleared.

Marlin sailed as the sun came up. A lively, spume-laced sea was waiting outside the shelter of the bay and she was soon thrusting a dipping, heaving way, spray drenching along her length, while a gusting, chilling northeast wind clawed at her flag and sang through her aerial rigging. Decks vibrating as the big twin diesels drove her on, the slim grey shape swung west and quickly left the mainland astern.

Webb Carrick had the watch but Shannon was in the command

chair with a full bridge team around him, a planned schedule as tight and complex as a railway timetable ahead, and a crew who knew he was determined to keep to it for his own personal satisfaction. In the chartroom, Ferguson was in charge of a pile of sealed black metal ballot boxes and carefully labelled bundles of voting papers. Jumbo Wills and Clapper Bell had a boat's crew huddled ready in the shelter of a deck house aft and any man aboard who had a hangover knew the best thing to do was keep quiet about it.

The first of the six islands on the delivery run appeared ahead exactly an hour after *Marlin* had cleared Feanport. An isolated dot on the radar screen became a green hump of land, a scatter of houses and a man with a horse waiting on a white strip of shell-sand beach.

Using the bridge glasses, Captain Shannon watched impatiently while the fishery cruiser's boat tossed through the surf to land the first of the ballot boxes and voting papers. The transfer was made, the horseman waved farewell, and as soon as the boat was back aboard, *Marlin* got under way again.

At the next island it was the same, except that there was a small stone quay where an old van and a young driver were waiting. Then the fishery cruiser turned on a new, southwest course for almost another hour through the lumping seas till it came in under the lea of a spectacular sea-bird cliff of black volcanic basalt.

The transfer there was made by rocket line while screaming hordes of disturbed gulls and terns wheeled overhead. The island was called Harvaig, eighteen adults and four children lived there, and even small boats could only land on it about once a month in winter, when tide and weather were exactly right.

As a rehearsal for the Thursday night collection run, Harvaig was the furthest west and most difficult of the six islands to be visited. *Marlin*'s wake curved south as she left, and Shannon ticked off one more point on the mental pattern of geometric lines he had decided on to cover the fishery cruiser's task in minimum sailing time.

They passed other islands and saw many more on the radar screen—but they were empty, inhabited at most by a few winter grazing sheep.

It had been different once. Ruined steadings, abandoned villages, occasional tumbledown castles told an earlier story. But of the five hundred islands in the long Hebridean chain only about a hundred were now populated and of that hundred only seven could boast a population of over two thousand. Beauty was one thing. Harsh economic reality had left only those isolated handfuls of people while the descendants of earlier emigrant generations were scattered far across the world.

The delivery run kept on. The fourth island, the largest, had almost a hundred inhabitants and a long, modern pier—built by the navy for wartime use, now home for a couple of forty-foot long-line boats. That left two tiny communities of lighthouse keepers and crofters, where the ballot boxes were landed by boat again.

It was noon, they had been at sea for a shade over four hours, and only the straight run back to Feanport remained. As if in agreement, the weather began moderating and the fishery cruiser's pitching roll settled to a regular vibration. Captain Shannon retired to his day cabin to go over his calculations again and the atmosphere on the bridge immediately relaxed. Ferguson disappeared and a little later Jumbo Wills arrived to take over the watch.

As soon as he'd been relieved Carrick left the bridge and went down to his cabin. He shaved for the first time that day, tapped the pack of cigarettes taped to the mirror as if it was a barometer, then went along to the wardroom.

The lunch menu was cod steak and a tasteless pudding but he was hungry. Andy Shaw, the chief engineer, was there too, ate with him, then dragged out his cigarettes as he finished.

"Still off them?" asked Shaw. He grinned at Carrick's nod, lit a cigarette, flicked the used match into the emptied coffee cup in front of him, and sat back. "I had the Old Man round my neck again about the *Rachel*—soon as he got back from that bun-fight last night."

"Saying what?" Carrick watched the smoke rise from the cigarette with a stony face.

"Saying nothing, just asking the same questions he did before," complained Shaw. "But how the hell do I know what happened when anything you might call evidence had vanished—cylinder, feed pipe, the lot? Laddie, I'm just a simple engineer."

Simple engineers were a bloody-minded race apart, decided Carrick. But there was another approach that sometimes worked with Shaw.

"I suppose it would need a fair amount of skill to rig an explosion," he mused. "But suppose we were talking about an engineer, someone who had that kind of skill?"

"Skill? The way I'd have done it would have blown the whole backside off that boat. No, from the looks of things this was different. Amateur style and—" Shaw stopped, eyes narrowing, and swore softly. "Conned me again, haven't you?"

"Well?" invited Carrick. "What's amateur style?"

"A couple of minutes aboard and a half-turn or so with a shift key," said Shaw. "That way, you'd get a pin-sized leak of gas that would take time to build up. But eventually you'd have a pool of gas waiting, and the smell wouldn't be noticed in the stink aboard the average fishing boat. Then if someone went below and struck a match to light that stove—wham."

"And the cylinder?"

"Depends," shrugged Shaw. "It could have been just the freed gas, maybe the cylinder didn't explode at all." He scowled and rose. "But I deal in facts, remember—I leave guesswork where it belongs, on deck."

Grinning, Carrick watched him go, then poured himself another cup of coffee and sipped it slowly. The chief engineer's theory made sense. But put it against the way in which any evidence had vanished and the whole situation went straight back into the melting pot.

He was still thinking about it a little later, when he made his way back up to the bridge. Captain Shannon was back in the command chair, Jumbo Wills had been relegated to a stance beside the radar screen, and a v.h.f. feed from the radio room was muttering away on the bulkhead-mounted loudspeaker.

Hanging back for a moment, he looked around. *Marlin* was still on schedule for the run and they were back in the Brannan Sound, on the approach towards Feanport again. The distinctive mainland bulk of Broch Point was to starboard. Over to port, about half a mile away, lay the flat, glistening shape of the Witchrock.

Shannon saw him and beckoned him over.

"Nicely timed, mister," he said. "We've company about a mile ahead—Feanport boats. Tell me what you make of them. Mister Wills hasn't any helpful ideas."

Sheepishly, Jumbo Wills handed Carrick the bridge glasses. Standing in a stiff-shouldered way, the duty helmsman seemed to be trying to pretend he didn't exist. Wondering what was going on, Carrick focussed the glasses on two broad-beamed, dark-hulled motor fishing vessels. They were travelling very slowly, about fifty yards apart, their trawl warps visible and running taut into the water at an odd angle astern. Figures were running back and forward on their decks, a small cloud of seabirds circled low overhead, and he took a guess at the rest.

"Pair-trawling," he suggested, putting down the glasses. That part was easy enough—pair-trawling, two boats operating a single net, was a reasonably common way of fishing. "They're trying to haul in—but it looks like they've caught themselves a problem."

"It sounds like it too," said Shannon, thumbing towards the loud-speaker. "They've asked for another boat to come out and lend a hand." He leaned forward. "Helmsman, alter course—steer fine towards them. Mister Wills, let's not make it look like a cavalry charge."

Crossing to the telegraph control, Wills raised his eyes to heaven in silent appeal.

*   *   *

It was an almost unbelievable scene that met their eyes minutes later. *Marlin* had come alongside the pair-trawl boats and lay about a ship's length distant, her diesels lazily holding steerage way—and over there, between the boats, the great net bag of their trawl showed hauled almost to the surface.

Swollen and bulging, it held a close-packed struggling mass of fish of every kind. Wriggling silver and brown shapes frothed the surface of the blue-green swell in a frenzy amid the constant raucous excitement of the circling gulls overhead.

"What a jackpot," said Jumbo Wills in an almost bemused voice, staring down from the bridge wing. "If they get that lot ashore—"

"That's their problem," said Captain Shannon, elbowing a way between Wills and Carrick with a battery-powered loudhailer in his hands. "Too big a catch, and they can't haul it in."

Life seethed within the net's confines—cod and coalfish, grey mullet and spotted dogfish struggled and thrashed with a score of other species. There were larger shapes there too, a giant skate that easily topped the two hundred pound mark and a young blue shark among them.

"So what'll they do, sir?" asked Wills, puzzled. "Let some of them go, or—"

"Throw away money?" Shannon shook his head, raised the loudhailer to his lips, and his voice boomed metallically across the water. "Captain Shannon, Fishery Protection—can we assist?"

A figure wearing overalls and a green tam o' shanter hat emerged from the wheelhouse of the nearest boat carrying a hailer.

"No need, but thank you," he bellowed back. "We've burned out a winch, that's all. There's another boat on the way now—we'll brail some o' the catch, then cope with the rest."

Brailing meant the third boat would come in with a small scoop net and remove some of the weight from the overloaded trawl bag. Looking down at the two bobbing fishing boats and the burden straining their trawl warps, Carrick knew it was about the only course open to them.

Pair-trawlers worked with one main legal limitation—the trawl they dragged between them mustn't touch the sea-bed. But once the trawl had been "shot" then the arc between them gradually tightened and normally both ends were transferred to the one boat to haul in. With a catch like this one they'd been in trouble from the start. One boat couldn't have handled it, and an overstrained winch packing in completed their predicament.

Shannon wasn't finished. Leaning his elbows on the rail, a glint in his eyes, he used the loudhailer again.

"You're in the money, skipper," he shouted through the rasping amplifier. "Ever had a run like this in the Brannan Sound before?"

The figure in the tam o' shanter didn't answer for a moment, then they saw him shrug.

"Sometimes you're lucky, captain," came his bellowed reply. "We had a hunch, that's all. No need to stand by us—we'll be fine."

Carefully, Shannon switched off his loudhailer, waved an acknowledgement, and scowled at Carrick.

"Luck and a hunch," he snapped sarcastically. "Damned liars. Mister Wills—"

"Sir?" Jumbo Wills blinked.

"Resume course and speed. Log the sighting and their registration numbers." Going into the bridge, he dumped the loudhailer on a signal locker, then beckoned Carrick. "Come with me."

The fishery cruiser was already getting under way again as Carrick followed him into the cramped space of the chartroom. Grunting under his breath, Shannon dragged out a large-scale Admiralty chart of the Brannan Sound and spread it on the table.

"You know what I'm thinking, mister?" he demanded.

"Fish-herding—Milne Vullan's way," said Carrick quietly.

"He told us he only needed a few more days." Shannon frowned at the chart, then gave a satisfied nod. "Yes, and these two were pair-trawling north. Take a look and see how you read it."

It took a few moments study of the chart before Carrick understood, then it suddenly became clear. The chart's depth readings showed an average of thirty fathoms of water in most of the Brannan Sound. But there was an exception, a deep, narrow undersea valley of eighty fathoms marked as running slightly west of centre from near Fean Bay all the way south until it reached the Witchrock, which sat like a marker where the valley widened out.

"If he used his electrical system from the *Sea Whip* somewhere north of us, in this trough—" Carrick ran his finger down the chart, paused, and raised an eyebrow at Shannon.

"Add two skippers who would help and keep their mouths shut," nodded Shannon. "He'd start the fish running south, down the trough—most of them would prefer to stay in deep water. That trawl net would be sitting waiting like a cork in a bottle."

"Then where is he?" asked Carrick, puzzled.

"How the hell should I know?" snarled Shannon and scowled out of the chartroom window. The two fishing boats had vanished astern and the fishery cruiser was cutting her way through the swell at a steady, thrusting pace. "He's probably back home at Fean Island by now—the skippers can tell him all he wants later."

"And they'll tell him that his fish-herding worked," mused Carrick. "If that's a sample of what he can do—"

"Then it's not fishing," said Shannon, cutting him short. "It's the next best thing to vacuum cleaning the sea, mister. And I'm old-fashioned enough to think that's a damned sight worse than witchcraft."

V

A faint dusting of snow still whitened the hills above Feanport as *Marlin* returned to harbour and eased back into her berth at the south quay. Milne Vullan's *Sea Whip* was moored further along, empty and deserted, and there was one new arrival among the other craft in harbour. The twice weekly mailboat from the Outer Isles, making its inward run from Stornoway, had tied up at the north quay and a small squad of dock workers were unloading an assortment of cargo from her holds.

Webb Carrick went ashore almost as soon as the fishery cruiser's gangway had been run out. He took Clapper Bell with him, and a brief talk session in the scuba compartment beforehand had brought *Marlin*'s bo'sun up-to-date with the main outline of the shaping puzzle hanging over the Brannan Sound. Now, with Captain Shannon's wary blessing, the first call on their list was to be the harbourmaster's office.

An extra ingredient had been added to Feanport's usual atmosphere while they'd been away. With less than a day remaining until the election booths opened, some of the political parties seemed to have decided to make at least a token attempt at wooing the fishing village's voters. Two sound trucks were braying slogans and tape-recorded messages at the harbour gates, trying hard to compete against each other and the steady rumble of the quayside crane working at the mailboat.

"Noisy sods," said Clapper Bell dourly, ambling along beside Carrick. "That's two who wouldn't get my vote."

Carrick grinned. "It's called involvement, Clapper. Back your choice and hope you've picked a winner."

"Not me." Bell kicked an old fish head which was lying among the litter on the quayside. As it flew, a gull swooped and snatched it up. "Any time I vote, it's to keep somebody out, not to put anyone in."

The sound trucks were still duelling as they entered the harbour-master's office, a small single-storey brick building with a flagstaff that needed a coat of paint and a noticeboard that looked ready to crumble away with age. Inside, they found Shuggy Morrison seated beside a glowing anthracite stove with a mug of tea in one hand and a tattered comic book in the other. Behind him, a v.h.f. receiver tuned to the fishing waveband murmured away.

"You two." The elderly, red-faced harbourmaster gave them an uneasy nod, set down the comic book, and stayed seated. "What do you want this time? I thought I tol' you last night—"

"That you keep your nose clean," agreed Carrick wearily. He considered the shabbily dressed figure and shook his head. "You've got a comfortable number here, Shuggy. It's a shame to spoil it."

"Eh?" Morrison heaved to his feet, alarmed, tea slopping from his mug. "Meaning what?"

"You might have problems," said Carrick. "For instance, if Fishery Protection made complaining noises to the harbour trustees about you. Nothing specific, just noises—"

"I've seen it happen," said Clapper Bell sympathetically. He picked up the discarded comic book and glanced at its pages. "Then your bosses move in. Checkin' your paperwork. Awkward questions about things like whether any skipper ever hands you a present for favours. They'd want everything tightened up, smartened up—hell, they'd maybe even make you wear a clean shirt every day."

"All because you didn't want to help," mused Carrick. "Yes, it's hard luck."

Morrison swallowed, stared at them for a moment, then capitulated with a groan.

"So what is it this time?" he asked warily.

"Friendly co-operation." Carrick exchanged a solemn nod with Clapper Bell. "Let's start with Vullan's *Sea Whip*. How long since it came in?"

"Half an hour maybe," shrugged Morrison. "He brought his wife an' John Marsh over from the island. If you want him, try the village hall—he's fixin' up things for the voting tomorrow." He saw Carrick's raised eyebrow and added hastily, "He looked in wi' a message for me to pass on to one o' the mailboat passengers when she docked."

"Tell," said Clapper Bell, flicking over a page of the comic book, not looking up.

"His name is Chester—he's here to see Dorothy Vullan." The harbourmaster took a gloomy swallow of tea. "You just missed him."

"Ever seen him before?" asked Carrick then, as Morrison shook his head, flicked a thumb towards the radio. "Two of the local boats have a problem. You heard?"

"Caught too much fish." Morrison managed a lopsided grin. "They made enough noise about it."

"Are the skippers friends of Milne Vullan?"

"Maybe not friends—" began Morrison.

"That's a hell o' an answer," sighed Clapper Bell, his voice a masterpiece of solicitude. "I'm sorry for you, Shuggy."

"What I mean is they—well, they maybe help him out," said Morrison hastily. "The word is the Witch of the Isles puts a good catch their way to square the bill."

"Then I want to know next time they're doing it," said Carrick grimly. "These two, or any other boat going out for that kind of reason. You get word to me on *Marlin* the moment you hear."

"I'll try." Morrison spread his pudgy, broken-nailed hands in resignation. "I can't guarantee it."

Carrick turned his back on the man and went over to the grimy window, looking out at the harbour scene. One of the sound trucks had driven off, the crew of the other seemed to be having a coffee break.

"Seen anything of Angus Grant or the MacLeans this morning?" he asked suddenly.

"They were around." Morrison gave a woebegone nod. "Willie MacLean is out o' hospital, bandaged like a mummy but healthy enough."

"Three men had a try at beating up Donnie MacLean last night." Carrick paused and looked round. "He claims he doesn't know them, or why. But I met a little man called Lampeye—"

"Him?" Morrison snorted at the thought. "Lampeye isn't the physical type—even when he's drunk. He talks, but I know his style. More likely he'd—" he stopped short, as if regretting what he'd almost said.

"More likely he'd do a sabotage job on the *Rachel* or release a truck handbrake?" suggested Carrick. He saw he wasn't going to get an answer and switched back again. "All right, but there were three men and they were set to give Donnie MacLean a hammering."

"I haven't heard," said the harbourmaster uneasily.

"But?"

The man shrugged. "There's Archie Campbell, another o' Angus Grant's old crew. He works at a garage in the village now—and he's big enough and thick enough to fight anyone. He doesn't talk much, but he has as big a grudge against the MacLeans as Lampeye." He licked his lips, suddenly aghast. "Look, I didn't tell you that—"

"You didn't say a word," murmured Carrick. "Just remember, if any boat leaves here to help the *Sea Whip* you get word to us."

"Fast," said Clapper Bell cheerfully, and tossed down the comic book. "Thanks, Shuggy. I'll come back and finish the story—find out if the girl ever gets her clothes back on."

"Don't hurry," said Morrison bitterly, and turned away to brew himself a new mug of tea.

*　　*　　*

Outside the office, the remaining sound truck was producing metallic throat-clearing noises. A girl member of its team, wearing tight jeans and a sweater, seemed to be making non-political progress with a couple of admiring fishermen. Clapper Bell threw an appraising look in her direction, then glanced at Carrick.

"Want me to find Campbell?" he asked.

Carrick nodded. "Try him. Then ask around about the Mac-Leans—how other people feel about them. But don't make too many waves, Clapper. Not yet."

They parted, the big Glasgow-Irishman taking a route which took him closely past the girl at the sound truck, Carrick heading up the climbing road which led to the village.

When he reached the hall the main door was lying open and a couple of workmen were erecting screens for a set of polling booths inside. Further back, Milne Vullan was standing talking to an elderly woman, who was spreading papers on a table top. Vullan saw him, exchanged a final smiling word with the woman, then came over.

"Decisions, decisions," he murmured. "She wants a screen in front of the table, so men won't look at her legs. At her age, that's being hopeful." He paused, stuck his hands in his pockets, and asked, "How did the delivery run go?"

"On schedule." Carrick shrugged that part of the morning aside. "We met a couple of boats pair-netting on the way back—they'd hit a jackpot." He raised an eyebrow. "Or maybe you knew?"

"Let's say I'll be talking to them later," temporised Vullan easily. "I told you, Webb—I only need a little more time and believe me, after last night I'm being careful."

"No more visitors?"

Vullan shook his head, looked past him, and brightened. "Not the way you mean. But there's someone I'd like you to meet."

He led Carrick further up the hall to where Dorothy Vullan and a stranger stood looking up at a stained glass window. The Witch of the Isles wore slacks and a white rollneck sweater, an outfit which only emphasised her striking looks. The stranger, a tall, thin, sandy-haired man in a dark sports suit, laughed at something she said, then the conversation ended as Vullan and Carrick arrived.

"Meet Robert Chester," introduced Vullan. "A wandering Englishman—he came in on the mailboat."

Chester smiled and gave Carrick a firm handshake as the introductions were completed. He had strong white teeth and boyish good looks and at a guess Carrick placed him in his late thirties.

"Robert is in the antiques game," said Dorothy Vullan. "That's how we met. He's up from London on another of what he calls his restocking trips—which means a plundering expedition."

"I'm the one who feels plundered," said Chester. "They drive a damned hard bargain among the islands."

Milne Vullan grinned unsympathetically. "You'll still show a profit. How much did you buy this time?"

"A little here, a little there," shrugged Chester. "I've five crates being unloaded from the mailboat to be sent south by road. Though—" he glanced significantly at Dorothy Vullan "—I'm still open for business."

"No," she said firmly, then ran a hand over her copper-bronze hair and chuckled. "We'll still give you lunch. But any bits and pieces at Fean House stay there—you've been told that before."

"So I keep trying." The sandy-haired man shrugged at Carrick. "She has some Jacobean glass I'm after, but she's stubborn."

"They're all stubborn," said Carrick fervently. "Staying long?"

Chester shook his head. "Just long enough to check those crates. I'll be driving south before dusk."

"Then we'd better get you across to the island," said Milne Vullan and frowned around the hall. "Where the hell has Lampeye gone?"

"He vanished out the back door when Fishery Protection appeared on the scene," said Dorothy Vullan. She eyed Carrick with unconcealed curiosity. "I'm not sure why."

"We've some unfinished business," said Carrick. The little one-eyed fisherman was obviously going to prove difficult to pin down. "You can tell him I haven't forgotten."

"It's—well, nothing to do with last night, is it?" Milne Vullan was incredulous. "I mean, that would be crazy. Lampeye's harmless—and he spends half his time helping me on the *Sea Whip*."

"No, it's something different," Carrick left it at that.

Satisfied, Vullan nodded. "Maybe you could tell Captain Shannon I'll visit him later. There are some details about tomorrow I want to check again. Dorothy—"

"Yes," she agreed. "We'd better move. What about John Marsh?"

Vullan shook his head. "He's staying at the seaweed plant for the afternoon."

They nodded goodbye. But as Vullan led Robert Chester away Dorothy Vullan hung back for a moment.

"Do you know anything more about last night, Webb?" she asked bluntly.

"Nothing concrete," he admitted. "But—"

"I hope it stays that way," she cut him short, her voice quiet and earnest. "I mean that. I'm hoping Milne is right—once he has finished these trials it may all just fade away."

"They've got the election to talk about for a day or two," mused Carrick, not totally convinced. "After that—I just don't know." He smiled at her sympathetically. "It could work out."

"The Witch of the Isles is hard to forget." She said it bitterly. "That shotgun business was out of the past, even if it was only some drunk trying to frighten me. But it could go on from there—I know that too. I've seen the rowan branches on some of the boats, to fend me off. Then there are the others—the ones who have left baskets of fish on the jetty at the island in the night. You know why?"

He shook his head.

"The other old belief, it's those that give that get." Her voice was tighter, strained. "Some of the skippers have always asked for a witch's blessing on their boats. But that's tradition, it was never serious—till now. And I want it finished."

Suddenly, the Witch of the Isles turned on her heel and hurried to join the two men waiting at the door of the hall. She left with them without a backward glance.

Carrick stayed where he was for along moment, disturbed by the vehemence that had been behind her words. Then, shrugging, he went out the same way. The elderly woman he'd seen earlier was carefully pinning a tablecloth so that it would hang down to ankle length at the front of the voters' roll table. When he smiled at her, she gave him a cautious nod. Everybody had their problems.

*   *   *

The *Sea Whip* had gone from the harbour by the time Carrick got back there. Thankfully, the second sound truck had also quit its location and he walked round past the dockers unloading the mailboat's cargo, heading for the repair slipway.

This time there was no grouping of spectators around the *Rachel*'s damaged hull and no work seemed to be in progress. But he saw Angus Grant and the bandaged figure of Willie MacLean standing under the shadow of the fishing boat's stern, and scrambled down to join them on the slime and weed-coated slipway. Their greeting was restrained, a deliberate nod from Angus Grant and a neutral sounding grunt from MacLean, whose face was partly hidden by the bandages.

"How do you feel now?" he asked MacLean.

"Singed at the edges," answered MacLean. "But it's better than being scraped off a bulkhead. I'm not complaining." He scowled along the *Rachel*'s hull to the hole in her side. "Not when I see what happened."

"She'll mend," said Angus Grant. "We'll maybe get one or two other wee jobs done too. I've told the lads, they'll be fishing again soon enough and in a better boat than before."

"Don't say that too loudly when the insurance surveyor comes around," said Carrick. He switched his attention to MacLean again. "Where's the rest of your clan, Willie?"

"Up in the village, havin' a beer." MacLean made a clumsy job of lighting a cigarette between his blistered lips. "Skipper, if you're finished here I've got a thirst of my own."

Grant nodded, but Carrick stopped the fishing hand as he turned to go.

"Tell Donnie I'd still like to know if he has any thoughts about who his friends were last night."

"That?" MacLean shrugged slightly. "I reckon we'll just take care of it on our own."

He went off, and Carrick heard Angus Grant sigh. He watched the big, bearded fisherman run a hand down the *Rachel*'s hull, that weathered, beak-nosed face hard to read. Then, suddenly, Grant turned to face him.

"You had a busy time last night," said Grant. "Here and—and on the island. When Shona told me about that business with the shotgun—" tight-lipped, he shook his head.

"It could get worse," said Carrick. "Someone might get really hurt next time."

"No." The word rasped from Grant. "I—there are ways of making sure of that."

"A few words in the right ears?" Carrick saw he wasn't going to get a response and nodded. "Good. Does it also include ending the war with Dorothy Vullan?"

"Maybe that's another matter, Chief Officer," said Grant. "A man's feelings are his own." Then his manner changed. "You'll have a dram with me tonight, when you come for Shona?"

"If it's offered," said Carrick carefully.

"Aye." An odd smile crossed the fisherman's face. "It'll be waiting. That girl would give me hell if it wasn't."

Carrick nodded goodbye, left him, and made his way back round the harbour to *Marlin*. An elderly M.G. coupe was parked beside the gangway. Though there was no clue to its owner, the petty officer on gangway watch stepped forward as he came aboard.

"Chief," he began, "Captain Shannon—"

"Wants me," said Carrick resignedly.

He headed for the day cabin, knocked, waited for Shannon's grunt, then went in and gave a grin as he saw who their visitor was.

"Don't look so damned pleased," said the man standing beside Shannon's rubber plant. "I only came here for the car mileage."

"And maybe that isn't a joke," said Captain Shannon. *Marlin*'s commander was also on his feet, but over by his desk, and the atmosphere in the room wasn't totally cordial.

They'd worked with Detective Inspector Malcolm Henderson before. He was thin and tall, had a dark, drooping moustache, and affected a habitually sad expression. As usual, he wore a leather jacket over slacks and a sweater but with a new acquisition, a long, hand-knitted wool scarf which reached down almost to his knees.

Carrick closed the cabin door and glanced at Shannon.

"I radioed Department and told them we could use some discreet assistance from the local police," said Shannon, ignoring Henderson for the moment. "Call it breaking a promise if you want, mister—to my mind that's incidental."

"And my bosses sent me because I'm not known around Feanport," said Henderson, unperturbed. "The trouble is—"

"The trouble is, he wants everything laid on a plate," snarled Shannon. "Hard fact evidence all the way, or he isn't interested."

"I didn't say that," soothed Henderson. "Suppose we re-run some of it now that Carrick is here?"

Shannon slumped down into a chair with an ill-tempered shrug. Flickering a grimace in Carrick's direction, Henderson cleared his throat.

"Start with Constable MacKenzie's death," he began, all humour suddenly gone from his manner. "There was the usual post mortem, with death certified due to drowning. Webb, the facts all fitted—MacKenzie took his boat out, it came ashore overturned. There's just one simple, natural conclusion, that he had an accident of some kind out there."

"He was a good swimmer," said Carrick quietly.

"Yes," admitted Henderson.

"There's also where his body was washed up," said Shannon. "He usually went fishing in the bay. He turns up on the rocks at Broch Point. How did he get down there?"

Henderson frowned. "Captain, you admitted it could happen. That the tides and currents around here—"

"Made it possible, not probable," snapped Shannon. "There's a difference."

Henderson shrugged. "The medical examiners still said drowning, and up here they've plenty of experience in that area. The body was released to relatives and MacKenzie was cremated—finish. So next you've got his quarrel with Dorothy Vullan. She created hell at Headquarters about that break-in at the seaweed plant, but Mac-

Kenzie's story was that he hadn't any real proof who was responsible."

"And afterwards?" asked Carrick.

"Nothing that Headquarters know about." Henderson stuck his hands in the pockets of his leather jacket. "Any prowling MacKenzie was doing, any questions he was asking about the Vullans or the *Sea Whip* was in his own time. I don't know what he was after and he didn't leave any hint behind him on paper. We've had his records brought in and checked as a matter of ordinary routine."

"But what about the rest of it?" demanded Shannon wearily. "The explosion on the *Rachel*, the shot fired at Fean House, every other damned thing that's going on around here? Do you want to just wait and see what happens next?"

"No. But I've got to hope the lid stays on things for another couple of days." Henderson sucked a stray end of his moustache and looked to Carrick for understanding. "It's this lousy by-election—just about every spare cop we can scrape together is needed to stand sentry outside the official polling stations. They'll be there like so many wooden Indians and about as useful, but that's the law. Get the by-election out of the way and then we can move in. But not before, not unless all hell really breaks out." He shrugged apologetically at Shannon. "Sorry, but that's how it is."

Shannon got to his feet.

"I saw a witchcraft panic once before, over on the Northeast coast," he said in a quiet, controlled voice. "Years ago, when you and Carrick were probably still at school. An old, half-mad woman cursed a boat and it sank in a gale, with all hands. I saw nets burned on the quayside, because crews thought they were bewitched. I saw grown men act like—" he paused and sucked his lips "—well, they were ready to burn that woman like they'd burned the nets. Except a doctor had her certified and carted off first."

"And what's happening here could be different, maybe worse?" Henderson nodded slowly, with understanding.

"I'm not laughing, and I'll be back. Tomorrow if I can, but the day after that at the latest—and I'll maybe check a few things before then."

Shannon studied him for a moment, his manner gradually thawing. Then he held out his hand.

"Do that," said *Marlin*'s commander. "And tell your bosses they could have sent worse."

"Thanks." Henderson grinned, shook hands with him, and turned to Carrick. "Walk with me to dry land?"

Carrick glanced at Shannon, drew a nod of agreement, and left the cabin with Henderson. The lanky detective inspector said nothing until they had reached the head of the gangway leading down to the quayside.

"Really got him, hasn't it?" he suggested, stopping with his hand on the rail. "How far do you go along with him?"

"All the way," said Carrick.

"That just might make three of us." Henderson scowled at the thought. "Headquarters are going to love me when I log this one, Webb—but if there is anything behind it, your lady Witch of the Isles could be playing a funny game of her own. Don't lose sight of that one. Or that, from what your Old Man told me, the trouble seemed to start just around the time this character Marsh arrived on the scene."

"You could check him out," mused Carrick.

"You know, I'd never have thought of that," said Henderson with sarcasm. He took a deep breath of the harbour air and grinned. "If I come up with anything, you owe me a drink."

He headed down the gangway, climbed into his little car, and a moment later it snarled away along the quayside. As it vanished, Carrick turned and made his way up towards the bridge. His intention was to spend some time in the chartroom, seeing for himself what Shannon had said about the tides and current in the Brannan Sound. But as he reached the bridge he found Jumbo Wills and the fishery cruiser's radio operator huddled in consultation over a stripped-down piece of equipment.

"Mice?" asked Carrick.

The radio operator grinned but Wills wasn't amused. His freckled face wore a worried look and one finger was gashed and bleeding where he'd cut it with a long, thin-bladed screwdriver.

"The echo-sounder's packed in," he reported unhappily. "I didn't notice till we were back in harbour, and I haven't even told the Old Man yet." He chewed his lip anxiously. "I was playing around with it when I had the watch and—"

"And now you'd better get it fixed before you tell him," said Carrick. The echo-sounder did just that, threw a sound signal down from under *Marlin*'s keel, picked up the echo that bounced back from the sea-bed, and gave a depth reading vital in the kind of inshore patrol work which was the fishery cruiser's regular routine. "What's gone wrong with the thing?"

Jumbo Wills sucked his bleeding finger and left the radio operator, a tow-headed youngster who spent his spare time playing Country and Western numbers on a home-made electronic guitar, to do the talking.

"Circuit overloads and a burn-out," he said laconically. "I can fix it—I think. If you want the technical detail, Chief—"

"No." Hastily, Carrick shook his head then had second thoughts. "Hold on. One question, one answer. Do you mean it got—well, some kind of electrical shock from outside?"

The youngster grinned and shook his head. "No, nothing fancy like that." He glanced at Wills. "It's the kind of thing that happens if— uh—well, like the second mate says, he was playing around with it."

"I see." The answer was diplomatic but plain enough. Carrick had other problems. "All right, but get it working."

He left them, went to the chartroom, spent enough time there to understand Shannon's reluctant agreement that tides and currents might take a body from the bay to Broch Point, then went back down to the main deck in time to see Clapper Bell ambling back aboard. The burly bo'sun waved a greeting and came over.

"I had a wee bit o' luck, sir," said Bell with a grin. "I found that character Campbell, the roughhouse expert Shuggy Morrison told us about. He's workin' in a garage, like Shuggy said—we had a talk round the back, private."

"It looks that way." Carrick eyed the red bruise wealing one side of Bell's face. "Friendly persuasion?"

"Self-defence," said Bell with an outraged innocence. "He hasn't my easy kind of nature."

"His misfortune," agreed Carrick. "Well?"

"He admitted he took a couple o' pals along and jumped Donnie MacLean last night," said Bell. "But Campbell's story is they only intended to scare him an' that they ended up gettin' the biggest fright when we piled in. And—uh—he says it was Lampeye's idea."

"Why?" asked Carrick, frowning.

"They reckon if they chase the MacLeans out o' Feanport they'll get their old jobs back on the *Rachel*." Bell rubbed his chin, puzzled. "Does that make any kind o' sense to you?"

"As much as anything has since we got here," said Carrick. He used a thumbnail to pick at a blister of paint on the metal beside him. "Apart from that, how do the MacLeans rate with the locals?"

"They don't mix much, keep out o' trouble—they just stay outsiders." Bell had something more important on his mind. "You know, we did say we'd get some diving time while we were here. How about it—right now, this afternoon?"

Suddenly, it seemed a good idea. Carrick felt in need of some peace and underwater was as good a place as any to find it.

"Get the gear ready," he nodded. "I'll clear it with the Old Man."

*   *   *

Captain Shannon agreed, in a way that made it plain he felt the same way too. Half an hour later, wearing black rubber wet-suits and with their scuba gear piled aboard, Carrick and Bell rasped their way out of the harbour aboard one of *Marlin*'s small outboard-powered Gemini boats.

As the little inflatable cleared the breakwater Clapper Bell swung her head north and opened the outboard's throttle. They foamed on, fairly close to shore, and Clapper Bell thumbed briefly towards a small jetty and a huddle of buildings at the far end of the village. The work-boat with the strange bucket-grab at its bow was clue enough for Carrick and he took a long, curious look at the seaweed plant as they went past.

The north end of the bay came next, the narrow, shallow passage between the mainland and Fean Island. It was easy enough to imagine how it would dry out at low tide as they slowed and murmured through, the bottom rock and shingle clearly visible close beneath as the inflatable passed through and out beyond the white rim of surf which marked the start of the open sea.

The waves were bigger, the sea a deeper shade of blue as the outboard engine opened up again and drove them swiftly on along the empty, rugged coastline. Then, two miles north of the bay, their goal appeared ahead—a sea-cliff cove where the wreck-chart shielded on Carrick's lap marked the resting place of the *Martha Pym*, a torpedoed cargo ship casualty of World War Two.

They brought the inflatable in, beached her at the foot of the cliff, then dragged the lightweight craft high and dry on the shingle. A white farmhouse on a distant hill and an off-shore stack of basalt rock gave them the compass marker points they needed.

It was to be a practice dive, nothing more. But Carrick and Bell still approached the drill involved with the total, careful routine which had long since become second nature. Once in their aqualung harnesses, the big twin air cylinders on their backs standard eighteen hundred p.s.i. jobs, they checked the air supply, fastened the weight belts round their waists, and were ready.

Carrick led the way, wading out, meeting the first, familiar chill of the sea as it seeped into the rubber wet-suit. The sea-bed sloped steeply, a few steps brought the slopping waves up to their chests, and Carrick paused, checking the compass on his wrist. Then, with a nod to Clapper Bell, he pulled on his face-mask, bit on the breathing tube, and duck-dived under.

They followed the sharp downhill slope of the sea-bed, demand valves clicking regularly, twin trails of air bubbles pluming from their masks while they finned along in a steady, kicking crawl-beat. The light faded slowly in the clear water, while small fish scattered from their path or darted into the shelter of the gently waving forest of long green kelp weed which beckoned from below.

Carrick's depth gauge registered ninety feet when the slope levelled out in a bottom layer of rock and weed. At that depth, it was a twilight world of undersea life, strange crawling shapes and flickering shadows. But suddenly Clapper Bell kicked closer to him, tapped his shoulder, and pointed to their left.

They'd found the *Martha Pym*. In another minute they were swimming along the length of her broken hull.

The old cargo ship lay on her side, a single funnel which had broken loose lying half-buried in shingle and ooze, upper decks a shambles of broken, tangled fittings, the tip of one of her boilers protruding from a giant rent in her side. Swaying weed sprouted in profusion along her old-fashioned, rivetted plates, which were encrusted with barnacles and limpet shell-fish.

Exploring on, they saw they weren't the wreck's first visitors. Her propellor had been cut away—commercial divers got good money for scrap bronze. And the *Martha Pym* had well-established tenants. As they reached the rent in her side a bad-tempered angler fish, a large, sharp-toothed mouth in a modest-sized body, came out to challenge their intrusion but disappeared again as Bell released an extra bout of air bubbles.

Any wreck along the northwest coast became home for a variety of creatures, from conger eel onward. A few young, innocent cod showed next, timidly following them as they continued to examine the rusting hull and reached the bridge, with its shattered glass and silt-covered controls.

At ninety feet, the standard diving tables gave a maximum underwater time of thirty minutes without decompression stops. Carrick let twenty minutes pass, then gestured to Bell and thumbed towards the surface. But Bell waved a negative, pointing down towards the seabed.

A large, fat lobster was scuttling along between the bottom weed. They finned down together, then Bell grabbed the lobster in a sideways swoop and waved it triumphantly under Carrick's face-mask, like a trophy.

That was when it happened. Carrick had a glimpse of something that looked like a great, wide cloak sinking down on them from the twilight above, their escort of tiny cod tried to scatter, he saw Clapper Bell's eyes widen—and before either of them could attempt to kick clear a great swathe of weighted net enfolded them.

Settling mesh tangling around the air cylinders on his back, more of it catching at his arms and legs, Carrick was dragged down on his hands and knees among the bottom weed. The same thing had happened to Clapper Bell, who had tumbled just out of reach and was struggling to get up off his back.

For a moment, Carrick knew raw fear as the tough nylon wrapped itself more and more around him, end weights sending up clouds of seabed silt. Then, suddenly, he became conscious of his rasping, hurried breathing, felt a warning tightening in his throat, cursed himself for a fool, and stayed still for a moment.

Clapper Bell was doing the same. It was the grim discipline of underwater work. Never rush, think positively, breath regularly. Carefully, tugging against the mesh, Carrick forced his right arm down until his fingers gripped the diving knife in his leg sheath.

Carefully, slowly, he used the sharp blade to saw through a first small section of mesh. That gave him more freedom and a better grip on the knife as he worked on, steadily gaining more slack, and gradually widening the hole in the mesh until his arm was free. Then, ignoring his numbed fingers, he began the steady process of hacking and sawing his way out of the net.

It took time, but he had company. Clapper Bell was busy in the same way as the minutes dragged past. Carrick beat him to freedom, kicked across, and helped the burly bo'sun slash the last strands of mesh around his air-tanks. They were over their thirty minutes and Carrick tapped his watch for emphasis before he thumbed upward.

They took their first decompression stop at twenty feet from the surface, where the water was bright and their arrival scattered a small school of silver mackerel. Then, resisting temptation, they shared another stop at ten feet—and finally they broke surface, spitting out their breathing tubes, shoving back their face masks.

The sea-cliff cove was empty. But out beyond it a small fishing boat was heading away, engine a murmur, hull little more than a black speck in the sea. Clapper Bell began cursing and Carrick's feelings were the same. It could be any boat. At that distance, there was no way they could ever identify it again.

They floated together for a moment longer, the speck still receding, then turned and swam back towards the shore.

The inflatable was where they'd left it and hadn't been touched. Rummaging in a haversack, Clapper Bell produced a flask of rum and they sat in silence on the shingle till it was finished.

"An' that turned out a real practice dive," said Clapper Bell after another moment. "What do you reckon? That they tracked our air bubbles, then made their net cast?"

Carrick nodded, a cold shiver going up his spine at the memory. The weighted net had been a callous, deliberate attempt to trap them down there beside the *Martha Pym*, leave them to a horrifying, lingering wait for death.

Bell sighed, stuck a cigarette between his lips, and lit it with a grunt of sheer pleasure.

"S.o.b.'s," he said conversationally. "What do we do about it?"

"Remember," said Carrick. "That's all we can do. Someone must reckon we're becoming a nuisance, asking too many questions."

"You know the worst of it?" said Bell morosely. "I lost my supper down there—that damned lobster." He contemplated the peaceful water of the cove and his mouth twisted. "I'll tell you this—I don't feel like goin' down for another one."

It was dusk by the time Carrick and Bell motored the little Gemini inflatable back through the Feanport breakwater entrance and into harbour again. The mailboat had gone, a small, neat lighthouse supply tender flying the Northern Lighthouse Commissioners' flag had taken her place, and the last of the rapidly fading daylight was already being challenged by the street lamps in the village above.

Once they'd nudged alongside *Marlin*'s hull, Carrick left Clapper Bell to see to the Gemini being hoisted in. Going aboard, he started in search of Captain Shannon but met Jumbo Wills instead.

"He went ashore about half an hour ago," Wills reported cheerfully. "He wanted to talk to the skippers of those pair-trawl boats. Webb, they got the catch in and you should have seen it being landed! They had the buyers queuing."

"That should make a happy time at the Anchor Watch tonight," said Carrick, undismayed at the delay.

"I was thinking that," said Wills. His freckled face shaped a grin. "Ferguson is duty officer tonight. How about you and I—"

"Another time," said Carrick, shaking his head. "Sorry. I've got plans."

"I think I saw her in the village this afternoon." said Wills. "Look, about that echo-sounder fault. It was some kind of overload and we had the spares to fix it. But—ah—I haven't mentioned it to the Old Man yet. So I was wondering—"

"I saw nothing, heard nothing, know nothing," Carrick said flatly. "But if you don't tell him, he'll find out."

As Wills sighed and plodded off, Carrick headed aft towards his cabin. A few minutes later, having stripped off his black rubber scuba suit, showered, and dried himself down, he lay back on top of his bunk and relaxed for a spell, trying again to make sense out of what had happened out at the wreck of the *Martha Pym*.

It still came down to a frightening bid which could have left them both to die under eighty feet of water. It had been no simple grudge against Fishery Protection—unless they were dealing with a madman. Which left only one other immediate possibility, that someone felt too many questions were being asked around Feanport.

Questions that were bringing very few sensible answers.

He gave up at last, rose, and dressed in shore-going civilian slacks, shirt and tie and a sports jacket. As he transferred money and other oddments to his pockets the cigarettes taped to the mirror tempted him again. On an impulse, he untaped one side of the packet, then quickly slapped the tape back in place and stood back as he heard a knock on the cabin door. The door swung open a moment later and Captain Shannon walked in.

"Shore rig, eh?" Shannon's eyes showed a brief, surprisingly humorous twinkle. Then, crossing over, he plumped down on the edge of Carrick's bunk. "I've talked to Clapper Bell. Any notion why it happened?"

Carrick shook his head.

"Then don't waste your time asking around," said Shannon. He drew out his cigarettes, then scowled at the pack taped to the mirror and tucked his own away again. "I forgot. You're still a no-smoking zone—a burden to the rest of humanity. Anyway, don't waste your time asking. I've just learned that lesson again."

"The pair-boat skippers?" asked Carrick.

Shannon nodded. "Innocent faces and sly smiles. But your harbourmaster friend says they sent a box of fish across to Fean Island almost as soon as they berthed. A token of thanks to the Vullans."

"And it's easy enough to guess why," mused Carrick. "Vullan more or less admitted it."

"Yes." Shannon rubbed a hand over his beard. "We know, mister. But as far as they were concerned who did they think they were really thanking? Milne Vullan or the Witch of the Isles?" He sighed. "Enjoy your shore time, but try not to stir up anything. I'm going to stay in my cabin and pray no idiot gallops in to tell me he's seen something strange flying across the moon. God knows, we've had just about everything else."

*   *   *

Carrick left *Marlin* at seven-thirty. It was a mild evening, the moon framed by thin wisps of cloud and the wind still light and from the west. Walking along the quayside, he passed a few groups of gossiping fishermen who were passing the time while their boats loaded ice and took on fuel and he noticed that the lighthouse supply tender at the north quay was preparing to sail.

The fishermen ignored him. But as he reached the harbour gates a car which had stopped outside flashed its headlamps at him. It was a dark blue Volvo station wagon and as he went towards it Milne Vullan and John Marsh climbed out. At the same time the driver's window was wound down and Dorothy Vullan smiled out at him.

"I thought it was you, Chief Officer," she said triumphantly, then glanced scathingly at her husband and Marsh. "Men—they didn't recognise you out of uniform."

"My infallable wife," murmured Vullan and winked at Marsh, who grinned dutifully. "Having the evening off, Carrick?"

"It could be my last chance here," said Carrick, then paused. "I didn't see your boat in the harbour."

"We came across to the seaweed plant jetty," explained Dorothy Vullan. "I wanted to pick up the car. We keep it at the plant, and I'm having the evening off too, a gossip session with a girl who lives inland."

"When Dorothy says 'girl' she means any woman up to pensionable age," said Vullan.

"And any woman is a girl till she decides differently," countered Dorothy Vullan. She reached over and opened the passenger door. "I'll give you a lift, Chief Officer. I think I know where you're heading."

"It isn't far," said Carrick.

"Let her deliver you," said Vullan and made a vague gesture. "John and I have to visit that damned polling station again, to make sure everything's ready. It opens for business at eight A.M."

"If anyone turns up," mused Marsh.

"Even Feanport has its political faithful," said Vullan. "They'll be there. But we might as well take care of things at the harbour, while we're here."

"Like seeing a couple of fishing skippers?" asked Carrick.

Vullan chuckled. "Maybe. But I promised Dorothy's friend Chester, the antique king, we'd double-check that his crates are properly stored. It'll be a couple of days before the truck arrives to move them south."

"One man's junk, another man's fortune," said Marsh.

"So do I give you a lift or not?" said Dorothy Vullan with a slight impatience.

Obediently, Carrick boarded the Volvo. Starting the car, Dorothy Vullan set it moving and he had a last glimpse of her husband and Marsh heading in through the harbour gates.

The Witch of the Isles drove with more zest than skill and Carrick winced as she took a corner with a squeal of tyre rubber.

"I saw Shona this morning and she said she was seeing you to-night," said Dorothy Vullan, unperturbed. She glanced sideways at Carrick, the car veering across the narrow road in the process. "I'm fond of that girl. She's the only blood relative I've got."

"Is that a warning?" asked Carrick.

She laughed, gave a blast on the horn as a dog escaped from their path, then changed the conversation abruptly.

"Milne's made me a promise—no more fishing trials after this week. At least, not anywhere near Feanport, ever."

"It should help," said Carrick, then winced as she took another corner. "What about tonight?"

"I won't be late back, and John Marsh is staying at the house," she said with an almost aggressive cheerfulness.

"Good." Carrick was glad they were already almost at the end of the village. "Your friend Chester got away on time?"

"He left hours ago," said Dorothy Vullan. "He planned to drive to Inverness to catch the evening 'plane out of there for London. It's a long drive, but he can make it and leave the hire car at the airport." A slight edge entered her voice. "Time is money to people like Robert Chester. I'll bet he already has customers lined up for every antique in those crates he brought back from the islands."

As she spoke, she braked the Volvo and stopped it at the side of the road. Angus Grant's cottage was a short distance ahead, to the right of a fork in the road.

"I'm heading north," she explained. "Anyway, it wouldn't help your popularity with a mule-head like Grant if he saw me dropping you off." Then, suddenly, her hand rested lightly on Carrick's arm.

"You know, I reckon I was very lucky to find a man like Milne. Shona could use some happiness too—temporary or otherwise. That's all I'm going to say."

She brushed aside Carrick's thanks, then set the blue station wagon moving again as soon as he got out. The Volvo took the left fork, swinging north, and as the red tail lights vanished Carrick walked the short distance down the other road towards the cottage.

When he knocked on the door, Angus Grant opened it. The big, bearded fisherman was in his work clothes, which was a surprise, and had a new almost aggressively brisk air as he invited Carrick in.

They went through to a small living-room furnished in a faded, old fashioned style but neat and clean and with a peat fire smouldering in a polished iron grate.

"You'll have a dram," said Grant and made it a statement of fact, going over to a table where he had a bottle and glasses waiting. "Shona says she's almost ready—though when a woman says that, it can mean anything."

He poured the drinks neat, brought the glasses over, and smiled gravely as he saw Carrick looking at a framed photograph of an attractive, dark-haired woman in a wedding dress.

"Aye, that was my wife, Chief Officer. A bonnie woman—Shona had to get her looks from somewhere, eh?"

Carrick nodded, took the offered drink, raised the glass in a silent toast, and sipped the whisky. It had that clean, special edge which usually meant a high-grade illicit still.

"I'm leaving in a minute," said Grant. "Fishing again—I've arranged things with one of the local skippers. My own crew and his boat. She's the *Duchess*, a forty-footer, smaller than my *Rachel*, but better than none. He'll use her by day, I'll use her by night."

"Shift work?" asked Carrick.

Grant nodded. "If it can be done with a factory, it can be done with a boat—for a spell, anyway, till the *Rachel* is ready. His crew need their rest, mine need the work."

The room door opened as he finished and Shona came in. Her long hair was caught back in a silver clasp, and she wore a figure-hugging cocktail dress of light cream wool, a tiny silver necklet on a thin chain at her throat. She was carrying a heavy Black Watch plaid shawl over one arm.

"Aye, you'll do," said Angus Grant gruffly.

"Anywhere," agreed Carrick.

She smiled at them, then faced Carrick.

"Ready when you are," she said.

Carrick finished his drink. Draping the shawl over her shoulders, Shona turned to her father.

"Be careful out there," she said quietly. "You'll be on a strange boat."

"A boat is a boat and fish are fish, girl," answered Grant patiently. "We'll be back in before dawn."

He went with them to the door, then, as he said goodnight, Carrick stopped him.

"Any idea where the MacLeans were this afternoon?" Carrick made the question a casual one. "I was looking for them."

"I'm their skipper, not their keeper," said Grant, some of the warmth fading from his voice. "I couldn't tell you."

He gave them a nod, went back into the cottage, and closed the door. Shona didn't seem to have noticed the change in mood. Taking Carrick's arm, she led the way round to the side of the house, where a small grey Volkswagen was parked.

"Borrowed—like father, like daughter," she said, handing Carrick the keys. Her eyes twinkled in the moonlight. "You drive, I'll navigate, and you'd better not count on eating for a spell. The only place I could think of is about twenty miles south of here."

"I'll survive," said Carrick with a grin, helping her in on the passenger side. "I can always turn cannibal."

She laughed and sat close to him once he'd got behind the wheel.

*   *   *

The road south was narrow, winding, and varied between stretches that clung to spectacularly moonlit lengths of coastline and other sections that ran inland, between the hills and through passes blasted from the rock. Once the Volkswagen's headlamps showed a deer on the tarmac ahead for the brief instant before it raced off. Other wildlife abounded, from small, scurrying rabbits to larger, anonymous shapes which were simply a momentary glimpse of a pair of bright eyes.

But the traffic was light, not much more than a few cars and an occasional giant refrigerated fish truck on the overnight haul to the cities. Carrick set a relaxed, unhurried pace and Shona was content to curl up on the seat beside him, saying little and equally at peace.

The twenty miles took about forty minutes, then a glow of lights showed ahead. Following his passenger's directions, Carrick turned off the road and the car crunched down a gravelled path. The path took a bend and ahead of them lay a long, low building, brightly lit, which faced out towards the silvered water of the Brannan Sound.

"That's it—the Clanstop," said Shona, pointing ahead. "One of the big hotel groups built it as a motel complex for the summer tourist trade. But the way things worked out, the bar and restaurant side keeps busy all the year round. Like I said, it's the only place you can eat out for miles around here."

There was a well-filled car park to one side. Carrick coasted the Volkswagen towards it and found a parking slot, close to a sign that said "Marina" and pointed down towards the shore. He smiled a little at that. There were a few places like the Clanstop being built along the coast, hoping to catch a share of everything from the winter skiing trade to the yachting extroverts who ventured that far north. But Shona was right. Most of them were surprised to find that their real business came from the locals—who had year-round money and a new generation outlook about what to do with it.

They locked the Volkswagen and left it, heading towards the Clanstop's neon-topped doorway. But halfway across, Carrick slowed and gave an involuntary grunt of surprise.

"Something wrong?" asked Shona, puzzled.

"Stone in my shoe." Stooping, he made a show of flicking a piece of gravel out of one shoe then rose, took her arm, and they went on.

But he'd taken the chance to have a second glance, and he'd been right. Dorothy Vullan's dark blue Volvo station wagon, the car she'd taken out of Feanport saying she was heading north to visit a friend, was parked in the row next to the one they were passing.

Which, Carrick told himself, might be none of his business. Except that after the last couple of days he was left with a feeling that he couldn't afford to ignore anything that concerned the Witch of the Isles.

In another moment they were in the carpeted warmth of the Clanstop's lobby. There were clan badges on the walls and the drapes were tartan but everything else was chrome and plastic. The motel section was to the left, the main bar, softly lit and with music coming from it, was to the right, and the restaurant doorway was straight ahead.

Still thinking about what he'd seen, Carrick steered Shona towards the bar, where a waitress in a tartan mini-kilt and a cutaway blouse found them a table. The place was as busy as the car park had suggested, crammed by a mixture of young farmers and fishermen and their girls plus a sprinkling of army men in from a mountain warfare course. The blast of music came from a guitar, bass and drums trio with an electronic hook-up and the postage stamp sized dance floor was filled.

"It isn't exactly candlelight and quiet," said Shona almost apologetically. "But—"

"I like it," he said easily. "Show me some food soon and I could even get to love it."

He ordered drinks, and by the time the waitress brought them he had made sure that Dorothy Vullan wasn't anywhere in the crush. But she was still very much on his mind. Paying for the drinks, he shoved back his chair.

"Two minutes and I'll be back," he promised. "If I go missing, try the men's room."

She laughed and nodded and Carrick went back out into the lobby. Going across to the restaurant entrance, he reserved a table and looked around the diners at the same time. Again, there was no sign of Dorothy Vullan. That left the motel section and he turned towards it then hesitated, telling himself again it could be none of his business.

Next moment, cursing under his breath, he took a quick side-stepping shuffle behind the shelter of a display stand boosting the tourist attractions available around the Clanstop's location. Dorothy Vullan had just emerged from the corridor which led to the motel rooms— and the man by her side was Robert Chester, who should have been on that night 'plane out of Inverness on his way to London and his antique deals.

The couple went straight across the Clanstop lobby and out into the night, towards the car park. Carrick stayed where he was, making a pretence of studying the display board, and after a couple of minutes Chester returned alone and vanished back down the same corridor.

Feeling like a tame spy, Carrick in turn went out into the night and walked over to where the Volvo had been parked. The space was empty.

*   *   *

He forced a grin back on his face when he returned to the bar and joined Shona again. When they'd finished their drinks they went through to the restaurant where the food and service was good but the menu prices were high to match. He joked and talked his way through the meal, but what he'd seen was still on his mind and it must have shown. He caught Shona eyeing him oddly a few times, but she made no direct comment.

Afterwards, they went back into the bar, staying there for another drink and a few dances, and in the process he got Dorothy Vullan out of his thoughts. It wasn't too hard, he decided, as the calm grey eyes opposite met his own.

It was around midnight when they left. Carrick was driving the Volkswagen north again along the same empty road when whatever patience Shona Grant possessed suddenly snapped.

"Webb, I want to know what happened back there," she said unexpectedly. "Something did—I know that much, and I want to hear about it."

Carrick gave a sideways glance. Her face, softly lit by the instrument lights, showed a firm determination. He shrugged, then sought a handy refuge from the truth.

"Sorry. I started thinking—about that character with the shotgun last night and what's maybe going to happen next." He paused, taking the car round a sharp bend, then added grimly, meaning it, "*Marlin* sails from Feanport after tomorrow. That could be like taking the lid off the pot and I don't like the idea of you still being around."

She moistened her lips. "That's all?"

"I'd call it enough," he said wryly.

She sat still for a moment, saying nothing, her face grave, watching the grey ribbon of road in the headlamps.

"Webb, pull in," she said suddenly.

He stopped the car on the verge and waited. She looked at him carefully, as if reaching a decision.

"Take me home," she said at last and gave him a quiet smile. "If we've only tonight, I don't want to waste it."

He leaned over, kissed her, then started the car again.

It was almost one A.M. by the dashboard clock when the lights of Feanport showed ahead and minutes later Carrick let the Volkswagen coast to a stop outside the darkened little cottage. Shona got out of the car first, waited until he joined her, then took his hand.

They were a few paces away from the front porch of the cottage when a figure stepped out of its shadow.

"Hello, Webb," said a dry, all too familiar voice. It was Ferguson, and he was in uniform. The middle-aged junior second mate had a veiled grin on his dried-up face as he came forward. He nodded politely to Shona then turned to Carrick. "I don't expect you to like this, but I've been hanging around that porch since midnight. The Old Man wants you back aboard."

"Now?" Carrick glared at him.

"Right now. The moment you show up." Ferguson glanced sideways at Shona. "Sorry if it breaks up your evening, but—" he gave a thin-shouldered shrug and ended it there.

Carrick mentally damned Ferguson and Shannon with an equal ferocity. But there was nothing he could do about it.

"Tell him I'm on my way," he said.

Ferguson gave a nod, and strode off briskly. Sighing, Carrick turned and looked at Shona in the moonlight.

"You'd better go," she said, then smiled. "But tell your captain he just lost a lot of popularity."

He managed a resigned grin, kissed her lightly, then hurried down the street after Ferguson.

*   *   *

Marlin seemed as dark and silent at her quayside berth as the other vessels around the harbour. But a petty officer was waiting just beyond the gangway as the two officers came aboard and directed them straight away to the fishery cruiser's tiny wardroom.

The deadlights had been closed over its portholes, it was brightly lit, and Captain Shannon was seated at the head of the wardroom table with some scribbled notes in front of him. There was a coffee pot on the table and some used cups around it showed that the wardroom had seen an earlier meeting.

"About time," said Shannon scathingly as they entered. His eyes showed a lack of sleep but the small, bearded figure was otherwise aggressively alert. "Sit down, both of you."

Obediently, Carrick and Ferguson took two of the chairs, settled, and waited. Ferguson still had the same expression of amusement on his face, but whatever he knew, he said nothing.

"We've had a visitor," said Shannon. He lit a cigarette with a match and tossed the match into an already overflowing ashtray. "Morrison the harbourmaster came sneaking aboard late tonight." He paused, his expression hard to read. "Morrison claims you threatened him, mister."

"Unfortunately, he doesn't have any witnesses—apart from our bo'sun," murmured Ferguson.

"And I don't give a damn," said Shannon. "Morrison says there's a fishing boat leaving harbour at five A.M. to help Vullan on a fishing trial."

Carrick stiffened. "Does he know where?"

"No," admitted Shannon. "But she's the *Sandworm*, one he has used before—and the skipper has already loaded a trammel net supplied by Vullan. The net must be laid by six A.M. and the *Sandworm* is to head back to harbour. I presume that means Vullan will show up just after that. Tomorrow is one day when he can't waste time."

Carrick nodded. With the Feanport polling station opening at eight A.M., Milne Vullan had a tight schedule ahead. But the trammel net, a long, floating curtain of mesh which could be paid out and left buoyed, was one type of fishing gear that could be collected later.

"I'd like to be out there," he said.

"You're going to be," said Shannon. "I want that net checked, I want to know what happens when Vullan comes along—and I don't want him to know he has an audience. You'll have the patrol launch, with Ferguson and a couple of hands as surface back-up."

Ferguson nodded. "Clapper Bell is briefed, the scuba gear is already in the launch. I've picked two men and—"

"And the rest can wait," Shannon cut him short and looked up at the wardroom clock. "We'll make it an 0430 muster. That, Mister Carrick, gives you about three hours sleep." He paused, and for a moment his bearded face showed a trace of amusement. "That's maybe not what you had in mind when Ferguson found you, but that's the way it's going to be."

    *   *   *

Three hours in his bunk was better than none. But Carrick didn't find it easy to sleep. He lay in his cabin, part of his mind puzzling again and again over Dorothy Vullan's meeting with Robert Chester, the rest of his thoughts on Shona Grant. He could still picture the moment Ferguson had stepped out of the shadows at the cottage porch, a moment when he could cheerfully have strangled him.

But sleep did come. And it seemed only minutes later when a seaman shook him awake again. Yawning, Carrick gulped down the mug of coffee the man left him then pulled on a sweater and slacks and went on deck.

The fishery cruiser still lay dark and silent under the faint moonlight. The temperature seemed to have dropped too and he shivered slightly, listening to the creak of their mooring lines and the soft lap of the sea against the hull. Then he spotted a small group of figures huddled below the bridge and joined them. The first he recognised was Clapper Bell, who winked a greeting but said nothing, then Ferguson pushed his way forward.

"It's starting," said Ferguson in a low voice. "The *Sandworm* is over on the north quay, to your left. The crew seem to be arriving."

Carrick looked across the harbour and saw tiny, moving lights twinkling aboard one of the black shapes of the fishing fleet.

"Anything else?" he asked.

"One boat came in about half an hour ago and tied up."

He nodded. "The *Duchess*—Grant had her out. What about her crew?"

"They went ashore," shrugged Ferguson, then gave a satisfied murmur as the first sound of an engine starting up came from the other quay. "Not long now. I'll let the Old Man know."

He went away and returned in a couple of minutes with Captain Shannon, who was still in his pyjamas with a duffel coat over his shoulders and the pyjama legs stuffed into seaboots.

Another few minutes passed. Then the *Sandworm*'s navigation lights came on, her engine note changed, and she began easing away from her berth. They watched in silence as the fishing boat headed out of the harbour but as her stern lights passed the breakwater Shannon came to life.

"Now," he rasped. "And keep it quiet."

The group of seamen around sprang into action and the patrol launch was quickly and carefully lowered. She was hardly in the water before Ferguson and his two deck hands were aboard, followed by Carrick and Clapper Bell. Ferguson started the engine with little more than a whisper of sound, they cast off, and in another moment they were inching away from *Marlin* with Shannon still watching from above.

A black shadow in the night, running without lights, the patrol launch murmured out past the breakwater. To the south, the *Sandworm* was a silhouette in the moonlight as she headed down the coast, gathering speed, and in the little cockpit of the patrol launch Ferguson glanced at Carrick and raised a questioning eyebrow.

"It's follow my leader," Carrick told him. "Keep your distance—just don't lose visual contact."

One of the crewmen was at the helm, the other was already checking their radio link with *Marlin*. Both were among the fishery cruiser's most experienced hands, and the patrol launch, with her low, compact lines, had been designed for just this kind of work. Carrick had little fear of the *Sandworm* spotting the fact that she was being shadowed. He glanced around the cockpit again, past the echo sounding gear to the compact, short-range radar. Neither was much use on this mission. Visual contact was more important—when the fishing boat got to work it was going to matter to know exactly what she did.

He left Ferguson and went below, into the tiny cabin, where Clapper Bell had begun the task of getting into his scuba suit. Carrick did the same, working by the dim light of a shaded bulb, while the patrol launch murmured on, pitching a little as she cleared the bay and met the more boisterous swell of the Brannan Sound.

When they had finished, they relaxed. Occasionally, Ferguson stuck his head down into the cabin to report progress. The fishing boat ahead kept to a southerly course, keeping to the middle of the Sound, and the only real change was that after twenty minutes her running lights blinked out.

Clapper Bell dozed. Carrick, too, felt his eyes gradually begin to close as the murmuring rhythm of the launch engine continued unchanged. Then, suddenly, it altered, slowed, and Ferguson stuck his head down again.

"We've arrived," said Ferguson. "Better come up."

He kicked Clapper Bell awake and they went up into the cockpit. The patrol launch was almost drifting in the swell and the *Sandworm* was clearly visible about half a mile ahead, moving slowly and making a curving turn to starboard.

"Position?" asked Carrick.

Ferguson gave a humourless grin. "She's just east of the Witchrock—we should have guessed it."

One of the crewmen handed Carrick glasses he'd been using. Carrick trained them on the fishing boat, seeing the tiny figures working near her stern, then the white streaking of disturbed water which told the rest. The trammel net was being laid.

They stayed clear, watching, until the fishing boat was finished. Then, at last, the *Sandworm* began heading for home and went past them, the beat of her engine loud across the water.

"Six A.M.," said Ferguson, glancing at his watch. "Like a railway timetable—only better. Our turn?"

Carrick nodded. The patrol launch began moving again and soon they were close to the bobbing line of marker floats which supported the waiting trammel net. Quickly, Carrick and Bell got into their scuba harnesses, made a last check of their gear, and clipped on the underwater lamps which had been added for the occasion. Then, when they were ready, Carrick beckoned Ferguson nearer.

"Remember Vullan is on his way," he said. "If the *Sea Whip* shows while we're down—"

"I'll ease off and collect you later," nodded Ferguson. "I'll be on radar watch."

Pulling down his facemask, Carrick signalled to Clapper Bell and they went into the water, duck-diving down to about twenty feet, then switching on the underwater lamps to get their bearings. The fine, wavering curtain of the trammel net showed immediately and Carrick ventured right up to it.

As far as he could see, it was an ordinary net with an ordinary mesh. A solitary dogfish had already been trapped in it near where Clapper Bell was making a similar examination, the fish wriggling in the pool of light from Bell's lamp.

But Vullan had supplied the net. Carrick kicked his way over to join Bell, signalled, and they dived deeper, down to the heavy bottom rope. Then they stopped, equally puzzled. A small cylinder of white plastic, about half the size of a beer can, was attached to the rope by a plastic toggle. Bell finned to the left, exploring, then came back and beckoned, leading him further along the net. Another of the white plastic cylinders was there, but mounted higher up.

They parted, Carrick swimming to the left, Bell taking the right-hand sector. It was a slow process, but by the time Carrick reached his end of the trammel net he had located six more of the plastic cylinders. Treating the close proximity of the mesh with respect, he cut one of the cylinders loose with his diving knife, shoved it into a pocket of his scuba suit, and moved clear before he began swimming back towards the centre.

As he swam, he suddenly found himself shivering, ignored it, then realised something else was happening, an odd, singing sensation had begun building in his ears. The shivering increased and, puzzled, he checked his air supply, found it normal, and had begun to swim again when a silver shape like a small torpedo slammed into his body.

It was a large cod, and it blundered off him, swimming straight for the net. Almost immediately, other fish were around him, all heading in the same direction, some colliding with him, while the shivering sensation began to rack his body and the singing in his ears became a high-pitched wail.

And the fish came on, large and small, fleeing from an unknown something in a way that sent them into the waiting net as if it didn't exist. For Carrick, they were just one more element in a nightmare which still held no pain, only bewilderment and a total weakness while he felt his body go out of control.

Bemused, he stared at the way the plume of air bubbles from his scuba mask had begun to bend and curve. It was a moment before his disorientated mind fought through to what that meant, that he was rolling over and over in the water. When he tried to right himself, the air bubbles began to dance while he slipped sideways instead, like a drunken doll.

Then, suddenly, it was over. The shivering died, the singing vanished from his ears, all that was left was total exhaustion and a sickness. Ignoring the curtain of trapped, struggling fish, mustering what strength he had left, he struck upwards, towards the surface.

As soon as his head was above water he tore off his face mask and vomited. It was a moment or two before he even remembered Clapper Bell—and then a retching noise from his right and the sight of another head bobbing on the surface not far away showed that Bell had been affected in exactly the same way.

Yet otherwise the sea was empty apart from the bobbing, mocking floats of the net.

Too exhausted to talk, they swam towards each other, cracked the little CO_2 cylinders which inflated their life vests, then lay back and floated, waiting.

It was ten minutes before the patrol launch nosed in and picked them up. They had to be practically dragged aboard then, while the two crewmen helped them out of their scuba gear, Carrick managed a weak grin as Ferguson bent over him.

"What the hell happened to you?" demanded Ferguson, his thin face tight with anxiety.

"It can keep," Carrick told him in a dull voice. "What about up here?"

"Vullan," said Ferguson. "Almost as soon as you went under we picked up a radar trace on the five-mile scan, heading here fast. I eased clear, like we arranged then—well that damned *Sea Whip* stopped about half a mile off, then manoeuvred back and forward as if she was trailing something." He shrugged. "Four or five minutes of that, then he just got under way again, slamming back for Feanport."

"Four or five minutes?" Carrick echoed the words in near disbelief. Under the water, it had seemed an age. "Anything else, anything at all?"

"Well—" Ferguson hesitated and scowled "—just one thing I can't understand. We were using the echo sounder, because we were on the edge of the channel and—"

"And it packed in? Total failure?" Carrick struggled up on his elbows, staring at him.

Ferguson nodded.

"We've been conned," said Carrick bitterly. "Shannon, all of us we've been conned." He dragged the white cylinder out of his thigh pocket and stared at it. "Electric fish-herding—like hell it was."

"What do you mean?" asked Ferguson, bewildered.

"I mean we get back to *Marlin* and dig the Old Man out of his bunk," grated Carrick.

Clapper Bell was fumbling with a pack of cigarettes.

"I'll have one," said Carrick.

"You've stopped," croaked Bell.

"Mind your own damned business," Carrick told him, then grabbed a cigarette and lit it. "This is medicinal."

Ferguson gave up, turned, and nodded to the crewman at the controls. Shuddering to life, the patrol launch swung round and began carving a broad white wake as she headed back towards Feanport.

*   *   *

Dawn comes late in the northern Scottish winter. There was still just the beginning of an iron-grey hint of light on the horizon when the patrol launch slipped into harbour, came quietly alongside *Marlin,* and was smoothly hoisted in.

Ferguson had radioed ahead. As soon as Carrick and Bell were aboard they were summoned to Captain Shannon's day cabin where that small, fiery individual stared at them for a moment under the light. Then he swore softly and angrily.

"Sit down before you fall down, both of you," he ordered with a frown that came close to concern. "That damned fool Ferguson only said you'd had problems, not that you looked half-dead." As they obeyed, he brought out glasses and a fresh bottle of his prized single-malt, then poured two of the largest whiskies either of them had ever seen. Then came another order. "Get those into you."

They did, while Shannon watched in silence. Then he nodded.

"All right, report."

"Vullan isn't electric fishing. He's using high-frequency sound, ultrasonics—something like that," said Carrick wearily. He handed a disbelieving Shannon the white cylinder he'd cut from the trammel net. "Whatever is inside that thing should prove it."

Shannon hefted the cylinder, chewed his lip, then shrugged. "Well, if we're thieving, let's see what we've got."

It took a knife to cut the plastic seal but after that the cylinder unscrewed and out fell a small, metal-cased box which might have been a photographic light-meter—except that it wasn't and the needle on the tiny dial had stopped at a scale reading.

"You said sound." Shannon's voice grated on the word. "Go on, mister."

Carrick did, while Clapper Bell nodded an occasional agreement and Shannon's attitude gradually shifted from initial scepticism and silence to thawing acceptance and an occasional question. When Carrick finished, Shannon paced the cabin for a moment then suddenly swore, headed for the bookshelf beside his desk, and pulled out a thin, black-bound book. Apparently ignoring them, he thumbed the pages while Clapper Bell sat with his eyes almost closed and Carrick fought down an urge to yawn and keep yawning. Whatever had happened to them, Carrick had never felt so tired and weakened in his life.

Shannon turned, saw them, and said searchingly, "Can you two stay awake long enough to listen for a moment?"

They straightened a little and nodded. Shannon slapped the book shut.

"Extracts from papers at a recent oceanography conference in Boston," he said. "One of them is on sound, fish behaviour and fishing. Experiments on the use of specially designed fishing gear with a low underwater noise level—so that it doesn't frighten the fish away."

Clapper Bell gave a semblance of a grin. Shannon saw it and sniffed.

"Bo'sun, I'm about to improve your education. Fish can hear—you know that much. It happens they can hear damned well. On a calm day they'll hear a ship's propellor when the ship is miles away. Some of the marine boffins have proved that a fish can even hear an aircraft flying over its patch of water—and I don't mean just low-level stuff." He glanced at Carrick. "Agreed, mister?"

Carrick nodded slowly. He didn't know much about it, but it was certainly long established that fish "talked" underwater. He'd once heard a tape recording of twitters and grunts which amounted to the courtship build-up for one species. Other fish were said to home in on sounds when searching for prey.

"Mind you, as usual, the fishermen knew it long before the boffins made a fuss," grunted Shannon. "When I was a boy, any fisherman bringing a net alongside got a lad to thump on the side of the boat with a hammer—so that the noise would scare the fish, keep them in the net till it closed. But this—" he shook his head. "How far from the net was the *Sea Whip* when it happened?"

"Ferguson says about half a mile," said Carrick.

"My God," said Shannon softly. "And Vullan talked about small-scale field trials. If it still knocked hell out of you two—"

"An' blew the echo-sounder, sir," reminded Clapper Bell sleepily.

"I hadn't forgotten." Shannon scowled. "I'm going to have to talk with our Mister Wills about the first time that happened—which he still hasn't bothered to mention." He drew a deep breath. "Stay quiet about this for now, both of you. We've satisfied our own curiosity about what Milne Vullan is doing. No wonder those damned fishing skippers didn't believe his prattle about electric fishing—not when this sort of thing was happening."

"But it doesn't change anything else," said Carrick quietly.

"No, it doesn't," agreed Shannon and shook his head. "They'd call it witchcraft, mister. There's a whole village ripe for trouble around this harbour. What's happened already could be nothing compared with—" he stopped short and shook his head again. "That's enough for now. Get out of here. Just looking at you is making me feel tired." He paused and added almost absently, "You did a fairly good job, both of you."

Which, Carrick decided, ranked close to a citation. They left the day cabin, parted, and he yawned and stumbled his way aft.

When he reached his own cabin, he had to fumble to open the door. He managed to close it again, reach the bunk, and then his legs buckled.

Still fully dressed, he was probably asleep before his head landed on the pillow.

VII

Jumbo Wills wakened Carrick at noon and didn't find it easy. At last, cursing between yawns, Carrick levered himself out of the bunk, crossed to the cabin mirror, and scowled at the unshaven, bleary-eyed face that stared back at him.

"Do you feel as bad as you look?" asked Wills politely.

"Go to hell," Carrick said.

"The company couldn't be worse there than it is around here," answered Wills indignantly. "Maybe you had a rough time, but I've been skinned and gutted by the Old Man—"

"The echo-sounder business?" Carrick grinned.

"That, and anything else he could think up," complained Wills. "Now we've got Detective Inspector Henderson back aboard. He's with the Old Man, and they want to see you."

Carrick raised an eyebrow. "Why?"

Wills shrugged. "I forgot. You wouldn't know. That little character Lampeye was fished out of the harbour this morning, drowned. Looks like he got stoned last night and—"

"You're sure it was Lampeye?" demanded Carrick, cutting him short, the news jarring him totally awake.

"I was there when they carted him off," nodded Wills. "He'd been jammed between the quayside and one of the fishing boats."

"Tell the Old Man I'll be along directly," said Carrick.

Wills nodded and went out, banging the cabin door behind him. Going over to the cabin porthole, Carrick looked out. The sky was almost clear of cloud, the harbour scene appeared unchanged—almost peaceful. But now, after the reality of his own personal nightmare, Lampeye was dead.

He washed and shaved quickly, stripped off the crumpled clothes he'd slept in, and got back into uniform. Then, taking a deep breath, he set off to answer Shannon's summons.

*   *   *

Captain Shannon and Malcolm Henderson were standing at a table, studying a chart, when Carrick reached them. They broke off as he entered the day cabin, Shannon scrutinising him carefully, the tall, thin policeman contenting himself with a twist of a smile from under his dark, drooping moustache.

"Fit for duty?" asked Shannon after a moment. "The truth, mister."

Carrick nodded and a glance that held a shade of relief passed between the other two men.

"You've heard about Lampeye?" asked Henderson.

"Yes." Carrick glanced at the chart. It was the one Captain Shannon had used to map out his ballot box collection run. "So—what happened?"

Henderson shrugged. "He turned up when one of the fishing boats started to move out not long after first light. We know he was drinking heavily last night, we know he usually ended up sleeping it off somewhere around the harbour—that's about it, so far."

"Except this time I imagine the post mortem will be toothcomb style," said Shannon.

"It will." Henderson's thin face flushed a little. "We don't make the same mistake twice."

"Twice?" Carrick seized on the word.

"George MacKenzie," admitted Henderson. "I've talked to the pathologist who performed the autopsy. He—well, he admits a couple of small details puzzled him."

"How small?"

"Signs of a fairly hefty blow on the head, and some small cuts on the soles of his feet, as if he'd been walking barefoot on rock." Henderson sucked an end of his moustache defensively and scowled. "But he could have taken a crack on the skull when he went overboard, anything can happen to a body when it's in the water—and there's no doubt about the thing that matters, Webb. He drowned."

"But how?" asked Shannon.

Henderson flared at the inference. "Captain, that's on my mind too. It also happens he was a cop, so don't get any notion that it doesn't matter to me."

"We know it does," soothed Carrick while the two men glared at each other. "Look, come back to Lampeye. There's at least one major difference. MacKenzie was feuding with Dorothy Vullan, but Lampeye was working for her husband. There's no chance of the Witch being blamed this time by the gossip squads."

"I wouldn't bank on it." Henderson had doubt in his voice. "Take a walk past the harbour gates, Webb. There's a new slogan painted on a wall up there—'Burn the Witch'."

"That could have been any small boy with a paintbrush," muttered Shannon. He rested his knuckles on the table, frowning absently. "All right, we won't know till the post mortem. But the odds are that Lampeye's death was the way it looks, an accident. I still feel slightly better knowing what Vullan has really been doing out there—and that it's probably just about over now."

"This ultrasonic fishing stuff?" Henderson rammed his hands in the pockets of his leather jacket and scowled. "Maybe it explains a few things, but that's all."

A fishing boat glided past the day cabin's window, heading out to sea, and the three men watched in silence until she had passed. Then Carrick had a question of his own.

"Did you check out John Marsh and the MacLean tribe?" he asked Henderson.

"I did, and so far I haven't got anywhere," shrugged Henderson. "I'm still trying."

"Do me a favour," said Carrick slowly. "Add Robert Chester, a London antique dealer, to the list." He saw Shannon raise an eyebrow and added cautiously, "Dorothy Vullan met him last night— that's maybe none of our business, but I'm curious about him."

"Will do," sighed Henderson. "As for the rest of it, I'm still hoping that today's damned election will keep most people quiet for a spell."

"It helps," said Shannon. "At least we know where Milne Vullan will be most of the day. As local Returning Officer he'll have to stay close to the Feanport polling station."

"Where I've got two large Highland constables on official duty," said Henderson with a faint grin. "Vullan's there right now, with his wife—I looked in on the way here."

"And the polling stations stay open until nine tonight." Shannon eyed Carrick thoughtfully, and tugged at his beard for a moment. "Mister, we'll be sailing an hour before that time, on the islands vote collection run. We won't be back much before midnight."

Henderson nodded. "I'm going to try to be around, Webb. But I told you before, until tomorrow there's not as much as a spare police cadet available."

Carrick said nothing, waiting, but with a feeling he knew what was coming. A moment later, Shannon confirmed it.

"You look like you could use a little extra time ashore, mister," said Shannon. "I'm going to leave you behind. You'll have the bo'sun and a couple of hands—call it a shore patrol, if you like. But you'll also have the patrol launch, and we'll think up a cover story so the whole thing doesn't look too obvious."

"Settled," said Henderson. He glanced at his wrist-watch and winced. "I've got work to do, but I'll try to get back to Feanport before dusk, and I should have the post mortem report on Lampeye by then." He grinned at Shannon. "Thanks again."

He left the cabin. Once the door had closed, Shannon settled in a chair and gave a sigh which held some relief.

"The *Sandworm* went out again at daylight and brought back Vullan's trammel net," he said. "They landed the fish, then returned the net to Fean Island. I did something too, mister. I radioed a report to Department—in code, telling them what happened." His mouth tightened. "I've had a reply, though I didn't tell Henderson. I've been more or less told to mind my own damned business."

Carrick frowned. "So maybe they knew about it already?"

"Perhaps." Shannon built a slow, deliberate steeple with his stubby fingertips and considered it. "High frequency sound, ultrasonics— maybe you were luckier than you knew this morning. If that's what Vullan is working with, it's a damned dangerous tool."

"They use it in medicine—and industry," mused Carrick.

"And you can cut a man's throat with a scalpel," snapped Shannon. "You don't fool around with ultrasonics." He paused, and his manner changed. "I'll get Clapper Bell to spread the word we're leaving some people ashore to make sure there's no hitch when we bring those ballot boxes back—it's weak, but it'll do. I'll think up an excuse for the patrol launch later. Eaten yet?"

"No, sir."

"Do that," said Shannon. "Then you're off watch as far as this ship is concerned." A faint twinkle showed in his eyes. "If you happen to meet a certain young woman, that's none of my damned business—as long as you remember the rest of what you're supposed to do."

*　　*　　*

It was three o'clock by the harbour clock when Carrick went ashore. A lobster boat was unloading its catch but otherwise it was a quiet spell on the quayside, a few fishermen mending nets or washing down decks while transistor radios blared tinny music from a couple of fo'c'sles. Shuggy Morrison was standing at the door of the harbourmaster's office. He gave Carrick a dour nod, turned on his heel and went in. Grinning, Carrick walked on, passed the harbour gates, then stopped short.

"Burn the Witch." The painted slogan Malcolm Henderson had talked about was daubed in almost man-sized letters on the wall just ahead. As he stared at it, he heard a chuckle and turned.

"It's a notion, isn't it, Chief Officer?" Hands in his pockets, a sardonic grin on his face, Donnie MacLean strolled towards him from a group of fishermen. The lanky fishing hand swept back a lock of his long dark hair then thumbed at the writing. "Daft—but it might get as many votes as anything those politicians are brayin' about."

"It's one way of wasting good paint," Carrick eyed him stonily. "Where's the rest of your clan?"

"Brother Willie had to go to the hospital to get those burn dressings changed—cousin Lachie went with him," shrugged MacLean. "Still, what's a burn or two? You heard about old Lampeye?"

Carrick nodded.

"It's gettin' so it's even unlucky to work for the Witch," said MacLean and jerked his head towards the other fishermen, who had slowed, waiting on him. "At least, that's what the lads are sayin'."

"Tell them not to say it too loudly, or they might have problems," Carrick told him. "How did Angus Grant make out with his borrowed boat last night?"

MacLean grimaced. "We didn't bring back enough fish to pay the fuel bill. But we'll keep tryin', Chief Officer—an' we're not lookin' for favours from Fean Island."

He went back to his friends and they went away while Carrick headed up towards the village.

It might be election day in the Lochard constituency and a lot of
political fortune might hang on the result. But Feanport's share of the
excitement came down to two bored policemen standing outside the
village hall on polling station duty, plus a solitary National Party
supporter with a tartan rosette who was being watched by a large Al-
satian dog which looked too tired to yawn.

Going in past the policemen, exchanging a nod with a voter who
was ambling out, Carrick found the polling booths were empty. The
grey-haired woman with the modesty curtain in front of her table
looked up hopefully, saw he wasn't a customer, and went back to
reading her book. Milne Vullan was standing further back, talking
seriously to a young man who wore tweeds and a clerical collar.

A clatter of crockery guided Carrick to a side room. He went in and
discovered Dorothy Vullan and Shona in a small kitchen, making
coffee.

"Look what's turned up," said Dorothy Vullan. Like Shona, she
was dressed in slacks and a sweater. "Can we rise to an extra cup,
Shona?"

"No way." The girl wrinkled her nose at him in a mock disdain.
"Staff and friends only."

"I qualify," said Carrick. "I've drawn shore duty for the day."

"Staff," agreed Dorothy Vullan. "Give him a cup."

She turned as she spoke, brushing against the table. A large leather
handbag lying at the edge tumbled, the contents spilling as it hit the
floor.

"Damn," said Dorothy Vullan and got down on her knees to
gather them up.

Stooping to help her, Carrick retrieved a lipstick from under the
table, handed it over, then reached under again and brought out a
small, unlabelled bottle filled with small white tablets.

"Give me those." Dorothy Vullan almost snatched the bottle from
him. It disappeared back in her bag, then she gave him a slightly
forced smile. "Painkillers, Chief Officer—for middle-aged muscles
and creaky joints. Witchcraft by prescription, and I don't shout about
it."

They located the last of the handbag's contents then rose and
Shona brought over two cups of coffee.

"What about Milne?" she asked. "Will I take him one?"

"Wait till he's finished with the local church." Dorothy Vullan
glanced at Carrick. "You've—well, heard about Lampeye?"

Carrick nodded.

"He didn't have family, so Milne wants to take care of the funeral arrangements." She shook her head slowly. "Poor Lampeye. I'm afraid it's easy enough to guess what happened."

"John Marsh says he saw him near the harbour last night, early on, and he'd already had a few drinks," volunteered Shona. "He was an odd little man and he drank too much—but most people liked him."

"I've heard worse obituaries," said Carrick quietly. He turned to Dorothy Vullan. "Is Marsh here too?"

"No, at the seaweed plant," said Dorothy Vullan with a note of disinterest. She sipped her coffee for a moment then said suddenly, "So Shona took you to the Clanstop last night. Did you enjoy it?"

"Yes." Carrick met her green eyes and nodded calmly. "What about your own evening? How was your friend?"

"Gossiping—as usual." Her eyes held his own for a long moment as if probing, suspecting. Then she seemed to relax and shrugged. "You said 'shore duty'. Does that mean you won't sail with *Marlin* on the ballot box run?"

"Captain Shannon doesn't believe in taking chances," lied Carrick. "He's leaving a berthing party for when he gets back in. Then we get those boxes up here." He grinned. "I'm not complaining."

"He sounds as bad as Milne," said Dorothy Vullan resignedly, setting down her cup. "Milne says he'll stay on here until the island votes arrive. Still—come back up here once the polling stops, Chief Officer. It won't be much of a party, but I've more sandwiches, and a bottle or two of something stronger than coffee." She saw Carrick hesitate and added dryly, "Shona will be along too."

"It's the best offer I've had," said Shona.

He grinned, agreed, then watched Shona turn and collect her shoulder-bag, which had been lying on a chair.

"I'm meeting my father," she explained. "He wants me along with him when he sorts out the insurance claim form for the *Rachel* with the local agent."

"Then take your wandering sailor when you go," suggested Dorothy Vullan, pouring herself more coffee. "I've enough problems."

Carrick didn't argue. They said goodbye to the Witch of the Isles and left. Outside the hall, past the policemen, Shona gave a sigh as they walked along the street.

"There's one thing she didn't tell you," she said quietly. "She knows about that 'Burn the Witch' slogan at the harbour—a damned fool of a cleaning woman told her first thing this morning. Milne knows too, and John Marsh. That's why the *Sea Whip* is berthed at the seaweed jetty again. She thought it would be better not to bring the boat into the harbour—not today, after Lampeye's death."

"Nobody's blaming her for that," said Carrick.

"She's expecting it," said Shona. Then she touched Carrick's arm and gestured ahead. Angus Grant was waiting at the next corner, a grim expression on his face. "He's in a raw mood, Webb. Because of Lampeye—though he won't admit it."

They reached Grant a moment later and the bearded fishing skipper greeted them with a nod.

"Got those insurance papers, girl?" he asked.

"In my bag," she said.

"Good." He made an impatient noise. "Then we'd better get along. I've a busy day—and a boat to work tonight."

"Taking the *Duchess* out again?" asked Carrick.

"Aye, but trying further south," said Grant. "There's a better chance o' decent fishing down there."

Giving another curt nod as a farewell, Grant hustled Shona away. Left alone, Carrick stuck his hands in his pockets and watched them heading along the street for a moment. Then, with his own plans in mind, he set off in the opposite direction through the north end of the village towards the seaweed plant.

It took about ten minutes, then the low clutter of huts and the jetty appeared ahead and a moment later the distinctive, totally unmistakeable odour of drying weed hit his nostrils. The smell grew stronger, almost overpowering, as he reached the wire fence which surrounded the plant and went in through the opened main gate.

He found the plant office, one of the nearest of the huts, and looked in. It held a couple of desks and some filing cabinets but it was deserted so he closed the door again and walked on, exploring as he went. Some of the huts were the equivalent of open barns, holding stacked bales of dried, compressed weed ready for shipment. Machinery was thudding somewhere near but there was still no sign of life.

Carrick turned towards the jetty. Great mounds of green, recently landed weed were stockpiled near it which meant the smell was even fiercer and the air thick with flies. The light breeze from the sea made things slightly easier once he reached the jetty and he walked out to where the *Sea Whip* was tied up. He called out, got no answer, and on an impulse stepped aboard.

The launch's for'ard cabin door was locked. It was the same when he tried the other cabin aft. Taking another glance round the deck, he shrugged and stepped back on the jetty again—to find John Marsh standing there, eyeing him quizzically. A few paces behind Marsh was another figure, a tall, thick-set workman who had a scowl on his face, a badly split lip and one eye blackened and almost closed.

"We keep her locked up, Carrick," said Marsh casually, a faint amusement on his lined, sallow face. "There's too much valuable laboratory gear installed aboard for Milne to want to take chances."

"I had that notion." Carrick thumbed at the burly figure beside the plant manager. "Is that Campbell?"

"Who had—ah—a disagreement with your bo'sun?" Marsh nodded. "But he's not the type to hold a grudge."

Campbell managed a battered grin and shook his head.

"As fights go, I imagine you could have sold tickets for it," mused Marsh. "Still, that wouldn't bring you here."

"I came looking for you," said Carrick. "Mainly to talk about Lampeye—the word is you saw him at the harbour last night."

"Late on," agreed Marsh. "After he'd been thrown out of the Anchor Watch." He paused and shrugged. "I reckoned he'd just sleep it off, as usual."

Campbell nodded, scowled and said, "Shouldn't ha' happened. Stupid wee sod."

"Campbell was a lodger at Lampeye's hut," explained Marsh. "We've just been down there, but I'm afraid anything Lampeye left behind comes down to old clothes and empty bottles." He shook his head sadly. "You know, he didn't particularly like you, Carrick."

"He didn't seem to like many people," said Carrick softly. A small cloud of flies from the seaweed dumps buzzed around him for a moment, and he brushed them away. "Did he say anything to you last night?"

"He ranted on," shrugged Marsh. "About the usual—how the MacLeans had done him out of his job with Angus Grant but that he'd get his own back on them. Nothing that—well, made sense."

"Anything about who was stirring up things against Dorothy Vullan?"

Marsh frowned, turned, and jerked his head at Campbell, who gave an unperturbed shrug and ambled off.

"Well?" asked Carrick.

"No." Marsh's thin mouth tightened. "Carrick, there's more than one way to stir up this Witch of the Isles business. Trying to be helpful could be one of them. Milne Vullan's an old friend—I think I can cope. Tonight, for instance. I'll be over here with him. But Campbell will be doing a stint as watchman over at Fean House."

"He's big enough," said Carrick.

"Agreed." Marsh considered him for a moment with an odd, almost sympathetic expression. "Carrick, I'm leaving Feanport in a few days, heading south again. That won't upset Dorothy Vullan, I can tell you. It's time I moved and—well, Milne's fishing trials are over, he can cope with the weed plant till he gets someone else."

"I'm more interested in their other problem," said Carrick. "How they're going to cope with the local 'Burn the Witch' brigade."

"That'll die off," said Marsh confidently. "Maybe not overnight, but with things back to normal—well, people have short memories."

"In this part of the world?" Carrick was more than doubtful.

"I'll bet on it," declared Marsh. Giving Carrick a friendly nod, he turned and walked away.

* * *

There was a guffawing, catcalling audience of fishermen on the quayside when Carrick returned to *Marlin*. The reason for their delighted amusement was in the water alongside the fishery cruiser— the patrol launch, coughing and spluttering and emitting occasional bursts of sick blue smoke while Clapper Bell and one of the deck hands bent over the engine with apparent puzzled concern. It travelled a few yards, spluttered, stopped and drifted to more delighted comments from the quayside.

But as Carrick went aboard *Marlin* the petty officer on gangway duty winked at him. Captain Shannon had promised there would be a valid reason for leaving the patrol launch at Feanport and the pantomime was his answer.

He saw Shannon a little later, the latter wearing a clean white shirt and his best uniform and ready to go ashore on a final, formal visit to Milne Vullan as Returning Officer prior to the ballot box run. They talked briefly, Shannon's thoughts obviously on the immediate task he had ahead, then the fishery cruiser's commander set off at the same time as the patrol launch ignominiously spluttered in towards the quay, astern of *Marlin*, and tied up.

Clapper Bell's continued performance as the irate bo'sun lasted while he left the launch and returned aboard *Marlin*. But as the quayside audience drifted away he relaxed and grinned at Carrick.

"Couple o' swopped-round plug leads was all it took," he said cheerfully. "Uh—the Old Man detailed Harris an' Edwards for to-night. Suit you?"

Carrick nodded. They were the same two experienced hands who had manned the patrol launch on the trammel net expedition. For once, Shannon was being as helpful as possible.

The afternoon drifted on and gave way to early evening. Shannon had been gone for about an hour when Malcolm Henderson's elderly sports car threaded its way down the harbour and stopped at the fishery cruiser's berth. The lanky detective inspector unfolded from behind the wheel, ambled aboard, and restricted himself to amiable noises until he was alone with Carrick in the wardroom. Then, slouched back in a chair, a drink in one hand, he explained why he had come.

"It's just a look-in, to bring you up to date—then I've got to go and sort out a domestic drama inland, a farmer who tried to feed his wife sheep-dip. The usual—their one and only shepherd was last seen scurrying for the hills." He paused and shrugged. "The main thing I've got for you is the autopsy result on Lampeye. He had a skinful of liquor, like we guessed, and the official report says death by drowning."

"But?" Carrick sensed there was more.

"The same again. Signs of a thump on the head, though it could have happened before or after he went in." Henderson sighed despairingly. "Any other time, and I'd have written it off. Right now—I'm damned if I know, but it'll have to wait." He took a gulp from his drink. "Feanport—hell, anyone who towed the place out to sea and scuttled it would be doing me a favour."

"Did you run a check on Robert Chester, like I asked?"

"Uh-huh. I telexed the London Metropolitan boys. They've no listing for any antique dealer of that name, but it means nothing—it seems plenty of these characters buy and sell without ever really setting up shop."

"The MacLeans?"

"Still zero—either they've been white as the driven snow or they've never been caught at anything. But—" Henderson leaned forward, nursing his glass, "—I've one little surprise for you. Remember you told me that Vullan and John Marsh were brother officers in the wartime navy?"

Carrick nodded, puzzled.

"I tried making the usual friendly noises about Marsh to the Ministry of Defence—how I'd be grateful for any information about this former officer." The grin took on a lopsided edge. "Ten minutes later I had a call from our Chief Constable, and got the deep-freeze treatment. A direct order to forget about friend Marsh and keep my mouth shut. Nice to have friends, isn't it?"

"You know what you're really saying?" asked Carrick, feeling as if the lanky figure opposite had just dropped a bomb on his lap.

"Me?" Henderson shook his head. "No comment. But if you want to play guessing games—"

Carrick nodded. If John Marsh was under Ministry of Defence protection, it threw a totally new light on his role beside Milne Vullan—and on Vullan's sound fishing experiments.

He remembered how he'd felt when the ultrasonic effect had hit him in the water, the way it had blown at least two sets of echo-sounding equipment, and the mad underwater stampede it had caused among marine life. Suddenly, with a startling clarity, he realised how the same effect, translated from what Vullan had termed "small-scale trials" into larger scale possibilities, had possible major implications in terms of submarine weaponry.

Whatever Milne Vullan had set out to achieve. Even letting Vullan work away on his own, far away from any limelight, made security sense—and other things tied in too, from the way Department had told Shannon to mind his own business to John Marsh's declaration that now the trials were over he would soon be leaving.

"That's it, and I've got to move." Finishing his drink, Henderson set down his glass, got to his feet and crossed to the wardroom door. Then he paused and glanced back. "Just remember I didn't tell you, right? I've still four payments to make on the car, so I'd like to keep working."

He left. Carrick was still standing in the wardroom, still slightly dazed at what he'd heard, when the little sports car growled away from the quay.

But, by the time Captain Shannon returned aboard a little later, Carrick had decided one thing. He would say nothing to Shannon for the time being—and from the edgy mood in which that small, bearded figure began storming around the fishery cruiser it was the right decision. When he did tell Shannon the result of the post mortem, the sole response was a grunt.

Dusk arrived, to an accompaniment of renewed coughs and splutters from the patrol launch as Clapper Bell made a further brief show of trying to repair the engine. Then, a little later, as the grey became night and the moon appeared, a trickle of boats began to leave harbour for their night's work on the fishing grounds.

Leaning on a deck rail near the bow, Carrick watched them murmur past. One of the last to leave was the little *Duchess* with the tall, unmistakeable figure of Angus Grant in the dimly lit wheelhouse, his face impassive as granite as he steered his borrowed charge past *Marlin*.

Turning away, leaving the rail, Carrick almost collided with the shadowy figure of Clapper Bell.

"All set, Clapper?" he asked absently.

Bell nodded. "I've switched the leads back the way they should be on the patrol launch, sir. Uh—just one thing, when we're ashore. How about using the Anchor Watch as a base?"

"We're being left to do a job, not to organise some extra drinking time," said Carrick. Then he relented a little. "I'll settle for you working a rota with Harris and Edwards. One man always down at the harbour, keeping an eye on the launch, the other two—"

"You'll know where we are an' we'll turn out fast enough," promised Bell with a grin and left him.

Marlin sailed on schedule, at 20.00 hours. Minutes before the harbour clock came round to eight P.M. Carrick went ashore with Bell and the two seamen. The gangway was hauled aboard, the fishery cruiser's twin diesels came to life moments later, the little group on the quayside cast off her mooring lines, and she edged out with a soft putter of exhaust from her squat funnel.

They waited until the slim grey shape, little more than a silhouette apart from her navigation lights, had cleared the breakwater entrance. Then they left, Harris drawing first watch on the launch, Bell and Edwards heading for the Anchor Watch, and Carrick settling for a stroll around the village.

A few late voters were still trickling into the polling station when he passed the village hall but otherwise the streets were quiet. On an impulse he walked from there to the seaweed plant but it was dark and deserted, the main gate padlocked. Feeling like a cop on the beat, he returned to the harbour, checked with Harris at the launch, and then headed for the Anchor Watch.

The bar was as busy as ever and Clapper Bell and Edwards had broken down the barriers enough to get into a darts match with a couple of fishermen. He watched till it finished and the sidebets were settled, bought Bell and Edwards a drink, then gossiped with them for a spell until Bell nudged Edwards and thumbed towards the door.

The seaman went off to take his turn at the harbour. From the deceptively innocent expression on Bell's face, Carrick had the feeling that the bo'sun's turn down there would coincide with the Anchor Watch closing for the night. But it was nine-thirty, voting at the polling station had ended half an hour earlier, and it was time he got there.

"Any problems, an' we'll come and get you," promised Bell. "But I'm bettin' on a quiet night."

It looked that way when Carrick reached the village hall. The door was closed, the two constables weren't in sight, and only the lights at the windows showed the hall was still occupied. He knocked at the door, and it was Shona Grant who opened it and let him in.

"If many more people turn up, it's going to be standing room only," she said dryly, leading the way.

One glance around and he saw what she meant. With Milne Vullan as local Returning Officer, the polling station procedure at Feanport seemed to take a fairly elastic view of the rules now voting was over. There were about thirty people standing around gossiping and drinking coffee, including the two constables who had shed their tunics and were in an obvious off-duty mood.

"Good evening, Chief Officer. Come to join our little party?" beamed the elderly, grey-haired woman who had manned the polling table. "Do you know, we had a sixty-eight percent poll, a full two percent higher than last time—"

He mumbled a polite reply, then was rescued by Shona who piloted him through the other groups into the side-room kitchen he'd visited before, leaving most of the babble of conversation behind. Dorothy Vullan was there, presiding over a bubbling coffee urn while her husband sat back in a chair, his feet up on a table and a cigarette dangling between his lips.

"Hello, Carrick." Milne Vullan grinned up at him without shifting his position. "I heard *Marlin* got away on schedule. Well, all I've got to do now is wait till she gets back."

"Captain on the bridge, stopwatch in hand," said Dorothy Vullan. Like Shona, she was still in sweater and slacks. "Who's going to take another coffee pot out to that waiting horde?"

Chuckling, Shona took the waiting pot and went back out into the hall while Dorothy Vullan leaned against a counter, sighed and ran a hand over her short, copper-bronze hair.

"Take a break and put someone else to work," suggested Carrick. "From the size of the mob outside, you've earned it."

"I'd settle for a drink," she declared. "And I don't mean coffee— but there's nothing left."

"Hold on till John Marsh gets back," soothed Milne Vullan.

"Gets back?" She stared at him oddly. "I thought—I thought he was still here."

"I left a couple of spare bottles of gin on the *Sea Whip*," said Vullan amiably. "Just in case—he slid out about ten minutes ago to get them."

"I see." Dorothy Vullan turned away from them and fiddled with the coffee urn for a moment. Then, suddenly, she faced them again. "Milne, you should be out in the hall, circulating, making 'thank you' noises." Her lips tightened slightly at her husband's amused reaction. "I mean it. Take Webb with you, introduce him to people. Move—I want to tidy in here."

Looking slightly startled, Vullan got up and beckoned Carrick to follow.

"Never argue with a woman in a kitchen," he said sadly, as they entered the hall. "It's too damned dangerous."

For the next few minutes, Vullan led Carrick around, introducing him to a variety of names and faces till he was called across to the other side of the hall and left Carrick talking to a farmer in leather-patched tweeds. Then Carrick saw Shona standing near, beckoning urgently. He escaped from the farmer and joined her.

"Something wrong?" he asked.

"I don't know." She moistened her lips. "I—it's Dorothy. She's gone—"

"What do you mean, gone?" Carrick asked quickly.

Shona shook her head, bewildered. "I went back into the kitchen and she quizzed me about John Marsh—if I'd seen him leave, if he'd said anything. Then—well, she said she had to go out, that she wouldn't be long and I wasn't to tell Milne. I—there was something about her, Webb. Something I've never seen before." The girl gripped his arm. "It was as if she was frightened."

Carrick swore under his breath. "What about earlier on—how was she?"

"The usual, I suppose. Maybe slightly edgy, but she's been here helping Milne." Her grey eyes met Carrick's anxiously. "Webb, I just have a feeling—"

"That makes two of us," said Carrick softly. "All right, just get me out of this place quietly."

"I'll get us both out," she retorted. "I'm coming along too."

He nodded, knowing arguing wouldn't have done much good. Easing through the chatter and laughter, they reached the hall door and slipped out. Pausing, Carrick glanced up and down the empty, darkened street and thought of Clapper Bell at the Anchor Watch. Then he shrugged. That might be wasting time, and he still didn't know what was happening.

"If John Marsh was going to the *Sea Whip*—" began Shona.

"We'll head there too," he agreed.

They set off through the village, Carrick setting a fast pace and the girl having to move at a near trot to keep up with his longer stride. Only a few people were out and about, none paid them any attention, and at last the dark, jumbled outline of the seaweed plant showed ahead. It still seemed in total darkness but as they reached the outer fence Carrick gave a soft grunt of satisfaction. The previously pad-locked gate lay slightly open.

"Somebody's still here," he said quietly. "All right, so we go in and look. But that's all."

She nodded and they went into the plant yard, skirting the black shapes of the storage huts. Shona caught Carrick's arm and pointed. The door of the office hut lay open, light streaming out of it.

They walked towards the door then stopped dead, a low moan of disbelief coming from Shona. They had found the Witch of the Isles. Dorothy Vullan was on her knees in the centre of the brightly lit office, bending over the sprawled, motionless figure of John Marsh.

Shona moved first, darting forward, and Carrick followed. As they entered the hut, Dorothy Vullan looked round at them with despair on her face—and at the same instant the door was kicked shut behind them.

"Thanks, Mrs. Vullan," said a sardonic voice. "Now all your friends have to do is stay peaceful."

Carrick turned slowly to meet the mocking face of Lachie Mac-Lean and the double-barrelled menace of the shotgun the stockily built fisherman held in a rock-steady grip.

"Get over beside her," ordered MacLean. "Move."

Powerless, they obeyed. Bending over Marsh, Carrick saw that he was unconscious but still alive—and winced at the ugly, broken welt across the man's scalp, a welt which still had blood oozing along its edges. He glanced up at Dorothy Vullan, who was standing gripping Shona's hand.

"I'm sorry," said the Witch of the Isles in a dull, listless voice. "It's my fault, all my fault, but—"

She stopped there as the hut door was flung open. The man who came in was Robert Chester but the alleged antique dealer was dressed in a fisherman's jersey and slacks and his thin face was a cold, calculating mask.

"You shouldn't have stuck your nose in, Carrick," he said almost sadly. "You or the girl—and I had a man watching the gate."

"Another of the MacLeans?" asked Carrick bitterly.

Chester nodded, glanced around the office, and shrugged. "I didn't expect any of this. But we can cope." He turned to Lachie MacLean. "Another five minutes should do it. Just keep them here and keep them quiet."

Shona Grant had been staring at the two men, total, shocked bewilderment on her face. She took a half-step forward, ignoring the menace of the shotgun.

"If the MacLeans are here, what have you done with my father?" she asked desperately. "They—"

"Your father's aboard the *Duchess*, making a one-man fishing trip," said Chester, cutting her short. He thumbed at Dorothy Vullan. "Ask her. She knows."

He went out, closing the door. Moving over, Lachie MacLean leaned against it in a way that was relaxed but watchful, the shotgun held steady. Wide-eyed, still bewildered, Shona turned desperately to Dorothy Vullan.

"He said you know." She gripped the older woman by the arm. "What is it, Dorothy? You've got to tell me."

"It shouldn't have involved any of you," said Dorothy Vullan wearily. "None of this was meant to happen—"

"But it has," said Carrick grimly. "Do I make a guess at it to save time? That the Witch of the Isles did a deal to sell out her husband's ultrasonic work—and that Chester is stripping everything he needs from the *Sea Whip* right now?"

"Yes." She saw the shocked disbelief on Shona's face and added quietly, "Your father was helping me, Shona. He—well, he understood." She managed an attempt at a smile. "Angus Grant isn't an easy man to convince. But he agreed—and all the rest between us lately has been play-acting."

"Play-acting?" The girl moistened her lips and pointed to Marsh lying on the floor. "Is that what you call it?"

"I didn't know he'd come here tonight," said Dorothy Vullan earnestly. "It shouldn't have happened. As soon as I heard, I—I tried to go after him and stop him." Bitterly, she looked at Lachie MacLean. "But I was too late."

"What did you expect, when he came chargin' in?" queried MacLean, unperturbed. He eased the shotgun against his hip and gave Carrick a fractional grin. "Hell, the old biddy still thinks the boss is just buyin' a new fishing gimmick."

It didn't seem to register with Dorothy Vullan and Shona was still in the same state of almost complete bewilderment. Carrick drew a deep breath, knowing they hadn't much time, certain he had to find out more because it was likely to decide what lay ahead for them.

"You've a right to know—now." She clenched her fists and looked down at them, her voice low and far away. "Just over six months ago, two things happened at the same time. Milne turned down an offer from a European fishing combine who wanted his sound fishing system and—and I got the results of a hospital test he didn't know about."

Something in the way she said it made Carrick understand.

"Those pills?"

She nodded.

"How long?" he asked gently.

"Under a year, they said." She made it sound unemotional. "You could call me lucky. When it happens, it'll be quick—I'd hate to be one of those long-time-a-dying people. But you see, I had to do something, for Milne. That's when I got the idea."

Carrick glanced at Shona and saw she was listening intently, the shock and bitterness gone from her, their place taken by a guarded compassion. Even MacLean, standing guard as before, had wiped the grin from his face.

"Tell us about it," encouraged Carrick. "Go on."

"Milne wouldn't know how to earn a living any ordinary way," said Dorothy Vullan. "He—well, he works on his own and doesn't even try to understand about money. And forget those stories you'll hear—the Witch of the Isles hasn't any fortune tucked away. There are things like death duties. He'd have to sell Fean House, and afterwards—" she shook her head. "I decided I wasn't going to let that happen."

She stopped there, bending quickly over Marsh as the man stirred a little and groaned. But it ended at that, and she rose again slowly, sighing.

"You said you went to my father," reminded Shona. "Why?"

"That was later." Dorothy Vullan moistened her lips, choosing her words. "First, I—well, I decided what to do. Milne was determined not to sell the sound fishing process, or whatever you'd call it—even though he said he'd talked to our own fisheries people and they weren't particularly interested. But I knew about the offer, and I knew it would still be open."

Carrick swallowed hard. "So you contacted them—"

"Yes. One of their people had read an article by Milne in some scientific journal. He hadn't spelled out what he was doing, but they'd guessed. They—well, they agreed it could be done my way, offered me a hundred thousand pounds, and sent Robert Chester to see me. We planned a way." She turned to Shona. "That's when your father came into it. I needed him."

"I'd have thought he was the last person," declared Carrick, wondering how much longer it would be before Chester returned.

"He was the very first—maybe the only one," said Dorothy Vullan firmly and glanced at Shona. "Angus Grant and I understand each other—and I told him everything. There was going to be a hate stirred up against the Witch—I knew that wouldn't be too hard. We needed a boat and Chester needed his own people in Feanport. Well, that wasn't so easy. But when Angus agreed, that meant we had his boat. Then he brought the MacLeans in as his new crew. At least—" her eyes strayed to the man at the door "—that's the name they call themselves, whoever they really are."

Lachie MacLean shrugged but didn't answer.

"And tonight?" pressed Carrick.

"Seemed the ideal night," she said sadly. "Everyone busy with the election—while some unknown fishermen with a spite against the Witch would steal the *Sea Whip* and—"

She stopped there, as the office door was flung open again. Chester came in, gave them one glance, then nodded to MacLean.

"Move them out," he said curtly. "We'll take them with us. I want to be clear of here before anyone else shows up." A flicker of tension crossed his thin face. "Carrick, you and the girl bring Marsh. You come too, Mrs. Vullan—and don't waste my time arguing."

"Where are you taking us?" asked Shona.

"A boat trip, so you'll be less of an embarrassment." He dragged a small automatic from his pocket. "Now move."

They left the office hut in a small procession, Chester first gripping Dorothy Vullan by the arm. Carrick and Shona followed, carrying the limp weight of John Marsh between them, and Lachie MacLean brought up the rear prodding them along with the shotgun. Chester led them through the dark shadows of the huts to the jetty, and the figures of the other two MacLeans appeared out of the night on the *Sea Whip*'s deck.

"Get aboard." Chester shoved Dorothy Vullan across as he spoke. As she stumbled on the deck, Carrick and Shona were prodded after her, still carrying Marsh.

Carrick saw a rubber boat with an outboard engine lying on the launch's deck near the bow. Some plastic wrapped packages were piled together in the cockpit, mere shapes in the faint glow of the binnacle lights.

"Aft," ordered Chester. "Donnie, you and Lachie shove them in the cabin. Willie, start her up and cast off—"

"Tell me something," said Carrick grimly. "Who are you working for, Chester?"

"People who pay good money—on delivery." Chester twisted him a humorless grin in the darkness. "I don't need to know how this gear works, just get it to them."

"And what about anyone who gets in the way—like a village cop or a little drunk like Lampeye?"

Chester's face was a harsh, mask-like silhouette in the night for a moment. Then Lachie MacLean-dug Carrick viciously with the shotgun and hustled them off. They carried Marsh in after Dorothy Vullan through a low, narrow doorway into the inky blackness of the after cabin, the door slammed shut, and they heard a bolt slap into place.

"Find a bunk," said Carrick, as he heard Marsh give a new, sighing moan. "Shona—"

"To your left," she told him.

Almost blindly, with only a faint trace of moonlight coming through the cabin's tiny portholes, Carrick let her guide him, then between them they laid their burden on one of the cabin's bunks. Dorothy Vullan had been clicking light switches, but they didn't work.

"There's a torch somewhere," she declared, and began feeling her way around the cabin, colliding with Carrick in the process. "At least, there was—"

"Chester would check." He stopped her and guided her over to sit on the bunk on the other side, bringing Shona over too. At the same time, the *Sea Whip*'s engines began to murmur and footsteps hurried along her deck. "Finish what you were telling me back in the cabin. What was the rest of the plan?"

"To take the launch out into the middle of the bay, then set her on fire," said Dorothy Vullan. "That was —"

"That way, she'd blow up when the fuel tanks caught—while they got clear in the rubber boat, with the ultrasonic gear," nodded Carrick. "Then what?"

"They'd rendezvous with Angus Grant, land Chester down the coast—and Angus would sail back into Feanport from a night's fishing with a full crew." She paused as the *Sea Whip*'s engine note changed and the cabin took on a gentle sway. They were starting to move. Then, making a strained effort to keep her voice under control, she added, "These crates Chester has on the dockside are full of rubbish, not antiques. Milne's equipment would go in them and nobody would think twice when they were moved south."

Marsh was groaning again, his limbs twitching. But Carrick listened for a moment to the *Sea Whip*'s engines as the launch nosed away from the shore. Chester was keeping her speed to a crawl.

"So what do you think they'll do with us?" he asked.

"Land us somewhere," suggested Shona.

"No chance," he told them. "There's a slogan on the harbour wall—Burn the Witch. That's all they've got to do. Just leave us locked in here, and when the launch goes up that's the problem solved."

"They couldn't," protested Dorothy Vullan.

"They killed George MacKenzie and Lampeye." Carrick hardly paused to let her digest that. "You may have thought you were selling a load of new-style fishing gear, but it's something a damned sight more important, whatever your husband told you. And John Marsh isn't just a friend who overstayed his welcome—as far as I know, he's Ministry of Defence, here to keep an eye on what was going on."

"Oh, God," she said in a low, trembling voice. "But—but there's Angus Grant—"

"So they get rid of him too," he said brutally. "Which means only one thing matters now—that we get out of this."

"How?" asked Shona.

"How about witchcraft?" he said sardonically. "The only way out is that damned door."

They stared at each other, Carrick with a feeling of total helplessness.

"You're wrong," said Dorothy Vullan simply, making them swing round. "It looks that way, but you're wrong. Milne altered all sorts of things aboard—and he took five feet off the rear of this cabin to make a special battery compartment."

Carrick moistened his lips. "Can we get into it?"

She nodded in the darkness. "The rear panel is on clips. Then there's a hatch that will take you out on deck. But—"

The murmur of the engines increased a shade and the *Sea Whip* lurched as she answered her helm. Carrick peered out one of the tiny portholes and saw the lights of Feanport twinkling. They were already a good distance from shore. Once they got out beyond the middle of the bay any time left might come down to seconds.

"Help me," he said quietly. "We haven't much time."

The rear panel was a single sheet of plyboard and came off easily, then Carrick squeezed through into the battery compartment, felt his way past the racked batteries which had fed Milne Vullan's experimental gear, and found the hatch. Easing it open a fraction, he took a deep breath of salt air then looked around.

The stern of the launch was deserted. One man was in the cockpit, at the helm, another was working at the rubber boat near the bow, and a faint glow of light from the for'ard cabin showed where the other two must be.

Opening the hatch wider, he wriggled out and crawled along the deck. He could hear the man in the cockpit whistling to himself as he steered. It was Lachie MacLean, and the binnacle lights showed the man's shotgun propped beside him.

Quietly, Carrick reached the door of the aft cabin, slid the bolt, felt the door push open from within, and murmured a warning. Then, on hands and knees, he crawled towards the cockpit and the unsuspecting helmsman.

A small brass fire extinguisher was clipped to the rear of the cockpit combing. Crouching, Carrick gauged his distance, then sprang. As he landed in the cockpit he grabbed the fire extinguisher, pulled it free, then as the startled helmsman swung round, mouth opening, Carrick brought the fire extinguisher down hard on the man's head.

He caught Lachie MacLean as he fell, lowered him to the deck, then realised the steering wheel was spinning loose. Cursing, he grabbed for it—at the same time as the *Sea Whip* lurched and a frantic shout came from the man at the bow.

A moment later, Chester erupted out of the for'ard cabin with Donnie MacLean hard on his heels. Hurling the fire extinguisher at them, Carrick swung round to reach for the shotgun. He didn't make it. The automatic in Chester's hand barked, a fierce lance of pain ripped into Carrick as the bullet slammed into him high, near the shoulder, and he felt himself falling.

But someone else was suddenly in the cockpit beside him, seizing the shotgun, bringing it up in a single smooth movement. On his knees, Carrick looked up in a daze and saw the tall, commanding figure of the Witch of the Isles.

The gun in Chester's hand barked again. Dorothy Vullan seemed to smile, to grow taller, surrounded by a strange power and purpose.

The shotgun in her hands slammed its first barrel and Robert Chester uttered a strange half-scream as he spun on his feet like an agonized doll and vanished over the side. She fired again, precisely, unhurriedly. Framed in the light of the for'ard cabin doorway, a fuel can in his hands, Donnie MacLean gave a high-pitched screech and fell backwards.

The man at the bow had frozen where he was, hands raised in surrender, as Carrick hauled himself back on his feet. The Witch of the Isles didn't help him. Still strangely tall and remote, she was staring at the for'ard cabin.

Little tongues of flame were appearing. In a moment, they were bigger, then a roaring mass of fire. Carrick saw a smile on her face and clutched at her.

"Get out," he croaked. "Shona and Marsh—"

Then, when he took his hand away from her, he saw it was covered in blood. His blood or her blood, he wasn't sure which. He saw the man at the bow dive overboard and start to swim. Swallowing at the pain it caused him, he dragged a groaning, stirring Lachie MacLean upright in the cockpit and switched off the *Sea Whip*'s engines. As the throb died and the launch began drifting he heaved MacLean over the side.

Dorothy Vullan was already at the aft cabin door. Shona was there, the racing flames making the scene bright as daylight while she dragged John Marsh along the deck towards a liferaft container.

Moving in a half-dream, half-nightmare, singed by the heat and flames, Carrick helped them release the liferaft. It inflated with a whoosh as it hit the water. Then they half-fell, half tumbled aboard, dragging Marsh with them, and pushed away from the burning hull.

Shona had the liferaft's paddles. He took one, she used the other, and they struggled to get further away from the floating inferno. At last, they stopped, and Carrick looked at her, nodded, and felt a new wave of weakness coming over him.

Marsh was lying at their feet, moaning again. Dorothy Vullan was sitting upright, staring at the night. He touched her, and the arm which had been resting on the raft's side fell limp, fingers brushing the water.

A white-cored blast came from the *Sea Whip* as her fuel tanks exploded. He felt the hot wind of the explosion against his face . . . . . . and the darkness that followed was deeper than the night.

* * *

It was two days later, when he was sitting up in bed in Feanport's cottage hospital, that Carrick heard the final verdict in it all.

He'd had earlier visitors, earlier conversations which had helped him put most of it together. How the flames had brought the patrol launch hammering out from Feanport to find the liferaft—and to pick up Willie and Lachie MacLean from the water.

John Marsh would live. He'd been operated on for a fractured skull, but was recovering. The same surgeon had later removed the bullet from Carrick's shoulder, with grunts about what would have happened if the wound had been a couple of inches lower and to the right.

But there was nothing anyone could do for the Witch of the Isles, and Carrick's version of what had happened was greeted with sympathetic scepticism.

"You see," the same surgeon had said patiently. "The bullet penetrated the left ventricle of the heart. There is such a thing as volitional movement, but I'd say the odds are thousands to one she should have died instantly, so—"

Carrick hadn't argued. He knew, while police uniforms and Malcolm Henderson came and went, while Captain Shannon bustled around in a grim-faced, earnest way, and particularly when Milne Vullan came in, stood beside him silently, then quietly went out again.

But there was a different mood about Captain James Shannon when he entered Carrick's hospital room on that second day. Grunting, he plumped himself down in a chair by the bedside, tossed a bundle of magazines on the covers, then surreptitiously slipped a whisky flask under the pillow.

"That's from Clapper Bell," he said gruffly. "I've got to do everybody's dirty work. All right, how are you feeling?"

"Reasonable." Carrick eased his bandaged shoulder. "Another few days—"

"I heard." Shannon dismissed the subject. "Well, we're tidying up. The two MacLeans are talking—they killed MacKenzie because of the way he was sniffing around. Lampeye was different—he was making too much noise about them. And on it goes." He stopped and shrugged. "The real problem is Angus Grant, and what the hell we do with him. He didn't know about the killings, he only sailed a boat up and down, and Milne Vullan won't have him touched. That's the way it's likely to stay."

"Good," said Carrick softly. "You know why he helped?"

Shannon nodded.

Carrick had heard it from Shona, the previous evening. Dorothy Vullan had told her in the desperate moments while they'd waited in the cabin and Carrick had been out on deck.

There had been several reasons. But the one which had mattered was that Dorothy Vullan had only one blood relation. Shona would be the next Witch of the Isles—and the eventual owner of Fean House.

"So"—Shannon broke the silence with a heavy throatclearing—"what's left isn't much, except for a couple of things. I've talked to Vullan about this ultrasonic thing. Frequencies, harmonics, amplifiers, God knows what. The Ministry of Defence boys swooped on him after that paper, and hit him over the head with the Official Secrets Act. He went to work for them, and Marsh as resident guard-dog, like you thought."

"And what happens to it now?" asked Carrick grimly.

"Now?" Shannon's bearded face twisted in a sardonic grin. "Nothing—because the series of final tests proved it doesn't work anywhere except around that damned Witchrock area. Something about underwater rock formations, acoustic echoes—hell, I didn't even try to understand." He saw Carrick's expression, and nodded. "Marsh was going down to London to tell his bosses to forget it—that's the irony of the whole mess."

Unable to think of anything to say, Carrick watched him get to his feet. Shannon crossed to the window, looked out for a moment, then came back.

"I said a couple of things. The other is this—" He paused, scratching his beard. "Now we've finished that damned election duty, *Mar-*

lin's going back on normal patrol. We'll be working the Barra Head area for a couple of weeks. Then we'll come back to Feanport and collect you. Understood?"

"Understood," said Carrick softly.

Shannon gave him a surprising wink, turned, and went out.

Carrick lay back, and for the first time in two days he smiled. He had another visitor due. They had things to forget, things to remember.

But two weeks was plenty of time . . . even for a brand-new Witch.

THE END